R.L.

QUIET NEIGHBORS

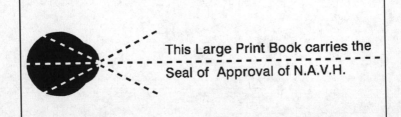

This Large Print Book carries the
Seal of Approval of N.A.V.H.

QUIET NEIGHBORS

CATRIONA MCPHERSON

THORNDIKE PRESS
A part of Gale, Cengage Learning

GALE
CENGAGE Learning®

Farmington Hills, Mich • San Francisco • New York • Waterville, Maine
Meriden, Conn • Mason, Ohio • Chicago

LIBRARY OF CONGRESS CATALOGING-IN-PUBLICATION DATA

Names: McPherson, Catriona, 1965– author.
Title: Quiet neighbors / by Catriona McPherson.
Description: Large print edition. | Waterville, Maine : Thorndike Press, 2016. |
  Series: Thorndike Press large print mystery
Identifiers: LCCN 2016020197 | ISBN 9781410492807 (hardcover) | ISBN
  141049280X (hardcover)
Subjects: LCSH: Large type books. | GSAFD: Mystery fiction.
Classification: LCC PR6113.C586 Q54 2016b | DDC 823/.92—dc23
LC record available at https://lccn.loc.gov/2016020197

Published in 2016 by arrangement with Midnight Ink, an imprint of Llewelyn Publications, Woodbury, MN 55125-2989 USA

Printed in Mexico
1 2 3 4 5 6 7 20 19 18 17 16

For Audrey and Wendy, with all my love.

Books make such good friends and quiet neighbours.

ONE

It was the last thing on her mind when she fled across London. She had her passport and meant to take a train to the airport then buy a ticket for the farthest place on the departure board, to put time zones and maybe the dateline between them. If she could have, she'd have blasted off and gone to Mars.

But the northern stops on the west coast mainline caught her eye — PENRITH, CARLISLE, LOCKERBIE — and she remembered a face, kindly and curious, peering round a door with a conspiratorial smile. Before she knew it, she was on the Glasgow train, in the corner seat of an empty four in the quiet carriage. On the sunny side, as though it were meant to be.

Who runs away to a *bookshop*? she asked herself as the train rattled through grimy suburbs. That place was the only bright spot of the whole two weeks, she answered herself. And then: I should have twigged right then that something was wrong.

For a start, it was the first time he'd suggested a quiet bit of Britain for a break instead of flying south for the sun and some culture. She'd thought it was romantic; what it really was, of course, was cheap. And ✓Max didn't want to be spending money just then. She'd wondered if he had a big splurge planned for her fortieth.

So they'd had a fortnight in a cottage of laminated signs — DO NOT POUR OIL IN SINK, LEAVE WET BOOTS IN PORCH, NOTHING BUT PAPER IN SEPTIC TANK — and on the middle Saturday he had suggested a day trip to Scotland's Book Town. He hated it. Maybe he thought it would have five branches of Waterstone's, a WH Smith, and an Amazon warehouse. Whatever. When he saw the quiet square of Georgian buildings, the antiquarian map shop, the Women's Studies specialist, the dragon's dungeon, and the rest of it, he'd checked his watch and said, "Quick look round, since we're here?"

Which had made Jude want to stay until the last tea shop cling-filmed its scones and rolled the blinds down. From cussedness, from complacency, she'd checked out not just the maps and the feminist poetry, but

10

also pictorial histories of the ancient world, guidebooks to places she'd never go — Southport, Oban, Roxburgh — and sermons by Victorian ministers with comic facial hair and tragic prose. Then she found Lowland Glen Books. It was no more than a doorway onto the street, opposite the clubhouse of the bowling green in the central square. The green-keeper had taken the chance of this single sunny day to feed his precious grass, and now he was pressing it in with a hand-roller, a cloud of flies following him, drunk on the pungent stink of manure. Jude sat, gagging, on one of the benches around the edge of the green, drinking bad takeaway coffee while Max paced up and down near the car and glared at her. *Such* complacency. More like oblivion.

From her vantage point, the Lowland Glen sign had beckoned. It was hand-painted, suspended from the two upstairs windows by means of washing rope tied to the pull-loops on the insides of the frames. The windows, consequently, were open a little at the bottom and the gaps were stuffed with what looked like bundles of cloth. EST. 1972 the sign said. Jude had drained her cup, repelled by the thought of what lay behind a sign like that after forty

11

years, drawn to find out like a moth to a candle.

She walked past the door twice, bewildered. There were two shop fronts — a children's books cum toyshop and a crafts specialist with one wall of books and three walls of knitting wool — but the door between them looked so much like the entrance to a house that she dismissed it until, on the third pass, she noticed that one etched-glass panel had a letter L amongst all the leaves and barley-twists and the other a letter G. She grasped the brass handle, still expecting to find a householder in slippers with a teacup halfway to their lips, to have to retreat with apologies. She pushed the door open anyway.

Books. Wavering, tottering piles of books. Brick-stacked towers of books. Woven dykes and leaning spires and threatening landslides of books. Unsorted. Fs upon Bs upon Ns, paperbacks and hardbacks, outsize to *Mr. Men,* novels and cookbooks and crosswords and plays. Jude snapped her eyes away and faced forward.

The passage was perhaps five feet wall to wall; the way through the middle of it, defended by carriers full of books wedged like sandbags into the bulges of more books behind them, was eighteen inches and not a squeak more.

She let the door close at her back and stood in the sudden quiet as the street sounds were shut out. The books, in an instant, had deadened everything. She could hear her breath in her head and her blood in her ears, the swishing she used to think was the sea when she held up a shell to hear it. Max had taken that away, telling her on one of their first dates that it worked just as well with a cupped hand, nothing to do with the sea at all.

Twelve feet ahead of her, a faded brocade curtain was drawn over the width of the passageway and a little soft light showed around its edges. Jude turned sideways, clamped her bag tightly under her arm, and edged forward. She could feel particles of dirt shaken loose by her brushing past, could feel the motes drift through the air between the books and her body and lodge in the weave of her clothes, settling in the folds of her ears, nestling among the roots of her hair.

The curtain let out a complicated puff of dust as she drew it aside. All of its life was there in the mix of sweet pipe tobacco, harsh cigarettes, boiled food, cooking oil, the faint suggestion of one small rodent somewhere in the long years, and most of all, of course, the books: the must of their pages and the reek of their old leather covers, crumbling or mouldy; the touch-stains of countless fingers on their buckram-covered boards.

Jude smothered a sneeze, compressing it into a grunt in case it sounded, to the bookseller, like judgment. But when she looked up to check, there was no one there. A big old teacher's table was set across the entrance to a back room to form a counter and there was a lamp on it, casting light on piles of papers and coils of old till receipt. A heavy grey computer was whirring, its fan at full tilt, straining against the dust in its innards. Pushed back from the desk was an empty chair, duct tape over the splits in its vinyl covering, a ring cushion on its seat, and a fawn cardigan slung over its back.

Fawn, Jude said to herself, nodding. It wasn't taupe or stone or oatmeal; it wasn't even beige. It was an honest-to-God fawn cardi and, without knowing why, she was smiling as she turned away to look at the nearest shelves.

ARCHAEOLOGY said the label on the edge, and above it were crammed railway timetables and rolled LNER posters tied with faded pink auditor's tape. She slipped around the desk and sidled into the small room behind it. GARDENING, COOKING, HANDICRAFTS was printed on an index card pinned above the door, and volumes of military memoirs stood in two tall stacks just inside. Jude ran her eyes down the nearest pile and up again, looking for something — thematic, alphabetic, chronological? — and finding nothing at all. She slid volume five of Churchill's WWII out of its place and wiggled it in between volumes four and six a few books higher up. That slowed her breath and, before the absence of the first three could quicken it again, she turned away.

Her eyes came to rest on a glass-fronted case full of Scottish fiction. She knew it was Scottish fiction; she would recognise those sets of Scott and ugly seventies Muriel Sparks anywhere. And on the third shelf down, after the Marion Chesneys but before the Dorothy Dunnnetts, there was one single book smaller than all the others, with a custard-yellow jacket and a rust-red logo at the bottom of its spine. Was it . . . ?

Jude surged forward. It was!

She opened the front of the case and drew the little book out with something between a gasp and a whoop, pressing it to her chest with her eyes closed, giving thanks for it before she started to inspect the jacket and

15

binding and state of the pages. It might be no good after all — ex-library, grubby and stamped, glue from old tape on its end papers. But the yellow of its jacket was so bright, even the spine unfaded.

She opened her eyes and screamed, dropping the book.

The man, noiselessly sprung from nowhere, dipped and caught it in one deft hand, like a crocodile snapping its jaw on a gobbet of tossed meat.

"That's my favourite sound," he said. "I mean, dear me, of course I mean the gasp, not the shriek. The cry of a book lover sighting a treasure." And he bestowed on Jude a wide grin, revealing strong, yellow teeth, stained in grey stripes from coffee or tobacco. He was undoubtedly the owner of the fawn cardigan and the haemorrhoid cushion. A tall man, egg-shaped from sloping shoulders and a comfortable paunch, with frizzy, iron-grey hair slicked down and brushed back but escaping its bounds this late in the afternoon and beginning to form a halo around the high dome of his forehead and the double sickle of his roughly shaven jowls. His eyes, bright above extravagant dark pouches, twinkled at her for another moment before he looked down to see what he had saved from falling.

"Ah," he said, smoothing the little book in his large, papery hands. "Miss Buchan. I join you in your gentle delight." And with a bow that detached another few strands of hair from their Brylcreem binding, he put the book in Jude's hands.

"O. Douglas," said Jude, looking down to check she had not made a mistake. Right enough, there was O. Douglas's name in the familiar font over the sentimental drawing: a family gathered at a fireside, sewing basket, terrier, little boys in shorts and jerseys.

"Oh quite, quite," said the large man. He had exactly the sort of accent people said *oh quite, quite* in. "But, dear me, she's John Buchan's sister, you know. Of *The Thirty-Nine Steps* renown? She eschewed the allure of his reflected glory. Like dear old . . . dear old . . . Nicolas Cage and the Coppola connection."

Jude had been so primed for the name of dear old scholarly someone she'd never heard of that it took her a beat or two to understand him and then she laughed, as delighted with this oddity before her as she was with her find.

"Do you have any more?" she said.

"Douglases?"

"In Nelson editions with jackets in good shape."

"Not at the moment," he said. "Which are you missing?"

"I've only got *The Setons* and *Pink Sugar*," said Jude.

"Well then you've barely begun!" the man said, his voice rising almost to a shout. "You've years of small adventures in store. Unless . . ." He put a hand to his mouth. His shirt cuff was frayed and his nails, like his teeth, were strong and yellow and striped in darker lines, but they were clipped short and very clean. Jude could imagine a manicure set to match the pair of brushes he must use to swipe at his hair, a velvet pad for buffing his nails every Sunday and Wednesday evening.

"Unless what?" she asked him.

"There's always that thing," he said, cocking his head toward the desk, where the computer sat whirring. "You could have the lot. *Plop, plop, plop* on your doormat." He looked at her with a wide-open gaze.

Jude wrinkled her nose and immediately, he wrinkled his too, looking ratlike as his lips drew up above his front teeth.

"Exactly!" he said. "Where's the fun in that?"

He wrote her a receipt in illegible hand-

18

writing, tore it from a receipt book with carbon papers between its leaves, and put her purchase, along with a bookmark, in a pale-grey paper bag bearing a logo just like the L and G etched into the glass of the shop doors.

"Where have you *been*?" Max shouted to her from yards away when she was back out on the pavement again. "I wanted to get a jump on the rush hour." Jude looked around the square. There was a tractor with a trailer of silage crossing the top and two boys on bicycles, riding hands-free so they could eat their crisps, freewheeling down the far side.

"Rush hour?" she echoed.

"Where *were* you?" said Max.

Jude looked at the fiction and knitting shop and the children's and toyshop, her gaze passing over the door to Lowland Glen Books again.

"The Leaky Cauldron basically," she said. "But let's get going. I need a shower."

"Of course you do," said Max.

She hugged the pale grey bag close to her as she followed him to the car.

That was the last day of the holiday that it didn't rain. When they got back to the cottage, the sky was just above the tree tops, the air thick with threat. The first few drops fell, sweet and dusty, as they carried the supermarket bags from the open boot to the cramped little kitchen. By the time the kettle had boiled and the cold stuff was packed in the fridge, sheets of water were pouring down the windows, rods hammering on the roof.

For the five days they had left, as Max prowled through the three rooms trying to get a decent signal on his phone, Jude stayed curled on the nubbly brown tweed of the armchair nearest the front window and read *Penny Plain,* from beginning — "It was teatime in Priorsford" — to end — "I'll go out of the world cheering". And it *took* four days, such a short book, because half the time she wasn't reading at all; she was staring into space. Into the blank spaces of a typical holiday cottage, cleaned every changeover and kept bare to deter theft. It soothed her: the empty mantelpiece where ornaments would normally be; the lack of junk mail needing sorting; the neat shelves of books and games without the detritus of life that might otherwise gather there. There were no batteries, no cracker prizes, no phone chargers or dead remotes. And in the kitchen, no twists of cardamom bought for one curry and left to moulder, no sticky pots with one spread of jam left, no single gherkins swimming like sharks in jars of

20

vinegar. And outside, just the sodden grass and dripping trees, nothing to weed, nothing to prune, nothing to turn from. So she gazed out at it and, while she did, she was thinking of a kind face and that cautious, semi-strangulated voice — *Oh quite, quite. Gentle delight. Years of small adventures* — and laughing again every time she remembered *dear old, dear old . . . Nicolas Cage.*

From Lockerbie, she took the Dumfries bus full of schoolchildren headed for late-night Thursday opening, and care workers in their polo shirts and tabards starting their shifts in the red sandstone villas, full of the elderly now that the merchants were gone. There was no chance of a bus all the way to Wigtown though, and the only taxi firm she phoned told her it was a big night, Thursday; she'd be lucky to get a driver to waste his time. So she went as far as she could, to Castle Douglas, deserted but for the pub-front smokers once the shops were closed, and spent the night in a room above the bar at the Something Arms, listening to the men downstairs bedding into their night's drinking, and the phone calls of the salesman next door, loud over the sound of his television through the thin dividing wall.

She had no change of clothes and was

ashamed to go into breakfast in the same black suit and grey shirt the staff had seen the night before, so she bought a pasty in a paper bag on the way to the bus stop and then spent the journey to Newton Stewart with the empty bag folded in her hand, wishing she could throw it away. She saw nothing of the scenery, turned away from it with her eyes closed, in case the memory of her and Max on this very journey the summer before should bring her to tears.

Tears felt close this morning. She had showered, but without her own tubes and bottles, her skin felt rough, her hair limp, and the tights on their third day had half moons at the heels where her new shoes had rubbed them. She didn't usually wear tights, hadn't known not to buy cheap ones.

She had never been on a journey without a companion, one so carefully chosen she wanted the road to be longer, the destination farther. Travelling bookless was a kind of purgatory, the monotony broken only by her constant, then frequent, then carefully spaced peeks at her phone. Every time she looked the only change was the little blue battery draining to black while her inbox remained empty. Ten miles from Newton Stewart, the blue turned to orange. She put her phone away and started sorting the contents of her wallet. She wouldn't need her library card here, or her gym card, and she was determined not to use their joint credit card either. These three she zipped into a pocket of her bag. She kept her Boots, Tesco, and Caffé Nero cards handy, but then, when the bus drew into Newton Stewart station and she looked at the family solicitors, takeaway pizza, and the kind of ironmonger with brushes hanging in the doorway, she felt foolish and tried to ignore the ache in her throat that told her tears were close again.

It was only eight miles down the country road to Wigtown, although hours until a bus, but the taxi firm near the bus station didn't bat an eye and so it was just after lunchtime that Jude stood opposite the etched-glass doors as the cab drew away and she tried to think of an opening line.

The toyshop had gone, replaced by a tarot and crystals outfit. It and the wool shop were closed, cardboard apologies propped in their windows. When Jude crossed the road and tried the handle, she half expected to find Lowland Glen locked too and was ready to sit in the bus shelter, then retrace her journey to Newton Stewart, Castle Douglas, Dumfries, with a night in one of the tired hotels clinging on in a tired town,

23

then a train south and the tube home to face the music.

But the door opened.

There were one or two more carrier bags stacked in the passageway, but otherwise nothing had changed. Well, the light was different — no sunshine competing with the lamp behind the curtain — and there was Calor Gas as well as tobacco and dust in the bouquet today as she pulled aside the heavy brocade and stepped through. Also, this time, the man was at his desk, sitting with the fawn cardigan around his shoulders and a cup of greyish coffee steaming.

"I —" said Jude.

"I'm just —" he said, sliding something into a drawer and turning back to face her. He pushed his reading glasses halfway up his forehead. "Aha!" he said, slamming the drawer shut. "Ha-ha-HA!" He turned to the other side and rummaged in a pigeonhole. "It came in September. I saved it for you."

Jude stared, then stepped forward and picked it up. *The Day of Small Things,* it was called. A bright dust jacket, the sandy pink and blue of a beach scene; that same brisk young woman, or one just like her, in a warm jacket and beret, larking among the rock pools with the terrier.

She didn't even know she was crying until

24

he stood and hurried round the desk to remove the book from her hand, brushing at a teardrop before it could soak in and dimple the shiny paper. When he had set it down well out of the way, he turned back and, taking a large, ironed, cotton handkerchief from the pocket of his trousers, held it out to her.

She dabbed her eyes with it still folded. She really wanted to shake it out, bury her face in it, and howl, but, breathing carefully in and holding the breath, she managed to stem the flow.

"Is everything all right?" the man asked her.

"No," said Jude. "Nothing."

"Good for you!" he cried, making her look up. She had bowed her head for the shame of it all. "I admire honesty above all things," he declared. "Quite right to give a pusillanimous question the answer it deserves!"

And then she was lost. Exhaustion and embarrassment were in there; fear too, and dread that she hadn't run far enough away. O. Douglas in the Nelson edition tugged hard, reminding her of the last happy day, but what finished her was someone sounding pleased and giving praise. If he only knew, Jude thought, he would throw her out, lock the door, call the cops. But he was smiling at her and now the pain was coming up inside her like the dark yolk in a lava lamp, trembling and eddying but always rising, until it burst out in a long howl, bringing hot gusts of fresh tears and leaving her hacking and jerking, her seam of grief cracked wide.

"Shush now," he said, wrapping his arms around her. And, "There, there." He rocked her as she shrieked into his cardigan front somewhere near one armpit. "Oh my," he said. "Dear me. Shush now."

Jude cried until her scalp was sweaty and her stomach quaking, then she drew back, unfolded the handkerchief, and blew her nose hard.

"Now, *that* must feel better, surely," the man said, sounding pleased with her again, even though all she'd done was wreck his hanky.

"Thanks," she said. "Thanks for the book."

"It's a gem," he said. "And if you like it as much as I know you will, the happy news is that there's a companion volume. *The Proper Place.* Now dry your tears and I shall give it back to you."

Two

It was still hard to explain what happened next.

"I'm so —" Jude started to say

"Don't apologise."

"— tired," she finished. That's what people said when they were going to kill themselves. One of the women at work did a weekly night shift with the Samaritans, and she'd told Jude all about it. *If they say they're angry or sad or desperate, you can talk them round. But the ones who say they're tired . . . Well, what can we do? More talking when they're exhausted already?*

"I could close up early and drive you home," said the man. Jude blinked herself back to the bookshop; she'd been in the tearoom at work, listening to the hard words, deciding she'd never call the Samaritans again. "Although, dear me, I do have my assistant coming at four, but as long as I pay him . . ."

"Home," said Jude, and her eyes filled again.

"I rather thought, last time, that you were a guest," he said, looking her up and down. Now that he wasn't embracing her, he had stepped back to a more normal distance. "A tourist, as used to be. *Tourist* has gone the way of *passenger* and *patient,* I rather think. Everyone's a *guest* now. Can't see that it makes a scrap of difference, can you?"

Jude nodded then shook. "Home's London," she said. "I ran away."

He took that in with a series of slow nods, his lower lip stuck out and his mouth turned down. "I ran away *to* home a few times," he said. "From school." When Jude said nothing, he tried again. "What happened?"

How could she even begin to tell him? "Funeral," she said, spreading her arms to display the cheap black suit.

"Who died?" he asked gently.

Jude hesitated. She didn't know and couldn't bear to imagine. She had spent the journey not looking at the headlines on other people's papers, had let the long hours yesterday evening in the sad hotel room limp past without putting the telly on.

"My parents," she said and, because it was true and because she hadn't thought of them since she left the crematorium two days ago, she could feel her face begin to melt again. One tear, the only one she had left inside her maybe, crept out and down her puffy cheek.

"Oh, you poor child," said the man. He rummaged in his trouser pockets, eventually drawing out a second handkerchief that he inspected and then dismissed. He cast his eyes around, but by the time he had concluded there was nothing else absorbent he could offer, she was calm again.

"I'm just so tired," she said. It wasn't meant to be a plea. She would have said it in an empty room. But he drew up his brows and chewed his lip.

"Could you manage a five-minute walk?"

She shrugged.

"Here," he went on, lunging for the desktop and snatching up a bunch of keys. He worked a strong yellow fingernail into the double ring, freeing one of the smaller keys in the collection. "My house is round the corner. Have a drink of water and lie down. Try to sleep."

"I can't — You don't —" she said.

"Help yourself to whichever bed or couch you fancy," he told her, pressing the key into her hand.

"Why would you let — ?"

"It's quiet and the shutters close."

"We don't even , ."

He turned her round and gave her the gentlest of pushes. She turned back.

"Why would you trust me?"

"You're not in London now," he told her, looking at her over the spectacles, which had fallen back down from his forehead.

"I could leave my wallet here as . . ."

"Surety," he supplied. "Unnecessary, my dear."

"I can't just . . ."

"Very well," he said. "Your wallet for my latchkey."

She opened her bag and then closed it a little so he wouldn't see her passport in there. She drew out her purse and handed it over.

"You won't ghost my cards, will you?"

"My dear girl, I have a schoolchild coming at four whom I must pay handsomely simply to add books to the catalogue on that loathèd appliance. No, I shan't 'ghost your cards.' And you shan't ransack my family silver. None of Miss Buchan's admirers would be capable of such a thing."

She managed a smile.

"Follow the left fork round and down," he said, pointing. "And it's left again at the end. Jamaica House. You can't miss it."

"What flat number?" she said.

"Hm?" said the man, then he smiled. "No, no, you misunderstand. Dear me, no. Not a celebration of the Windrush by the local authority. No, I'm sorry to say it's rather earlier and much more unseemly."

"What?" She was swaying with exhaustion and couldn't follow the patter and waft of his voice.

"Never mind," he said. "Jamaica House. On the left. I'll see you once you've rested, and we shall talk then." He slipped the copy of O. Douglas into her bag. "In case you have trouble dropping off," he said. Then he held out his hand. "Lowland Glen."

Jude blinked, took his hand, and shook it. It was dry and warm and she didn't want to let it go.

"My mother's maiden name was Lowland," he said. "But, still, schooldays were a trial. These days, thankfully, people call me Lowell. You see? There's always a solution."

She tried to smile again but failed this time. "I'm Jemimah, for my gran," she said. She choked on the second name, still not sure what to say.

"Oh dear!"

"But I get Jude."

"You see? Jude!" he cried. "Nothing is ever as bad as it seems."

She nodded and turned away before he

31

could see the shadow pass over.

Outside, the weak winter sun had turned the street into a dreamscape. Or perhaps Jude's lightheadedness only made it seem that way. She was dizzy from sobbing, from lack of food, from lack of sleep, from the horror of the last three days, the two coffins side-by-side and the squeak of the rollers behind the velvet screen as they were borne away. The undertaker had urged her to have music and she had refused. If he had told her why, she'd have known better. That muffled squeak was stuck in her head like a jingle.

There was a corner shop coming up. She crossed the road to avoid its windows but found herself outside a newsagents and didn't look away in time. She saw the headlines, then relaxed. Clinton, Europe, immigration. But when she looked up the street for the left fork he'd told her was coming, what she saw stopped her dead then made her sink against the wall at her side as her legs weakened.

Two police, shoulder to shoulder, were strolling towards her just twenty yards away, heads like searchlights, turning and watching, seeing everything. Like always.

They'd seen her stumble, and now their

eyes fixed on her as they strolled forward. No rush, they seemed to say, and no escaping.

"Everything all right?" one of them asked when they drew near. "Need any help?"

"You're not driving, madam, are you?" said the other.

Jude shook her head. "New shoes," she managed to say.

"You take care then," said the first, mouth smiling, eyes cold.

Jude felt her stomach rise. "Thanks," she said. She took a step but they were still standing four-square. "Hope you have a quiet shift," she said. And at last they started moving, swivelling their gaze again for whatever else might happening farther along.

"Safe bet, round here," one said.

"Mind how you go," said the other. "Get yourself a coffee, eh?"

She made it to the corner and out of sight, then leaned back against the wall, sick and whimpering.

"Come on, come on!" she hissed at herself. If they came back and saw her like this, she was done for.

But they didn't and the street was deserted. No bookshops round here. When she could walk again, she found herself passing along between rows of stone cottages, the smallest ones just a door with a single window beside it, another tucked under the eaves. They must be tiny inside, but even the meanest of them would be a real home, thick stone walls and a working chimney. Not like London, with the chipboard that divided a mean little house into two even meaner flats at the front door. She put her hand in her bag and stroked the jacket of the book. *The Day of Small Things* now and *The Proper Place* to hope for. As she turned left again onto a broader road, nothing but flat fields on its far side, she felt, unaccountably, a lifting inside her. It was probably just the fresh air and the simple act of putting one foot in front of the other after two days of travelling. Or perhaps not.

She had talked about rock bottom for months, always thinking she could feel it, cold and unyielding under her. And then there would be another lurch and another drop and she would tell herself that this time she was there. The funeral. Was there anywhere lower to fall after a double funeral? By that midnight she couldn't have touched it with her middle finger if she'd stood on tiptoe. Now, in three-day-old clothes with unbrushed teeth, with tears and worse dried into her cheeks, she saw the gateposts for Jamaica House and, cops or no cops, thought she'd passed rock bottom and was on her way up again.

The house matched the vowels and the ironed handkerchief: stone steps leading to a pillared portico and banks of tall windows. It wasn't quite castellated, but there was a ridge running round the edge of the roof like the crust of a pie, and chimneys and finials were spaced out along it so that the silhouette was more like a castle than any house Jude had seen before.

She looked at the black iron keyhole in the front door, big enough for a mouse to pass through, and then at the small modern key in her hand and the leaves blown into the porch. Then she walked round the side of the house to look for another entry.

The garden was winter neat, the grass so short she could see worm casts dotted over it and the roses pruned down to skeletal hands. At the kitchen door, reached through an arch into a cobbled courtyard, there were clay pots with the first green nubbins of snowdrops showing through and, in the centre of the cobbles, an urn with a small bright bush in it; impossibly fragrant purple flowers, like sugar ornaments for cupcakes, crowded on its bare branches.

It misled her and she wasn't ready when

she opened the door. She felt her throat soften with disgust. The inside of Jamaica House went with the grey teeth and the duct taped chair and the bulging carriers full of unsorted paperbacks. Jude stood on the threshold and did what she knew.

There was no dog, she told herself, and the drain and bins were okay. It was just the contrast with the little purple sugar flowers that made the air in the house so flat and stale.

Then she stepped inside and couldn't ignore it. The tiled floor was stained with spots and trails where someone was in the habit of slopping tea as he walked. And there were teacup rings on the windowsill too, and desiccated flies from summer.

But she was so tired and his words came back to her on a new wave of fatigue. *Take whichever bed or couch you fancy.* She was turning to close the door at her back when the clamour of her mobile made her jerk and set her heart rattling. She fumbled it from her bag and swiped with clumsy fingers. The voice started up high and tiny before she could raise it to her ear.

"Jude? Jude? Where *are* you?" It was Natalie, her sister-in-law. Holding her breath, she listened. "Jude? Oh my God, at last! Have you *heard*?"

She pressed the button to power down and stood staring at the black rectangle, her heart banging high in her chest. They could still trace it when it was off, couldn't they? Could they?

She went back out to the courtyard. Behind the door there was an old-fashioned iron boot scraper set into the ground. Jude brought the phone down hard on one of its curled ends, so hard she felt the knock all the way up her arm to her jaw. The phone came apart in three jagged pieces. She lifted the battery clear and tried with both hands to bend it, putting deep red scores in the heel of each palm but leaving the little square intact. She looked around. There was a tin watering can sitting under a dripping copper tap in the wall. She could hear the plink of each drop falling. She walked over and slid the battery into the can, leaving it there for as long as it took her to grind the SIM card to crumbs under her heel then gather the crumbs and the shattered fragments of phone together.

She put all the pieces in the greasy paper bag from her morning pasty, then she plunged her hand into the can of water, gasping at the cold, and fished the battery out again.

There was a puddle now, but the ground

37

was damp everywhere and the extra would soon soak away. Jude searched around the little yard, then down a back drive, where she saw what she was looking for. She glanced in both directions, but there were no neighbours, no windows. She hurried down, dropped the paper bag into one corner of the wheeliebin, heard it hit the bottom, and then trotted back to the kitchen door.

She had a technique for things like this — for public toilets and lifts in multi-storeys — and she employed it now. "Not here, I'm not here, I'm not here," she said as she walked through the house from the tiled corridor to a carpeted hall, up a curving stairway, and into the first door on the upstairs landing.

It was his bedroom; she knew that right away. There were clothes heaped on an armchair beside the high fireplace and a pair of trousers slung by its braces from one post of the dressing mirror. There was a jumble of prescription bottles and crumpled handfuls of receipts on the chest of drawers, a coffee cup with cold dregs beside a newspaper folded open at the crossword on the bedside table.

She slipped out of her shoes, let her jacket slide to the floor, and pulled back the covers, old-fashioned striped flannel sheets and woollen blankets edged with bands of faded blue satin.

She pushed her stockinged feet down the cold bed and lowered her head into the dent in the pillow, smelling hair tonic she hadn't noticed when he hugged her. She closed her eyes and waited for her pulse to slow, waited for the *smash!* of the phone and *plunk!* of the battery to stop sounding in her head, for the breathless urgency of Natalie's voice to stop running through her like a shudder.

But even when she was sunk in a pit of sleep with sheer, steep sides and a soft, clawing floor that held her snugly, even then, in her dreams, the glass and plastic shattered and the cold disc of water gulped what she fed it and Natalie's voice, strung taut, kept repeating *Jude? Where* are *you?*

THREE

Birdsong woke her. She opened her eyes onto a soft greyness and the sound of something not a sparrow or a pigeon. Not a London bird at all. Its liquid treble was unconcerned with food or squabbles, as though it sang from pure joy at the morning. Jude was lulled back towards sleep by it but then, shifting, she felt the nylon toes of her tights and the waistband of her skirt and, turning her head, her cheek brushed the satin edge and then the rough wool of the blanket and she sat up abruptly, a gasp escaping her.

The first thing she saw was her wallet on the bedside table. Then, looking past it, she glimpsed Lowell Glen sitting in the arm-chair, its load of clothes dumped in a heap at his side. His legs were stretched out in front of him and crossed at the ankles — he still had his shoes on — and his arms were folded over his front. His head had dropped back until his mouth was wide open and he breathed in uncomfortable, choking snores that set Jude's pulse rattling. Then she took in the rest of the scene. The trousers hanging by their braces, the till receipts and coins, the coffee cup, the newspaper. They were all still there, and shoes shoved under the wardrobe that she hadn't noticed before. She felt her throat begin to close and lowered herself gently back down again, trying to stare at a blank section of the ceiling and ignore the dark bulbs in the centre light, the fly resting in the bottom of the shade. But the bed was old and creaky. The snoring stopped, and when she glanced over he was smiling at her.

"You slept all night," he said. "It's almost morning."

"What about all the other beds and couches?" she said, sounding terse, feeling guilty.

"I was worried about you. I decided to keep watch." He rubbed his chin and laughed a little. "Dear me, I fell down on the job rather." Before Jude could answer, he sat up and smacked his hands. "Coffee!" he exclaimed. Then at her silence, "Tea?"

"Coffee would be wonderful."

He got up, levering himself out of the armchair with both hands, groaned and

41

stretched, then shuffled away. Jude watched his reflection in the dressing mirror. He stopped at the top of the stairs and spoke over his shoulder.

"That's . . . ahh . . . that's a bathroom with the half-glass door, my dear. I'll use the downstairs carsy." Then he descended, his hair — like a seed head from his night in the chair — catching the first light from the landing window.

Jude swung her legs round and stood. She thought she caught a whiff of odour as she moved. Funeral, Wednesday night hiding with her heart in her mouth, fleeing across London scared to look behind her, hours in the station, hours on the train, the raucous commercial hotel, the bus, the weeping, and then — she glanced at her watch — fifteen hours in a stranger's bed, dead to the world like a princess with vines grown up around the castle.

No wonder she stank.

As if he had heard her thoughts, Lowell spoke again. She glanced at the dressing mirror and could see him hovering on the half landing, eyes down to shield her privacy.

"There's always lots of hot water in the morning," he said, "if you should want a bath. And um, second door along from there, if you rummage in the wardrobe there are clothes and things . . . Look in the chest too. There are . . . Well, clothes and what have you, you know."

Jude was intrigued. She waited until he'd gone, then tiptoed out and along to the second door to investigate. It hadn't been used recently. Dust lay thickly on the dressing-table top and even furred the tufted trim of a cushion on the armchair, but there was nothing out of place. If she could have brought a Hoover in here and worked round from the door, floor to ceiling, following the swags of cobweb and nudging into every fold, it would be perfect again in minutes. She dragged her feet across the carpet as she walked and then picked the grey rolls from the soles of her tights and pocketed them.

The wardrobe door was a snug fit and it squeaked open, letting go a breath of old wood and faded lavender. Jude ran her hands along the row of plastic department-store hangers, little cylindrical beads on their necks showing the sizes. She was no expert, since jeans were jeans and tee-shirts were tee-shirts, but these clothes looked decades old. She could remember a teacher at her primary school wearing one of those long cotton skirts with tassels of silk along the hem and tiny mirrors stitched on like patches, could remember the cheap green dye rubbing off on their homework as Miss Pol-something sat with worksheets on her lap and told the children how well they'd done, how pleased she was. The blouses made Jude think of Miss Pol-whatsit too. They were loose and smocked with bell sleeves and drawstrings through the necks, the strings bound at the ends with gold thread or finished off with bells. There was a shop in Camden where you could still buy it all, this and incense sticks and cheap brass elephants, but it wasn't real. It wasn't from the seventies, and some of it wasn't even Indian. Jude pulled at the neck of one of the blouses: 100% viscose, made in Korea.

She took a dress exactly the shade of green she remembered from Miss Pol . . . perran? kennan? . . . and a quilted waistcoat and turned to the dressing table. The top drawer was a tangle of beads, sunglasses, and hair bands, sitting in a rubble of cheap outsized earrings and loose change from before the Euro. Jude saw some pesetas and francs and got as far as smiling at the memories they loosened before the guillotine fell.

She opened the next drawer. It had bras tucked into dome shapes and pants folded in squares, and she knew their owner washed everything together — cheap Korean tie-dye and white cotton undies — because everything in the drawer was a uniform murky grey. But if the choice was a fourth day in her own or someone else's clean, no matter how halfheartedly clean, she didn't have to think for long. She lifted a pair of the thickest socks and a pair of paler (and so perhaps newer) knickers, decided not to trouble with a bra because they all looked enormous, and ventured to the bathroom.

Twenty minutes later, she followed the smell of coffee downstairs and through a door beside the passage she had flitted along the night before.

Lowell was standing with his back to her, bent over a toaster with a pair of wooden tongs in his hand. Jude cleared her throat and he turned.

The flare in his eyes came and went too swiftly for her to give it a name.

"Ah," he said. "Excellent. That's better. Sorry I don't run to a hair dryer." He gestured vaguely towards his neck as though apologising for Jude's wet hair on hers. "You could perhaps wrap it up in a towel."

"It won't take long," Jude said. "I'm not blessed with luxuriant tresses." She could feel her mouth twisting up and could hear the bitterness in her voice. She saw a sheet of shining black spread out on a wooden floor and then, thank God, the blade came down again.

"Marmalade, honey, jam," said Lowell, ferrying jars from an open cupboard to the kitchen table. "Or, dear me, perhaps not." He squinted into the jam jar, then opened a bin with his foot and dropped it in. "Marmite," he said. "And Nutella, my guilty pleasure."

Jude sidled into a seat as he put a plate of toast and a cup of coffee, dark as treacle, down in front of her and pushed a butter dish forward.

"Thank you," she said.

"I'll just nip up and . . ." said Lowell, waving his hand around again to display his stubble and messy hair. "I don't suppose you left the water in?" And then, at her look, "No. No, of course not. I can't think why I said that. I . . ."

"Do you have sisters?" said Jude, taking pity on him.

"That's it!" he said. "Exactly. Thank you."

She looked around the kitchen while he was gone. She was fine. She had decided in the bathroom that she needed to get out of here, decided as soon as she saw the towels, the soap scum on his razor, the plughole. The kitchen was one last thing to be endured, and then she would leave.

It must have been impressive once, with its high ceiling and flagged floor. She could imagine a cook in an apron and a little hat, bossing maids and garden boys around. But someone had ruined it with units in walnut veneer, lights under the top cupboards, and little quarter-circle shelves at the ends of the rows, finished off with tiny fences to safeguard the decorative jugs and tureens that were meant to be displayed there. What *was* displayed there, or shoved there anyway, was envelopes rucked open by someone's thumb, yellowed fliers, faded seed packets with clothes-pegs holding them shut, FedEx packets with their rip-strips hanging in ringlets. Jude turned to face the other way, where bottles of oil and sauce and cooking sherry sat along the back of the hob, grease-spattered and dust-furred, a single charred oven glove stuffed behind them.

"I'm not here," she said, sipping her coffee.

Then Lowell was back, hair combed and chin smooth, in a different though identical shirt and the same trousers.

"How long have you lived here?" she asked him.

"Born here," he said. "I went away to

school and university, travelled a bit, but, dear me, yes, more or less always, I suppose you'd say."

"It's got that feel about it," said Jude. "Solid."

Lowell wrinkled his nose. "My mother wrecked this room," he said. "When I was a little boy, Mrs. Dawson used to bathe me in the big sink and warm my nightshirt on a rail above the range. And in my father's day, there was a pump in the middle of the floor. All very swish. No going out to the yard for water. *He* remembered *his* mother saying it would spoil the maids. Turn them soft, you know."

"Your father was born here too?"

"He was the doctor," said Lowell, nodding. "The *young* doctor. My grandfather was the doctor and then the *old* doctor, and my father was supposed to become the *old* doctor in turn, because of me." His face fell and he tried to hide it by taking a bite of his toast and chewing it thoroughly.

"That's not fair," said Jude. "That's too much to ask."

"Of someone who faints at the sight of a cut finger, certainly!" Lowell said.

"What about your sisters?" said Jude. "Were they press-ganged too?"

"No sisters," said Lowell. "Or brothers.

48

Only me." He took another bite of toast and looked fixedly at Jude until he had swallowed. "I shouldn't have grabbed that lifeline you threw regarding the bathwater. I don't have the wits to see it through." Then he opened his eyes very wide. "Sorry!" he said. "Unforgivable! Forcing you to pity me. You must forgi— Oh dear." He took a draught of coffee and tried again. "And what line of . . . It's quite all right to ask this of a young lady these days, isn't it? What line of work are you in, ah, ah . . ."

"Jude."

He closed his eyes, pained again by his failings. "What does your family run to, *Jude*? Butchers, bakers, candlestick makers?"

"Well," said Jude, "before they died —"

Lowell groaned and passed a hand over his eyes. "I am the biggest —" he began, but Jude stopped him.

"No," she said. "I want to talk about them. My dad was a foreman at the Swallow's Works until it closed down, and then it was backshift at B&Q, and my mum had her own hairdressers until the works closed, then she went mobile. They retired last year. My dad got his lump sum — he'd deferred it till he was sixty-five — and they were all set."

49

Lowell tutted. "What happened?"

"They got one of those big . . . like a caravan but with an engine? I can never remember the name."

"Winnebago," said Lowell. "It comes up in crosswords."

"That's it," Jude said. "They were going to tour in it. I was surprised at my mum, to be honest. She was always a one for little things. Natty things. Likes of a doll's house? So I could see her in a camper-van. A VW caravanette." Jude knew her voice was rising. "But it was so stupid! Winnebagos are made for empty freeways not Cotswolds B roads."

"Did they have a crash?" asked Lowell gently.

Jude shook her head. She was still angry with them, still embarrassed and ashamed of her embarrassment and angry at being ashamed.

"You don't have to tell me. Dear me, I didn't mean to pry."

"I have to tell someone," Jude said, and the note in her voice frightened her; so strained and high, she was almost singing. "I have to tell someone something," she said, trying to breathe out and speak on the fall. She turned her thoughts away from the memory of all those people she thought

50

were friends. Friends of the family. All that barely concealed delight at the funeral. Everyone who had snatched at the pay-out when Swallows closed, jeered at her dad in his B&Q tee-shirt and back brace, then looked round the tourer with a smirk on their lips, pretending to care, while her mum showed off the little fridge and the shower room.

"Use my phone," said Lowell, misunderstanding. "Call a friend."

"They built a high garage to keep it in," Jude said. "Is it okay if I tell *you*? Friends are . . . Friends have been . . . They built a high garage."

"People can be thoughtlessly unkind."

"And they tried it out the night before they set off: showers, cooking, telly, had the heating on. The whole bit. But they didn't want to drain the power pack."

Lowell put a hand up to cover his mouth and Jude looked closely, but his eyes were wide. He wasn't hiding a smirk, she was sure of it.

"Yes," she said. "In the garage with the engine on. Stupid —"

"Oh, my dear child," said Lowell again, as he had the day before. "Oh, my dear!"

"It was in the paper," said Jude. "It was on the news, at the end, where they have the talking dogs and quintuplets."

"My *dear.*"

"I mean, no one reading the news actually laughed."

"But I understand completely," he said. "No *wonder* you ran away."

Jude stared at him. Every word was true. It was the truth and nothing but the truth, and he was happy with it. She could leave it at that and say no more. She was a poor dear child and he understood her.

"I just snapped," she said. Also true. "I think you can get to a point where you just snap. Don't you?"

"Of course," he said. "We've all been there, my dear, and for lesser reasons than you."

She didn't believe him, of course. Everything about his life said otherwise; from the etched-glass initials in the shop door to the ironed hanky to the memories of his grandparents' servants, spoiled by the luxury of a water pump in the kitchen.

"I ran," she said, trying it out. "In the clothes I stood up in. Left my job, left my home."

"Are you a hairdresser too?" Even that showed the world he lived in, where children follow their parents through quiet lives.

"Librarian," she said. "Possibly. If I've got

a job to go back to after taking off like this."

"Local authority?" said Lowell. She nodded. "Well then . . ."

"It's not like that now, though," said Jude. "Not with all the austerity and everything. I'd phone them if I could think what to say."

"Don't you have bereavement leave?" said Lowell. "I've always thought council workers . . . The county buildings are at the bottom of the street, you know. We meet at lunchtime and some of them are customers."

Jude nodded from behind the guillotine that had once again come thundering down. Or maybe it was a portcullis, but the edge of it was sharp and it whistled as it fell, cleaving her life in two pieces, sliced cleanly apart on Wednesday.

"I've used all my leave up," she told him. "If I don't start again soon my cataloguing days are over."

"Cataloguing?" said Lowell. "Well now, how interesting. I've lost my schoolchild, you see. He's gone to Safeway, for the bright lights and big money. He told me yesterday." He gave her a solemn look. "I don't mean to make light of your difficulties, my dear, and I don't mean to imply serendipity or even timeliness, given what brought you here, but if you really *have* found yourself free and if you happened to look around up at LG Books yesterday . . . I mean, *if* you've no one to rush back home to."

Jude felt her eyes fill, and Lowell went so far as to jump out of his seat and come round the table towards her.

"I wish I could say this isn't like me," he said, shifting from foot to foot, "but it is. It's *absolutely* like me. Absolutely *typical* of me. 'No one to rush home to!' I'm a fool. I'm so very sorry, my dear. You told me. Your parents! The funeral. You *told* me!"

Jude nodded dumbly. She *had* told him. And he believed her. It was the truth and nothing but the truth, and it seemed to be plenty.

FOUR

Suddenly she was living in an Anne Tyler novel. A world where you can set down one life, walk away, and pick up another. It was almost too easy.

"I don't have any references," she said. "I don't have my National Insurance number."

Lowell's eyebrows shot up. "No? No. Well, dear me, I was thinking of cash in hand, to be perfectly honest," he said. "Yes. Um, National Insurance, quite."

"I don't mind if you don't mind," said Jude.

"And your work is your reference," said Lowell, spreading his arms. "I mean, I can tell already."

They were round in the shop by this time. Jude had walked through the ground floor twice and calculated the stock there at twenty-five thousand volumes, the shelf space at capacity minus thirty percent. It didn't seem like any kind of substitute for a letter of recommendation, but she wasn't going to argue.

"I only hope it won't be too dull for you," said Lowell, peering at her.

Jude almost laughed. "I'm literally tingling," she said, trying out more honesty on him. "My skin is itching." He frowned and shook his head, and she smiled to suggest that *literally* had meant, as it usually did, anything but. "I mean, it's an adventure playground. For a cataloguer."

"And would you mind serving the odd customer if I'm abroad?" He caught her look. "In the old-fashioned sense of 'from home' not 'overseas.' Dear me, no, not these days, at my advanced age. But there's a sale coming up in Edinburgh, you see."

She opened her mouth to refuse, but then wondered. Two cops had let her slip through their fingers when she was pale and shaking. They'd hardly question her behind a counter. If they ever came in. And, in her experience, cops were not big readers.

But still. Besides that, there was the reason she'd ended up in Cataloguing, where all the books were spanking new and creaked at the spine on first opening. It had hurt her heart up on the desks to see them coming back coffee-stained, old bus tickets and envelopes left in their pages. People had some filthy habits. Once, she'd found a condom wrapper. At least here, if someone took a book away, picked their nose and wiped their fingers, they wouldn't be bringing it back again. And if any of the books already in here were past saving . . .

"Problem?" asked Lowell.

"Can I chuck them out if they're vile?"

His eyes widened. "It's a small town," he said, uncertainly, "and many of them are neighbours."

Jude took a beat and then laughed. "Not the customers," she said. "The books. Grotty books. I mean, I see you've got a bit of a backlog, but you must chuck *some* out, right? Right?"

"As you see fit," said Lowell, although there was an odd note in his voice. "I leave it in your hands, my dear. The one thing I will stipulate is that you mustn't . . . I mean, dear me, there's no need for you to trouble yourself with . . . this material."

He turned to the walnut document chest that sat to the left of his table and waved his hand at the ranks, floor to shoulder, of shallow drawers.

"Maps?" said Jude.

"Photographs," Lowell said. "And very dear to my heart. I mean, I'm fond of the books, but these are my true passion."

"I'll steer clear," said Jude. "Cataloguing pictures is a specialism anyway. I wouldn't know where to start."

"Splendid," said Lowell. "That's all settled then." He tugged one of the brass handles and Jude stepped forward, assuming he was going to show off some of his collection — his true passion — but he was checking that the case was locked. "And, dear me, dear me, how can I put this?" he said. "As soon as you're ready to return to London, you should feel absolutely free to go."

He meant it to be reassuring, but it caused a small weight to settle inside her chest.

"Likewise," she said. "As soon as you want the place to yourself again, just say the word." He nodded, but he looked even glummer than she felt. "Or if it starts getting too expensive."

"Ah! Ah! Money!" he said. "Yes, quite. Well look, here's some for now." He took out a black leather wallet, fat and shiny like an aubergine, removed the notes without looking at them, just shoved them at her. "And, oh, here's . . . Yes." He rummaged in one of the cubby holes at the other side of his desk. "Ah, yes, I thought so. This is the spare key for the car. The garage is never locked, so just help yourself. For Marks and Spencers or Tesco, or anything you like. I

58

mean, dear me, I think you look very pretty. Delightful. But if you want to pick up some of your own . . . things too. Dear me, yes of course, you'll want to pick up some of *those.*"

Jude was half sure he looked at her chest as he spoke, and she rounded her shoulders to let the thin dress fabric fall clear of her bare breasts. She counted the money for something to do and then raised her head.

"There's more than four hundred pounds here," she said. "That's far too much to hand over like petty cash."

"Oh, ah, yes, well, mm," said Lowell. "Petty cash. Well, it's not really bookshop money, I don't suppose, strictly speaking. It's more the picture side. But yes, you're right. We should keep things ship-shape for the tax man."

"Sorry," said Jude, "I didn't mean to be picky. I don't know the first thing about running a business, never mind two."

"Two?" said Lowell.

"The photography," Jude said.

"Oh! No, no, no," Lowell said. "I don't take photographs. Dear me, no. That spot of cash . . . well, I keep it handy for *buying* them. I'm a collector. No, I mean, L.G. Books is as poor as a church mouse, it's true. As poor as a bookshop mouse, we could say. But Lowell Glen himself is well, dear me, not to be vulgar, but I'm fairly comfy. I can indulge my passion without too much sacrifice."

Jude tried not to raise her eyebrows. She had noticed that his shoes, like his chair, were mended with duct tape, and his towels had been as frayed as his cuffs.

"I live quietly," he said, acknowledging that her eyebrows had risen anyway. "And my grandmother, my mother's mother, never forgave her for marrying a doctor. She was delighted with me — she saw me as a scholar, you know — and left me all her loot, in a trust, which I eventually managed to get my mitts on, despite some opposition."

Jude nodded as if she understood trusts and bequests and a doctor being an undesirable match.

"So let's call that a little gift, shall we?" Lowell said, nodding at the banknotes.

Jude hesitated. She loved Anne Tyler, of course. All those instant new lives. But still she hesitated. Was this too good to be true? A friend, a job, a house, a wad of cash. No questions, no strings? Forty years of London rose up inside her and threatened to break through.

Before she could speak, though, the shop

door opened at the other end of the passageway, beyond the curtain, and a voice muttered, "Mess of the place! He must be turning in his grave."

"Oh dear," Lowell whispered. "Well, this is a bit much for your very first morning. You can slip away into Crafts and Cooking, my dear."

"Customer service training?" said Jude, but she stepped back into the dark doorway.

"She's not exactly a cust—" Lowell began before the curtain was swept aside.

"*Mis*-ter Glen." The voice was clipped and tight, and Jude thought its owner must be from some other part of Scotland. She sounded nothing like the cheerful publicans and shopkeepers whose soft friendliness had charmed her last summer. She looked the same, though: an elderly woman, dressed as though for church in a coat with a brooch pinned to the lapel and a swipe of bright lipstick, like the Queen.

"Mrs. Hewston," said Lowell.

"I'm here to help you, Mr. Glen," she went on. "It's that mess of briars on the fence."

"That mess of briars is a beautiful *Rosa rugosa*, Mrs. Hewston," Lowell said. "And it's on my side of our common fence, and perfectly pruned."

"There's a bird's nest in it," the woman went on, sounding as though she were landing the knock-out blow.

"I saw it," said Lowell. "Finch, I think. A thing of wonder."

"A source of infection," said Mrs. Hewston. "I know you decided against a career in health, Mr. Glen, and so it's up to me to watch out for you. I never mind what I do for the good of the community."

Lowell shared a glance with Jude at this, and Mrs. Hewston swung round, following his look.

"Oh!" she said. "*You're* back, are you?"

Jude stepped forward out of the gloom, and as she moved from silhouette into full light, the little woman put her hand up, fluttering, to her neck.

"Oh!" she said again. "I beg your pardon." She blinked and suddenly all the sharpness fell away, leaving her face naked and young-looking, although the liver spots and webs of wrinkles round her eyes put her well over seventy. Perhaps it was just that vulnerability always makes us think of infants, Jude decided. Tearful eyes too. And Mrs. Hewston's eyes were swimming.

"I'm getting old," she said, "and it doesn't come itself." She turned to Lowell as though he had argued. "I'm fine! I'm coping better than many half my age."

"I don't doubt it for an instant," said Lowell. "Mrs. Hewston, allow me to introduce my colleague, Jude. She's come up from London to help me with a special project for a while."

"*London,* is it?" said the woman, back to what Jude felt sure was her true self, sharp as a tack. "A special project at the house? Because I'm always happy to help if you need me."

"Here at the shop, Mrs. Hewston," said Lowell. "Jude is a book person. There's nothing happening at the house."

"I can't say I'm sorry for that," Mrs. Hewston said. "I like my peace. Although something will have to be done someday. But for now, how do you do, Jude?"

"I'm pleased to meet you," Jude said.

"Oh my! *That's* London and no hiding it," said the woman and left without a word of goodbye.

Once the door had shut, Lowell let all of his breath go in a sigh that was halfway to a groan.

"Mrs. Hewston. From next door. You'd better get used to her."

"Her house can't be that close to your place," said Jude, thinking that Jamaica House sat in the middle of gardens so generous you would almost believe you were right out in the country.

Now Lowell groaned for real. "It's worse than you think," he said. "Her house *is* my place."

"She lives with you?"

"No! Good grief! Heavens, no. Gosh. She lives in the bungalow. It was the surgery. My father built it in the sixties, state of the art for the time. It was supposed to be ready for me when I qualified and joined the practice. Then, when he retired and went south, he fitted it up as a house. It really is quite dreadful. The worst the decade could provide in the way of pebble-dash and what have you. And then he rented it out to his practice nurse for sheer spite because she'd always hated me."

"Can't you — ?"

"She's a sitting tenant with a lease like the Magna Carta. If she weren't, you could take up residence."

"Oh, I'll sort something out," Jude said. There had to be a bed-and-breakfast near here somewhere, she reckoned. A cheap B&B run by someone house-proud but not inquisitive. It was an unlikely combination, she knew. Women laid-back enough not to wonder about their guests were too laid-back to clean. But she couldn't live at

Jamaica. She knew that coffee cup was still in Lowell's bedroom near the newspaper. She knew he hadn't rinsed out the mouldy jam pot before he'd thrown it in the bin.

"Dear me, that's a thought, actually," Lowell said. "I *am* a chump, wittering on about Tesco and references. But I tell you what: go back round to Jamaica, right up to the top, up again from the bedrooms. See what you think."

He refused to say anything further, and so Jude left with no more than an hour's work done for her four hundred pounds. If nothing else, she could take care of the coffee cup and the jam pot. He surely wouldn't mind if she did all the dishes and gave the kitchen a wipe round.

As she walked, though, she stopped thinking about it. The sea wasn't close enough for her to hear the tide, but there were gulls circling and salt in the air. And she was rested too. She was wearing soft, bright clothes quite unfamiliar to her, the way the skirt eddied about her legs and the soft kiss of wool against her cheek from the borrowed scarf. Even her hair felt different. Washed with Lowell's big bottle of supermarket shampoo and left to go its own way, it blew lightly back and forth across her brow, clean and dry, like the skeins of pale sand that sheet across a beach in a breeze. Her feet in the wool socks and borrowed clogs looked ridiculous but felt wonderful, the blisters from her funeral shoes cradled and unprotesting.

This time, she noticed the surgery because she was looking. Dr. Glen had done his best to turn it into a home. There was a tacked-on chimney and a tacked-on porch, but its origins showed in the ramp up to the front door, the tubular steel handrail, and the row of small windows along the front wall, perfect for a dispensary, consulting room, and waiting room, perhaps, but mean things to live behind.

As she walked around the side of the big house to the kitchen door, she caught one glance through a smeared window of faded curtains drawn back roughly, a jumble of spectacle cases, binoculars, books, magazines, and wine glasses on the inner windowsills. She turned to the rose beds instead, drinking in their neatness, feasting her eyes on the cobbled yard and breathing in the scent of those little purple flowers.

"Not here. I'm not here."

She let herself in, thinking she would see what he meant about going up another floor then start the search for a B&B. How close was the nearest Travelodge? That would be

66

anonymous *and* sterile. How far would four hundred pounds go?

But then, at the bottom of the dark stair-well, she looked up and was surprised to see, high above, a clear and pale brightness. It grew as she climbed the stairs and, as she turned and climbed again, it opened and admitted her. She arrived on a little landing with white walls turned blue by the cold winter sunshine.

There were two doors, one on either side. In the left-hand room, the walls were yellow and the window, tiny and deep-set, looked out over the front garden and across the fields and *there* was the sea! A low, slack ribbon of still water in a bay. There was a kitchen corner in here, with a small, square china sink on metal legs like something from a laboratory or — she realised — a medical surgery. And on a wooden counter beside it, a small fridge and a two-ring cooker were plugged into a single socket on a big square adaptor. There was no other furniture in the room and no carpet on the floor, just the bare, broad floorboards and the light bouncing around the coombs and angles, making a hundred shades of sun-shine yellow.

Jude stepped across the landing. This room was painted a pale medical pink and

67

was utterly empty. It didn't even have a window, just two small skylights, one on either slope of the ceiling. She imagined lying on a mattress on the floor looking up through them at the stars, knowing that, even if someone heard she was here and followed her north, in this room, at the top of this tall house, with its windows facing the sky, they still wouldn't find her.

FIVE

It didn't take Mrs. Hewston long to sniff her out. She got four days of peace — long enough for a shopping trip to Stranraer in Lowell's ancient Volvo, long enough to choose a bed and a couch, a table and chairs to set about in the pale attic rooms; not to fill them, but just so that she could spend her days inside their emptiness. She cleaned the bathroom, boil-washed the towels. He didn't mind; she suspected he didn't notice. She put some of the tasselled, mirrored clothes from downstairs into a cupboard out on the landing, took some of the dishes and glasses Lowell pressed on her — "far too many, dear me, I never have dinner parties these days" — and, of course, she selected some books.

Without a television, a computer, a phone, or even a radio, the small stack on her bedside table was a miser's hoard of gold. O. Douglas was at the top of the pile, small and perfect with the fringe of a blue leather bookmark curling softly out from between its pages. Under it was a green Penguin of a Margery Allingham, one of the playful ones; a reprint of *Midnight's Children* with a jacket like an album cover (she had always meant to read it one day); an old cloth-covered *Rebecca,* with fine floppy pages like a Bible; and one more, chosen solely for the picture on the jacket. It was the kind of book that didn't exist anymore. It wasn't a mystery, nor a romance, nor even what Lowell called Literature. It was simply a story, a ripping yarn, a tall tale of derring-do. It had an inheritance, a misunderstanding, and a small plane crashing in a desert, throwing two people together, man against wilderness and woman with man. The picture on the jacket, in perfect condition forty years later, showed the aftermath of the crash: sunset and scrubland and two people, the man strong and suave and the woman with a streak of dirt on one cheek and her hair escaping a chignon. She had even found time to tie her shirt in a knot just under her bosom and turn up the hems of her khaki trousers to show off her slim, brown ankles.

Not what most people looked like as they hauled themselves away from the brink of near disaster and stood reeling, catching their breath. Not what Jude looked like as she tackled the bookshop, one room at a time, with rubber gloves and buttoned cuffs, her hair in a scarf and a paper mask on her face.

By the fifth day, though, the shadows were gone from under her eyes and those odd yellow streaks that might be what people meant when they said "pinched" were gone from the sides of her nose too.

"Ho!" said Mrs. Hewston, standing in the kitchen doorway. "You're looking well on it."

"Guilty," said Jude. "It's the sea air."

Mrs. Hewston said nothing but smirked and bridled so much that Jude took her upstairs to show her the little bedsit to prove she was sleeping alone.

"Of course, I haven't been here much since the doctor died," said Mrs. Hewston, looking round the bedroom landing with the quick, angled glances of a blackbird, although the doors were closed. "He was one of the last true gentlemen. Always treated me quite like one of the family. Chocolates on my birthday, brandy at Christmas, always lifted his hat when he drove past."

Jude couldn't think of anything less like family membership than lifted hats and neutral gifts on expected days, but she said nothing. She didn't even realise she had missed the cue until Mrs. Hewston offered it up again in a different form while they were climbing the second set of stairs.

"Yes," she said with a sigh, "you don't come across his like much anymore. And it was a mutual regard. He called me the salt of the earth. 'You're the salt of the earth, Nurse Hewston,' he'd say."

What with her age and all the talking, she was labouring before they reached the attics, and she sank into one of the kitchen chairs in the yellow room as soon as Jude opened the door.

"It was the great sadness of his life that this one didn't follow him into medicine," she added, taking three breaths to get through it.

"Lowell?" said Jude, confused enough to look around for who else she might mean. The Scots with their *thises* and *thats* caught her out ten times a day.

"It's *Lowland*," said Mrs. Hewston. "He was named for his mother's family. They were gentleman farmers down Whithorn way. A great big spread. They looked down on the doctor when he went courting Miss Lowland. Can you believe it? But there, the family died out and the farm's away. Sold

72

on to a bunch of bankers and they're living off cheques from Brussels, like all farmers these days."

Jude nodded, barely listening. The fields around the edges of the town were dotted with sheep and cattle, she thought, and the shops were full of lamb and beef; it didn't seem like much of a con to her. But then, Mrs. Hewston would look at a babe in arms and see a grifter. She was still sneering at man of sixty because he didn't want to take up medicine when he was a boy.

The woman had seen Jude's attention wandering and changed the subject. "And so what's brought *you* here?" she began.

"Like Lowell said," Jude replied evenly, "I'm helping out with a project in the bookshop."

"All the way to London for consultants!" Mrs. Hewston said. "That's the mother's side. A fortune they let slip through their fingers. And all that land. The doctor built up his practice from nothing and retired very comfortably. It *was* London, wasn't it?" she added. Jude nodded. London was a big place. "And you jumped at the chance, did you? Ah, well. I've seen it too many times not to know it again. Galloway is just that kind of place for some reason."

"What kind of place is that?" said Jude,

sounding less even now, she knew.

"Galloway attracts runaways," Mrs. Hewston said. "I don't say it in judgment, dear. But when you've been a village nurse like me, you can't help seeing clearly." She beamed at Jude, delighted with herself.

"I did need a break," said Jude. "So the timing was good, it's true."

"We never had 'breaks,' the doctor and me," said Mrs. Hewston. "We left school and started our training, worked our forty years, took our statutory leave, enjoyed our public holidays, and did our jobs. Grateful for the privilege, we were. None of this 'gap year' and 'downtime.' '*Me* time.' "

"But you're surely much younger than Lowell's father, Mrs. Hewston." Jude didn't mean to flatter; she only wanted to kill the Greatest Generation talk before a second wind.

"Cut from the same cloth," said Mrs. Hewston vaguely. "No running away for either of us, no matter what life served up. You wouldn't understand. I don't say that meanly, dear. It's just different times."

Jude couldn't help herself. "My parents died," she said. "In an accident. Their funeral was a week ago."

Mrs. Hewston cocked her head up to one side and looked at Jude from the corner of

74

her eye. The blackbird again. "No," she said. "I'm not trying to contradict you, dear, but that's not it."

Jude felt a flush begin to spread up over her neck from the collar of the peasant blouse, flooding her cheeks with heat and her eyes with tears. "My mother and father both passed away in a freak —"

"I don't doubt it," Mrs. Hewston cut in. "But that's not all that's going on. That's a clean thing, if you take my meaning." She sat back after she spoke. She had completely recovered her breath now, quite comfortable after the climb, and she took the chance while Jude was speechless to have a proper look round, blandly cheerful as she noted the dishes and the pans.

"Clean?" said Jude at last.

"Bereavement," Mrs. Hewston said, "is an open thing. You gather friends and family round you. You clear the house and do the paperwork. Bereavement isn't trouble. Bereavement isn't . . ."

"Dirty?" said Jude.

"Now, now," Mrs. Hewston said. "There's no need to be upset. We're just talking." She stood up and placed the kitchen chair very carefully under the table. "But I'll take my leave. Plain talking has gone the way of hard work, I sometimes think. I don't mean that

75

to hurt, dear. But I was a nurse when nursing was more than looking at a screen and dressing in pyjamas. And being a doctor meant more than signing notes and passing people on to specialists. He did tonsillectomies downstairs in the dining room, you know."

"The good old days," said Jude, still recovering.

"I hope you don't mind me saying something to you before I go, dear," Mrs. Hewston said. She pointed to the shelf of crockery. "Those are full sets of good china you've broken apart. Some of those plates were wedding presents."

Jude tried to laugh it off to herself once Mrs. Hewston was gone. "China shaming!" she said out loud, shaking her head, but the woman's words had spoiled the peaceful rooms, and although she had been planning a quiet morning, she decided to go to the shop instead and tackle another bay there.

Lowell was gone, in search of a possible Audubon. "A renowned birder," he'd said that breakfast time. "Moved to Galloway from the Essex marshes specifically to work on his list. I tried to get a squint at his library when he went into sheltered housing five years ago, but his daughters would have none of it. We'll see."

"When did he die?" said Jude, watching him count out a thick stack of twenties and fold them into his inside pocket.

"Tuesday," Lowell said. "So they'll be past the shock and just getting round to packing. The housing trust will have mentioned a final bill. The undertakers might have sent an estimate already. Definitely the florists."

"Right," said Jude. "This is a new side to you."

Lowell only grinned, wolfishly, and patted his pocket, the pad of banknotes making a dull, smacking sound through the wool and the lining.

She had never been alone in the shop before, although Lowell had given her a key that very first day, and she felt a flip of excitement in her belly as she unlocked the door and hurried in out of the rain. Excitement or something similar, anyway. The long passageway to Lowell's desk seemed welcoming now, a primrose path to certain pleasure.

Soon she would work her way through each of these bags, up one side and down the other, sorting, dusting, wiping the books, stuffing the empty carriers into a bin bag, and then sweeping and mopping the floor, washing down the walls with long firm swipes. Maybe, she thought, once the floor was clear, Lowell could hang some of his photograph collection on the walls, make a display.

For now, she turned sideways and edged along towards the curtain. Were the photographs framed already, she wondered, and she pulled the little brass handle on one of the shallow drawers. Still locked. She turned away and surveyed her battleground.

She was winning. There was enough order to warm her librarian's heart, still enough disorder to gird her librarian's loins. To the left of the desk, where Lowell could see them, the large and expensive Art and Architecture volumes were now arranged on the deep shelves where they could stand upright, as their beauty deserved. To the right of the desk, the side room was cleared, and everything of local interest — gathered from three floors and every corner — was stacked in there by subject matter, the shelves lately scrubbed with a soapy cloth and now dry again, waiting to receive them. The small room behind the desk, where that single Scottish Fiction case had been, held all the Scottish Fiction now. She had named it Miss Buchan's Boudoir and added the poetry too, of which there was much, Galloway being the sort of place that drew poets and shook out poems from the usually prosaic as they strode the shores and stood on the headlands.

Jude had decided the arrangements after interrogation. What did most people come in for? Fiction. Did those buyers browse other sections? Yes, they often did. Who didn't, if anyone? Tourists. Coach-trippers looking for the printed equivalents of coasters and key rings. And who were the most avid readers of all? Who were the rabid ones, the frantic ones, the bookworms who'd lost all sense of proportion completely? Crime fiction fans, Lowell told her. Mystery and horror and sci-fi too. And amongst the nonfiction? The bird-watchers, as one would expect, although there were increasing numbers of hard-bitten quilters and knitters these days too.

It made sense then, she explained to him, to have Local Interest and Scottish Fiction — the coasters and key rings — nearby, so the bus-trippers' bunions wouldn't be troubled by too long a walk and their old knees (or new knees) wouldn't protest at the stairs.

General Fiction and Literature were in the two big draughty rooms on the next floor, the rooms above the neighbours' shops, with the tall windows onto the street, the good daylight letting discerning customers read pages and pages, whole chapters at a time, before they made up their minds.

Exiled to the top floor were Natural History, for those unhinged twitchers; all the Handicrafts, for those beady-eyed quilters; and the whole dark kingdom of Fantasy, Horror, and Crime. Lowell insisted that Children's Books be tucked under the eaves up there too.

"I'm not so sure," Jude cautioned. "Parents might not want their little ones climbing the stairs."

"Good," said Lowell. "Plenty of children's bookshops around. Mine are for collectors but, dear me, there's a stink if you say so."

The stairs. Jude lifted the latch on the door between Coasters and Key Rings (the name had stuck) and Miss Buchan's Boudoir and began to climb. Each rise was steep and each tread was shallow and the turn was tight and the rail was loose, and if ever a health and safety inspector came near the place, Lowland Glen Books would be gone forever.

"I get the odd claustrophobe," Lowell had said. "But if they tell me what they're after, I can dot up myself and bring it down to them. I made a mint from a very . . . Ah, a very . . . Well, quite a solid Canadian lady who wasn't so much claustrophobic as in real danger of getting jammed — Winnie-the-Pooh-style, you know? So she sat out the back in the shade of the apple tree and I brought everything we had on the Russian royals. An Anastasia complex opens the wallet wonderfully."

"I was just going to say what a sweet man you are," Jude told him, straight-faced and twinkle-eyed. "But then you kept talking."

Russian royals were still in need of a permanent home. All the royals were, come to that; Biography in general, and History too, and Travel and Non-Scottish Poetry, and Plays and all the really dusty stuff like Theology, Philology, the Humour that was never funny, and the now heart-breaking Reference section. As she emerged from the staircase, there on the landing was a beautiful set of the poor old Encyclopaedia Britannica, half calf, buff buckram, tooled in gold, tissue over the woodcuts, clicked into Wiki-oblivion.

I know how you feel, she said silently to them, trailing a hand over their gilt-edged pages as she passed. You and me both, Britannica. Then the portcullis came down.

Up here it was easier to see that Lowland Glen Books had once been someone's home. There were fireplaces in Fiction and

Literature. Shame they couldn't be lit when the wind whistled in around the rags plugging the windows. Jude looked at a shelf or two in each and tried not to form a view. John Irving and his brothers were in Literature; Sarah Waters and her sisters in Fiction. She turned away from both and from the awkward conversation she might need to have with a kind man who'd taken her in, given her a roof over her head and a bed to sleep in, and filled her pockets with tenners.

The little back room above Miss Buchan's Boudoir that Jude had earmarked for Poetry and Plays, since its shelves were so narrow, was actually a bathroom. It had a plate screwed over the old toilet hole, but the washbasin was still there, filled with Beatrix Potter, heaped up against the taps, held together with cobwebs. She could look at it, holding one wrist in the other hand, and feel her pulse slow and steady, like a lizard's. One day soon she would have to empty that sink, and then she would soak herself pruny in scalding water in the cavernous Jamaica House bath as every stitch she'd had on sloshed around downstairs in the drum of Lowell's washing machine.

The room next to it, above . . . Jude wasn't familiar enough with the layout to say . . .

but the next room was a bedroom decorated in the sixties with those emetically cute rabbits on the wallpaper — long lashes and little satchels — and Blu-Tak marks from where posters had been removed. As though the child that chose the bunnies had been stuck with them into the pop group years and had covered them with posters.

She was at the landing window, by the foot of the stairway to the attic floor (even steeper, even narrower, behind an even smaller door), when she heard something. It was a short *chunk* of sound halfway between a squeal and a groan, and it stopped dead after less than a second. Jude cocked her head and, as she turned, she thought she saw something too. Just a flicker of movement and nothing to concern her since it was outside, glimpsed through the half-bare branches of the yellowing apple tree down there. As she moved closer to the tiny grimy pane to take a better look, though — *bam bam bam!* Someone was pounding the front door loud enough to shake the building's rickety bones, stirring dust and setting the mice in the walls — silent till now — scurrying and scrabbling. Jude heard the beat of wings and wondered if gulls had risen from the roof or if some-

83

where in the eaves of the attic floor an owl or even a bat had been woken.

SIX

Bam bam bam!

Police! Jude thought. Who else would pound on a door like that? But police usually shout through it too.

And as she thought it, the shout came. "Hurry up and let me in — I'm drowning!"

Jude fumbled the door open and was bundled aside, staggering against the nearest carrier bag of paperbacks as a woman, coatless despite the drizzle, hurried inside.

"What a pigging awful day," she said, shaking the two flaps of her cardigan. She had poolside flip-flops on and the toes of her socks were wet from the puddles.

"He's — I'm — We're not really open," Jude said.

"I'm not buying," said the woman. She was perhaps sixty, but her hair was older than the rest of her, from years of home perms (or at least cheap perms) and a colour chosen when she was young and

85

never noticed again. "Maureen," she said, wiping her hand on her jeans and holding it out. "From the Cancer. Charity shop," she added, seeing Jude's eyes widen. "I'm overdue for a rootle."

She strode off along the corridor, clicking on lights, quite at home.

"Lowell lets me have his Dan Browns and I give him our Bookers."

"Well, okay, if you're . . ." Jude said. She had never lived in a small town. "How do you know where to start?" she said, looking up and down the choked passageway and thinking about the three floors around and above them.

"You're not wrong!" said Maureen. "I could have danced a jig when I heard you'd arrived."

"Me?"

"To take a shovel to it." Maureen turned sharp left at the desk, into the short off-shoot by Art and Architecture, where Lowell kept a kettle and some mugs on a counter. He filled the kettle from a spout above the tiny washbasin in the toilet and Jude tried not to think about the pipes, nor about the coffee-crusted spoon in the sugar bag and the sugar-crusted spoon in the coffee jar. She would take them back to Jamaica House and soak them. Better, she would buy plastic ones at Tesco. He might not notice that either.

"Can I get you a cuppa?" she asked.

Maureen shuddered, making her smile. Then she batted back a curtain just beyond the kettle counter, another of Lowell's curtains, and opened a door Jude had never seen. She followed to the doorway and peered in.

It was a room about ten feet square, stacked high with carrier bags, wall to wall, all the way from the back to the door.

"I — I didn't —" Jude said.

"O-ho!" said Maureen. "He's kept this bit quiet, has he?"

Jude let her eyes travel over the mound of bulging bags. It filled the room, washing up the walls and brushing the ceiling. She had seen something like it once before, an illustration in a history text about the third Reich. Inside a bookshop, it was obscene.

Some of the bags were tied shut, but most gaped, showing a coxcomb of yellowing paperback pages, the odd flash of colour from a jacket or glint of gold from an embossed title. Jude couldn't bear to imagine the bottom layer — crumbled bindings, torn pages, crushed spines.

Maureen had fished out her phone and was scrolling through her pictures.

"Here we go," she said. "This is the only way I can do it." She held the phone out and showed a photograph of the room taken from exactly the same spot where she was standing. "Three new ones," she said, comparing the image on the screen with the view before her. She slipped her phone back into her cardigan pocket and poked open a Safeway bag halfway up the front of the pile.

"*Casual Vacancy, Bake Off, Fifty Shades,* Picoult," she said. "This is your typical Supermarket Sadie. Save a fortune if they'd just put their name down at the library. I'll just bob up and check Lowell's got these already before I nab them, though. I know where to look."

Jude nodded dumbly. She pulled at a thin, yellow carrier that had bulged out of place at floor level like a lumbar disc. Jilly Cooper's *Riders* was just visible inside. If it had been discarded after one reading by another impulse buyer that meant there was roughly thirty years' worth of mouldering paperbacks in here. And she had actually thought she was *winning*.

"I'll leave the Picoult." Maureen had returned. "But he's got the rest. Well, not *Fifty Shades*. Ask him why not if you want a laugh sometime." She had rechecked her phone and was reaching up to a second bag.

"Now then, what do we have here? Oh, this is different. Yellow hardbacks. I know better than to touch them."

"Gollancz edition," said Jude. When she'd first started in the library, the long stretch of yellow Gollancz Michael Innes was something to navigate by when she was shelving. Like the soft pink block of Mazo de la Roche and the fat spines of the Susan Howatch blockbusters. All gone now.

"And . . ." said Maureen, stretching to the final new bag, ". . . comics. I'll tell the lads up at Kapow! Lowell can't be fashed with comics."

Jude barely heard her. She had walked away to Coasters and Key Rings. "I'm not here, I'm not here," she said.

"That's me sorted, hen," said Maureen, coming to join her with a short stack of books under one arm. "Do you want to get the door after me?"

Jude nodded and smiled, over her slump already. It was all good. That's what the happy people were saying these days to anyone who'd listen. *It's all good.* Yes, there was an extra week's work in there; a fortnight's maybe. But that meant an extra fortnight's pay and an extra fortnight's — she tried to stop the thought before it was finished, but it came anyway — safety.

"I'll let you out the back if it's easier," she said to Maureen. "This weather! Are you parked out that way?"

"Parked?" Maureen said. "There's no parking out there. It's a garden."

"But didn't you come round?" said Jude. "I thought I saw you."

"Round where?" said Maureen. "There's nowhere to . . . you thought you saw *what*?"

"Doesn't matter," said Jude. She walked briskly and opened the front door, then watched as Maureen scuttled up the street with the paperbacks held tight inside her cardi. Then she locked the door again and wandered slowly back through to the Boudoir. It had been a laundry room once, or whatever a utility room had been called in those days, with a door to the drying green.

Jude opened it as quietly as she could and thought she saw, was almost *sure* she saw, through the high stalks of old hollyhocks and the lowest branches of the apple tree, that same flitting movement again.

She *knew* she heard the sound; the squeal that was more like a groan. But this time it ended with a sharp *smack*. Jude made sure the laundry room door was propped open, misusing a tattered copy of *Highland Verse Vol II* that lay on the floor, and picked her way down through the tussocky November grass, feeling the cold and wet begin to seep in at the seams of her shoes. The apple tree had outgrown its space over the years and now filled the garden side to side, like a bouncer in a nightclub doorway. Jude ducked under its lowest boughs but must have brushed against at least a twig because she showered herself with droplets and shivered as she straightened again.

When she got to the end of the garden, she knew what the noise had been. There was a door in the high, stone wall. Peeling paint and sodden wood with an iron handle rattling loosely on its one remaining screw. And, on the path, an arc where the moss had been scraped down to the stone as the old door opened as far as it would go. Jude tried it, just to make sure, and there was that noise for a third time. She poked her head out and looked up and down the lane, but it was empty. Just clusters of wheelie-bins standing in groups like gossiping housewives and no noise but the rain, heavier suddenly, pattering on their plastic lids.

Someone, Jude thought, had been in the garden, creeping around until they were startled by Jude coming out the back. They were gone now, leaving nothing behind but a single footprint in the mud at the edge of the lane, the toe distinct but the heel a skidding swipe, like the mark left on the path. Jude felt in her pocket, ready to take a picture — already the print was softening in the rain — then remembered her shattered phone.

The rain had soaked through at her shoulders and the top of her head was cold, so, with a final glance both ways, she shoved the gate shut and hurried back up the garden again.

Police wear Docs, she told herself, not Nikes. But plainclothes police — detectives — could wear anything, could leave a footprint exactly like that one. But detectives wouldn't run at the sound of a loud knock. It was probably kids. One kid, she corrected herself, and felt her spirits lift. Police detectives went round in pairs, and it was definitely a single flitting figure she had glimpsed.

Back inside, with *Highland Verse* kicked away and the door locked behind her, she leaned against it and closed her eyes. Concentrate, Jude. What had she really seen? Something dark. Very dark. Black, in fact. Too long to be a face, too narrow to be a piece of clothing across someone's shoulders, and too high to be a cat, which was what it had looked like most. The glossy flank of a black cat.

Trick of the light, she told herself. Trick of the gloom; trick of the rain.

"Lonely?" she said, in answer to Lowell's hearty greeting. He had returned before lunch, the hoped-for Audubon carefully wrapped in brown paper and a bagful of Ian Flemings (unexpected and so extra-welcome) slung over his shoulder. "I haven't had a chance to be lonely. I had Mrs. H. just after breakfast and then Maureen popped in for a rummage. And someone was in the garden too."

"Maureen?" said Lowell, and shifted a little. "Ah. Yes, right. A rummage. Did you . . . ?"

"I did," Jude said. "You're lucky I stayed. Lucky it's raining."

"But of course I didn't ever mean the dead room to be part of your remit," Lowell said. "Shut the door on it and pretend it doesn't exist. That's what I do."

"I believe you," said Jude. "But I was joking. Now I know it's there, I'll have to dig in."

"Nonsense," said Lowell. "I couldn't possibly ask it of you." He was unfolding the brown paper with great delicacy.

"It's that or leave," Jude said. She was be-

93

ing honest. It had worked once. "It'll keep me awake at nights." Lowell unwound the last turn of the parcel. "Occupational hazard," she added, shrinking back into the comfort of lies. "Twenty years a book wrangler, you see."

"Well, well," said Lowell. "I'd have said a librarian and a bookseller were kissing cousins." He looked around himself. "Perhaps not though."

"Anyway, the *dead room*?" asked Jude. "Is that what you said a minute ago?"

Lowell gave her a shrug and a sheepish smile. "I can't say no," he said. "Sometimes the relatives still have tears standing in their eyes when they bring the bulging bagfuls round. I can't just say 'no time to sort them; take it all to the dump,' now can I? But once I've accepted them, I can't let the grieving children see the books just lying around."

"So what's all that then?" said Jude, pointing at the choked passageway.

"Kindles and divorce," Lowell said. "They don't count." He had finished unwrapping the Audubon, and he took his spectacles from his breast pocket and hooked the wires round his ears. "My precious," he said in a voice that left Jude halfway between laughter and alarm.

"You're an enigma, Lowland Glen," she

said. "So do you get many grieving children coming round?"

She never forgot it. Those words were still hanging in the air when the street door opened. The words were in the air, Lowell was wearing his reading glasses, and she, Jude, had just decided she could cope with the "dead room." Was patting herself on the back for taking it in her stride.

"Oh! Oh!" Lowell said. He slumped in his chair and his face drained until it matched the fawn cardigan on the seat back.

"Ah!" said Jude. She recognised it as the girl turned away to close the door. It was too small to be a jacket and too long to be a face; it was a sheet of hair as black as a witch's cat, still wet at the tips from her skulking in the garden.

As the girl turned back to face them, Lowell pushed his spectacles up his forehead and rubbed one of his large, papery hands over his jaw.

"Dear me," he said. "You remind me of someone I . . ." Then the words died in his mouth.

She was ethereally thin, small and bird-boned, but her belly stuck out in front of her as round as an apple.

"No," Jude breathed, and she knew from the twitch of Lowell's forehead that he had

95

heard her.

The girl picked her way towards them between the books. Her eyes were wide with fear and her chest was hitching with each breath, but she spoke with a voice as clear as a bell, liquid and warm, with an accent Jude couldn't place.

"Are you Lowell Glen?" she said. Jude saw him nod once and saw too that the hand resting on the Audubon was shaking. "Well, then, I think you're my dad."

SEVEN

For the next few hours Jude was underwater. Or no, not that exactly. More as if she'd been put in Plexiglas. She was the decoration in a paperweight, and everyone could see her and she could see out and she could almost hear too, but a dull plug of sour plastic filled her and a dome of it surrounded her and nothing could touch her through it and even if she hurled herself at a wall, nothing would shatter her free or even make a crack she could scream through.

As soon as the girl spoke, Lowell leapt to his feet and led her by one of her pale tapering hands to his chair. Was she warm enough? Could he put a hassock under her feet? She was fine; her ankles were fine. Lowell nodded, frowning. He knew she might want her feet up, but he didn't know why.

As she was settling herself back, patting

97

the rosy cheek of the apple, Jude turned away — lurched away, really — and filled the kettle, splashing her face with cold water and drying it on the tea towel, always slightly sour from the way it hung in its damp folds from a cup hook.

"Tea?" she said, coming back with a smile.

The girl nodded. Her shoulders dropped; even her eyelids drooped as she relaxed, and she took a huge gusty breath in and almost laughed as she let it go again. All from a smile Jude didn't really mean.

"I was bricking it," she said. "I nearly didn't come in."

"My dear," said Lowell, as he had to Jude so recently. "My dear."

"Eddy," the girl said. "Eddy Preston."

"Preston?" said Lowell. He was searching her face so intently that Jude itched to remind him his spectacles were still halfway up his forehead. He could use them to take a better look.

"My step-dad," said Eddy. "For a bit." Jude watched the emotions passing over Lowell's face like clouds in a high wind. Disappointment then relief. Guilt, finally. "My mum," Eddy went on, and then paused, Lowell still as a stone, waiting. "I'm Miranda's daughter."

"But —" said Lowell, then caught it.

"Miranda," he repeated, and his cheeks showed a very faint pink flush. "Of course, dear me. My goodness. How is she? Is she *here*? Is she with you?"

Eddy's lids lifted again, her eyes larger than ever, and Jude knew what she was going to say. But Lowell kept the same mild expectant look on his face, and it hit him like an anvil.

"She died," said Eddy. "Three weeks ago."

Through all the hurt that was coming in the days ahead, the one thing that kept Jude from running away, even walking into the sea, was that right then — a moment after learning he had a child, the same second he learned his lover had died — Lowell remembered about *her* parents, about her. He flashed her a look of concern, just a flicker, before turning back to Eddy again.

"Why did she keep you from me?"

No *ums* and *ahhs*. No *dear me* this time.

Eddy shook her head, staring. "I was hoping you could tell me."

"Miranda," said Lowell again and then, "Didn't you ask?"

"I didn't bloody *know*," said Eddy. "She only told me when she was dying."

The water was starting to bubble.

"What do you take?" asked Jude, but Eddy didn't hear her; didn't answer anyway.

Then the kettle clicked off and Jude filled three mugs, pushed one into Lowell's hand, and set another one down beside the girl.

"I didn't know if you wanted sugar," she said, "so I haven't stirred it."

Eddy was staring at Lowell, who was staring back. They were drinking each other in. It had never seemed true enough to deserve becoming a cliché, but Jude understood it now.

"I always thought you were —" she said. "I mean, I thought *he* was dead. Then really late on her last night she told me, 'Lowland Glen — it's a bookshop.' I just assumed it was the painkillers. Then a bit later she said, 'Lowell is your father.' I didn't even put the two things together till days later. Lowell and Lowland. I Googled you."

"Painkillers?" said Lowell.

"Cancer," Eddy said. "Pancreas. She tried so hard. She wanted to see the baby." She took two slow breaths, through pursed lips in a silent whistle, the kind of breaths learned in baby classes, then sipped the tea and gave Jude a watery smile. "Lovely," she said. "Just how I like it."

No one likes their tea half sugared and half not, Jude thought, and her heart softened. The poor kid was walking on her eyelashes, choking down horrible tea, scared

100

to ask for anything.

"I'll leave you two to it," she said, thinking it would be easier on the girl not to have two of them gawping at her. Telling herself that was what she was thinking anyway.

Last she heard as she turned the bend in the stairs was Lowell asking, "And is your, um, I mean, dear me, yes, are you all alone on this trip?"

Jude stopped.

"Trip?" said Eddy. Then she gave a little laugh. "My 'um'? I'm not married or anything, if that's what you mean. It's just me."

Jude started walking again and her feet on the bare wooden steps covered the voices even though the close walls deadened their echo.

She walked back and forth between the two front rooms and barely heard a murmur. Just once, Lowell's sharp bark of a laugh startled her, and she dropped the book she had reached for. It fell flat — *smack* — on the floor, and for a moment there was quiet downstairs.

"I'm okay!" she sang out and the murmuring began again.

She could no longer deny it, the thing she had been trying not to see. Joyce Carol Oates in Fiction, Daphne Du Maurier in

Fiction; John Steinbeck in Literature. Mighty Hunters and Ladies Who Pen. She searched for Iris Murdoch as a litmus test but couldn't find any.

Engrossed, she had almost forgotten them when Lowell came and stood in the doorway. He had the dazed look of someone very drunk who can hold it well, or someone newly concussed and not diagnosed, still going about his business. Then he blinked and came back. He grinned at her.

"My dear, you have the most delightful streak of dirt on one cheek," he said. "Let me." He shook out a handkerchief and wound it round one finger, advancing. Jude wiped her face roughly with the back of her hand before he reached her. But the dazed look had come back and he didn't notice.

"I'm going to take Eddy — that's really her name, you know; it's not shortened from Edwina or Theresa. Extraordinary! — I'm going to take her round to Jamaica and make her rest."

I walked there by myself when it was me, Jude thought but didn't let it show.

"Only, I wondered — could I borrow my spare key back? I'll get another cut of course as soon as I can slip up to Newton Stewart to the cobblers, but I don't want to leave the poor child stranded. Do you see?"

"Of course," said Jude. Blood, she thought, was thicker than ink. And babies trump everything.

Stop it, she told herself. Don't be that person. Look where it led you last time.

"How long is she staying?" she asked, and then added hurriedly as she saw him frown, "She's Irish, right? What a journey in her condition. She'll need a good long break before she travels again."

Lowell's brow cleared as he decided she was being kind.

"Northern Irish," he said. "Miranda's family was from Cork, but she seems to have settled in Derry, of all places. Poor soul, poor soul. It's hard to believe. She was a good bit younger than me, you know."

"But pancreatic," said Jude. "That's one of the worst."

"And as to 'home'," Lowell said. "She's quite alone, you see. And she's on her gap year, as they say. Not twenty yet. Dear me. Quite alone. And I didn't want to push too hard too soon and startle her, but I really think, dear me, I really do think she might stay."

Jude nodded. Of course she would stay. Who wouldn't? Nineteen, pregnant, and suddenly not alone after all. "I'll clear out soon as I can," she said.

He came back without a hitch. "Not a bit of it. Why, the house is large even for three of us. No need at all, my dear. In fact, it'll be just like the old days. I had friends all around me in the good old days. Beach picnics, music parties, every room occupied."

"But she's not just a friend, is she?" Jude said. "You and she need to . . . bond."

"We've bonded!" said Lowell in a happy shout. "Already I feel I've known her all my life. She looks . . ." He shook his head and his eyes were shining. His whole *face* was shining. "I'm a father and I'm going to be a grandfather in a month's time. We have a wonderful hospital at Ayr, although it's rather far away. Well, well. We shall just have to see what the doctor says. I shall ring and make an appointment."

Jude dug in her dress pocket. She was wearing a smock today. Bell sleeves and ten cuff buttons, a square of embroidery on the front like a breast plate, and these capacious pockets. She held out her hand.

Lowell blinked.

"The key," she said. "So Eddy's not stuck in the house."

"Ah." He took it and patted her hand. "Well, I'll probably stay with her, don't you know? There's not much on today and there's no foot trade when it's raining. I might just stay."

Once they were gone, when Jude went downstairs again, she noticed the prized Audubon sitting not quite unwrapped on his desk where he had left it, the girl's half-empty mug on top and a drop of milky tea drying into its jacket in a tiny puckered dome.

She had found five volumes of Nevil Shute in various places and gathered them together in Fiction. (Fiction, not Literature. These were yarns as yarn-like as the tale of the burning plane, by her bed.) Five was a nice collection, she thought, and most were in good shape — although one had a bright yellow sticker on its jacket, proclaiming it to be "53", whatever that meant — but she was almost sure she had glimpsed another in that bag protruding from low in the heap in the dead room . . .

It was disorganised and disorderly, a disgrace to library science, to go truffling after it. And she was at least as repelled as she was attracted to that lurking mountain-ous wrongness behind the locked door, crouched there like a toad, growing in the dark like a tumor.

She was close to nausea when she found

herself sidling back in and feeling around for the light switch.

She was right. The bag — thin plastic, years old, and even crisper than it had begun — was just where she remembered it, and inside it, as well as the Jilly Cooper, there was indeed a garish, shiny-jacketed *On the Beach*. The same edition as the one upstairs, but this time without the sticker. Jude plucked it out, stiffened briefly as the toad resettled itself, and then bore the volume away upstairs to the others.

It was in good nick for its thirty years, none of its pages ever folded and no tears at the turn of the spine from being forced into an overpacked shelf. It was only a reprint for a book club, but book clubs back then put out well-made volumes, and it was still an attractive object to the right person. Jude flipped it open and saw that the owner had written his or her name on the flyleaf in that careful old-fashioned script so familiar to her from her grandmother's birthday cards: *T. Jolly* it said, in fountain pen ink. Jude wrote £5 in one corner with her soft pencil and flipped to the back flyleaf. She tutted. T. Jolly was a note-taker and had filled the back boards with his (or her) thoughts about *On the Beach*. Jude twirled the pencil like a six-shooter, rubbed out the 5, wrote

2, and inserted the book into the run, along with its stickered mate, between *No Highway* and *Requiem for a Wren.*

She worked steadily until half past four and then could no longer ignore her stomach rumbling. She would, she thought, stop in at the newsagents and buy a picnic of junk food to eat in her room, not get mixed up in the love-fest downstairs.

The fact was that without a store cupboard of oil, salt, pepper, flour, and all the things you never think of, without a sieve or a grater, it was pretty hard to make food up there, and she didn't know how long the four hundred might have to last her. Those women in the Anne Tyler stories didn't seem to need garlic presses or measuring spoons. Maybe they ate ready-made from the cook-chill, but Anne Tyler didn't seem the type.

Before she left, she took a look around and, despite everything, felt a small nut of satisfaction, plump and shiny, inside her. She'd winkled out all the short story anthologies and semi-fictional memoirs and, feeling less compunction about Lowell than before, had made her own decision about the Ladies and the Mighty Hunters, Fiction and Literature. Doris and Toni were in;

Nevil and Nick were out. And every book she touched got a wipe and felt the soft caress of her pricing pencil.

If only, Jude thought as she killed the light and sank the room into greyness exactly the colour of the water in her book-wiping bucket.

If only what? she asked herself in the little toilet as she poured the water away. If only Eddy had stayed put in Derry all alone? How selfish could she get?

She pulled the street door closed. The rain had stopped and Wigtown was nestled in cosily for the evening with lit lamps and smoking chimneys. The lights of the Co-op and the newsagents shone out across the still-damp pavements, making them gleam.

And Lowell had told her straight: "Plenty room in Jamaica House for three." There was no reason not to think he meant it. She tried not to look at the tabloids arranged on the low shelf in front of the newsagent's counter, kept her eyes trained on the glass cubicle of the post-office section while her mind circled. Eddy wasn't pushing her out either. Jamaica House was still a haven. As long as she was happy to go from treasured guest to tag-along, she was welcome to stay.

It took a good few minutes to register what she was reading.

108

FOR RENT: KIRK COTTAGE, WIGTOWN.
FULLY FURNISHED, PETS BY ARRANGEMENT
£200 PCM. TEL 01988 612932

The postcard was yellowed and there was a square brown stain where the first generation of Sellotape had aged and died. It was stuck to the glass with replacement tape, but even that was hardly young. Jude stared at it. Rented by the month? There was no reason she shouldn't spend some of the money Lowell had given her. The asking price was reasonable. Beyond reasonable. The holiday cottage just big enough for Max and her had been five hundred for a fortnight.

Someone had spoken.

Jude turned round to find the shopkeeper, a smiling woman in her late sixties. Another one. The whole town was peopled by grannies. This one was giving her an expectant look, twinkling but not smirking.

"Thinking on Digger's Cott, are you?" she said.

"Kirk Cottage?" said Jude, scanning the notices for another one.

"Aye, that's right," the woman said.

"It seems cheap," said Jude. "Is there anything wrong with it?"

"Naw, it's a couthie wee hoosie. Todd kept

it braw and betimes your man's been a guid steward since he was taken."

There had been quite a few exchanges like this one since Jude had arrived. Of course, everyone's vowels were mangled, but most spoke English despite the strange sounds. Every so often, though, Jude would come up against a wall of vocabulary, grammar, and rhythm — plus the vowels — that made a person's speech no more than music to her. *Couthie wee hoosie. Betimes your man.*

"Has it been empty a while?"

"Ocht, aye. Your man's no Gekko and there's them as canna thole it."

Jude smiled, understanding one word in ten, and wrote down the number while the woman rang up her Ginsters and Pringles.

"But then there's always them as relishes the peace and quiet," the woman went on, twitching a flimsy carrier off the hook to pack Jude's purchases. "And whatever befalls you at Digger's, you'll never have rowdy neighbours, will you?" She rewarded herself with a deep chuckle as if at her own wit — although Jude was guessing — and handed the bag over the counter.

"So is it Kirk or Digger's?" Jude asked.

"It's baith. And Jolly too. It was always Jolly's Cott when we were wee and Todd was hale."

"Jolly?" said Jude, staring in amazement. "Todd Jolly? T. Jolly? He lived there?"

"Owned it outright," said the woman. "Why?"

"I've just been sorting his books," said Jude. A true Londoner, she was thunderstruck.

"Aye, he was a great reader," the woman said, not struck at all, of course.

"Incredible," Jude said. "What a small world."

"Damn right it is in Wigtown. Books to the boy and hoose to the man and naeb'dy the wiser on either. We've never seen Jollys since."

"Right," said Jude, back to being mystified again.

"I'm Jackie, by the way," the woman said at last, perhaps sensing the encounter was almost over and wanting to prolong it.

"Jude," said Jude, shaking her hand.

"Aye, that's what I'd heard. But I thought you were fixed. And here you're flitting."

EIGHT

Jude tried the number from Lowell's land-line as soon as she got in, standing in her coat in the hallway by the big black rotary phone. When the line went dead after a series of clicks, she felt the little bubble that had grown in her chest deflate again. It was no surprise. If someone was too disorgan-ised to make a go of a cute little cottage — there was no picture; she was only guessing — why would they pay a phone bill?

She climbed the stairs to the landing, pull-ing herself up by the banister rail, weary from disappointment rather than work. Before she could start on the second flight up to her attic, though, Lowell popped his head out of one of the bedroom doors and summoned her with a crooked finger.

"Can we have a chat?" he whispered. "I mean, not if you're tired, my dear, you look rather tired, but perhaps later."

"Is Eddy in there?" said Jude, whispering too.

He smiled at the sound of her name and he stood back, opening the door wide. Jude tiptoed forward and peered in, seeing Eddy on the made bed but covered with a quilt and propped up with two pillows at her back and three in front, including one Jude had been using upstairs as a cushion in an armchair.

Lowell slipped out, latched the door without a single sound, and led Jude away with a gentle hand under her elbow.

Down in the kitchen he grew boisterous, clapping his hands together and announcing that the evening called for champagne. It was mostly high spirits, but Jude looked closer and thought she saw a frenetic edge, as though he were keyed up, dreading something.

"Pretty amazing," she said. "First me then Eddy. Not that I'm — I mean, she's your daughter. I know that's something else again, but it doesn't seem ten minutes since you were watching me sleep when I turned up out of the blue."

"It's like I told you," said Lowell. "Back to old times. Miranda and I weren't here alone. There were at least three of us all that summer and more usually. At the weekends

113

anyway, and for August."

"She lived here?" A daughter who turned up on the doorstep had made Jude think of a one-night stand.

"The summer of '94 until the spring of '95," said Lowell. "That was my, well, dear me, that was my wild year."

Jude tried not to look too calculating, but he guessed anyway.

"Yes, you're right," he said. "I was over forty. Rather late in the day for wild years. But it was my first chance, and look how well it turned out eventually."

Momentarily, he had forgotten about Eddy and as the thought of her came back to the front of his mind and struck him anew, he beamed again, helplessly, like the bowl of a fountain filling with water and spilling over.

"So um, yes, well anyway, dear me," he said, after a moment. His smile had dimmed, although he couldn't turn completely solemn while he had such happiness inside him.

Jude felt her pulse quicken, sure she didn't want to hear whatever it gave him such trouble to say.

"I'm getting on like a house on fire with Fiction and Literature," she blurted out. "I've switched categories for quite a few authors. Less biological." She was, she admitted to herself, trying to start a fight, trying to put a distance between them to help her cope with what was coming.

"Good, good, good, excellent," Lowell said. "Recategorise to your heart's delight, my dear. It was never my forte. In fact, I think my father did the foundation of the organising. He took an interest in Lowland Glen briefly the year he retired. Thirty years ago, by jove. But returning to my point, my dear. I don't want to suggest, not a bit, not for a minute, that Eddy arriving changes a thing. Not a jot, not a scrap."

"But?" said Jude, thinking *here it comes.*

"Well, yes. This is the thing. You see, I showed her round. I wanted to show her where her mother slept and everything she touched. The asparagus bed! That was Miranda's doing. She loved the garden. And the thing is, Eddy — I suppose I'll get used to that: *Eddy!* — has rather fallen in love with the attic rooms, you see." He sat back, slumped with relief for finally having said it.

Jude nodded and hoped her face looked less blank and cold than it felt, because it felt like putty.

"She didn't take at all to the notion of staying downstairs and sharing *these* rooms, but as soon as she saw the attics her little face lit up. Well, I suppose that's because you made it every girl's dream. It is looking very pretty."

Jude nodded again and managed a smile; one twitch out to both sides at the mouth and nothing at all in her eyes.

"So you see, dear me, yes, I have a proposition for you. I own a cottage, you see. Not the bungalow, another one. Minutes away and it's empty and you can have it. It's quietly situated and really very — What is it?"

"Jolly's Cottage?" said Jude.

"Kirk Cottage," said Lowell, with a start of surprise, "but yes they call it that in the village."

"You own it?" said Jude, but even as she aired her disbelief she felt things shift into place. *Your man,* Jackie had said, meaning Lowell. *Your man's a something steward.* And of course she couldn't ring that half-familiar number from his landline! She laughed and, though he couldn't know why, the fountain basin spilled again and he laughed too.

"And the rent's really —" she began, but he shushed her.

"Tush, no stop, no really, not a bit of it. I insist. You're doing marvels at Lowland Glen and I've yet to make it up to you for

116

the discovery of the dead room. So not another word about rent, I implore you."

"When can I go and see it?" Jude said.

"Tonight by torchlight," said Lowell. "Or first thing tomorrow." As he spoke, a squall of new rain hit the kitchen window and the voice of the wind sounded in the chimney. They grinned at each other.

"Tomorrow," said Jude.

"You won't be lonely," Lowell said. "You must come to Jamaica every evening after work for supper."

"Thank you, Sir Thomas," said Jude. *"Sense and Sensibility,"* she added at his frown, and he laughed again.

"Well yes, dear me, but wait until you've seen it, my dear. It's nothing like the one they used in the film."

"So if it's not Jane Austen," she said, "whose novel will I be walking into tomorrow?"

His face might have clouded, or it could have been her imagination, or even just the unwelcome reminder of Literature and Fiction. Perhaps he had been stung by her insinuations after all.

"I'm sorry I was irritable," she said. He shook his head with his mouth turned down in a carp pout, denying all knowledge of any such thing. "I was . . . I felt . . . jealous,

I suppose. I was envious of Eddy."

"Oh my *dear,*" said Lowell. "There's absolutely no need for you to feel that way. I told Eddy all about you — you don't mind, do you? And of course the dear child is only relieved to have someone here who understands. I do my best, but what use is an old codger like me? All passion spent, don't you know."

Jude stared at him. "What do you mean?" she said. "What are you talking about?"

Lowell blinked. "Your parents, of course. Her mother. I've been through it too, as I say, but so long ago now and, well, um."

"Of course!" said Jude. "I mean, it's very different after a long illness and with a baby coming. You threw me. But of course."

"What did you *think* I meant?" said Lowell, eyeing her.

Jude didn't answer for a while. She looked around the kitchen at the pile of *National Geographic* beside the battered old sofa, a pile high enough to serve as a side-table and actually that minute holding the customary plate and mug from Lowell's breakfast. She looked at the gimcrack kitchen units and the rippled vinyl on the floor, at the straggling pot of parsley on the windowsill and the balled-up J-cloth, dark with coffee grounds, stuffed down behind the taps.

While she was staying here under his roof she had kept the portcullis down, bolted to iron rings that were driven deep in the ground. She had to; if she lifted it just an inch and snakes sprang out, slithering into every corner, if filth poured out and coated every surface, if insects swarmed out in clouds to fill the air . . . what would she do? She couldn't clean Jamaica House from roof to cellar every day without him noticing.

But if she was going to Jolly's Cottage (and despite Lowell's warning, the picture in her head was the golden haven from that beautiful movie with a green meadow and women in muslin), she'd have a retreat from his prying eyes and his clever questions. Maybe it was one of those tiny cottages with a door and two windows. Maybe she could clean the whole place every day before breakfast and again before bed. Then she could let all her hard-fought recovery float away, give up on breathing and coping and hurting, and just go back to the comfort of the only thing that really helped. She could pull it even tighter round her this time, without Max to placate. She could clean the inside of the keyholes with cotton buds soaked in white spirit, like the girl in her group therapy used to do. The nurse had scowled, but everyone else in the group, the six of them, seized the tip and felt richer.

So maybe, just maybe, she could let a bit of it go.

"My parents dying was the last straw," she said. "My husband left me last summer — well, made me leave him, actually — and Eddy said she was single too. I thought you meant that. Alone."

Lowell nodded. "Mrs. Hewston guessed as much," he said. "And shared it, of course. Just to be helpful, you understand. She waylaid us on the way in."

"Was she asking questions?" Jude said, her mouth suddenly dry.

"I wouldn't answer them even if she did," said Lowell, smiling.

Jude, with great effort, tried to think of what she'd say if she had nothing to hide. "What did she make of Eddy?"

"I shoved her inside out of harm's way and kept my hand on the door to stop Mrs. Hewston barging in after her."

"I'm sorry," said Jude, "I know she's an old family friend, but she really is . . ."

"Ha!" Lowell said. "You should have met her before she mellowed with age." He sighed. "But she was my father's nurse and she was very kind to him. Loyal and so on, you know. What can one do?"

"I'm delighted you're such a pushover of

a landlord," said Jude, and Lowell raised his glass to drink to that. She hoped he wouldn't question whether anyone meeting Eddy and hearing her tale would be thinking, first and foremost, that she was single.

NINE

It was in her head as soon as she opened her eyes, proof that "sleeping on it" works even when you don't know it's there to be slept on.

Kirk is Scottish for church. The thought was as clear as if someone lying beside her had whispered it in her ear. And the other name that Jackie in the shop had said was *Digger.* But it was too PG Wodehouse for his name to be Jolly, and so she didn't believe it until she saw it with her own two eyes.

She drove Lowell's Volvo, with him directing. Eddy was having a bath.

"I'll shave my legs," she'd said, not noticing Lowell turning pink. "I look like a cactus. I've only got a shower in my flat and I'm so awkward now, like a bloody hippo."

She was wearing a pair of men's pyjamas with the legs rolled up to show her little pipe-cleaner legs, as smooth as peeled peaches. She looked about as awkward as a faerie sprite, not even pregnant amongst the folds of the striped pyjama jacket.

"Be careful," Lowell said. "Don't stand up in the water. Just stay sitting down safe and sound until it's drained, then put the mat thingy in the bottom and shuffle onto it."

"I'll be fine," Eddy said. "Don't worry."

"You said you were too awkward to shave your legs in a shower," Lowell chided her. They were both enjoying themselves. Jude could tell. Loving the stern fatherly words and the pose of a child bridling under the yoke.

"Fine! Whatever!" Eddy said.

"Well good then," said Lowell, and he went over to where she was leaning, standing on one leg like a stork with the other foot against her calf. He made as though to hug her, then as though to kiss her, but in the end he patted her head, stroking her hair down and back as if she was a dog. Jude would have winced to have that large hand dragged across her hair that way, but Eddy either had a sweeter temper or better manners because she only gave him a shy smile and nudged his arm with her knuckles, the faintest ghost of a friendly punch.

"See you soon," she said. She took a breath to say more but stalled.

"I thought we agreed on Pa-*pa*," said Lowell.

"Pops?" said Eddy

"Pater!"

Jude said nothing until she and Lowell were out on the cobbles and then only, "She'll get there. You can tell already she wants to."

"I want her to call me Daddy for a few years until I graduate to Dad," he said. "She's only nineteen and I shouldn't like to have completely missed *Daddy.*"

"I suppose you're sure —" Jude began before she was aware of deciding to. Then she managed to stop.

"Oh absolutely," Lowell said. "It never even crossed my mind. When she walked in, I thought I'd seen a ghost."

"But you didn't know Miranda was —"

"Not Miranda!" Lowell said. "Gosh, no, nothing like poor Miranda at all apart from her colouring. All that black hair. And some of her expressions and whatnot. In fact, it took me a moment or two to realise *who* exactly she reminded me of — one's brain does turn to absolute mush as the years pile up, my dear. But it's my mother. She's like my mother come to life again. Nothing of me in there, thankfully for the poor child."

He was bubbling over with the fun of tracing lineage in a loved one's face. Jude wouldn't have been any less excited, if it was her.

"Can I tell you a — Well, dear me, not a secret exactly, but a shameful thing?" he said.

They were at the car. Jude nodded encouragement but hoped by the time they were settled and belted, the mood would have left him.

"I'm hoping," said Lowell, clicking his seatbelt and tugging it tight, "since Eddy looks like *my* mother, that the baby, when it comes, if it's a boy — dear me, yes, my goodness, only if it's a boy — might take after its poor old grandpapa."

"That would be lovely," Jude said.

"But only if it's a boy," Lowell repeated, flipping down the sun visor and peering at himself in the cracked mirror there. "I wouldn't wish this face on a little girl."

Jude was busy with the seat and mirrors — she was a foot shorter than Lowell and always had to adjust them — then with the ignition, which didn't have much zip left, and she didn't notice for a moment that he was sitting in his seat, staring up at the visor.

"What is it?" she asked finally, when the engine was running.

Lowell pointed with one wavering hand at something tucked into the perished elastic strip beside the little mirror.

"That's hers," he said. "I never sit here and I never — Well, there's never enough sunshine in Wigtown."

Jude squinted up at it, a small gold cylinder, tarnished and dusty.

"A cigarette lighter?" she said.

"Lipstick," said Lowell. "Heavens above. Miranda's lipstick. Good grief. I can see her now, fag in one hand, putting her . . . What did she call it? Putting her . . . ?"

"Slap on?" Jude was guessing, but Lowell shouted with joy.

"Slap!" he cried. "That's it. Good heavens, I wonder what else is still here. Eddy will be charmed, don't you think? To see her mother's things. Don't you think that would make the poor child feel at home?"

"I should put her clothes back," Jude said. "I'll wash them all and return them."

Lowell dragged his eyes away from the lipstick tube and looked Jude up and down.

"Those aren't Miranda's," he said. "She's Am — Dear me, she *was* Amazonian. A Valkyrie. Twice the size of you."

"Oh," said Jude. "That's good then."

"Eddy showed me a photograph," Lowell said, in a very different voice. "One of the nurses took it. Eddy was on the bed and Miranda was in it. Both of them were smiling, but dear me, I shouldn't have known her. All her hair was gone to wisps, like straw. She had a mane of black hair. A *pelt* of hair. I kept finding them all over the house for years. And she had a high colour too, lips as red as cherries. Even without that." He nodded at the open sun visor and then, seeing his face there and seeing upon it the pain of the memory, he snapped it shut again. "The woman in the bed was withered away to nothing," he said. "When one looks at the very elderly or the very ill, one forgets they're not some exotic tribe, but just ourselves at a different moment."

"I suppose so," said Jude. "I've never really . . ."

"There's a tradition in care homes," Lowell went on, "to keep a portrait of each resident prominent in their rooms, to remind the staff that they once were young. It never works. Portraits of youngsters dancing the Charleston looked like museum exhibits to me, and I daresay snaps of me dancing the jitterbug will look like history to whoever spoons mush into my toothless gob when the time comes."

"Which way will I go?" said Jude, after a moment of silence. Perhaps the moment wasn't long enough, because Lowell shook his head, bewildered by the question. "To get to the cottage," she added, and he started back to life and leaned forward, pointing.

She saw the steeple as they made the final turn, driving between brambly hedgerows, leaving the last of the paved streets behind them. The road, rough now under the wheels, led to a pair of weathered-sandstone gateposts, bright with lichen, and stopped there.

"Now the kirk itself isn't used every week," Lowell said. "Just Good Friday, Easter Sunday, and Christmas Eve. We have the new kirk in town for everyday services, Boy Scouts, and whatnot. So it's extremely peaceful here."

It was as though he hoped she wouldn't notice, Jude thought, as they rolled in through the open gates onto the gravel and drove around the side of the church where Lowell was pointing. As though the rows of gravestones, some of them ancient and wind-scoured, corners softened like half-used soap bars and lettering reduced to mossy dents, were not worth mentioning. They leaned like drunks this way and that, several lying flat, passed out; a few were broken where they fell.

Every so often, though, there was a newer one, in sparkling granite with black letters and even sometimes a pot of flowers wilting at the base. Jude turned to look at one of them as they passed but couldn't read the writing.

The cottage was towards the back, beyond it just two ranks of free-standing gravestones and one final row against the far wall. She tried to look at it with a Londoner's eye. A detached stone-built house, full of period charm, hers for buttons, or even for free.

And to be fair, it was lovely. Like something from a fairy tale. It had two big windows below and two little windows above and it showed its ecclesiastical connections by having its door on one gable end like a chapel, sheltered from the weather by a tiny black-and-white-painted wooden porch that made Jude think of a lych-gate. She wished she didn't know, or at least she wished she hadn't remembered, that the lych-gate began as a place to keep coffins while the graves were dug.

The charm diminished as they grew near enough to see the blisters in the paint, the missing roof slates, and the line of damp around the base of the single chimney. The windows were dappled where rain had run through summer dust and this, along with the darkness inside, left the place looking closed and yet watchful. A fairy-tale cottage indeed.

"Yes, dear me. Well, I haven't been out here for a while," Lowell said, climbing out.

"Why do you own it?" Jude asked. "Shouldn't the diocese —"

"Presbytery in these parts," said Lowell. "And yes, of course, indeed, they did. But they sold it to Todd Jolly, who was the last groundskeeper here, and he left it to my father, and so it came to me."

"How long has it been empty?" Jude asked. She was out of the car but put her hand back on the door, thinking to climb in and drive away. She couldn't remember when Lowell said his dad had died — or was it Mrs. Hewston who had told her? — but she knew it was decades ago, and if the doctor had inherited this from its last inhabitant . . .

"Gosh well, dear me, um," said Lowell. "Let's have a look then."

They were parked under a single tree still studded with shriveled red berries — she fought the absurd notion that the very birds of the air didn't come near here — and Lowell, after some fussing with a pair of identical keys, threw the front door open.

Jude let a held breath go, almost laughed

as she did so. Todd Jolly had obviously had what estate agents call "pride of ownership," which was code for "no taste but lots of time." The living room, opening straight off the porch, had stairs climbing up its back wall and had been brought bang up to the minute sometime in the seventies with a pink and burgundy carpet that washed up to the first ledge of a complicated fireplace. The recesses under the windows, deep from the thickness of the old walls, had been turned into drinks cupboards with frosted glass doors and, Jude would have taken a bet on it, lights inside. The furniture consisted of a three-piece suite in a rusty red that screamed holy murder at the carpet and a coffee table of orange pine with a tiled top, each tile a different city of Europe painted Gypsy-style and labelled in jaunty black script: *Roma! London! København!*

"I'm very interested," Jude said. She heard Lowell let go a mammoth breath of his own. "It only needs Hoovered and wiped down. There's no detritus . . ."

"In that case, I'll ah . . . I'll ah . . . Well, dear me, yes, I think I'll potter off and let you explore," he said, holding out the house keys. "I need to pop into LG and then ahh . . ."

"I can walk back," said Jude, trying to

131

swap the car keys for the house keys.

"No, no, no, no, no," said Lowell, backing towards the door. "It's gathering itself to rain and I need the fresh air and umm." He patted his stomach, looking sheepish, and then he was off, striding up the weedy path to the gravel track, practically trotting when he got there, back to Eddy and the baby and everything that mattered to him.

Jude took a minute, sitting on the red sofa, which gave up a cough of dust but no smell of mice or damp. She had to let it go. It was nothing whatsoever to do with her past or her future that Lowell — her employer — had a daughter or that that daughter was having a child. She still had work for a while and a friendly boss, and now she had a whole house instead of a scraped-together pair of attics. A dead house, she couldn't stop herself thinking, instead of those airy, light-filled rooms with the long view to the sea, where Eddy instead of her would now be lying looking up at the stars, her father sleeping below her and her baby curled inside her.

Jude stood up. She hadn't even looked at the view from upstairs here. And it was only one flight, not the long slog to the top of Jamaica House. Wasn't it odd that a heavily pregnant girl wanted to hide herself away

132

up there instead of staying down with her father, who would wait on her hand and foot?

The kitchen made her wonder if T. Jolly had been in the Navy before he took a job as a gravedigger with a cottage thrown in. There was something about the neat arrangement of homemade cupboards and shelves, even the cup hooks at strict intervals and the spice racks and knife racks precisely centred on the only spot of bare wall, that made Jude think of a submarine. When she started opening drawers and found that one was an ironing board and one was a breakfast bar, she felt almost sure, and when she opened the back door and noticed the stout rubber block that let it get an inch away from the spice rack then stopped it dead, she decided not only that T. Jolly was an old seadog, probably an engineer, but also that she liked him. She imagined him, elderly but still upright, with shiny shoes and a clipped moustache. But that was the Army, wasn't it? A sailor would have the rolling gait that kept him steady on a high sea, and he'd have a white beard trimmed close.

He had never married, she decided, never been entangled in messy emotions at all, had left his estate to his doctor in gratitude for . . . Actually, it was hard to explain, unless Dr. Glen had found the cancer that the specialist missed, or had been through the war with Jolly and had carried him over one shoulder from a battlefield. Not in the Navy, she told herself, and shook the daydreams away.

She stepped out onto a small patch of paving at the back door. There was a single clothes pole at the far end of it and a cleat on the cottage wall. Jude could imagine a line of shirts and tea towels waggling in a stiff breeze, tugging at their pegs, and a row of geraniums and petunias planted in the thin strip of soil hard against the house. And despite the gravestones three feet away, she could imagine sunshine — no matter what Lowell said about Wigtown — and clean windows and something like happiness.

Then a gust of wind blew the kitchen door shut and, with timing she couldn't help finding malevolent, the rain that had been threatening all morning finally began. One drop hit her head right in the parting of her hair and the paving stones were spotted and then blotched and then, as the heavens opened, Jude hunched her shoulders and ran round the cottage towards the front door.

Halfway, despite the shower, she stopped. The black letters on one of the newest gravestones had caught her eye, glittering in the wet. Jolly, it said.

IN LOVING MEMORY OF
TODD ROBERT JOLLY
BELOVED HUSBAND OF THE LATE
MARGARET PAYNE
AND ADORED FATHER OF TODD AND ANGELA
"HE SEES EACH SPARROW FALL"
31ST DEC 1905 — 21ST MAY 1985

She stood there until a convergence of raindrops ran down the bridge of her nose and dripped from its tip, then she shook herself, hurrying under the porch and back in at the living room door.

Now she could see Margaret Jolly neé Payne everywhere: in the choice of pink and burgundy for the carpet and in the whimsy of the tiles on the table. What she couldn't see was why a father of two children — an adored father — would disinherit them and give the cottage to Dr. Glen.

She had noticed a roll of kitchen paper, yellowed and rather brittle-looking, but she had no option, so she went through and used it to blot her hair and wipe her face dry, wadding some up and putting the pads under the shoulders of her shirt to soak up the rain there before it chilled her.

Then, newly intrigued by T. Jolly, she climbed the stairs.

They must have moved here once Todd Jr. and Angela were grown and off their hands; there were only two bedrooms, a large one above the living room and a small one at the far end of the house sharing space with a bathroom. This had been T. Jolly's library. It was lined with shelves, handmade by the same careful workman who had built the kitchen cupboards. Jude's librarian heart thrilled to see them. He had planned them meticulously; there was a single folio shelf near the floor by the doorway and a low run of quarto all around the rest of the room. Above them were six shelves precisely sized for octavos and above the window a couple of very shallow slots for maps. The only furniture in the room was an easy chair drawn close to the light, a side table beyond it, a standard lamp behind it, and an upholstered footstool before it with two heel dents in its plump dome.

Even before she looked in the big bedroom — where T. Jolly had made a fitted bed head to rival the fireplace downstairs, replete with nooks and shelving and integral lights and deep drawers below that still ran smooth and silent all these years later — Jude knew she wanted to live here. And not just for the month or so it would take her to finish the overhaul at LG Books. She could imagine a *life* here. She walked into the bathroom — tiled all over; every tile still square and flat decades after T. Jolly had spaced and grouted them — and the window decided her. It was plain glass; no reason for it to be frosted when it looked out over nothing but endless miles of rolling gorse-dotted grass, dark trees in the dips, and pale rock breaking through at the gentle summits. This was better than hiding in a garret with a skylight. Here she was safe not because no one could see in, but because no one would think to look.

Suddenly even the graveyard felt like a comfort. The railings above the wall and the tall gates that she could surely close. The church like a bulwark hiding her cottage from view even if someone ventured along the dead-end lane.

Was it possible?

Soon, Lowland Glen would be licked into shape, and she hadn't dreamed that Lowell would keep her on forever to sit at the desk and read O. Douglas. But he *had* said that thing about being fond of the books but knowing the photographs were his downfall. No, not downfall, she corrected herself. Obsession. That wasn't right either, but it didn't matter. There was more to her plan than just that. She remembered the easy way he told her money was no object. And the way he beetled off back to Eddy. He wanted the girl to stay and, at least until the child went to school, wouldn't he rather be free to be papa and grandpapa? Wouldn't he happily pay Jude to take his place?

Not in fistfuls of twenty-pound notes, though. She leaned her head against the bathroom mirror, stopping the daydream. And so that would mean a bank account and the tax office and the end of everything.

Or perhaps not. Perhaps she was hiding for nothing. Perhaps if she Googled she'd find out everything was okay. She patted her pocket, forgetting for the hundredth time that her phone was shattered and gone. She'd buy a new one, once she'd stopped all this stupid worrying. She'd buy a phone, ask Lowell if she could stay. She was only a cataloguer, but Cataloguing had shared an open-plan office with Display and Events and she'd picked up some basics. Would Lowell's deep pockets hold enough cash to employ her as a . . . ? She didn't really know the name for it, which wasn't a glowing recommendation. But by hook or by crook she'd work, make friends, put down roots. She'd start the exposure therapy again, find

138

a group, and — this was her rest and her reward — she'd sniff out T. Jolly's library, as much of it as was left, and bring it home.

Home to the house he *didn't* leave to his adoring kids, she thought again, as she hurried through the rain to the car and turned the heater up as high as it would go. Were there radiators in the cottage? She hadn't seen them. If it was just the fireplace, she'd wear thick jumpers and toughen up.

Families were weird, she told herself, as she rolled over the gravel towards the back of the empty church, watching the cottage in her mirror. Miranda, for instance, was weird enough to keep her pregnancy a secret and only tell Eddy who her dad was on her deathbed, even though one summer with Lowell must have taught her he'd be the kind of father any girl would dream of. Some men were just made for fatherhood. She would start facing facts like that right away.

TEN

First, though, to LG Books to use the Internet — could she get WiFi at the cottage? — and to pluck *On the Beach* out of place again. Unless someone had bought it, she suddenly thought, putting on a little spurt as she drove along the road towards the first of the houses.

Turning into the main street minutes later, it seemed sadly unlikely. Her neat shelves and clear prices would entice anyone who made it over the threshold, as long as her cheerful day-glo yellow posters didn't annoy them — EXCUSE THE MESS WHILE WE MAKE OUR BOOKSHOP EVEN BETTER! — the way they had annoyed Lowell. He hadn't said much, only that some of his regulars were rather stuffy and would harrumph. But nothing she did inside LG Books would get someone into a car or onto a bus on a day like this. At least she got to park right at the door.

"Ah splendid!" said Lowell, seeing her. Her heart lifted. "I need the car to take Eddy to the surgery." And dropped again. "She mentioned exercise, but it's filthy out there. Great news, my dear. Tremendous news. She's definitely staying! She's going to have the baby here! And then *stay*!"

"That is wonderful," Jude said. "I'm absolutely thrilled for you both." Lowell beamed. "I love the cottage, by the way." He nodded absently. "Do I sign a lease?"

"Tush," said Lowell with a wave of his hand. "Pish-posh. Well then, dear me, I'd better shake a leg." He held his hand out for the car keys and was gone before Jude could ask about services or Internet or a phone number or a deposit or even if she would get a staff discount on the Nevil Shute.

She went upstairs, quicker than the first days, getting used to the rise and the turn and the low ceiling above her, and took it down from the shelf. "Tush," she said to herself, "I shan't hear of it, my dear child. Well, my goodness, of course, dear me, you must help yourself to anything. Pish-posh, not another word."

She didn't even mind the writing on the end papers now that she knew Todd Jolly. She sat down on the kick stool and turned to the back, wanting to know him better.

This is a very sad book, he had written. *I do not know if Mr. Shute is a widower as myself, but Dwight's sorrow for his wife is very sad. This was the wrong time to read this book. Poor M. would be upset to know what she had brought in to me to read to take my mind off my own troubles. She said it was about submarines and just my cup of tea. I need to tell Dr. Glen enough is enough. Archie Patterstone is dead.*

Jude stared at the writing. The familiar name was so unexpected that it took a minute for the last sentence to sink in.

"Archie Patterstone is dead," she whispered. But Archie was an old man's name back then, before its second vogue. There needn't be anything sinister about his dying.

But enough of what was enough? Was this mysterious note connected to Jolly's cottage being owned by the Glen family?

And who was M.? His daughter-in-law perhaps. Jude would have guessed a neighbour from the way he had written "brought in," but Kirk Cottage *had* no neighbours.

Giving the ink a final stroke, she closed the book and went down to the desk. However Lowell had ended up owning the cottage, it was his now and it could be her home. She took two deep breaths to pull courage down inside her, and shook the mouse to wake the computer. She would Google Max's name and find only his Sunday football team, his face tiny and unknowable, just one of twelve in a thumbnail.

She typed *Max Hamner* into the browser and waited and waited and waited, and then cried out, fumbled the mouse, managed to close the window, cleared the history, emptied the cache, all without taking a breath. Then she leaned back in the seat thinking she might faint, leaned forward thinking she might vomit, and couldn't get that string of numbers out of her head. They were printed on the back of her eyeballs, branded there: *414,326 hits*. All in "news."

Shaking, she started again. *Raminder Ha* — she typed and the browser, helpful as ever, finished it for her. She clicked on search. For some reason this one was faster, and she didn't have time to close the window. Or maybe the shock had slowed her reaction. *633,248 hits* she read, and flashed on a headline — TRAGIC NEW MOTHER — before she killed it.

She was wrong to think it was a portcullis. It was definitely a guillotine, at least this time.

Stupid. The cottage was empty and cold. She'd done no more than walk through it once on a miserable winter's morning and yet she felt as if the life snatched from her was something real. The line of shirts and tea towels dancing in the breeze, the geraniums and petunias in the strip of dirt, the rows of spines on the shelves in the little library — they were all more real than any memory of the life she had lived. She saw snowdrops in the tussocky grass at the edge of the churchyard, sheltered from the winds by the lee of the wall. Crocuses, daffodils, bluebells, and then she didn't know. Like she didn't know if geraniums and petunias were out at the same time or would thrive in the same soil and sunlight.

She knew there was one more search she ought to do. How many hits would come shooting out if she entered her own name? What words would the headlines use in place of "tragic" for her?

But she couldn't make her fingers type the words. She stood, walked unsteadily to the street door, and let herself out, locking the shop behind her.

■ ■ ■

"I hope you don't mind me closing," she called out, coming in the kitchen door at Jamaica House. "It's as dead as a doorknob and I'm too cold for a sandwich."

No one answered until she was along the passageway and right in the open doorway of the kitchen. It was warmer and brighter than she remembered it; cleaner too, and there was something bubbling on the hob. Eddy, dressed in one of Lowell's cardigans and a pinafore so large that the bib covered her stomach and the shoulder straps functioned like braces, was sitting at the table reading a gossip magazine, one slippered foot on the floor and one tucked up beside her so that her knee was practically by her ear.

It didn't seem a comfortable pose for a pregnant woman and, as Jude watched, Eddy shifted, putting both feet up on the rung of the chair opposite and slumping down a little.

"He's not here," she said. "He's gone to the town with the two names to get petrol."

Jude had never found a Northern Irish accent beautiful before, but everything Eddy said sounded like lark song. "Newton Stew-

145

art?" she offered, then added, "There's a petrol station in Wigtown."

"He said he got grit in his carburetor one time from that petrol and the engine cut out. He doesn't want the engine to cut out when he's driving me." She blew upwards with her bottom lip stuck out, as if to lift a fringe. Her raven hair, hanging in two curtains from a knife-edge parting, didn't move.

"Hang on though," said Jude. "If he's got enough petrol to drive to Newton Stewart, he's got enough to take to you the doctor's ten times over."

"I know," said Eddy. "He wants enough to drive me to London to the Lindo Wing in case my waters break while I'm in the car." She grinned. "I should tell him to chill, but he'll more likely listen to the doctor. And anyway, I like it."

Jude grinned back, but she knew from the look in Eddy's eyes that she hadn't managed to make it convincing. "Something smells good," she said, taking a quick peek into the bubbling pot.

"Just some broth," Eddy said. "Warmer than a sandwich, though. Go for it."

Jude helped herself to a bowlful, fished a spoon out of the clean dishwasher, and sat opposite the girl.

Once, a rat had died in their under-stairs cupboard when Max was on a double shift. It was high summer and the smell grew by the hour. Jude, hating every second of it but knowing she'd be glad when it was done, covered her hand with a bag and picked it up. She had tied a knot, thrown it away, and squirted air freshener.

She needed to do the same now. To stay here — to hide here — she needed Lowell's help. And this girl was the apple of Lowell's eye. Instantly. She had come along and bewitched him. No! Those were the very thoughts Jude couldn't allow herself to think, like she didn't allow herself to feel the weight of the rat, the soft rustle of its body in the bag as she tied it shut.

"We got off on the wrong foot," she said. Then she smiled and spooned up some of the broth. "This is delicious!"

"It's just peas and onions," Eddy said, "and herbs from his garden out there. Did you know he's got strings of onions hanging in the shed like a bistro? I told him he should have them in the kitchen but he said the steam would ruin them." *He* she called him. She couldn't bring herself to say *Dad,* but she wouldn't say *Lowell* either. "Anyway, how d'you mean 'wrong foot'?"

"Not you," said Jude. "Me. I was a torn-faced cow when you fetched up yesterday."

"I didn't notice," said Eddy. "I was shitting myself. I wouldn't have noticed if an elephant had been in the shop."

Jude wondered. Was that innocent? Telling her she was beneath notice then picking an elephant to compare her to? A unicorn would have worked just as well.

"And you'd just had a fright too," Jude said. "All that hammering on the door when you were in the garden."

Eddy grew very still. "The garden?" she said, turning to look out the side kitchen window towards the rose terraces and the asparagus bed at the far end, where the ferns, yellowing by now and bedraggled in the downpour, served as a backdrop to the sturdy figure of Mrs. Hewston advancing in a raincoat and short wellingtons with a plastic rain bonnet tied over her hair.

"Who the hell's this?" said Eddy, and her voice was an octave lower and a lot less bell-like in her surprise. Which, Jude thought, was unusual, since it normally went the other way.

"This," she said, "is another one of Lowell's hangers-on. You think *I'm* bad."

Eddy turned back to her and laughed. "I don't think you're bad," she said. "I don't know where you've got any of this from. I

148

thought you were his wife! I thought I'd got a step-mum for free and I was happy. I wish you'd believe me."

Jude said nothing. Either the girl had barely noticed her or she thought she'd stumbled over a brand-new mummy, but not both. And there it was again, like "elephant." Telling her she could be married to Lowell and ready to be a granny.

"It really *was* just me then," Jude said. "I'm sorry."

"So what's the scoop about Mrs. Wellyboots?" Eddy said. "Quick, before she gets here."

"Like I said, another one of Lowell's waifs. Well, his dad's waif that Lowell inherited, I suppose. Truly, Eddy, he's been in training his whole life for you turning up here."

Before Eddy could answer, Mrs. Hewston was lifting the latch.

"Knock knock," she called, as if saying it while she barged in would make it like she'd done things properly. When she came round the corner she pretended to be surprised at the sight of Eddy, but her acting was over the top and fooled no one. Besides, she had togged herself up head-to-toe in waterproofs and tramped through wet grass; she wouldn't have done that just to see Jude a third time.

149

"Oh!" she said and actually put her hand up to her cheek in a gesture of affected shock. "Company."

"Shall I introduce you?" said Jude.

"Aye, go on," said Eddy. "Unless you think we better wait."

Jude gave it some thought, unsure whether Lowell would mind missing the chance to drop Mrs. Hewston's jaw. She decided he was probably above such petty concerns. She wasn't, and she paused dramatically.

"This is Mrs. Hewston, Dr. Glen's old practice nurse and now Lowell's tenant from the bungalow at the bottom of the garden."

"Not tenant, dear," said Mrs. Hewston. "Neighbour."

"There's no shame in being Lowell's tenant," Jude said. "I am too." That caught the woman's interest. "I'm renting Jolly's Cottage now that Eddy's moved in."

"Eddy?" said Mrs. Hewston.

"This is Eddy," Jude said, gesturing. "She's Lowell's daughter. She's come to stay."

Eddy, with perfect timing, rose to her feet, held out one hand to shake and used the other to smooth her pinafore over the bump in her belly, pushing it forward as far as it would go.

Suddenly, Jude felt something like a sunrise spreading inside her, lighting up everything. *Everything.* She had no idea what Eddy was up to or where she thought it would end, but all of a sudden, Jude was sure what was going on here: why Eddy would want to sleep upstairs away from Lowell and any accidental sightings of her if her bedroom door swung open; how she could sit with her foot tucked up at eight months gone and why she moved when Jude saw her; why her belly was like an apple and no other part of her had an ounce of flesh on it.

It all made sense now.

ELEVEN

Mrs. Hewston didn't see through it, though.

Her hands hung slackly at her side, forcing Eddy to turn the proffered shake into a wave before sitting again. Mrs. Hewston took her cue and plumped down into another of the kitchen chairs with her mouth open.

"We're having some of Eddy's lovely soup," Jude said. "But you look like you need a cup of tea, Mrs. Hewston."

"Daughter," the woman said. "His daughter?" She was recovering but not rapidly. "What — What sort of age would you be then?"

"Coming up twenty," said Eddy.

"And starting young!" said Mrs. Hewston, almost back to her old self. At last she removed the plastic rain bonnet, shaking it and pressing her curls back into place with a cupped hand before she unbuttoned the raincoat and shrugged it off onto the back of the chair. She wriggled about a bit in a way Jude couldn't account for until she heard the soft plunk of the wellington boots, pushed off, hitting the floor.

"Well, well," she said, once she was settled. "Twenty, eh? So your mum would be . . . ?"

"Miranda," Eddy said.

"Was that the name?" said Mrs. Hewston, as if a girl would mistake her own mother. "I never did get them straight. The *harem,* they called it in the village. I don't join in with gossip, of course. In my position, I had to stay out of all that."

"Harem?" said Jude.

"What's that mean?" said Eddy

"Oh yes," said Mrs. Hewston. "Jamaica House was quite the place to be in them days. Parties, music, you name it. So you're that Miranda's girl, are you? Aye well, you've a look of her."

Eddy smiled politely.

"And how's she keeping? Is she here on the visit too?"

"I'm not on a visit, Mrs. Hewston," Eddy said. "I've come to stay. And my mum died, I'm sorry to tell you."

"Died?" said Mrs. Hewston. "And you not even twenty."

"There's a lot of it about," Jude said.

But Mrs. Hewston wasn't listening to her.

153

"Miranda's little baby all grown up," she said. "And Miranda gone."

Her next words split the air in the room. Cracked it wide open.

"I remember the night you were born."

"What are you talking about?" Eddy said, one eyebrow up and one down. "I was born in a village just outside Derry."

"You were born right here in Jamaica House," said Mrs. Hewston. "Your mother must have told you the story, didn't she? About how I heard you crying and came to help."

"You — You — *What?*" said Eddy. Both eyebrows were down now and there was a deep vertical score between them.

"I'm a nurse, like *she* said, and there's no mistaking the sound of a newborn's cry. But your mother will surely have told you all this." Mrs. Hewston looked annoyed. The youth of today not listening to their elders.

"I honestly have no idea what you're on about," Eddy said.

"She didn't tell you about me?" said Mrs. Hewston.

"Um, *no,*" said Eddy. She had recovered. The tune of her speech was back to air quotes and unspoken *duhs* again. Sarcasm as the default setting. "She told me about the night I was *born,* in a *yurt,* in a *village,* outside *Derry.*"

"Maybe she left a letter telling you?" said Mrs. Hewston. The sarcasm was lost on her.

"Telling me what?"

"*I* can tell you, if you really don't know." She straightened her jumper and crossed her arms cosily. "I was watching the telly — unusual for me to still be up by the ten o'clock news, but I made a special effort that night. Terrible doings in America."

Jude believed that bit. Mrs. Hewston would have been phoning cousins in Indiana on 9/11 hoping to hear they'd gone to New York to catch a Broadway show.

"So you were watching the telly at ten o'clock, minding your own business," Jude said.

"I was born in Derry," said Eddy again.

"And I heard you crying."

"Mrs. Hewston," said Jude, "don't you think Lowell would have known he had a daughter if she'd been born in his house?"

"He wasn't here," Mrs. Hewston said. "He was over *there* on some trip or other. See, the doctor stayed at home tending to the sick apart from his two weeks away. But sometimes it seemed the other way on with — Ho!" Her brain had caught up with her ears at last. "He didn't *know*?"

Jude could have bitten off her tongue,

stuffed the words back in her mouth.

"Well!" Mrs. Hewston said. "I knew that was the end of the party. The house was empty when I woke, but it never occurred to me that he didn't *know*. Mind you, it never occurred to me that he was the father. Your mum was just a child herself, here and there with all those lads that hung around, and *he* was gone forty. But then some men prefer youngsters, don't they?"

"What do you mean, *youngsters*?" said Eddy, looking sick.

"I don't mean kiddies!" said Mrs. Hewston. "I wouldn't stand by if *that* was going on. I just mean too young for him. Young girls and boys who didn't know any better. You two should watch out for yourselves, you know. You can't be too careful these days."

"For God's sake," said Jude.

"That's my dad!" said Eddy.

"Oh!" said Mrs. Hewston, and Jude was sure her cheeks reddened. "I wasn't thinking. I'm an old woman and I get mixed up sometimes."

"Aye right," said Eddy. "Cheers for making out my mum was some kind of slag too."

"When did I do that?" said Mrs. Hewston. "What did I say? I assure you I meant nothing of the kind." She was wriggling again as she worked her wellingtons back on. "I'm not interfering."

"God almighty," said Jude.

"I know my day is done and it's all changed," Mrs. Hewston went on, "but I really do have to say this." She turned to Jude once she had struggled her way back into the damp mackintosh. "You'd better not go taking the Lord's name in vain at Jolly's Cottage. I'm just telling you to be helpful, dear. You don't want your neighbours rising up to tell you what they think of you."

She left with her coat flying back in two wings behind her and her rain bonnet clutched in her hand. They watched her stumping down the garden until she disappeared between dripping fronds of asparagus fern.

"She's horrendous!" Eddy said. "Does she just barge in and go on like that all the time?"

"That was towards the top end, I think," Jude said. "But she's harmless, really." She said it to comfort herself. Truth was, Mrs. Hewston worried her. Straitlaced and always watching.

"She's barking mad!"

"Well, you can take everything she says with a pinch of salt anyway," Jude said. It seemed a smart move. Discredit her before she caused any trouble.

"Total crap! She heard me crying all the way from Ireland? She's as bad as that bint that can see Russia from her front step." Eddy sighed. "And I look nothing like Mum." She sighed again and rubbed her belly. "But I'm glad she came. *We're* pals now, aren't we?"

"We're pals," Jude said.

"And why weren't we?" said Eddy. "What was the problem before?"

Jude got up and took her empty bowl to the sink, buying time to decide what to say. She was just a kid, half Jude's age. Would she understand? She turned, leaned against the sink, and gave it a go.

"I was married," she said. "Then someone else came along and I was out on my ear. It brought back memories. That's all."

"But I'm his daughter," Eddy said. "Not a . . . Like a . . ."

"Rival," said Jude. "I know. And I'm an employee. It didn't make sense."

"So it wasn't me being pregnant then?"

"No way," said Jude. "To be honest, I thought that was a scam." Eddy stared. "You know," said Jude, "a cushion up your front?"

The girl stared for another minute then

stood and undid three buttons of her pinafore to show a patch of taut, waxy-looking skin streaked with purplish-red lines across the alabaster.

Jude chuckled and raised her eyebrows, turning her lips down in the expression that means "idiot," even to monkeys. She had seen it once on the telly.

But what she was thinking was that Eddy had chosen a strange way to show her. Wouldn't most people just have lifted their skirt up? Perhaps she was shy about showing her knickers. Or perhaps those plastic pregnancy bellies that fasten round the back with elastic straps, although they were very lifelike with the stretch marks and all, are more convincing if you can't see the edges.

"Satisfied?" Eddy said, when she was buttoned up again. "Jesus, I knew *something* was bothering you about me. But I can't believe it was *that.*"

Jude said nothing. Eddy's original story had been she didn't know anything was wrong at all.

"Shoot me," said Jude. "And, listen, thanks for the soup. I need to go and get my stuff packed up. Clear out and let you move in. I'll scrape it together now and get some boxes from Jackie later."

"Jackie?"

"In the Co-op," said Jude, knowing how pathetic it was to show off that she knew someone's name but unable to help it. "You'll be used to it, living in a village, but I'm still tickled pink, knowing everyone, everyone knowing me."

"I'm used to *that*," Eddy said. "Miranda didn't exactly blend into the background. Even in a new place, we were never incognito. And I don't suppose *I* will be." She made that same gesture again, smoothing her hand down over her front and tucking her dress in close, making Jude think of a duck preening its gleaming feathers.

"I'd say not," Jude said. "This doesn't strike me as a place you can keep secrets." A pretence of openness. That was a good move too.

"Good," said Eddy. "I'm here to get some answers, so that's good news to me."

Before Jude could reply, Lowell's voice rang out from the front of the house.

"Madam, your chariot awaits!" He arrived in the kitchen, sweeping off his hat and bowing low. "I've parked out the front. Those cobbles get terribly slick in the rain. I should wash them down with . . . Well, dear me, there must be something."

"Jeyes fluid," said Jude. "And get some grit before the first frost too."

"I'm not going to throw myself at the ground walking to the car," Eddy said.

"But it changes your centre of gravity, doesn't it?" Jude said, poking again, just gently. Shouldn't the girl herself be worried about those mossy cobbles and frost on stone steps?

"Do you want some soup?" said Eddy, and Lowell leapt across the kitchen for a bowl before she got to her feet.

"There's just time before your appointment," he said. "I'm taking Eddy to the doc to start the ball rolling," he told Jude.

"Is that right?" Jude said. A doctor's visit would put the pregnancy beyond doubt, she admitted to herself, and yet Eddy's answer set off all the alarms again.

"Yeah, it *is* right," the girl said. "So what?"

Lowell noticed nothing. "So how have you passed your morning?" he asked. Jude opened her mouth to apologise for shutting the shop, but he went on, "Besides making this delicious concoction."

"We've had a visitor," said Eddy. "Mrs. Whatsit."

"A surprise attack, more like," Jude said.

"Mrs. Hewston?" said Lowell, sitting. "Well, well. What did you say? I'm happy to field any enquiries from that quarter of course, dear child. Well, not happy, dear me, no, but at your service."

"Jude told her," said Eddy. "She nearly died."

Lowell choked a little, laughing through his first mouthful of soup.

"But you should have seen the recovery," Jude said. "She was all over it like a rash in ten seconds flat."

"Oh?" said Lowell. He was tearing lumps of bread and dropping them into his soup bowl. His manners were an odd mix of posh and revolting. Napkins in rings but open-mouthed belches with no apologies.

"She went straight from never clapping eyes on me to remembering the night I was born," Eddy said. Lowell's eyebrows shot up and he coughed, either from a second choke or because he hadn't recovered from the first one. Eddy laughed. "She — what was it, Jude? She heard the cry of a newborn baby but she just kept watching the telly cos she was glued to the news. And then the next day Mum had hooked it and was never seen again. She's barking, isn't she?"

"Mad as a brush," agreed Lowell. "Be ready for her to decide she was Miranda's bosom pal, won't you?"

"That's exactly what I thought," Jude said. "She was glued to the news because there was some scandal or disaster somewhere and she wanted in on it."

"Scandal," said Lowell, "not disaster." He wiped his face with his napkin and put his spoon down. "It's funny she should say that, actually. The last time I saw Miranda, she and I *were* glued to the news, as a matter of fact. It was the verdict on the OJ trial."

"The what?" Eddy said, and Jude and Lowell shared a look.

"She said it was America, right enough," said Jude.

"But it wasn't the night of your birth," said Lowell. "I can ah . . . I can . . . Yes, dear me, I can attest to that. Still." He cleared his throat, from embarrassment or yet more fall-out from the soup. "A grain of truth, eh?"

"What grain of truth?" said Eddy. "How can there be a grain of truth about me being born here?"

Lowell gulped.

"But wait," Jude said. "She reckoned you were travelling. She said you were in America. She was worried about you getting caught up in it. Were you?"

"What *is* an OJ trial?" said Eddy.

"Well now, dear me, yes," said Lowell. "There's that grain of truth again. I *was* travelling. I came home and found Miranda waiting for me."

163

"Oh, I get it," Eddy said. "You mean that was the night I was conceived? But how can you be so sure?"

"Because it was the, ahhh . . . It was the only, ahhh . . ."

"Seriously? I was a one-night special?"

"And what about the cry of the newborn baby?" said Jude, trying to change the subject before Lowell's blush singed his shirt collar.

"Oh, gad!" said Eddy. "Which one of you is the squealer? Toxic vomit."

"But I'd been in Plymouth at a maritime book fair," Lowell said, doggedly. "Not in L.A." He gathered their bowls and piled them in the sink on top of the morning's porridge pot and the chopping board from Eddy's cooking.

"I'll just show these the dishcloth," he said.

Jude didn't offer to help. She couldn't bear to dry what he washed. *Showing them the dishcloth* was all too accurate. She just kept an eye on the rotation and made sure to use plates *she'd* been responsible for washing.

"I'm sorry you were subjected to Mrs. Hewston quite so soon, dear child," he said.

Eddy shrugged. "It was nice to speak to someone who knew Mum, no matter what

164

they say about her."

"Oh? And what exactly did dear Mrs. Hewston have to say?"

Eddy sent a worried look over to Jude.

"Don't worry," Jude said. "He's heard it all before." She turned to Lowell. "Pretty much that your father was a saint and you were Hugh Hefner."

"Who?" said Eddy.

"And Raminder was no better than she should be."

"Who?" said Eddy.

Jude rolled her eyes, but this time Lowell joined in.

"Who's Raminder?" he said, and Jude felt the colour, all the rosy glow from the hot soup and shared laughter, leave her cheeks.

"Slip of the tongue," she said. "I meant Miranda."

"Although Raminder is a name, isn't it?" said Eddy. "Indian."

"I've never heard it," said Jude, recovering.

"Nor I," said Lowell. "Not round here anyway. Wigtown is many wonderful things, but a melting pot? Dear me, no."

"Well, if she's moved in, like you and me, Jude," said Eddy, "we'll soon know. No secrets here, like you were saying."

She spoke so lightly that Lowell, elbow-deep in suds at the sink, didn't even pause in his tuneless whistling, but Jude heard something under the tone and felt a chill crawl up her neck and shrink her scalp, leaving her tingling.

"Good luck at the doctor's," she said and was sure she didn't just imagine the girl's face clouding over.

TWELVE

Jude had only just gone back round to the shop to start her afternoon's work when they returned. It was clear something had changed.

"Glad to see you opened up again," Lowell said as he ushered Eddy in. He was holding an elderly golf umbrella over her, brought it right inside before drawing it away and shaking it out at the open door, shooting it into the umbrella stand when he was done. "Sandy at the doctor's said there's a coach load around somewhere." He turned to Eddy. "Since *Jude's* here doing *her* duty, I can take you home."

"I don't mind," Eddy said. "I keep saying."

"And actually, Lowell," said Jude. "I could do with concentrating, not bobbing down every time the door goes." In truth, she had been sitting blankly at the desk, summoning the courage to look at the Internet again and had only leapt up, grabbing her duster, when the handle rattled. She was aware of the desk chair slowly turning, one arm of the fawn cardigan hanging down.

"Ten minutes, then," Lowell said, clipped speech for him. "I need to find something in Biography."

Eddy took the chair and Jude settled on the bottom step. When his footsteps told her he was on his way to the top floor, she spoke.

"What happened?"

"I didn't like the doctor," said Eddy. "I didn't sign on."

"What was wrong with him? Her?"

"Him. I didn't like him. I don't want him delivering me and there's no practice mid-wife."

"But what was *wrong* with him?" Jude said. "Was he rough?" Poke, poke. "Or did he give you what-for for being pregnant?" she added as a distraction.

Eddy screwed one eyebrow up and dropped the other one down. "What? They can't do that. It's none of their business."

She was right, of course. Only, Wigtown was the kind of place where the doctor and the minister might well still dress you down for moral failings. With Nurse Hewston standing by, nodding.

"Is he a creeper?" said Jude. "We had a doctor when I was little called Dr. Goff and everyone called him Knickers Off Goff."

Eddy giggled. "We never got that far," she said.

Jude managed to sound surprised. "He never examined you?" The girl had handled it beautifully. If she had quibbled about seeing the doctor from the off, Lowell would have wondered why and might have got suspicious, but going along cheerfully and then claiming to have changed her mind for a reason she wouldn't make clear . . . Who could argue? She was good at this. If she was really at it.

"How come?" Jude said.

"He wanted to muck about with me," Eddy said. "Interfere for no reason."

"Examine you, you mean?" said Jude. "Are you weird about people seeing your body?" Poke, poke, poke.

Eddy snorted. "What century were you born in?"

"Okay, so what's the problem?"

"He wouldn't let me sign up for a home birth," said Eddy. "He was a right stuck-up shite about it, actually."

"A home birth?" said Jude, thinking of Jamaica House, dusty and draughty, with its creaking, sprung beds and its long slippery

169

bath, no handrails, no shower hose.

"Why not?" said Eddy. "I'm healthy."

"You're nineteen!" said Jude. What she meant was that nineteen-year-olds wore Playboy bunny tee-shirts and got Brazilian waxes and thought women's rights were for their grannies. She remembered a conversation in the staff room at the library when she said she wouldn't let a man pay for dinner, all the youngsters hooting with laughter and calling her a sucker.

But Eddy misunderstood her.

"Nineteen's when we should be pregnant," she said. "Nineteen's normal. It's not natural to wait till you're God knows how old like everyone does now. No offence." She paused, but Jude didn't respond with a *none taken,* so Eddy just stuck her tongue out and sailed on. "And I thought this was totally the kind of place they'd have all that water and chanting. I was dead chuffed when I looked him up and he was living here. Christ, it was like having Mum back again. 'Go to the biggest hospital you can find and get everything modern medicine can give you.' On and on."

"Really?" said Jude.

"Right? That's what I thought. I thought she'd be on my side because she was so . . . Never met a crystal she didn't believe in.

170

And she hated official things instead of homemade things. We had three kids living with us for a year once when their mum was in the bin. Mum was adamant we could cope. Instead of them going to a fosterer or into a group home."

"It's not really the same thing," said Jude.

"I know," said Eddy. "Anyway, Mum came from care, so that explains that. And apart from her one blind spot about me having this baby in a space-age laboratory, she was pretty sorted out about most things. At least, when I came looking for *him* I knew he wouldn't be an accountant or that. No offence."

"I'm a librarian," said Jude.

"Right," said Eddy. "Exactly."

"Speaking of which, I think I'll go and get on with it," Jude said. "Shout up if the rush gets too much for you."

She walked up the first flight making no effort to be quiet — making a bit of effort to be noisy, actually. Then she slipped off her clogs and padded as silently as she could up the second flight. A pregnant woman wouldn't climb these steeps steps if she didn't have to. A girl pretending to be one wouldn't, certainly.

Lowell was standing in the back room gazing around in dismay.

"What happened here?" he said. "There should be two shelves of military biography."

"Have you just been standing there this whole time willing them to come back?" said Jude. "What happened is I put them downstairs with all the other Biography in the L-shaped bit." She held up a hand to stem his protest. "Because they've all got the same Library of Congress and Dewey numbers, and I'm guessing the average age of the military buff is not twenty-five and I'm saving their poor old feet with corns from all the marching."

"What about my poor old feet?" Lowell muttered.

"You didn't tell me what you were looking for, for one thing. And for another, this isn't what's bugging you." She left a pause and then tried to turn her voice gentle. "What *is* bugging you?"

"What's *upsetting* me is I don't think Eddy's going to stay after all. As to what happened . . . Well dear me, I have no earthly idea. Not a clue."

"She doesn't think much of the doctor," Jude offered.

"She refused to listen to reason!" Lowell exclaimed. Then they both, with a look at the floor, realised how loud he was talking.

When he spoke again it was in a fierce whisper. "He's not against the notion at all — although why on earth any sensible girl would eschew medicine on the one day in her life she's most likely suddenly to need it . . ." His exasperation had left him breathless and he heaved and puffed before starting again. "But the doctor was sweetness and kindness. He explained how far it was to either hospital — Ayr or Dumfries — and how bad the roads are, and if she'd been at all in the mood to listen she would have seen the sense of it. If things go wrong there's simply no *time* for the journey. He was very clear."

"He doesn't seem to have been very clever, though, if he put her back up and made her dig her heels in."

Lowell was shaking his head. "She walked in looking for trouble," he said. "She made up her mind on the drive over."

"Oh? What happened on the drive over?"

"Nothing!" said Lowell, and they both glanced downwards again. "She spent the whole time poking at the tiny tyrant." Jude quirked her head. "The inevitable and dreary iPhone. One of your finest attributes, my dear, in my obsolete opinion, is that you do not possess one."

Jude registered the compliment, undeserved, with an absent smile. Had Eddy found something online that changed her mind? Had she got an email that put her off? Or had she, as Jude thought, always intended to dodge the doctor in the end? Or perhaps they were both wrong and she really was a fledgling earth mother, stung by the condescension of the Wigtown GP.

As Lowell pottered off in search of his prey, she decided that, since she was here in what was destined to be the Crime, Horror, and Fantasy section, she might as well do some work and clear some floor space.

Years of shelving in her past had left her with an instinct for it. She knew to leave plenty room for Cs in crime, Ks in horror, and Ps in fantasy, and when she started in on the nearest pile, knee-high and four-square, indeed there were endless Pratchetts, well-thumbed and grubby, endless Childs and Christies, and more Kings than she could believe.

Under a full set of the Inspector Wexford novels, she found a nice early edition of John Wyndham's *The Chrysalids* that got her thinking. A librarian doesn't consider value but, here at LG Books, was a subject-matter split enough? Should the tatty Pratchetts be shelved with that pristine Wyndham, or should there be a premium section for hardback, first editions, and rarities? What would something like this be worth anyway?

She flipped it open and felt a burst of warmth to see *T. Jolly* on the endpaper. Immediately she checked the back but was disappointed not to find any notes there.

Back on the ground floor, Eddy was sitting mulishly in Lowell's chair scrolling through messages, while he leaned awkwardly past her to look at something on the computer.

"Price, Lowell?" Jude said, holding up *The Chrysalids.*

"Ah, Wyndham," Lowell said.

Eddy rolled her eyes and Jude bit her cheek to hold back a smirk. It was a classic father/daughter relationship already in some ways.

"Underappreciated these days of course," Lowell said. "Dear me, now *The Day of the Triffids* is a fine piece of story-telling but not flashy enough for —" He broke off and Jude was sure the words he had swallowed were *the youth of today.* "Fifteen pounds," he said instead.

"For an old *book*?" Eddy squeaked.

"And look," said Jude, ignoring her. "I'm glad to see not everything he owned ended up in the dead room."

Lowell gave her a sheepish look and rubbed his jaw. "Well, dear me, yes, but you see he used to drop in. Bring me things, you know. He had none of the snobbery that leads a pedestrian mind to value the obscure."

"What the hell are you *on* about?" Eddy said.

"And he was the kindest man," said Lowell, absolutely ignoring her. "For instance, dear me, I had quite forgotten this and it's a charming story. When his daughter . . . Now what was her name?"

"Angela," said Jude, and Lowell registered his surprise with a startled look that dislodged his spectacles from his forehead and deposited them towards the end of his nose, which startled him even more.

"I read his gravestone," Jude said.

"Jesus," said Eddy. "Is there anyone normal in this entire town?"

"So you see, dear me, yes, Angela *wasn't* a reader. And so one Christmas, when she gave old Todd a book-club membership as a present — very thoughtful — he was distressed whenever he was sent a duplicate. It happened moderately often because, as I say, of his populist tastes: Trollope, Brontë, Wyndham."

"He wasn't exactly slumming it," said Jude.

"So he would bring the original to me. In case, you understand, Angela saw that there were two and felt her gift had been unwanted. The kindest of men."

"Sounds a bit uptight, if you ask me," said Eddy.

"You're saying his first editions are in stock or sold, and Angela's are all in the dead room?" Jude said.

"Well, as I say, she wasn't a reader and she'd moved to Christchurch, and so you see the next chapter of the story unfolds. In his last years he signed up for yet another book club. One hundred books to read before you die."

"Seems like the time to do it," Eddy said.

"Along those lines anyway," Lowell said. "Quite a few of the town's worthies joined, I think, since I've got multiple copies of some of the offerings. Of course, this was years before the true epidemic of book clubs, but it was annoying enough for a bookseller to notice."

"And what sort of age would he have been by then?" Jude asked.

"In his seventies."

"Jesus, good luck reading a hundred books!"

"And of course, my dear, among the hundred books to be read before — that is, while one *can* — were quite a few of the same again. *Barchester Towers, Wuthering Heights, Of Mice and Men.*"

"Sounds like enough to finish 'one' off," Eddy put in.

"And so we had a fair few of Angela's passing through our hands too," Lowell said. "But yes, I'm afraid to say, his entire final library awaits your attentions, my dear."

Eddy looked up, ready to protest, but when she realised that Jude was his "dear" this time, the scowl on her face dropped away, leaving it naked. She saw Jude noticing, though, and managed to close herself again, with a snap.

"Great story," she said.

Lowell levelled a look at her. "When I disappointed my father," he said, "which was often, he used to tell me that soon enough my son would be disappointing me. It strikes me, my other dear — my primary dear, my unexpected and utterly delightful dear — that as you sulk and mock, you can lay your hand upon the little one who, in days not far hence, will be sulking and mocking you."

Eddy stared glumly at him for a minute

before she spoke. "It would be less weird if someone was feeding you all this through an ear piece. Just coming out with it like that is freakorama."

"Speaking of fathers and sons," Jude said, "and daughters. Todd and Angela sound pretty tight."

"Tight?" said Lowell.

Eddy snorted.

"Not estranged in any way, I mean. Have you any idea why he left his house to your father?"

Lowell heaved an enormous sigh and rubbed his face with his hands. "Indeed I do," he said. "It's a sad tale. He was forced to let his wife go into a nursing home. She was very frail. Younger than him, but, as they say in these parts, she didn't 'keep well'. He visited her every day and she cried inconsolably when he left. After that — or perhaps he had always felt this way, in which case, dear me, it must have been even worse, so let's hope not — but after that he had a horror almost amounting to a phobia about ending up there himself. He left my father the house to thank him for letting Todd die in his own home."

"Is that ethic —" Jude began.

"Oh, but my dear, my father didn't know about it! He made home visits and organised nursing care because he was that kind of doctor. But when Todd died and the will was read. *Well!* Can you imagine? The BMA took a long hard look at him —"

"The *who*?"

"The British Medical Association. Yes, a very long hard look and there were rumblings about an enquiry. But three things saved him. One, he tried to refuse the bequest. Two, he had decided to retire. I think he was holding on as long as Todd held on. And most importantly, three, Angela, halfway around the world, and young Todd, only in London but further off in a way, put in a good word for him."

"And saved themselves trailing back here to crack out the binbags," said Eddy.

"Unkind but not untrue, dear child," Lowell said, and Eddy gave him one of her sunniest smiles.

"Sorry I was a mare," she said. "You're dead good at not reacting. Both of you."

"Are you commending or complaining?" Lowell asked her.

"I'm just saying you're weird," Eddy said. "*My* dad —" She stopped and Jude saw that Lowell had grown very still. "My step — Mum's — Well anyway, he'd have been throwing bottles."

Lowell stood up so suddenly that he

180

knocked a pile of invoices off his desk and sent them swishing out in a fan across the dead nap of the old carpet.

"He beat you?" he demanded. "This Preston fellow? He hurt you? What's his address?"

"He — No!" Eddy said. "Well, he smacked my bum when I was little if I was asking for it."

But all Lowell heard was *smacked*. "Where is he?" he said, even louder. "Have you a phone number for him?"

"It's just an expression," Eddy said. "*Throwing bottles*. Didn't your dad smack you?"

"Bottles?" cried Lowell. "He's an alcoholic, is he? He beat you when he'd been drinking?"

Jude was crouching to pick up the fallen papers and said nothing.

"No!" said Eddy, as loud as Lowell now. "Well, yes. Yes, he's a drinker and not a happy drunk, but he never lifted a finger to either of us."

"I'll still have his address," said Lowell, snatching a piece of paper out of a drawer and holding his pencil over it like a dagger.

"Lowell," said Jude, from her position on the floor, "you're upsetting her. Look at her. Her blood pressure must be sky high."

And although he continued to breath hard through his nose, nostrils whitening and reddening in time, at least he put the pencil down.

"Drunken brute," he said.

"Irish guy," said Eddy. "That's all."

"I am a Scot," Lowell said, "but I don't drink myself senseless then blame my birthplace."

"Can I ask you something?" Eddy said. "Changing the subject."

Lowell shrugged; a gesture he'd learned from her, surely.

"How did you know Mrs. Cottage cried for hours after Mr. Cottage left the care home?"

"Jolly," Lowell supplied.

"Right. How'd you know?"

"How observant you are!" cried Lowell, beaming again. "I worked there."

Jude said nothing, but Eddy cackled. "You? You worked in an old folk's home? Did you wear a polo shirt? *You?*"

"It was when polo shirts were worn for polo," Lowell told her. Jude knew from her face that she didn't understand. "But yes, me. After displeasing my father by rejecting medicine and before my grandmother died and left me her money, I worked in a care home."

"A care assistant," Eddy said. "God almighty, I've had some shitty jobs since I left school, but that takes the biscuit. Did Mum know? Cos she hated the system. You know why, don't you?"

Lowell nodded. "Jude, what the child is hinting at is that Miranda herself —"

"I told her," Eddy said.

"Did you?" said Lowell. Jude had never heard him so haughty. "Well, all I can say is that your mother and I both deserve some of the loyalty you're happy to show towards a violent alcoholic who abandoned you."

"That's not fai—" Eddy began.

"And as for your execrable jobs: I thought you were on a gap year."

Jude couldn't be sure why she said what she said next. She didn't usually jump to fill silences.

"Max was a drinker," she said. "There's a big difference between a drinker and an alcoholic, Lowell."

"You poor dear," he said. "Both of you. I am ashamed of my sex!"

"But I'm trying to *tell* you. It wasn't a problem. He worked hard, never drank the night before a shift. Never tried to hide it, never drank alone. Never puked on the carpet or peed in the wardrobe." She grinned. "If he hadn't dumped me, we'd

183

have been happy ever after."

"Sounds like it," said Eddy, not scornful or mocking, but more world-weary than any nineteen-year-old should be. "Sounds like Disney."

THIRTEEN

Of course, it was worse than that. True, he never *had* puked on the carpet, because she always put a bucket by the bed. And he had never peed in the wardrobe because he didn't wake up. She'd grown to dread the sound of a taxi engine in the street outside; grown adept at guessing, from the length of time it sat there, how bad he was, how unable to count out notes and open the door. Twice, only twice, but both times it crushed her, the taxi driver had honked his horn over and over and she'd had to go out in her dressing gown to help.

She laughed it off the first few years. Actually, the first few years she matched him glass for glass. The *next* few years she laughed at how she'd changed and he hadn't. Then, as she noticed their friends shaking heads and rolling eyes while Max stumbled around the dance floor at yet another wedding, face red, tie lost, she stopped laughing. She never turned into a nag, though. She even managed to turn it back on anyone who tried to patronise her. Some female friend — it was always a woman — would cluck and tut and say, "Max is hammered, Jude."

"Drunk as a skunk," Jude would agree.

"Can't you — I mean, don't you worry?"

"He's a big boy and I'm not his mum," Jude would reply. "He buys his own undies too." As if the clucking, tutting friend was a throwback housewife. That usually did it.

And if the friend, stung, lobbed another one — "So you just put up with it? I wouldn't." — Jude had the perfect put-down. "No one gets everything," she'd say, and then she'd watch the woman grow thoughtful, realising what *she'd* missed, what *she'd* settled for. And Jude would hate herself and wonder why she *didn't* nag and shout, sneer at his stains and stumbles instead of turning it out on everyone else.

That was when she'd tried to persuade him. They made deals. He made promises. She wiped the slate clean and waited, and then they made deals again.

Eventually, she gave up. She was too busy to be out there watching Max lurch towards the toilets, green and weaving. She had her job and she had the flat to look after. He drank and she cleaned. She bought a wallpaper nozzle for the Hoover, a fringe comb for the rugs, a wire tidy for the cables in the entertainment system. She learned how to dismantle a keyboard to clean it, from a YouTube video, how to freshen trainers with cat litter and degrease burners with vinegar and mouthwash.

Then he stopped. That was the bit she hadn't told Lowell and Eddy. She didn't ask him why. She didn't talk about him stopping any more than she'd talked about him drinking. She just quietly took the credit for playing it well and getting what she wanted in the end. It wasn't until the last night —

Jude caught herself. That was the first "last night." The night she thought might be the worst night of her life until the real worst night came along.

The book she was holding slipped from her hands and she sat back on her heels as a brand-new thought slotted neatly into a space in her brain she hadn't realised was there: even now, she hadn't had the worst night of her life. The night she had given that name to was just the first step to the big one that was coming.

She picked up the book again and shelved it. Lowell's distress at the shifting of his military biography had spurred her on to finish the section. At least they all had prices already, since he found Biography more worthwhile than Fiction. He wasn't going to be happy with her work though; she knew that already.

"How are you doing it?" he'd said. "Subject area? Century?"

"Subject area?" Jude echoed. "It's Biography."

"Yes, but . . . Military, political, royal, theatrical . . . ?"

"Alphabetically by surname," said Jude.

"But how would a man find, say, all the biographies of the Boer war?"

"Google it. Or I can put colour-coded spots on the bottoms of the spines."

"Colour-co—" said Lowell. "Why not handcuffs and love hearts? Why not have carousels and two-for-ones? Why not sell coffee?"

"Libraries don't sell coffee," Jude said. "It *was* libraries you were scoffing at, wasn't it?"

He might change his mind when he saw the neat shelves and started noticing all the sales he was ringing up, once people could find what they were looking for. Although Jude knew from Saturdays in a supermarket when she was a kid that you weren't supposed to make things *too* easy to find. You were supposed to make the ambience so appealing they'd want to stay, find what they were looking for and a whole load extra; more expensive, if you were lucky.

Browse appeal, she thought, looking round. Pick the right one to go face out in the space at the end of the row: Simon Weston, Paul O'Grady, Winston Churchill, that kind of thing. Then encourage people to linger. She had seen the perfect encouragement in the window of the charity shop as she'd walked to work that morning. A green velvet armchair and beside it a tiny octagonal mahogany table with a Tiffany lamp on top. It had made her think of T. Jolly's chair upstairs in her cottage. Reading perfection. She had barely sat on the rust-red sofa in the living room at all.

Assuming it was velour, veneer, and Tiffany-*style,* she thought, she could probably scoop the lot with petty cash and surprise him. She finished picking off another of the ubiquitous number stickers and headed downstairs.

Eddy was sitting at the desk, leafing through an outsize guide to natural childbirth.

"I should take this round to that doctor's and shove it up his arse," she said. "Then tell him he's got a thousand miles to go to the nearest hospital to get it removed." She slammed the book shut and spun round on the chair with her head back. When it stopped revolving, she was facing the bank of shallow drawers where Lowell kept his photograph collection. She tugged on a few of the handles then sighed and slumped back.

"Have you ever seen these?" she said. "He won't show me."

"There's no 'ever' about it," said Jude. "I've only been here a week." Eddy sighed louder. "And no. He's pretty possessive about them."

"That's one word," said Eddy. "They've got to be porn, right?" She spun round to face Jude. "Right? Else why's he so weird?"

"They could be anything," Jude said. "Landscapes, wildlife, tall ships. They're locked away from your grubby hands because they're valuable." Eddy was nodding. Slow, sarcastic nods. "I'm going out," said Jude. "And cheer up. There's bound to be midwives round here. Independent wacky ones. Doulas."

"How much would that set me back?" Eddy said.

"Tell Lowell you're staying and he'd cough up for a busload," Jude said.

"He knows I'm staying," said Eddy. "Where the hell else'm I going to go?"

She had no idea of her power, Jude thought, hurrying along the road with her head bent against a halfhearted drizzle. God help Lowell if she ever worked it out.

Maureen was alone in the charity shop, pressing a suit and ready for company.

"Stick the kettle on, petal," she said, leaning down hard on a cloth-covered turn-up. "I must be mad," she added, peering at Jude through a plume of steam. "No one appreciates it. Not as if some natty gent's going to buy it to wear with a collar and tie. It'll be a Goth wearing the jacket covered in badges with the sleeves rolled up and some punk in the trousers with a string vest and red braces."

Maureen, thought Jude, hadn't kept up to date with street tribes, but she was probably right about the natty gent. As she set about making the tea, she flashed on Max in his paramedic's uniform the day he'd qualified. Then, to take her mind off that, she checked the price tags in the window. £40 for the chair, whose back at least one cat had used as a scratch post; £20 for the table, which had a wedge of paper under one of its three feet to keep it steady; and £5 for the plastic lamp.

"I'll give you a round fifty in cash for this lot," she said.

"Typical Londoner," said Maureen. "You know it's for cancer, don't you?" Then she wiped her forehead with the back of her hand and fanned the neck of her blouse. "Go on then if you'll wait till closing so's I don't have to redo the window. And if you'll share any news you might have," she added, just a shade too innocently.

Jude smiled. "You've heard then."

"Heard and can't believe it!" Maureen said, setting the iron on its end and taking the cup Jude offered. She dropped into one of a pair of wicker garden chairs marked NFS and nodded at the other.

"Where will I start?" Jude said. "Eddy is nineteen. She's the daughter of Miranda, who used to stay at Lowell's away back."

"Twenty years back probably, eh no?"

"Good point. Back when Jamaica House was a bit of a bordello." Maureen raised her eyebrows. "According to Mrs. Hewston anyway."

"You need a pound of salt with anything she tells you," Maureen said. "She's never recovered from Dr. Glen leaving her. Lowell can do no right."

"So what's the truth?" said Jude, blowing into her cup. Maureen was one of those tea-drinkers with a cast-iron mouth; she was taking great gulps of it already

"I can't say for sure," Maureen said. "Twenty years ago I was busy with my girls and, nosy as I am, I couldn't spare the time. He did have a sort of open house, I suppose you'd say, once the old fella was gone and he got to start living. Had a party or two, had some lads camping on the lawn. Mrs. Hewston nearly blew a gasket. Folk came and they went. But, right enough, there were girl hitchhikers. Dressed like hippies — and this was years too late for real hippies, mind. Now, which one was it?"

"Miranda," said Jude. "I told you."

"Aye, but which one was she?" said Maureen. "There was a big one, big bushy head of black hair, big red lips, put me in mind of Raquel Welch. And a wee one like a prawn — no colour at all and never said much either."

"Miranda was the big one," Jude said. *Amazonian,* Lowell had called her. "She sounds terrifying."

"A right femme fatale I always thought, even with the cheesecloth and thon clompy shoes. And it would have taken one to get round Lowell."

"That's a bit odd, isn't it?" Jude said. "I mean, he's too old for me, but he's a kind man with a nice house and a job — sort of. Why's he single?"

"Oh mighty!" Maureen said. "He's far too old for *you*. He's . . . now let me see. He was a year behind my brother at the school and Alec's two years younger than me. And I'm sixty–five, or so the mirror tells me in the morning so . . . sixty-two he would be."

"Twenty years," Jude said, which didn't seem so much, really. Only Lowell with his monogrammed hankies was from another time, like the star in a black-and-white war film.

"And as to why he never married," Maureen said, "that's like I was telling you." Tea finished, she was wresting the lid off the jar of toffees she kept on the counter. When she had one unwrapped and stowed in her cheek, she spoke again. "Of course, we all thought he wasn't 'the marrying kind.' But that was just our ignorance here at the back of beyond. Just because he read books and loved his mother. Well, here we all read books now, since Oprah, and he was close to his mother because it was either her or the doctor."

"You're not one of his fans then," said Jude.

"Och, doctors had too much say, in the old days, and nobody saying anything back to them. It would turn anybody's head in the end. Same as coppers. A clip round the ear and no paperwork."

"Mrs. Hewston calls it the good old days. When nursing meant more than —"

"Reading a screen and wearing pjs, aye," Maureen said. "That's her wee catchphrase. Dr. Glen used to smack your arm before he put the needle in. And you only got a lolly if you didn't cry. Well, I cried because he smacked me and then I cried because I didn't get a lolly! Then the teacher tanned my arse and I cried more."

"The teacher?" said Jude.

"Small pox jags," Maureen said. "Dr. G. sat at the front of the class and did thirty of us. *Whack! Jab! Whack! Jab!*" She laughed and shook her head. "The good old days, my foot. He played a canny hand at the end, mind."

Jude gave her an expectant smile, hoping for more, but Maureen looked away.

"What we were talk — Oh aye! Lowell never married. If *that* was at the back of it, he'd be 'out' now, wouldn't he? These days we've all got a bit more sense in our heads. I mean, look at this Eddy that's rolled up. When I was a youngster Miranda getting in the family way would have been whispered about, and then the same carry-on with her daughter would be the tin lid. Unless that's just Mrs. Hewston stirring." She turned curious eyes on Jude.

"No, it's not just Mrs. Hewston," Jude said, only just managing to follow the thread. "Eddy's out to here. Which reminds me: she's not too struck on the current doctor and she's looking for a private midwife."

"Ocht, she's her mother's daughter right enough," Maureen said. "All incense and beansprouts. Aye, you can't spit in Galloway without hitting a healer of something or other. She'll not need to look far. And so is her mother with her? Will she be coming to help with the baby?"

"Oh God," said Jude. "I can't believe Mrs. Hewston didn't tell you this bit! Her mother's dead. Miranda died. That's what spurred Eddy on to come and find her father."

"Dead," said Maureen. "That lovely girl with her mane of raven hair?" She had been upgraded out of sympathy, Jude noted.

"And she only told Eddy about Lowell on her deathbed."

"The wee sowel!" *Soul* Jude thought she meant but it sounded better with two syllables. "And why was that then?"

Jude thought over all that she'd heard from Lowell and from Eddy herself and shook her head. "I've no idea, actually. Miranda was married at one time. Eddy had a stepdad, but he doesn't sound much cop and they were long divorced when she died."

Maureen rocked rhythmically back and forth for a bit, sucking the toffee. It wasn't a rocking chair, but the wicker was old enough to have some give. "Well," she said in the end, "maybe she'd had a bad experience with him and it put her off letting another man in on it. Fair play to her. Only, anyone who knows Lowell knows he's a good man."

"But *did* she know him? If it was a nonstop party that summer?"

"I see what you mean, but she was here a good while," Maureen said. "They came for the summer solstice down on the Rhins with all the rest, and usually that lot take off at the first nip of autumn. I mean, it's never that cold here but you've seen for yourself, petal, it's gey dreich when the rain starts and no stopping. But that pair stayed put and saw the winter through. The wee one like a peeled prawn was at her pictures — rocks, mudflats, never a bonny view; and the big one — that was Miranda you're saying? — was in the shop huddled over a paraffin stove, reading."

"And then they just left? Why?"

"Well, no one ever knew, did we?" Maureen said. "Just that she went and took her wee pal with her."

Jude considered it. When Lowell had talked about Miranda's last night at Jamaica House, them watching the news together, he hadn't mentioned anyone else being there.

"I don't think they left at the same time though," Jude said. "I think Miranda stayed on by herself."

"Makes sense," said Maureen. "Maybe her and Lowell only got close when it was down to the two of them. I honestly couldn't tell you. Wintertime here, you can go weeks without seeing a body. I'm thinking if I want to meet Eddy I'll need to come round for a rummage. How far on is the lass?"

"Pretty far," Jude said. "Eight months."

"And how's she carrying it?" Jude wondered if she was about to hear some old wives' tale about boy and girl babies sitting differently, or if Maureen was going to offer to swing a pocket watch. But she had misunderstood. "Some bloat and some bloom, and nobody every tells the bloaters they're not blooming! Like no one ever tells a man he's married a pig or a tells a woman her baby's a wee gargoyle."

Jude didn't laugh. The memory had come

back like a thrown knife. She met Raminder only once, at the ambulance station's family day, the charity picnic. She was wearing a sari and gold bangles, with a cascade of warm black hair bouncing against her back as she walked. Jude had spoken to her beside the chocolate fountain. Neither of them liked marshmallows. But Max hadn't introduced her, and Jude thought she was another wife until they were driving home.

"Who brought the glam Hindu?" she'd said.

"Sikh," Max had told her. "That's Mindy."

"*That's* Mindy?" said Jude, amused at first. "Mindy that you're on call with?"

She had got the impression that Mindy was a dumpy little frump. Partly it was the name but, as well as that, Max had said she brought food from home instead of eating in the canteen, and he'd said she wore her hair in a . . .

"A cake?" Jude had said, laughing at him. "You mean a bun?"

"Right," said Max. "A little cake on the top of her head so her baseball cap looks like it's floating." And he had laughed too and Jude had thought they were sharing laughter about a funny-looking woman he worked with, but really Max was laughing because talking about Mindy, even with his wife, made him happy.

"Why didn't you introduce me?" she'd asked, driving home from the picnic.

Max shrugged. "Get enough of her at work."

But of course he didn't get enough of her at work at all. That was a lie. He couldn't get enough of her without leaving his wife and spending every day and every night with her.

Everything else he had said was technically true. Her hair and the food and how she lived with her parents and made her own clothes. But Jude had taken the snippets and made a spinster out of them. The reality was *Raminder,* with her fall of warm black hair wound into a knot under her cap and her hand-stitched saris and salwar kameez and her delicious food brought in to share with the shift because no one would settle for canteen grub again once they'd tasted it. Just about as different from poor *Mindy* as a woman could be. Jude had looked at herself in the wing mirror the day of the picnic and somewhere deep inside she already knew.

"Not much time to waste then," Maureen was saying. "Tell her to ask in Pandora's. They've got a notice board in the back. Aye, you can get everything from breast milk to death spells off the notice board in Pandora's."

"Death spells?" said Jude.

"Oh God aye," said Maureen. "The wee minister from the happy clappy church keeps writing letters to have the whole place closed down, but it's a right laugh for a hen night."

"I'll tell her," said Jude, still not sure if Maureen was joking.

"She'll get a free prescription of birthstones and her own wee star chart. Me, I'd rather have the epidural."

Jude shared the good news as soon as she got back.

"There's a coven just across the road, apparently," she told Eddy. "Pandora's. There's a notice board where all the voodoo midwives put their phone numbers."

"No judgment, eh?" Eddy said.

"So get your star sign ready and warm up your chakras." She was rewarded with a small smile.

"Aries," Eddy said.

"Sagittarius," said Jude, to be companionable, but Eddy had stopped listening. She was staring at the desktop with a frozen look on her face. Jude peeked over the cubbyholes, but there was nothing to see except the blank sheet of the desk calendar Lowell never used.

"You okay?" she said.

"Yep," said Eddy. "This is going to sound daft, but you know what? I've just worked out why Mum was so nuts about me going to a hospital for the baby. It's because I nearly died when I was born. I was so early."

"What's made you think of that?" Jude said.

"Oh, because of how she used to talk about whether I should go by when I popped out or when I was supposed to. Cancer or Aries? How do you decide? Mum reckoned Cancer was a curse, so she went the other way."

"It's true when you think about it." Jude said. "*Cancer!* So . . . she didn't really believe in it then if she let you pick your own? Somehow I thought, living in a commune and all . . ."

"Oh yeah, she totally believed in it," said Eddy. "She believed in everything from Allah to Zoroaster. But not me. I went with Aries because the birthstone's a diamond, and why not, eh?"

"What's the one for Cancer then?" said Jude.

But Eddy just stared at her, eyes wide. "She'd have loved Pandora's," she said at

202

last. "Speaking of which, I might just shoot over there now. Ever since I read that damn book I'm convinced I'm having Braxton Hicks. Bet it's all in my mind."

She edged past Jude with an unhappy smile and, in the light coming through the open door to the Boudoir, there was a sick sheen to her skin.

"Are you sure you're okay?"

"Fresh air," Eddy said. "It's stuffy in here with all these books. Mouldy, probably."

Jude watched after her and then sat down in the vacated chair. What had just happened?

Nothing. A normal conversation. And then all of a sudden Eddy shut down, just as Lowell said she did on the way to the doctor. He described her scrolling on her phone and chatting then . . . a guillotine of her own. A portcullis to rival Jude's.

And this time she wasn't even looking at her phone. She was . . . As it hit, Jude felt like laughing. She was looking at a calendar and she said she was an Aries and then tried to change her story and say she was a Cancer. And she didn't know the Cancer birthstone.

When was the OJ verdict? Jude longed for her phone, but at the side of the desk there was a collection of reference books: Whittaker's Almanac, Concise Oxford, Norton/ Grove, Roget, Brewer, Bartlett, Burke, and a short 20th Century. She rifled through the index and found it. The verdict in the OJ Simpson case was delivered on October the third, 1995. If Eddy was conceived that night, she'd have been due in July, a Cancer. If she was born in April, under Aries, she would indeed have been premature and in danger.

Jude even thought she understood the problem with the doctor now. If Eddy really was pregnant — if! — then what would be the first thing her new physician would ask when he signed her on, with her beaming "father" right there beside her? Her birth date.

FOURTEEN

Jude's euphoria lasted less than an hour. It carried her through another few shelves of sorting and dusting in the Biography corridor and the perk she awarded herself at the end of it: choosing the volume she'd place in a pool of lamplight on the octagonal wine table beside the armchair when Maureen delivered them at the end of the day.

It had to be someone everyone loved, a national treasure. The problem with most national treasures, she thought, after discarding Alan Bennett, Victoria Wood, and Stephen Fry, was that the few who didn't adore them really loathed them. All that left was Stephen Hawking and Helen Mirren, and she hadn't come across them so far.

"Danny Kaye it is then," she said, plucking him out from between Kourtney Kardashian and Hedy Lamarr. "And Russell Brand for the under-nineties."

Then, checking that they were priced up,

she saw what she'd missed before: *T. Jolly* in the flyleaf of the Danny Kaye, and a book-club plate opposite the title page: *To Dad with love from Angela, Christmas 1979.*

She turned to the back and felt an unaccountable lift in her spirits when she saw a few lines of notes there.

There's something suspicious about a man who changes his name to hide his background, T. Jolly had written. *You'd never catch John Wayne at that game.*

Jude laughed out loud and then felt a cloud of sadness descend on her. In 1979, he was sparky and cracking jokes. Five years later when he read *On the Beach,* he was reduced to *This is a sad book* and *I miss my wife.* But then, *On the Beach* was nothing to joke about, really.

And grief did strange things to people, she told herself. Look what it had done to her.

To cheer herself up she went into the dead room and burrowed in behind the yellow bag with the Jilly Cooper, hoping for another review from his late period — larky and witty and proving that *On the Beach* was a blip. But the heap had settled for some reason — maybe Eddy had been in here rummaging — and none of her tugging and prodding worked.

As the sadness closed back in around her, even her brainwave about Eddy's birth started to crumble. There had to be a different explanation, because if Lowell and Miranda slept together on OJ night when she was already three months pregnant, wouldn't he have noticed? And what had Mrs. Hewston really heard and seen?

Probably no and probably nothing, she decided. Three months was too early, and Mrs. Hewston was mad. But she wished she was still staying at Jamaica House, where she could start casual conversations and not have to go round specially, looking nosy.

At six o'clock that night, when it was completely black outside the cottage, she heard the crunch of a steady tread on the gravel path and then a knock at the door.

Police! Instantly she was shaking. Before they could shout *Come out with your hands in the air,* before they could break down the door, she inched it open.

And of course it was Mrs. Hewston, unconcerned about looking nosy, saving Jude the trip and the trouble.

"I've come to see how you're settling in," she said, her head waving like a cobra's as she tried to see past Jude into the living room.

"Come in," said Jude, sweeping the door wide.

"Ah, he always kept it nice," said Mrs. Hewston, settling into one of the rust-red chairs and smoothing the nap of one arm. "Kept all those books of his nicely tidied away and not cluttering up the lounge. There's nothing like a book for trapping dust."

"Fair point," said Jude through the open kitchen door, thinking it was interesting to know that Mrs. Hewston had seen the upstairs of the cottage at some point. "It's nice to hear about him," she went on when she got back with the tea tray. She reckoned Mrs. Hewston was the type to appreciate cups and saucers on a tray.

"The doctor?" Mrs. Hewston said. "Yes, it's a pleasure to talk about him."

"Um, I meant Mr. Jolly actually," said Jude. "Keeping his books out of the way, you know."

"Oh! Right," Mrs. Hewston said. "I had wandered. When you get to my age you live more and more in the past."

"And yet your memories get sharper," Jude said, passing her a cup. "I remember someone saying that to me. Like your memory of Miranda's last night at Jamaica House. Twenty years ago and you remem-

208

bered so much detail. What was on the telly and everything."

"Shocking news," said Mrs. Hewston. "Yes, I remember that night. I was paying extra attention because his son had gone off and left strangers in charge. I had an ear cocked for trouble. Parties and what have you."

"He wasn't in America, though," said Jude. "Plymouth, apparently."

Mrs. Hewston sniffed. "I'm only going by what he told me. He'd gone off *somewhere* and left the monkeys in charge of the zoo. This was years before the music festival, of course. Wickerman! Nobody had even heard of such a thing before that nasty film gave us a bad name. But there had been 'raves' on the beach over at Port Logan, and I didn't want one messing up the doctor's nice house while his nibs had left them to it."

The passage of twenty years and the fact that there hadn't *been* a rave at the house after all didn't seem to count for much with Mrs. Hewston.

"And you really had no idea Miranda was pregnant?" Jude said.

"Not a bit of it!" Mrs. Hewston cried. "Not till I heard them at their nasty business."

It seemed to Jude she was beginning to conflate two stories now. *Nasty business* presumably meant the conception; a nurse would never speak of a birth that way.

"When you say you heard them," she began, but then wondered how to go on.

Mrs. Hewston bristled. "I never went snooping," she said. "That's not my way. I serve the community any way I can, but I don't interfere."

"I wasn—"

"The baby was born before I knew a thing. Afterbirth delivered and all."

Jude didn't want to put the woman's back up any more, but there didn't seem to be a delicate way to tiptoe towards it. "You didn't actually see Miranda in labour then? You just heard a baby cry."

"I heard a *newborn* cry," said Mrs. Hewston. "It's not like any other sound, the sound they make before they suck for the first time."

"And how long did it go on for?" Jude asked, thinking maybe it was a fox or a kitten.

"I reckon her milk wasn't in yet," said Mrs. Hewston. "That baby cried sore. Oh, a good twenty minutes."

"Poor mite."

"I agree. But there's always one that

thinks if you drink enough raspberry tea you don't need help from anyone!"

"You mean, she was all alone?" It would explain why, twenty years later, she was nagging Eddy about it, Jude thought. And Maureen *had* said Miranda was the last to go. Jude couldn't bear thinking about it: a woman alone and a baby crying. And the very person who should be helping — a nurse! — staying away. She had heard Max on the subject enough times. *You must attend,* he would say. *Doesn't matter if it's not your shift or you're on your holidays. If you're a medical professional and someone needs you, you must attend. The day we're told to stand back in case we're sued is the day I hang up my jump pads.* It used to thrill her. Her hero. Until she realised she was the only exception. If *she* needed him, she could raffle.

"It must have been quite loud for you to have heard it all the way down here," she said to Mrs. Hewston.

"Well, it was a lovely night," Mrs. Hewston said. "I had my curtains open to the last of the sunset. And my windows open to the let the scent of the flowers drift in. A beautiful night. He was always very particular about his garden — kept it full of blooms."

"Lowell's not doing so badly," Jude said, and Mrs. Hewston's face suddenly clouded and then crumpled. She put a hand up to her neck and fussed with the buttons of her blouse.

"Yes, well, the doctor was a very busy man. He kept things shipshape but he had no time for hobbies, did he?"

It took a couple of minutes for Jude to sort through what had just happened. The woman was confused. Mrs. Hewston was definitely slightly confused. She had remembered the lovely scent of the flowers and had credited her beloved doctor, as usual. It upset her to be reminded that it was Lowell and not his father who had planted them. Or maybe it just upset her to realise she was mixed up. And she *had* to be mixed up. No way the same person who had walked all the way from her bungalow to the graveyard to check up on Jude's doings wouldn't have poked her nose into a *birth.* Taking place *next door.* No more would she have kept quiet about it for twenty years either. Mrs. Hewston might have seen something at Jamaica House that night through her open curtains or heard something through her open windows, but it wasn't a baby being born.

"I hope you don't mind me being nosy,"

Jude said, "but can I ask you something else?" Mrs. Hewston nodded. "What did you mean by *nasty business*?"

"Well, that was hours later, of course," Mrs. Hewston said. "Out in the garden." Jude waited. "She was burying the afterbirth. Right there in his blessed garden."

"Get out!" said Jude.

"As sure as I'm sitting here." Mrs. Hewston was thrilled with the effect she'd caused. "She had the placenta in the doctor's washing up basin from the kitchen and she was burying it in the asparagus bed! She looked like a wild thing, hair all hanging down and blood on her feet."

"On her *feet*?"

"From the birth. She was like a savage. She wheeled around when she heard me coming, dropped the whole mess and then scraped it into the hole with her bare hands. She was all set to drop the basin in after it until I stopped her. I steeped it in bleach overnight and took it back in the morning. They'd all cleared out. She was the last of them. I had a right good go at the place before he came back from his wandering."

Another nugget Jude could believe: Mrs. Hewston probably *would* go barging in cleaning the doctor's house when it was empty again. Except Lowell had come home and spent that last night with Miranda. He hadn't mentioned Mrs. Hewston turning up with her dustpan in the morning.

"And I'll tell you this," the woman said, in a summing-up kind of voice, "that end of the asparagus bed was like Jack's beanstalk compared to the other. A good ten years the bumper crops lasted, and he puzzled and pondered more than once why it was and I never let on. Miranda asked me not to, and I never did."

"You're a good loyal friend keeping the secret that way," Jude said. The woman did that rolling wriggle of her shoulders that made Jude think of a plump little robin in a birdbath.

"I try," she said. "But this is a thankless place to move to. No matter what you do. I was nurse to young and old for twenty years and did plenty else besides for everyone. Brownies, whist nights, you name it. But I'm still an outsider."

"Well, what does that make me?" Jude said.

"You!" Mrs. Hewston cried. "You're a blow-through. Londoners never settle here. It's the quiet. It gets to them all in the end."

"I might surprise you," Jude said. But her heart wasn't in it. She would use every last minute of this stolen time the best she could, try to work out a way out of the mess that didn't involve bars and an orange jumpsuit. Or was that only on films? They didn't still have arrows on their clothes anyway. She was sure of that much.

Mrs. Hewston was still talking; on and on about this southerner and that southerner who hadn't made it through a rough winter or went back to Hampshire for the schools. Maybe it made her feel better, to compare herself with incomers who couldn't stay the course at all.

When she finally got rid of the woman, Jude found herself in the bathroom, scrubbing her hands in water hot enough to leave them pounding, trying to wash away Miranda, barefoot and bloody, wheeling round, and the basin of gore spilling onto the dark earth, the rich harvests for years afterwards. "I'm not here," she said. But she was looking right at herself and she didn't believe it. "It didn't happen," she tried instead, and that made much more sense.

It *couldn't* have happened. Eddy was born in April in Ireland. Whatever gore Miranda was burying in the asparagus bed in October, it wasn't a placenta.

But even the gore-burial couldn't be true, really. Miranda was waiting at Jamaica House on OJ night, three months pregnant

215

and hiding it, probably decked out in a loose negligee, certainly not — what? Killing a piglet that screamed like a baby to feed the soil?

Jude looked at herself in the bathroom mirror and was unsurprised to see that her cheeks were pale and her eyes purple all round, as if she'd been crying.

Book dust, she told herself, even though in all her years in the library, even when she was recataloguing the basement stacks, she'd never so much as sneezed. Books had never harmed her. Books were her friends.

She could see a portion of Todd's library reflected in the mirror, just a slice through the two open doors: Lauren Bacall and Salvador Dali had joined Danny Kaye: *A fine woman who deserved better* he had written, and *Out to shock for the sake of it like a wee boy swearing at his granny.* She had discovered a run of James Herriot paperbacks, the old Corgi edition with the cartoons on the covers, but without the line drawings inside. *A true gent and good company over a pint, I bet.*

And she had begun her own little collection on a separate shelf, just in a very small way. Finding a nice Collins copy of *The Thirty-Nine Steps,* she had put the price of it in the till and shelved it with *The Day of Small Things*, trying not to think about *Penny Plain, The Setons,* and *Pink Sugar,* stuck in London. Trying not to think of London at all.

FIFTEEN

Jude looked at the two books she held in her hands: Seamus Heaney and Samuel Beckett. Beckett's granite face would make a dramatic display for a shelf-end in Poetry and Plays, but who knew he was these days? Heaney would have legions of fans in Galloway, but he looked like an angry drunk, no getting away from it.

She was still trying to decide when she heard Eddy coming up the stairs with a slow, halting tread.

"You okay?" Jude called out.

Eddy arrived on the landing balancing two cups of coffee on a *Tiger Who Came to Tea* and holding two Twixes in her teeth by their packet corners.

"Nice tray," said Jude. "Don't let Lowell see you."

"I need to talk to you," Eddy said, spitting out the Twixes and handing over one of the cups. "I want to ask you something too. But,

218

seriously, there's something I've got to say."

"I believe you," said Jude. Coffee, biscuits, and a solemn face left no doubt. She watched Eddy settle herself in the new armchair. She was wearing another one of the colourful dresses from the wardrobe in Lowell's spare room, unflattering and complicated, with its wrap ties that poked through eyelets and its long, bell-like sleeves. Her breasts made it gape and Jude could see blue veins spreading in filigrees across the impossible underwater white of her skin.

Maybe she really was pregnant. Slim girls of nineteen don't have heavy breasts with blue veins showing. Jude glanced at the belly pushing open the skirt flaps. Eddy was wearing ribbed tights, the waistband pulled high, clear to the bottom of her bra, but her little lolly-stick legs still had wrinkles at the ankles. No swelling.

"I know," she said. "I look like a pile of shite."

"I think you look lovely." In truth, Eddy's hair could have done with a wash. It was dull and separating into hanks at the parting so that her scalp showed. And she didn't take all of her make-up off at night either; she had black dots from yesterday in the corners of her eyes and a rash of spots in each nostril crease. "Blooming."

It came from nowhere. She was thinking about Eddy and Eddy alone, and yet it hit her so hard she doubled over from the pain of it.

"Jude?" said Eddy, sounding very young.

She had doubled in pain the first time it hit her too. It was long after Max left that she worked it out. She calculated, from the news her soon-to-be-ex-sister-in-law *insisted* on sharing, that the day of the charity picnic when Raminder floated around serene and magnificent, brimming with health and hope, she was already two months along.

Max had stopped drinking. Jude had been telling herself they'd turned a corner, good times were on the way.

"Jude?" said Eddy again. "Are you okay?"

Jude straightened up and tried to smile. "Sorry," she said. "Maybe I need to talk to you too."

"You first," Eddy said. "I'm still trying to screw up the courage."

"I was married," Jude began. "We couldn't have children. Well, I couldn't. He could. He did. Now we're not married. Well, I'm not. He is." The way the words jerked out of her sounded comic even to her own ears.

"Scumbag," Eddy shouted. She had so much mascara on that her eyes, wide with

220

outrage, were like cartoon daisies drawn with a marker pen.

"You look like Twiggy," said Jude.

"Who?"

"Google her. And thanks for not laughing. If you'd laughed I might have broken up in little bits."

"Thanks a million!" Eddy said. "What did I do to get that? Why would I laugh?"

"It's not you," Jude said. "Look, what did you want to say?"

"I wanted to ask you . . ." Eddy chewed her lip. "But here's something else first. How come you're here when your parents have just died? How come you're not home sorting out all their stuff?" It was the same question Mrs. Hewston had fired at her.

"Council house, only child. Plus I'm a cataloguer. It was done and dusted before the funeral." She sat back on her heels. "But I cheated a bit. There was a post-mortem, so the funeral took three weeks." That was a distraction. What did it say about her life that a post-mortem on her parents was a polite way to distract attention from the really bad stuff?

"Why was that then?" said Eddy.

"They died in their car," said Jude. It was about as dishonest as the truth could ever be. She couldn't face telling Eddy what had really happened. Eddy had had what everyone deserves: a mother dying in a crisp hospital bed with cheerful nurses and a drinks machine in the corridor. No one would smirk at *her.* "Why aren't *you* sorting *your* mum's stuff?" she said. Another distraction.

"She didn't have any," Eddy said. "No possessions, like Lennon said." Then she grinned. "I haven't told him yet I was a commune kid. I decided before I got here to keep that bit quiet in case, you know . . ." Jude shook her head. "In case he got pissed off with Mum."

"About what?" said Jude. "It sounds like Jamaica House wasn't far off being a commune back in the day. Too close to one for Mrs. Hewston anyway."

"Well, cos it's one thing to cut him out if she was married all nicey-nicey, but it's a bit of a kick in the teeth to have nothing to do with him when anything *else* goes."

"I suppose," said Jude. She shelved a couple of books. "A commune in Derry?" Another book. "You'd think they'd all be in the west. Somehow. Sorry if that's a cliché."

"Sometimes it's handier to be in the UK and not real Ireland," Eddy said. "Some of the guys couldn't — you know — get over the border. Passports and that." She gave

Jude a knowing look.

"Dave Preston?" said Jude. If Eddy's stepfather had been one of the guys who couldn't legally get over the Irish border, Jude was losing respect for Miranda's taste in men. Leaving kind sweet Lowell for that sort was madness.

"Nah," said Eddy. "He'll never leave Fermanagh. He lives three streets from his granny. Mum stuck it out seven years, but she never liked it. As soon as she left him, we were straight back to the Community till she had to go to hospital. I think she made the right choice. I mean, a lot of it sucked, but they looked after her really well as long as they could. Dave would never have done that."

Lowell would, was what Jude was thinking. "She really kept quiet about Lowell?" was what she said.

"She never mentioned Scotland at all," Eddy said. "She talked about travelling in Wales, all over Ireland, Glastonbury and that. All before I was born. I was dead chuffed when I looked up LG Books and found out it was this close to the ferry over."

"And she finally told you right at the end? I've been feeling pretty sick about not speaking to mine for weeks before they died," Jude said. "But getting hit with a bombshell like you were . . ."

"I'm just glad I listened," Eddy said. "She was off her head on the morphine. And I was knackered too — completely zoned out. But she gripped my hand so tight my fingers went purple, so I knew it was important. She said my father's name was Lowell and he was good man. She said she'd done a terrible thing and she was sorry. And then I thought she said Lowland Glen was a bookshop in Jamaica. I was glad to get *that* straight."

"The terrible thing being that she kept you apart from your father?"

"I suppose so," Eddy said. "Or making me live in the Community."

"That bad?"

Eddy thought about it for a moment or two. She was pleating the skirt of her dress, pinching it up in two fingers to make a fan. "Nah. I mean, don't get me wrong, it was freezing cold in the winter and the food was terrible. We grew most of it ourselves."

"In Ireland?"

"Exactly. And we never got anything new. Jumble sales and hand-me-downs all the way. And a lecture about how we were everything that was wrong with the world if we ever moaned."

Jude felt something then that she couldn't

224

put a name to. She looked at the baggy pinafore and the wrinkled tights, at the clumped mascara and patches of oily skin, and suddenly she wanted to bundle Eddy into the Volvo, drive her to Glasgow, and buy her anything she pointed at.

"So . . . that's what you wanted to *ask* me," she said, winding back through the conversation. "What am I doing here. But what is it you want to *tell* me?"

Eddy let the pinched pleats of dress fall, put her hands up to her face, and hid it.

"Oh, you poor thing," Jude said. "I'm sorry."

The girl's shoulders were shaking. Jude looked around helplessly. She had no pressed cotton handkerchief in her pocket. She glanced at the duster, but it was filthy. Eddy's sobs grew louder with every breath.

"I've done a really stupid thing," she said. "It's about being pregnant." She pulled her hands to the sides of her face, stretching her skin, so that pink crescents showed inside her lower eyelids and her bottom lip turned out, shining and smooth, like the curve of a conch shell. "I don't know how to tell him," she said. "I don't even know how to tell *you.*"

"You don't have to," Jude said. "I guessed."

Eddy let her hands drop. Her marker-pen mascara was smeared into swipes of war paint over her cheeks. "How?" she said.

"I worked it out."

"How?"

"That's not the question, Eddy. The question is *why*? Why'd you do it?"

"I don't know," Eddy said. "I wasn't thinking straight, what with my mum and everything. And then it just sort of took on a life of its own — he was so thrilled! — and I don't know how to stop it without destroying him and making him hate me." She gave a big shuddering sigh. "How the hell did you guess? Are you some kind of psychic. Or — Hey! Have you been reading my texts? And why didn't you bust me?"

"Tell Lowell, you mean?" Jude said. "I haven't lived your life and I haven't had your troubles." It wasn't particularly true. "Mostly I didn't want to rock the boat," she admitted.

"No," said Eddy, with a new note in her voice. "You wouldn't, would you?"

It must have been her imagination, but Jude would have sworn the light on the Biography landing dimmed a little. It couldn't have. LG Books was decrepit but not so bad that the lightbulbs flickered if someone switched the kettle on. And be-

226

sides, Lowell — wherever he was — wasn't moving. The whole house was completely silent, no wind rattling the windows, no creaks as the boards and beams shifted, and outside not a car passed nor a child called out nor a single reversing delivery van made a sound.

"I snooped," Eddy said.

"Well, I deserve to be snooped on, I suppose," Jude said. "I slipped up, didn't I?"

"Yeah. Saying *Raminder.*" Eddy gazed at her. "You know they're looking for you, don't you?"

"I really don't want to be found," said Jude.

"I'm not going to tell."

"Why not?"

Eddy stuffed her empty Twix wrapper in her coffee cup and banged it down on the octagonal table. "Because here's why. You know what they called her, don't you? You know what Raminder called the baby?"

"Jade."

"Jade! Like you basically don't exist. Like it never even occurred to them. Jade and Jude! Bastards!"

"Thanks," said Jude.

"I scratch your back," Eddy said. She stared at Jude for a moment and then added, "I slipped too."

227

"Saying Aries," said Jude.

Eddy tipped her head, mock-saluting. "So it's not just this," she said, laying a hand on her stomach. "It's that too." She took a deep, shaky breath. "I'm not his. He's not a dad and he's not going to be a grandpa."

"I'm not going to tell," said Jude, trying a little impersonation of Eddy's accent, to make her smile. "I scratch yours too."

"I just wish I knew why she did it," said Eddy, the tiny smile fading. "Why tell me lies on her deathbed? Who does that?" Jude shook her head. "No psychic lightbulbs about that one?"

"Sorry," Jude said. "It doesn't make any sense to me any way I look at it. And I don't know what to do."

"Never say die," Eddy said. "We'll work something out, won't we?" She must have seen Jude's face fall, because she turned clamourous, insistent. "Come on! My mum managed to disappear, why can't you? And I'm not the only kid in the world with a dodgy 'dad.' Christ, I bet I'm not even the only one in Wigtown. And as for this?" She slapped her belly again. "We'll think of something."

Jude said nothing. When Miranda disappeared no one was looking for her, because she hadn't done anything. "I don't want to live in a commune," she answered at last.

"Ha!" said Eddy. "It'd kill you. They don't get many neat freaks in the Community." Then she laughed at Jude's face. "What? Was that supposed to be a secret too?" She pointed and cackled. Jude looked down at the Twix wrapper folded into a tiny square and wedged into the narrow end of the coffee-cup handle. "You know the one thing that bothers me?" Eddy said, sobering. "That Hewston bint. This place is perfect apart from her. She's the sort that'll ferret out anything she can get a sniff of and make up what she can't."

"She troubled me too, at first," Jude said, "but I don't think we need to worry. Two reasons. One, she's gaga. She was talking absolute crap to me when she came round and she's starting to know it. She got upset when she got confused."

"Good," said Eddy. "What's the other one?"

"She knows what side her bread's buttered. She lives rent-free in Lowell's house and she'd be a fool to wreck that, wouldn't she?"

"That makes three of us. He's a bit of a chick magnet, is old —"

"Dad," said Jude. "Just call him Dad,

Eddy. He'll never order a DNA test. He loves you."

And, even though she was young and in a fix, Eddy paid enough attention to hear something in Jude's voice. "I'm sorry," she said. "If I hadn't come along, you'd be well in by now."

"I don't think of him that way," Jude said. "He's just a genuinely good, kind, sweet man."

"Up a tree," sang Eddy. "K-I S-S-I-N — Yeah, I know he is." She sighed. "He used to work in a care home, for fuck's sake. And he keeps his creepy porn locked up where no one can accidentally see it."

"It's not porn!" said Jude. "It's a valuable collection of . . . something. Oh, I give up," she added as Eddy blew a raspberry. "And you've no need to apologise. I've got a house and a job and a friend. I'm better off than I could have imagined a couple of weeks ago. If I can just keep my head down till . . . It's easy on the telly, isn't it? Films and all that? People get new identities all the time. But it's not the same in real life."

"You don't need a new identity," Eddy said. "Mum used bang on about this all the time. You can call yourself anything you want and — say what you like about this country — you never need to show your

230

papers."

It was Anne Tyler again, but it looked like Eddy believed it. Jude smiled and tried to believe it too.

"That's right," she said. "I've got a home and a job and two good friends."

"Three," said Eddy, "counting Mrs. Hewston."

SIXTEEN

Except, in Jude's mind, there was a fourth friend and she wanted more of him. *After* some hard graft and a bit of desk work over lunch, she told herself sternly. She was supposed to be saving an ailing business here.

Spinning Yarns, the book and wool shop next door to the left, and Tilly's, the tarot and crystals operation next door to the right, had steady streams of customers. Jude could hear the Yarns shop bell ding whenever she was up in Mighty Hunters and the Tilly's wind chimes when she was up in Ladies Who, on account of the way the big front windows were always cracked open around Lowell's sign strings. She had gone to visit the proprietors, hoping to get some tips, but both of them — a retired Yorkshire social worker in the tarot shop and a young Polish mum whose husband worked at the fishery — told her the Internet was all that mattered and they only kept the shops because the rates were cheap and the rent was cheaper.

She took the last of her coffee into the dead room at two o'clock and surveyed the squatting toad, the book mountain. T. Jolly was thirty years deep. She could just dig in, throwing books over both shoulders like a burrowing mole, but she was too much of a librarian. She could deal with each bag from start to finish, sorting, cleaning, pricing, shelving . . . Except she could see into one of the front bags from here and it was three Asda cookbooks staring back at her: vegetables, chicken, and cheese. She would know that Asda cheese cookbook at fifty paces because there were two more upstairs in Home Crafts and Gardening; one pristine for a pound and one well-crusted — with cheese, presumably — for twenty-five pence.

Nothing, Jude thought, was twenty-five pence anymore, so God only knew how long it had been there. She was going to have to tell Lowell to send some of these to the pulper. He wouldn't agree; he would — he had! — start on about jumble sales and the free exchange of ideas and sending books to Africa. As though a village school in Africa would thank him for Asda's Book of Cheese.

In the end, she compromised by starting three towers just inside the dead room door, doing a bit of rough triage. Slowly, the book mountain grew a canyon as Jude removed bag after bag from its nearest slope. The three towers soared. But it was almost closing time before she saw something that said *T. Jolly* to her eager and practised eye. She tugged, felt the north wall of the canyon threaten to slip, and spent another patient twenty minutes excavating properly. She had just freed a tantalising Brentford Nylons carrier, packed three across and six deep with hardbacks, when Lowell sidled in.

"Golly," he said, looking at the towers and canyon. "Dear me, yes, it has rather run away from me, hasn't it?"

"Sell, pass on, RIP," Jude said pointing. "Don't look! Or if you insist on looking, don't argue. You've lived without all of them up till now. If I'm about to give the upside-down penny black to Maureen at the Cancer, it's no worse than it sitting here turning into coal."

"Fine, fine, no argument!" Lowell said, holding up both hands and backing away. "Do whistle if you come across anything called *Love's Labour's Won,* won't you?"

"Or *Cardenio,*" said Jude. "I'm a librarian, Lowell. I know about lost Shakespeare."

Lowell put a hand to his breast and bowed his head, a repentant knight.

"You can make it up to me by giving me a lucky dip price for this," she added, holding up the Brentford bag.

Lowell took a step closer, pulling his spectacles down from amongst his hair.

"Whoa! Whoa!" said Jude. "Lucky dip! I don't know what's in here and neither do you. That's the whole point."

"A pound," Lowell said.

"We'll call it a tenner," said Jude. "And take it out of my wages. Anyway, what can I do for you?"

"Tush now, you're already doing so much. Even the cottage is a weight off my mind, more than anything. Dear me, yes."

"What did you come in here just now to say?" Jude explained, trying not to speak so loud or slow he would have hurt feelings.

"Me? Oh! Ah yes indeed, quite. You flummoxed me with your hard-nosed hustling. I just wanted to ask where young Eddy had got to. I'm afraid she and I have had words."

"What about?" said Jude. And then followed it up with, "And since I'm being nosy, can I ask something else that's none of my business?"

"My business *is* your business," Lowell said. "Since you are bringing it back from the brink."

"In that case," said Jude, "it's about your

pictures. The photographs you've got under lock and key. Are you really just a collector or do you sell them too?"

Lowell was standing in the shadows, but he stepped forward then. "Funny thing," he said. "That's just what young Eddy and I were discussing so heatedly."

Jude tried to look surprised but suspected she had failed. Not least because Lowell was wearing his spectacles and could see her clearly.

"I'm not trying to make you sell them if you don't want to," she said. "I've only got as far as thinking you should frame them and hang them on the walls. In the corridor. Once it's cleared."

"No," said Lowell. "I don't think so. I don't think that would be wise."

"Are they valuable?" Jude said. "Would it be a security risk to have them on display?"

"Not exact — No," said Lowell. "I mean they have a value, certainly. Some of them."

Jude knew it was more suspicious not to ask and so she forced herself. "What *are* they?"

"Early work," said Lowell. "Victorian. Rare pieces."

"But what *are* they?" said Jude. "Landscapes, street scenes, portraits?"

"Portraits, yes," said Lowell. "In a way. I

mean, of a sort. Figure studies, I suppose one would say."

"Figure studies," Jude said. She trusted the low light to hide her change of colour. "And *are* you a dealer?" she said. "Or just an admirer?"

"Neither," said Lowell. "So far I'm a searcher, buyer, and locker-up in a drawer."

It sounded noble.

"So you're not gathering them with a view to putting them out in a collection?"

"A book?" said Lowell, with a sharp laugh. "I'm a used bookseller, my dear. No one knows better than I the folly of publishing."

"Did Eddy try to persuade you?" Jude said. "Is that why you argued?"

"No, no, nothing like that," said Lowell. "Dear me, I forgot about her. Where is she?"

"She shouted through a while back that she was going home. She was tired."

That was all it took. "Tired?" he said and was off, halfway to the door, shouting over his shoulder. "Lock up when you're finished, my dear, won't you? Good Lord, she shouldn't be wandering the streets alone when she's faint from exhaustion. What if she fell?"

He was gone and didn't hear Jude's answer. "If she fell on her 'belly,' she'd bounce

237

if it's foam and if it's feathers . . . soft landing."

It wasn't until Jude had lugged the lucky bag right to the cemetery gates that it occurred to her these might not be Todd's after all.

"Pillock!" she said to the nearest gravestone, glancing at the name.

"Not you, Archie," she added, passing on. "Me." Then she turned back and read the rest of the epitaph;

HERE LIES ARCHIBALD PATTERSTONE,
MASTER ENGINEER,
A TRUE FRIEND AND A MUCH-LOVED MAN
"SLEEP WELL, MY GOOD AND FAITHFUL
SERVANT"

No wife and no kids, Jude thought, so she couldn't have run into a Patterstone descendant in the town. Yet the name felt familiar. When she was in the bright kitchen of the cottage, lifting out the first of the books, reverentially, hardly daring to hope, she remembered.

"Archie Patterstone is dead!" she said, then shivered. *"I will tell Dr. Glen enough is enough."*

She looked down at the book in her hands.

It was a Patricia Highsmith: *the* Patricia Highsmith — *The Talented Mr. Ripley* — and when she glanced inside the front flyleaf her heart leapt. Immediately she turned to the back and couldn't help a chirp of laughter. *It's clever,* he had written, *but it's nothing to curl up with. Neither was Miss Highsmith if anyone's asking me. Since none but me will ever read these words, I'm giving the talented Miss Highsmith this review: she needs a night out.*

"Oh, Todd!" said Jude. "You've just broken every rule in the lit crit book and I love you."

She put the kettle on, took the casserole dish of leftover pasta-bake out of the fridge to come to room temperature, put the oven on for when it did, and settled down to unpack the bag of books like a child under the tree on Christmas morning.

There was *Rosemary's Baby* (*Blimey!*), *Gone with the Wind* (*She should have saved some of this and written a sequel, doubled her wage*), *Catch-22* (*He's been on the wacky baccy and no mistake*), *The World According to Garp* (*If this is New England, God help California*), and *I Capture The Castle* (*Not exactly action-packed and I could draw a ruddy floor plan*).

And that was just in H to L. Jude began to think she was being greedy keeping Todd Jolly to herself. LG Books should have his reviews laminated and stuck to the shelf edges.

And then she found another one. It was *Lolita,* a beautiful late edition, with a sugared-almond-coloured cover, powdery surface and all, and creamy silken pages. Todd had loathed it.

This book is admired because Mr. Nabokov uses a lot of fancy words for a dirty business but a plain man can sometimes see clearer than a clever one. M. tells me Etta Bell is fading fast and her family has been sent for. This plain man is sick of the world tonight.

Jude was staring at his words with tears pricking her eyes when the knock came at the kitchen door. For one wild moment she was scared to open it. Archie Patterstone was out there, and no doubt Etta Bell too. Todd himself was feet away from the doorstep. Who had come knocking this black night?

Then the door opened. He started apologising even before his face appeared.

"Filthy cheek barging in like this, my dear, but it's as cold as a well-digger's — That is, a witch's — That is, it's dreadfully cold, but I — What is it?"

"I was miles away," said Jude. "Well, years away. Communing with the dead."

Lowell nodded absently. "Eddy is missing," he said.

Jude sat down suddenly. "Packed and gone?"

"Just gone," said Lowell. "Left everything behind and fled."

"But she might just be out," said Jude. "Was there a note or anything?"

"She came clean," Lowell said. "Told me the truth about the pregnancy. My so-called grandchild. What an old fool I am." He had been studying the floor and so, when he suddenly looked up, he caught Jude's face before she could hide the thoughts plainly written there.

"She told me too," she said. "I'm sorry."

"I thought I took it well," he said. "I certainly didn't say anything to make her bolt. I mean, dear me, I was terribly excited about the idea of grandparenthood, but on the other hand it was almost too much coming at the same moment as sudden fatherhood. I was perfectly happy to take things one at a time."

"And you weren't angry with her for telling tales?"

"Not at all," Lowell said. "She wasn't to know I would approve, was she? Plenty men my age are perfect old fuddy-duddies. I might have dropped dead from the shock of it."

Jude had been nodding but as she tried to follow his words, she found herself frowning.

"Disapprove of . . . ?" she echoed. Of not being pregnant? Drop dead from the shock of a daughter turning up without a grandchild on board? What did he mean? "I think we're at cross —" she said and then the back door burst open and Eddy came flying in, muffled in a crocheted hat and a long afghan coat, looking like someone from Fleetwood Mac.

"Fuck-a-doodle-doo," she said. "How can you live here with all these bloody corpses?" Then she caught sight of Lowell and her face fell.

"Oh," she said. "You. I came to speak to Jude."

"It's all right," said Lowell. "I've told her I know. And I know you told her first. I'm not angry. I understand that you wanted to confide in a woman and someone nearer your own age than your old papa."

"I didn't confide," said Eddy. "She guessed the gist. I didn't tell her the details."

"*Someone* tell me the details," Jude said.

"Okay," Eddy said. "So you know I'm doing a surrogacy. What else? The dads' names are Liam and Terry. I'm going back to Derry for the birth, so's they can be there and so's I'm with the same doc and midwife I've had all along. That's it, really."

It was genius, Jude thought.

"They don't know I've taken off," Eddy added. "They don't even know my mum died."

"They'll understand," said Jude.

"Course they will," Eddy agreed.

"But it's right for you to return," Lowell put in, beaming. "The living — the about to be born, in this case — matter more than the dead. The celebration of life must take over from mourning. Babies come before us all!" He stopped. "My dear, have I said something to upset you?"

Jude didn't even know there were tears in her eyes until he mentioned them.

"Yes, Dad, actually you have," Eddy said. "Jude's shitbag husband knocked up some bint and that's why he left her."

"Oh my dear!"

Jude managed a stiff smile. It was so much more complicated than that. She stared at both of them, trying to catch the thought and examine it. The living tell the tales and the tales of the dead die with them. Unless, like Todd, they write them down and leave them behind. But that wasn't it either.

"We shall leave you in peace to continue your . . ." Lowell stopped talking and stared her. "What did you say when I arrived?" he asked. "Communing with the spirits of the dead?"

"Interleaved ephemera," Jude began. They were words to make ninety-nine out of a hundred listeners glaze over — Eddy snorted like a hog with hay fever — but Lowell was the hundredth, and his eyes lit up.

"Such a change of view in that quarter even in my lifetime!" he said. "Although, dear me, I'm getting rather old to use my lifetime as unit of short measure, I daresay. Forgive me."

"What for?" said Eddy.

"People do PhDs on it now," Jude agreed. "And not just Dickens' Shakespeare or Joyce's Dickens."

"I shouldn't have thought Joyce was a Dickens man."

"You just keep saying the same words over and over," said Eddy.

"Ephemera," Jude began, "is when —"

"I don't care," said Eddy.

"Well, anyway as I was saying, Lowell, I'm reading the book club notes of this lot's first owner and . . . it's hard to explain."

244

"Not to me, my dear," Lowell said. "Although the prevailing view is that the dead should go and one should commune with the living."

Jude looked uncertainly out of her window. It was a black square. Night had fallen like the snow in a fairytale and blanketed everything.

"I'm certainly better off for the dead than the living in this place," she said.

"Creeporama," said Eddy. Then she stood up very suddenly, from where she had been leaning against the sink. "Oh!"

"What is it?" said Lowell, leaping to his feet. "Pain? Contractions?"

"I just had a brilliant idea," Eddy said. "Dad, can you wait outside while I tell Jude something privately?"

He hurried out, falling over himself to do her bidding.

"Brainwave," she said when he was gone. "Jesus, I can't believe you never thought of it, living in a bloody graveyard surrounded by nothing but headstones!" She waited for Jude to catch on and then rolled her eyes. "Lowell doesn't know your second name, right? And Jude could be a nickname, right? And you want to start again, yeah? Well, look around." Jude glanced to either side. "Not the kitchen, Einstein! Outside. You

245

need a name and fresh start. Well the ground is full of people who don't need their names anymore, isn't it? Knock yourself out — you could be anyone!"

SEVENTEEN

Jude woke the next morning to a strong sense that she'd been dreaming of someone, but she couldn't remember who.

She stared at herself in the bathroom mirror, groping for it, knowing it was gone.

"Todd Jolly, Archie Patterstone, Etta Bell," she said to herself. The bathroom threw her voice back at her, cold and hollow. There was nothing in here to stop the sound bouncing around, just the painted floorboards, shiny-tiled walls, and bare window.

She knew it wasn't any of them she'd dreamed of. There was a face to go with the name. "Eddy, Lowell, Maureen, Jackie," she said, turning the taps on. The water thundered out and steam began to soften the air. Then there was Jen at the tarot and Ela in the knitting shop. She smiled as she dropped her dressing gown and lowered herself into the water. She was making friends.

And what of Eddy's brainwave? Could she really go to a big cemetery in Glasgow and look around for a Judith or Jennifer or even a Jane, born in the mid-seventies and soon after dead again? She had told Lowell that her name was Jemimah, but he might not remember. And she hadn't breathed her last name to anyone.

She felt her smile fade. Did they count as friends if they didn't know her last name or she theirs? Yes, she decided. First names all round was just part of the friendly Wigtown way. Except for Mrs. Hewston. No one ever called her anything else. Despite the hot water, Jude shivered suddenly.

She meant to ask Lowell about it as soon as he got in that morning. She was in Home Crafts, looking in the pitiful collection of interior design books for ways to warm up her bathroom and finding nothing, when he came slowly up the stairs sounding like a tired old man. He appeared in the doorway, like Eddy the day before, with two cups of coffee and two chocolate biscuits.

"Like father like daughter," Jude said.

He pushed one of the cups onto a shelf full of gardening books. Jude, proprietorial about the volumes she had sorted and wiped, couldn't help glancing at the single splash of milky Nescafé rolling down the spine of *The River Cottage Year,* a pest of a book you couldn't properly shelve in either Cooking or Gardening because it was exactly half of each.

"Ha!" she said.

Lowell, startled, slopped a good glug of the cup he was still holding, tutted, and rubbed it halfheartedly into the floor with his toe.

"I've just remembered what I dreamt about last night," she said. "Mrs. Hewston in the asparagus bed."

"With a scythe."

"Right. She . . . I don't even want to tell you what she said about it to me. But is she totally off her nut or is it true that one end's better than the other?"

"All true," said Lowell. "Dear me, yes, it's been an asparagus bed of two halves ever since we dug it. Well, I say *we,* but it was Miranda."

"And where would Mrs. Hewston have got the idea that she was out there in the dead of night burying . . . things?"

"Oh, no doubt she was," said Lowell. "She believed greatly in planting at the full moon and putting roadkill under the rhubarb. Oh yes, absolutely. She was tireless in the garden. Quite tireless. Shoveled barrowfuls of ordure, laid paths, moved enormous shrubs six inches to frame a view. Fan-trained all the fruit trees against the south wall. That was Miranda. I've only had to go over them with a pair of clippers to keep them trim — she was a marvel." He took a bite of his wagon wheel, looking disconsolately at the shelves closest by.

"She must have liked it here," Jude said.

"She loved it. I thought it was the crowd. That summer, you know. Inez and Gary and Tom Tres — Goodness, I've forgotten his name! Tom Tres-something. Cornish, you know. But it wasn't that, because, after they all left, after the end of that summer, she stayed on. I hadn't dreamed she harboured feelings and . . . Well, she went in the end, of course, and only visited once."

"What?" said Jude. "I thought you said when she was gone she was gone for good?"

"No, she'd been off on her travels for a while before her last visit. That last fateful visit." He raised his eyebrows.

"I see," Jude said. "Well, thank heavens for that. Otherwise, no Eddy." She knew Lowell was far from shrewd, but it was unbelievable that he had no doubts at all about this tale. Miranda had taken off, returned for one night only and then twenty years later her daughter turned up and claimed him. "Do you have pictures of your

250

mother?" she said.

"Miranda?" said Lowell. He had misheard her. "Yes, I've a lot of snaps of . . ."

"Of the summer of love?"

Lowell gave his bark of laughter. "It really was," he told her. "My father was dead and I filled the house with laughter at last. There was one particular week in July where every room was full and we had bunks in the drawing room too. The weather was beautiful and we sat outside every night until the small hours in the scent of the Lonicera.

"Of course I know they were humouring me. I know that *now.* Dear me, yes, I'm quite reconciled to that these days. They were all a good deal younger than me and from very different walks of life. But I had the house and I bought all the wine — filthy wine one drank in the country then, wouldn't clean brass with it. I shall indeed have a rummage for some photographs. Eddy would like to see them, I'm sure."

They sat companionably finishing their tea and then he stood, clamping one of his large hands on each knee and levering himself to his feet.

"I like the reading corner, by the way, my dear," he said, with a smile.

Jude peered at him. "You look different," she said.

Lowell snorted and then bared his teeth at her. They were gleaming like pearls. Like enormous mismatched magnolia pearls. "She ordered a preparation from the dreaded Internet and made me sleep with a mouthful of it. Like little strips of gaffer tape. It was most disconcerting."

"It's incredible," Jude said. "Is it safe?"

"The instructions weren't in English," Lowell said, "so I very much fear not. Anyway, if you come round for supper tonight you can help me resist another application, and I'll dig out my photograph albums. Toddle down memory lane, eh?" Then, when he was almost out of the room, he stopped. "Idiot. I forgot to give you what I came up for."

"You gave me tea and biscuits."

Lowell fished in the inside pocket of his jacket and drew out a small book. He was beaming.

"Oh!" said Jude. "Where did you get it? You haven't been to a sale." She wiped her hands on her jeans, and reached out, only faltering when it was in her hands.

"I — I thought it was a Douglas," she said. "I mean, thank you."

In fact, it was a field guide to British seabirds, a pocket edition from the middle of the last century. Jude supposed migration patterns wouldn't have changed much, unless global warming had knocked them off kilter, and here she was right at the coast in a wild place where miles of empty headland met miles of mudflats and estuary. It must seem silly to Lowell that she wasn't making the most of it.

He was laughing. "My dear, what do you take me for? I wouldn't give you a thing simply because *I* happened to like it. I had an uncle who collected coins and he gave me coins for every birthday between the ages of eight and eighteen. Postal orders at Christmas thankfully, but still. Ten dreary birthdays until finally I got a bottle of malt." He nodded at the book. "Look inside."

Jude opened it and smiled. *T. Jolly.*

"It's a sad tale, actually," Lowell said. "When he was getting very frail indeed, no longer going out and about, he began to cull the library somewhat. He did away with his natural history collection — too painful, one supposes, when he knew his days of spotting things were over. Or perhaps he needed the space. One hundred books to read before et cetera. Well, dear me, many of them are gone, but I found this for you."

Jude flipped to the back, but there was nothing there. As the pages turned, though, a piece of card fell out and landed at

Lowell's feet. He stooped with another grunt and swiped it up.

"Sighting list?" he said, but he handed it over without looking. "Interleaved ephemera, anyway," he went on. "And therefore yours, my dear. And I shall keep shaking my remaining brain cells for memories of more." He turned away and then turned halfway back. "He was an interesting man, Todd Jolly. I'm very happy that you're . . . honouring him, I suppose. I don't suppose . . ."

"What?" said Jude.

"I know all this" — he waved a hand at the disorder in the room, at the piles of books and the unpacked boxes of stock jammed onto what should be a display table — "will come to an end, and it's not exactly stretching you even at that. I don't suppose you'd consider just staying on, would you? No, of course not. Why would you? This backwater. Dusty old relic like Lowland Glen."

Jude honestly had no idea whether he meant the bookshop or the man.

"Only, heavens above, you make her laugh. You and she seem to be quite . . . in cahoots already."

"You don't need me to sweeten the pill, Lowell," Jude said. "She loves you. And you're all she's got."

Lowell couldn't hide his pleasure, but when he let in the whole of what she'd said, he shook his head. "I didn't mean that exactly," he told her. "I didn't mean that you should function as some sort of . . . Dear me, no. I simply thought perhaps the three of us could be happy."

Lowell was no less surprised than Jude herself when she stepped over and hugged him tight. He had the mugs in one hand but he pressed the other against the middle of her back and said, "Well, well," before he left.

She had never been the emotional type. She knew it had unnerved people at the funeral. They had come ready to find her broken, or even to witness her breaking, and they went away disappointed and disapproving. But just because her grief didn't come out as tears in the crematorium, that didn't mean it wasn't there. It had to be at the bottom of what came after. If she could have gone to work she might have been all right. Well, not to work exactly. But to the bindery.

She tried to ration herself to a couple of visits there a month, because of the glue fumes and the suspicious gossipy nature of the three bindery workers, who didn't know why she came. Why *did* she go? Because it was mesmerising: the bindery inbox filled up during the day with the grubby, slackened, bacon-greased books from all over the system, then at night Stella and her girls stripped their baggy plastic, bleached the stains, stitched the slackness tight and glued feather-light tape on the tears. They put the books in clamps and buffed the edges of the pages with a sanding block until they were white again.

After Max left her — after he made her leave him — she wished they would turn their talents her way. Strip her, bleach her, clamp her, buff her smooth and pale with finer and finer grades of sandpaper until the last stroked her like silk and left her gleaming

Anyway, she couldn't go and sit in the bindery in the middle of her bereavement leave. And so what came after happened instead. She wasn't in control. She was reverberating like Wile E. Coyote when he made for the painted tunnel and met the rock face. That would be the basis of her defence if it came to that. Reeling from the double funeral of her parents, her only family, poor orphan child.

If it came to that. But between a new name from a Glasgow cemetery and a change of hair colour too, maybe it never would. Maybe the three of them *could* be happy. Eddy, the cuckoo in Lowell's nest with her secrets and lies. Jude on the run, looking over one shoulder for the rest of her life, careful never to get her face on a screen or her name on the news. And kind, honest, open Lowell, saving the world from tame Victorian porn, suspecting but not caring that once again it was his house and his money and this haven of a town that were the real draw.

Finally, she glanced at the card he had handed her. It was one of those rectangles, shiny on one side and rough on the other, familiar once upon a time to anyone who worked in a public library. Youngsters finding them now would be mystified most likely. But Jude was just old enough to remember when pairs of tights came with one leg stretched precariously around them to show what "American Tan" or "Ecru" would look like on a leg of pure snowy white.

These were birding notes, as Lowell had suspected. On a single day in November 1984, Todd had recorded a robin, ten sparrows, four herring gulls, something called a dooker that Jude had never heard of and three oystercatchers. Oystercatchers? She was intrigued despite herself, charmed by the thought of something so exotic-sounding in Scotland in November. If she went down to the shore one of these days, if it ever stopped raining, would she see oystercatchers too?

She was just about to look in the index for a picture when the last few lines caught her eye.

A. PATTERSTONE
E. BELL?
L. MCLENNAN — NEXT?

"Archie Patterstone is dead," she said. *"Etta Bell is fading fast."*

She dropped the card back into the book and rubbed her hands on her jeans but could feel the echo of its glossy surface like a taint on the pad of her finger and thumb for the rest of the day, even after hours of shelf-washing, hours of dunking her hand over and over again in a bucket of lemon-scented water.

She tried to talk herself round. She already knew he was near the end by late 1984, housebound, mourning his wife, losing his friends. If he was a lifelong note-taker he might well jot all kinds of things down. And when two of his friends died, he might well wonder who was next. She only wished she could get the other sentence out of her mind. *I will tell Dr. Glen enough is enough.*

By closing time, she was filthy and exhausted, not much of a prospect as a dinner companion and so she stopped off at the newsagents to buy a box of mints as a sweetener, remembering Lowell's words: *I thought perhaps the three of us could be happy.*

"Nice to see a smiling face," said Jackie, as she walked in. She was tying up the unsold Sunday papers to set them out for recycling. "Nowt but torn coupons all afternoon. November, ken."

"Sorry?" said Jude.

"Halloween weeks back and a gey stretch to Christmas," said Jackie. "Everyone's mumping. And if they're stuck for somebody else, they mump at me."

"You sell them sweets and ciggies," said Jude. "I should think you'd be a friend."

"Not the shop," Jackie agreed. "They mump about the prices though, mind. Naw. The Post Office." She nodded to the glass cubicle, which had its shutter drawn down and a closed sign sitting on the counter. "Moan that it's shut, moan that it's open and I'm busy, moan that the lassie canna take a shot when they ken damn fine I'm

259

the postmistress." She pointed at the procla-mation of her status — a yellowed sheet with an official red stamp in one corner, stuck in the glass of the cubicle in pride of place amongst the small ads.

"Can I take the cottage advert down, Jackie?" Jude said. "It's let."

"Moan that they've missed the parcel van, moan that I canna do them a passport photo. Christ! They're in here every day of life. Think if there was a photo booth they'd have seen it, eh? Aye, go on, hen, rip it off. Lowell's not one to come moaning that I should have left it for him to take down since he put it up there."

Jude smiled politely, getting just the gist, as was usual with Jackie, and slightly less than the gist towards the end since she wasn't really trying. She had seen some-thing. She had noticed that the name of the postmistress, printed in ink on the dotted line of the form was *J. McLennan.* She took a chance.

"I've just been handling something that belonged to a relative of yours, I think."

"Oh?" said Jackie. "Has that wee besom been putting mair stuff out? I've telt her till I'm blue." She saw Jude's frown and at-tempted an explanation. "My brother's wife's cowping everything that came out of

260

my mother's house, the wee bitch that she is. I told her I would help her when I'm not stuck in here, but oh no!"

"I don't think —"

"She'll have the place stripped to the walls and everything she fancies away!"

"I don't think — it was a book, quite an old one."

"She's never!" said Jackie. She took a phone out of her overall pocket and started jabbing the buttons. When she put it to her ear, her face was thunderous, her mouth a line.

"No!" said Jude and put out a hand. "This was a book that's been in Lowell's shop for ages. L. McLennan."

"Oh!" said Jackie, killing the phone call. "Christ on a bike, hen! We'd've had World War III if she'd picked up. She's a nippy sweetie when she's riled."

"Sorry."

"L. McLennan? That can't be right, though."

"A different family?"

"No, no, that's my Auntie Lorna, right enough. But she's long gone."

"His stock doesn't exactly turn over," Jude said.

"Aye, but I'm talking decades," said Jackie. "Must be well past twenty years. She nearly saw a hundred, mind."

"A hundred? That's marvelous."

"*Nearly* a hundred!" Jackie said. "And then she died."

After Etta and Archie, in her turn, like the list said.

Something in Jackie's tone made Jude ask, "What did she die of?"

And the tone turned stronger and darker, like espresso, as Jackie answered, "She died of me having a job I couldn't walk away from and that useless bitch being too lazy to do a hand's turn."

Jude tutted, as though she understood. Which she didn't. Jackie gave a single nod, just a tuck of the chin, and carried on.

"Auntie Lorna was scared she'd die alone and *lie;* ken, for days, till the smell got bad? So she went into the home and right down-hill. She was fine in her own wee flat on the ground floor. But the minute she went into Bayview, she was on her way. She was too frail to be changing her diet and it wasn't good for her to be cooped up in that so-called social room — roasting hot and all of them passing their germs around. This was before the flu jabs came in. She'd always kept her window cracked at home, but there was none of that. In case they caught cold. Cold! Those folk went through the war on

262

mashed turnips and liquorice water. They weren't soft like some I could name."

"I'm forty," said Jude. "I'm not as tough as your auntie, but even I'm not as bad as the teenagers now."

"She missed her telegram by two weeks, the wee sweetheart," Jackie said. "We had the cake ordered. Would you believe that cold-hearted so-and-so kept it in her fridge and ate it slice by slice?"

Jude tutted again. "It's a thought, isn't it?" she said. "Going into a home. Mr. Jolly — you know, who lived in my house? — he managed to stay in his own place, didn't he?"

"Back when doctors still did house calls. It was better in some ways. Depending on the doctor anyway. The last thing you needed, when you were lying in your bed covered in chicken pox or running at both ends, was *him* barking at you, and the stink of his cigars."

"Dr. Glen?"

"I missed my sick bucket and got the sleeve of his jacket when I was four years old and he reminded me every last blessed time I saw him till his dying day. He made a joke about it at my wedding, the swine."

"Why was he at your wedding?"

"Ocht, he wasn't. But it was in the func-

263

tion room at the Masonic and he was in the public bar. Todd Jolly told him to shut his face. Just like that, one end of the bar to the other. Oh it doesn't sound like much now, but things were different then."

"I can imagine," Jude said.

"He was a fine man, was Todd." Jackie sighed. "He went fast at the end."

"After his wife died?" said Jude.

"What? Ocht, no. She was a sorry wee thing, barely saw her pension. It wasn't till after she went that he got his life under him. Ken the type? She was always ailing with something or other. What a life he had! Well, no life at all. No, it was when he was a widower that he started to live. Joined the bowling, joined the bridge, worked on the house. She'd kept him back — always in her bed with her migraines and didn't want the sound of a saw or the smell of paint. Then he had fifteen good years, just his own self. It's sometimes the way."

Jude wasn't acting when she shook her head in wonder. "I love that you know everyone," she said. "They're not really gone if someone remembers them, are they?"

"Everyone who?" said Jackie, giving Jude an odd look. Jude thought if she said nothing, Jackie would be sure to carry on, but when the silence started getting awkward she was forced to say a little more. With her throat slightly tight she said more than she had expected to.

"Well, Mr. Jolly. And . . . Etta Bell was another name I came across, and Archie Patterstone."

The woman blinked twice. "By jings, you're going back there," she said. "Etta Bell was my mother's age, and where the hang did you get Archie's name from? What did you say you were here doing? I thought it was just clearing out that midden. Is it a history of the town you're at?"

"Occupational hazard," Jude said. "I'm a cataloguer. If I come across a name I want to record it somewhere, cross-reference. Make it fit."

"Fit what?" Jackie said. Two clipped words. No family history, no side swipes at her sister-in-law, no local colour. And Jude had no idea how to answer.

"Auntie Lorna was a good age," Jackie said in the end. "And Etta and Archie and them are a long time gone. Resting easy."

Jude paid for her mints and left.

It had stopped raining, and a rising ground fog dulled her footsteps. Walking in the muffled quiet towards Jamaica House, Jackie's last words rang in her ears. *Etta and*

Archie and them. She repeated it to herself and found her footsteps starting to keep time to the rhythm. *Etta and Archie and them.* Like *Lions and tigers and bears.* Etta and Archie and who, though? Not Auntie Lorna because Jackie had just mentioned her. Etta and Archie and who? Todd Jolly was one more, but that still left someone missing.

EIGHTEEN

He had moved the onions to the kitchen. Festoons of them, neat braids of whitened stems and double rows of copper orbs, were hooked over the open ends of the drying rack high above Eddy's head. She saw Jude looking.

"Yeah," she said. "He didn't do it to make me feel guilty, so why do I feel guilty?"

"Use them up quick before they go mouldy," Jude said. "He loves your cooking. Where is he anyway?"

"Last minute eBay bid on a box of photos," Eddy said, pointing upwards. "He said to have a drink and he'll be down at seven when it closes."

Jude helped herself from an open bottle of red sitting in the middle of the kitchen table with two glasses. Eddy, drinking Coke from a can, lifted it to toast her.

"I'm not allowed any," she said. "Cos of the baby."

Jude gave her a quizzical look then shrugged. Maybe it was easier to keep the fake pregnancy going all the time rather than on and off.

"You'd probably do any baby more harm with that muck," she said.

"Don't drink wine anyway. And he's got no vodka, cos I've checked. I've been trying to work out what she was playing at."

"Who?" said Jude, after her first swallow.

"Mum," Eddy told her. "Who else?"

Raminder, Jude didn't say. She had spent a year trying to work out what Raminder was playing at. A good Sikh girl who lived with her family in Hounslow, dressed modestly, brought in food from home. She should have met her husband through a matchmaker and slept with him for the first time on her wedding night. Instead, she had picked up a married drunk heathen and got herself pregnant before he'd even left his wife.

"It's a funny expression, *got yourself pregnant,* isn't it?" Jude said with another mouthful of wine.

"Unless you're a stick insect," Eddy said. "Yeah, so I've been trying to work out what she was playing at. Because what I'm thinking is this: why did she send me back here if Lowell's not my dad? And the only answer

I've come up with is that the deed was done that summer, while she was here, *by* someone who was here. See? Someone who was at the big party that lasted all summer long. And sending me back here was the only way she could set me on the path to finding him. Maybe she never meant to say Lowell was my dad, just that he was here and he'd help me start searching."

"For some guy from a wild time twenty years ago?"

"I can try," Eddy said. "Lowell's going to show me his photos."

"Really?" said Jude. *"Seriously?"*

Eddy snorted. "Not those ones! What is wrong with him with that, right? Photos of Mum, I mean. Summer of '94. Perfect chance to ask everyone's name. You never know. And I might recognise him."

There was a creak upstairs and both of them stiffened. Then Jude looked at her watch.

"Only five to," she said.

"He'll be just getting on his marks," Eddy said. "You should see him. Hunched over the keyboard like a vulture. He goes bright red." She leaned back and hooted with laughter. "I'm not being rotten. I think he's great."

"So why not leave it?" Jude said. "He loves

269

you, like I said. And you're getting fond of him too."

"Because I'm normal," said Eddy. "Unlike you."

Jude took a careful slow sip from her glass and then made her voice as light as she could get it. "How's that?"

"Are you really not looking?" Eddy said. "How can you not be looking? How is that not killing you?"

"What at?" She remembered as she said it Jackie's two darts of sound earlier. *Fit what?*

"At the news! The Internet. All the buzz!"

Jude froze. It was her own fault, trusting a bloody kid.

"Look," she said in an urgent whisper, "I'll make a deal. I won't talk about 'Liam and Terry' if you don't talk about Max and Raminder."

"It's not the same though, is it?" Eddy said. She was right. Max and Raminder were real; hundreds of thousands of hits in the online news was how real they were.

"I didn't say it was. But I can't keep talking about it every time we're alone."

"Sorry!" said Eddy. "Jeez. But just tell me one thing and then I'll never mention it again. How right did the papers get it? Likes of, did you really go round to the house?"

And just like that Jude was back. She

270

could feel the cheap black shoes chafing her heels through the tights and the awkward tug of the ill-fitting jacket across her shoulders. She could taste the sourness in her mouth from three cups of stale coffee at the reception and smell the stink of her sweat, drying cold on the polyester shirt. She could hear the unfamiliar sound of her own breathing, muffled and close, panicky quick, and the *too* familiar sound of Max stumbling on his way up the stairs, opening the door to the bedroom. She held her breath. He had never, in all the years they were married, put his clothes away when he came home drunk. He would kick his shoes off, one toe against the other heel, and then he'd fall like a tree, facedown on the bed with his head hanging over.

"Say what you like about Max," a colleague had drawled once. "Doesn't matter how blattered he is, he's still a paramedic. Sleeps on his front with his airways clear."

She heard one shoe, the other, then at last she felt the floorboards shudder and heard the creak and thump as he let himself fall, knocking the headboard against the wall. In less than ten more of her frantic heartbeats, he was snoring. She'd stood, batted away the sweet folds of Raminder's clothes, careful not to jangle the coat hangers, and

271

opened the wardrobe door.

She drained her glass. "I can't talk about it," she said.

"Right, right, got it," Eddy said. "I'm only asking."

"Hail the conquering hero!" Lowell strode into the room and beamed at both them — briefly, before his face fell. "Oh my dears, I've done it again, haven't I? You were talking about your mothers."

"Not this time," said Eddy. "Scumbag boyfriends. How'd the auction go?"

"I triumphed," Lowell said. "Fifteen pounds within my budget. And I picked up a Richard Scarry in mint condition while I was waiting."

"Children's book?" said Jude, trying and failing to sound cheerful. "You'll only attract them if you keep buying books for them, you know."

"Mint Scarry?" said Lowell. "It's a *collector's* piece. I'll price it out of range of their grubby little fistfuls of pocket money." He glanced at Eddy's belly, particularly prominent in a skimpy skinny-rib polo neck. "Not that I'm speaking against children in general."

"You're off the hook, Dad," Eddy said. "This isn't your grandchild, remember?"

And she sounded just about as miserable

272

as Jude.

"Are you — forgive me, dear child — but are you going to be a part of its life at all? Am I? I'm not *au fait* with the rules governing this kind of thing. Dear me, no."

"Nope," said Eddy. "I'm just babysitting. It's not — Well, if you must know, it's not my egg. It's no relation to either of us."

"I see," said Lowell. "Yes, I see."

"The egg donor's a big high-flying lawyer or something and she didn't have time. If I'd known about you back then I would have been able to brag a bit more about *my* genes, but I didn't, so there it is."

Stop talking, Jude willed her silently. It was sounding more ridiculous by the minute. But Lowell didn't bat an eyelid.

"I shouldn't have thought I'd be any great recommendation," he said. "Doddery old bookseller from the back of beyond."

"Your dad was a doctor!" said Eddy.

"A GP, also in the back of beyond, with a third-class degree," said Lowell.

"Don't be like that," Jude said. "I mean, from what I was hearing this afternoon, he might have been a bit bossy, but he really took care of people."

"Ah," said Lowell. "Mrs. Hewston has been back, has she? Singing his praises. She really has got Queen Victoria knocked into

273

a cocked hat for posthumous devotion."

"You don't half talk a pile of shite," said Eddy.

"Jackie in the post office, actually," Jude said. "She said he made house calls and kept people alive. And you said yourself he didn't retire while any of his long-timers still needed him."

"What does Jackie know about it?" said Lowell. "And how on earth did it come up?"

"She was eulogising her Auntie Lorna."

"Eulogising!" said Eddy. "You're as bad as him."

Jude ignored her. "Saying she would have made it to a hundred if she'd stuck with Dr. Glen and not gone into the nursing home."

"Was that the nursing home you worked in?" Eddy said. Again, the notion seemed to tickle her. "Jeez, people couldn't get away from the Glen family and die in peace, could they?"

"How damning!" said Lowell. "Well then, let me see. Let's turn to something happier shall we? I fished this out earlier." He patted the pile at his side. There was the usual *Telegraph* folded in quarters and open at the crossword, the junk mail and magazines, but also now the bulk of a photograph album, one of the ones with a bulbous spine hiding thick internal rings and stiff pages covered with sticky clear plastic to clamp down the pictures.

Eddy took it and laid it on the table in front of her, pushing her Coke can away. Jude sidled into a chair beside her, and Lowell got to his feet and came to stand behind both of them.

"I'll get supper started in a minute," he said. "Bacon sandwiches okay? I'll have to toast the bread though. It's not in the first flush of youth."

Jude looked over at her box of mints meant to make up for being scruffy and felt a surge of happiness. It was the first time in her life a housekeeping shambles had made her happy.

"But I wouldn't mind a quick trip down memory lane first," said Lowell. He put a hand on Eddy's shoulder and patted it gently as she opened the front cover.

Someone — surely not Lowell — had gone to a bit of trouble here. The first page had a handmade label under the plastic. *Wigtown, Summer 1994,* it said. The top corners were decorated with water-colour paintings of bees and butterflies, long grass along the bottom edge with buttercups and plantain heads.

"They were so very young," Lowell said.

Eddy turned the page and Jude heard her let her breath go. There were four pictures in the double-page spread, but all were of the mud flats down by the shore. Different times of day from dawn until sunset and different weather days too: a periwinkle blue sky or angry banks of rolling grey thunderclouds. The photographer had caught the dimpled look of raindrops hitting the surface of the water and the dream look of the sky darker than the land.

"Bo-ring," Eddy said and flicked the page over.

These four were of the beach. Someone had lain flat on the sand to make a sandcastle loom in the foreground. First it was new and dark, with shells for windows and a feather flag on top, then pale and beginning to crumble with some of the shells lying around it. The third photograph showed it with the tide sloshing into the moat, and finally it was no more than a bump, shells and feathers long gone.

"Bloody hell," said Eddy.

"It was Inez's camera," Lowell said. "And she was more interested in —"

"That's better!" Eddy said. It was the same beach but this time with a bonfire in the foreground, the flames showing up as faint purplish wisps, and around it a ring of faces, all young, all reddened by the sun. The women sat cross-legged or Little Mermaid style and the young men, two of them and another hidden by the fire, just his legs visible, were stretched out. One had his head in a girl's lap, her long hair hanging worryingly close to the glowing tip of the cigarette he held clamped in his lips. He was laughing around it, his face crinkled and his hands wide as if he had just clapped them together with glee. And yet the girl who cradled his head was looking off to the side in the other direction, unsmiling.

"That's her," Eddy said. She pointed at one of the faces distorted by the heat.

All Jude could see clearly was an elbow and a knee, a tented skirt, and a rolled sleeve. And then with a gasp she recognised the pinafore Eddy had been wearing the day before. Eddy recognised it too and traced it with a careful finger.

"Who are the rest, Lowell?" said Jude.

"Well, that's Tom with the cigarette, and John . . . dear me, I've forgotten his name, with the guitar. He strummed it endlessly, never quite getting as far as what you'd call a tune but never quite stopping either. And the girl in the jeans was called . . . Diana. And the other two were . . . oh, I think they just joined us for the evening. I'm not sure I was ever introduced."

"Where are *you,* Lowell?" Jude asked him.

"I was there somewhere," Lowell said. "I think — Yes, those are my legs!"

Eddy began turning the pages again. There were shots of the empty road outside Jamaica House with a sea fog rolling across it, shots of cows standing in the rain by a field gate, shots of the garden, looking raw with tiny roses in yards of bare earth and new paths laid out in the muddy mess caused by their laying.

"That was all your mother's doi—" Lowell said, as Eddy whipped past to another page.

Every so often she stopped. Whenever there was a picture peopled with figures. Most of them were set pieces like the bonfire; another was of a supper table laid in the garden of the shop with fairy lights and lanterns hanging in the branches of the apple tree, and two rows of faces, red again, perhaps from wine this time, leaning in to be seen from both sides. Lowell was at the head of the table, with a paper hat on his head and his arms thrown wide.

"Such a wonderful evening," he said. "Two of the lads — Tom and . . . Golly, I wish I could remember . . . But they brought a little table-top cooker and set it up under the bin store. We made a feast on those two

278

rings you wouldn't believe. Well, Miranda did. Beef en daube and a —"

"Mum never ate beef!" Eddy said.

"Look at her plate!" said Lowell, pointing.

And even Jude could see that there were bones pushed to the side of the plate in front of Miranda. She was tapping ash into a small pool of something dark — sauce or gravy — and smiling broadly at whoever was behind the camera. Her hair was a cloud of absolute black around her head and her eyes were just as dark, the way the camera had caught her, only a pinpoint of light in each. Her mouth was wide open in laughter. Jude couldn't see the cherry-red lips Maureen had mentioned, but inside the wide mouth more points of light glittered. The phrase that sprang to Jude's mind was *she-devil*.

"One of the best nights of my life," Lowell was saying. "Which probably says quite a lot about my life, dear me, yes. But looking at their faces, perhaps it wasn't just me."

Jude looked closely then. And he was right; they were shining with more than heat or alcohol. Bathed in the soft light of the lanterns, they looked even younger than they had on the beach. Even Lowell looked young, his teeth lighter and his hair darker. And he had only a shirt on, missing the top layers of cardigan and jacket Jude had never seen him without.

"The wonder of it was that I knew it at the time," Lowell said. "I knew that very evening it was one of the special moments. Well, actually, I thought it was the start of something, but I knew how special *that* was. Better to have loved and lost than never loved at all."

"Bullshit," said Eddy. "What about what you don't know can't hurt you?"

"What are the names of them all?" Jude said. "Tom, I recognise. And John . . ."

"Talport!" said Lowell. "Johnny Talport. And Miranda looking marvellous there. Inez behind the camera, as usual. And that's a couple who cycled down from Edinburgh."

"Ouch," Eddy said.

"Calum and Sandra? Sarah? And those two were from Dumfries. Inez and Miranda met them when they went on a bus trip one day to see the Ruthwell cross. I have no idea what their names are."

"Another couple, were they?" Eddy said, peering closely. Jude knew what she was wondering — whether the man might have hooked up with Miranda — but Lowell squirmed.

"It might seem tawdry now, but it truly was not, dear child. It was a wonderful summer. Sunny and hot day after day. Inez

280

hasn't really done it justice, interleaving all the photographs of autumn when the rains came. There wasn't a shower from June to September."

"Tawdry?" said Eddy. "Like an orgy, you mean?"

"It was an innocent time," Lowell said. "Love was in the air. We were happy and the sun shone and young people came and went, sang and swam."

Eddy was almost at the end of the album now. There were more pages of the beach and the sky and the mud flats, then two double-page spreads of what looked like a village show: two young men shearing sheep while a ring of onlookers watched them; children jumping over lumpy grass in hessian sacks with their hair flying up; a beer-tent table covered in empty glasses with a wasp floating in the dregs of a pint; and a long trestle table with vegetables laid out in formation and a rosette in the foreground, bright yellow with the light catching its gold script: *Five potatoes of any kind, Commended.*

"She was a wonderful photographer, wasn't she?" Jude said.

"Best dead wasp I've seen today," said Eddy. "*Here's* one of Mum. About bloody time!"

281

"I took that," Lowell said.

And Jude could tell the difference. The background was half wall and half window, so that one of the women was silhouetted and one was not. Miranda stood against the white wall, grinning again, her red lips obvious this time. The woman she had her arms around showed up mostly as a nimbus of brilliant hair, almost pink in the light. She was tiny and Miranda's tanned arms, bare under a rainbow-coloured vest top, engulfed her.

"She looks so very alive," Lowell said.

Jude gave him a glance. To her the little pink and gold woman looked like a ghost, or an angel. But of course he was talking about Miranda.

"Yeah, that's the best one," said Eddy. "Can I copy it?"

"I wish I had made more of an effort," Lowell said. "I despise most modern ways, but it is rather marvellous to know whether one's pictures have failed before it's too late to try again."

"I miss going to Boots in the rain and getting the packet back though," Jude said. "Sitting in the car remembering what sunshine felt like."

"I miss the Christmas Day film," Lowell said. "The whole family — the whole coun-

282

try — all sitting down to watch something no one had ever seen before. Box of chocolates to pass around. Everyone dashing for the lavatory during the adverts, loath to miss anything."

"And all for sixpence if you showed your ration book," said Eddy, making Jude and Lowell laugh.

"Right then, Lowell," said Jude. "Let's shake these names out of your memory. They'll be in there somewhere."

"Why?" said Lowell.

"Because young Eddy here has had a wonderful idea," Jude said, ignoring Eddy's face going still. "She's going to try to get in touch with everyone who knew her mother throughout her life. Most of them will be in Ireland, of course, but some of them will be elsewhere, including some in Scotland from that summer. So."

"Tom, Johnny Talport, Inez and Miranda, Gary and Paula — good heavens. You could be a sergeant major, my dear. Your wish seems to be my command. Dear me, yes. Those I'm sure of, but as to the rest . . ." He shrugged.

"What was Gary's *other* name?" said Eddy. "Just for practice," she added, at Lowell's look.

"I've got a better practice for you," Jude

said. "Complete this list: Etta Bell, Archie Patterstone, Lorna McLennan, and . . ."

"Wait!" said Eddy. She grabbed Lowell's crossword pen from the middle of the table and started scribbling on the border of the *Telegraph.* Jude ignored her.

"What on earth?" Lowell said. "Those aren't my summer guests. Those are Wigtown worthies from days of yore."

Eddy threw the pen down again.

"Gravestone names?" she said. "Jude, I told you to go to Glas—"

"Tom Treserrick!" said Lowell, suddenly. "And I've just remembered that they put up a little talent show too. Inez made playbills. I must still have one, and there will be surnames there, certainly."

Eddy was on her feet before he had finished talking, and they left together. Jude heard them in the drawing room, drawers opening and shutting. She stood and crossed to peer in the fridge, see if she could scrape together something better for dinner than bacon sandwiches.

The fog was even thicker when she set off home. Deadening and clammy, it settled on her clothes and condensed on her face so she had to wipe it away. *The three of us could be happy.* Could they? Could a life made up of nothing more than nights like this one be a whole life? She thought so. Lowell would even have got the Volvo out and trundled her home, but he was over the limit after wine and whisky, and walking was safer when it was this bad.

Within minutes, she began to wonder. She had borrowed a torch but that only made it worse, a thick pale cone ahead of her like a candy floss and the dark even darker, so she switched it off and went into the middle of the road to walk the white line. It appeared out of the emptiness two paces ahead and disappeared under her feet while she fell forward. And although she knew there were houses on either side, the silence was so total and the hazy blobs of window light so faint that she began to feel like the only person here. The only person alive. She quickened her pace. Surely someone would be walking a dog or coming home from the pub, dragging a wheeliebin up or down a drive.

As she approached the turn-off to the cemetery she slowed down and moved to the edge again, waiting for the kerb to curve away at the mouth of the lane. It was further than she thought. She kept walking and then all of a sudden she found the road bending to the left and a lowered kerb with yellow painted studs to help wheelchairs.

She stopped dead. This wasn't it. She had taken a wrong turning somewhere.

She tried to laugh to herself. "Walk around London no problem and lost in Wigtown!" she said. But the muffled sound of her voice unnerved her, and when she turned around and retraced her steps she knew her heart was racing.

For twenty minutes she walked slowly and calmly. If she got back to the main street before eleven, she told herself, she would go into the pub and ask someone. But that was crazy! What would she ask? And anyway she couldn't *find* the main street. She had lost track of her twists and turns now. For all she knew she was out of the town completely and heading up the country road towards Newton Stewart, a sitting duck if anyone was driving the other way. She walked to the edge, saw the pavement and a glimpse of a garden gate, and knew at least that she was still in the town somewhere.

Just once she heard footsteps ahead of her.

"Terrible night," she called out. It was how the Scots greeted each other in bad weather and she was learning. No one answered, though. The footsteps only quickened as whoever it was hurried away.

"I don't suppose you could —" she called

286

louder and could have sworn the footsteps grew quicker again, the stranger running.

"Charming!" she said, trying to feel annoyed and failing. She was properly frightened now. A third time, she shifted to the side of the road, planning to march up the nearest path and knock on someone's door and, just like that, she saw the familiar manhole cover on the broad corner where the pavement turned and the telegraph pole with the rusted warning sign nailed to it and knew at last she was at the cemetery road.

Here the painted markings stopped but there were soft verges to either side, high with bracken, and she would feel the ground change underfoot if she veered off, so she strode along to the gates and slipped through them, feeling instantly safer to be inside the cemetery walls. She didn't know if she could really see the dark shape of the church looming ahead of her or if she only imagined it because she knew it was there, but she smiled anyway.

Jackie had forgotten something; all of them forgot something when they teased her or asked her, worried, if she was frightened to be there alone. This place was a sanctuary. It was out amongst the living that people could hurt you. Here, where all were

287

at rest, passion spent, troubles ended, she was safe.

She hurried around the path to her cottage. "Evening, Todd," she said. "Evening, Archie. Evening, Etta, wherever you are. I'll find you tomorrow if it's a nice day." She would buy some flowers, she thought. If she was going to live here permanently, she would learn everyone's birthday from their tombstone and make sure they had some flowers on the right day. There was nothing morbid about that. Then she remembered Lowell saying that the dead should be gone and the living present.

So perhaps she should forget Todd and Archie and them. Perhaps she should invite some living people round for a party, make some noise and mess. Did she know enough people to make what you would call a party?

She opened the porch door, clicking the light on and slipping through quickly, before too much of the chilly damp swirled in with her.

As she turned to lock up she saw a sheet of paper pushed part way through the letterbox.

See that? she told herself. One of your friends has been round while you were out. She plucked it free and opened it.

People say their blood freezes. Sometimes

that their heart is in their mouth. Jude felt it differently. To her, it seemed that all her blood raced to her middle and pulled her heart, heavy and bulging, down into her gut. Every other inch of her except that hot weight was empty and tingling.

NINETEEN

Let the dead rest.
— Norma, Elsie, Archie, Etta, and Todd

The paper was roughly torn from a pad, lined in blue with a red edge to the margin. The pen was a red biro, pressed in hard so that the words could be felt, like Braille, as well as seen. And there was a dark blob at the start, telling Jude this pen was not used every day, that it had been plucked from a cup or scrabbled out of a drawer.

Her first thought was a throwback to her life before. She turned to the phone to dial 999. Then she remembered she couldn't call the police. Not tonight, not ever again. She carried the note to the kitchen without shifting her grip, got a plastic sandwich bag from the rack — one-handed, thanking Todd for his nifty kitchen system — and dropped the note inside.

She washed her face, brushed her teeth,

290

and climbed into bed. The nooks and shelves of Todd's ingenious headboard were filled with books now as well as the little stack moved from the attics at Jamaica House: the Douglas, the Allingham, the plane crash, *Rebecca,* and *Midnight's Children.*

There was everything from the new Ian Rankin (bought at Tesco's and hidden from Lowell) to another O. Douglas find — *Eliza for Common* — got online by Lowell for her and lied about, she was sure. She had *Danny: Champion of the World* for comfort and *Gravity's Rainbow* for a challenge. There was *The Brothers Karamazov* to cure insomnia and two Ian McEwans to remind her of home, although to be sure his London was not hers. There was an early Anne Tyler — *The Clock Winder* — that she had somehow managed never to read and the last PD James, which she would save as long as she could bear to.

But she didn't so much as glance at a single one of them. She sat up against her pillows with the covers drawn to her chin, staring out the window at the blackness, thinking.

It had to be Jackie. *Etta and Archie and them,* she'd said. Who else could it be? But

291

why? What was going on?

She woke once in the night, starting awake after a dream. Her head had fallen sideways and her neck was stiff. She shuffled herself flat and turned the bedclothes away from her shoulders to cool off. She had been dreaming about the fog. Hearing footsteps and chasing after them only to realise that they were behind her and really she was running away.

She turned over on her side. The sky had cleared. Outside her bedroom window she could see two stars in the black and could hear the wind rattling the catch. She thought about getting up and stuffing it with paper, then thought about the note in its plastic bag, downstairs on the kitchen worktop. *Let the dead rest.* And the next time she opened her eyes it was morning, a glittering blue day.

She stood at his bedroom window and looked down. All the better to see what was laid out below. The tips of the grass were white with frost and all around, in a series of dots and loops, were footprints. Someone had walked on the grass in that drenching fog last night and the flattened blades had frozen in place.

God, for a phone to take a picture! Jude tried to memorise the placing of the foot-

292

prints and then bundled herself into warm clothes and hurried downstairs and out.

She told herself the feet could have belonged to a relative who came in the afternoon on an innocent visit, or even to a graveyard enthusiast. They existed, she knew. And she told herself that of course a visitor — relative or cemetery buff — would want to read the legible gravestones and would ignore those whose words had worn away. But she didn't believe it. For one thing, there was no stopping and starting in the prints, no evidence of a search.

There was no denying it after two trips up to her bedroom to look down again. The footprints led from the path to Todd, to Archie, to the grave of a Norma Oughton, to Etta Bell, to another one full of an entire family of people called Day, and then back to the path again, closer to the cottage, to deliver the note.

Jude put the kettle on and went upstairs. She leaned her head against the window and looked down, watching the sun come up behind the distant trees and the frosted grass warm and darken until the footprints melted away.

Norma Oughton, she had learned from the gravestone, was ninety when she died in 1983, the widow of the late Frank, who was

293

buried there too, along with a stillborn child from the spring of 1925. She was the beloved mother of Frances and Peter, and a grandmother, a great-grandmother, and *"blessed among women."*

There were even more Days in their plot. Following the patriarch Hamish in 1947, there was a wife, two young children, an elderly son in 1973, and finally the son's widow, Elspeth Day née McLennan.

Bathed and redressed a little later, she sat down at the table with her coffee and made a few notes: Bell, Patterstone, Day, Oughton, Jolly. She wrote McLennan in brackets because although Auntie Lorna had no headstone and hadn't been listed in Jude's note last night, it hadn't escaped Jude's notice that Elsie Day was a McLennan by birth. She added the dates, starting with Norma Oughton in December 1983 and ending with Todd himself in May 1985.

Then she looked at her watch and stood up. She should get into work. She needed to ask Lowell about this, if she could work out how to do it casually.

In the meantime, though, was she really going to leave these scribbles lying around when someone had been snooping last night? Of course, the footprint-maker hadn't been inside, but these locks were decades old. There was no way of knowing how many duplicate keys had been cut over the years and kept in drawers and junk bowls all over this friendly little town.

She took her own scribblings and the plastic bag with the warning in it and carried them upstairs. She slipped them both into the most innocuous, the least enticing, of Todd's books: the middle volume of three in a series of collected essays. He had won the set in 1915 as a prize for Sunday school attendance. No one would look there.

"Let the dead rest," she repeated to herself as she made her way to the middle of town, wondering again how she had managed to get lost last night. If the note hadn't been signed with those names she would have thought it meant her own dead. Except that she *was* letting them rest, wasn't she? She had kicked over their graves and run away, barely giving them another thought. Eddy was the one trying to bring the dead back to life, looking at photographs of Miranda and searching in her dark places for secrets. She remembered Lowell saying *although the prevailing view is . . .* How did it go?

Then, without her willing it, her feet slowed down. There was something tickling at the edges of her brain. She almost had it as she turned onto the main street. Then, distracted by a cluster of people outside the Post Office, she let go of the thread and the whole idea was gone.

There were four of them; five, counting a baby in its pushchair. The baby's mother was at the centre of the group, beside her a retired man with a bag of morning rolls in one hand and a *Scotsman* under his arm. Slightly aside were two women, dressed in velour for walking, with water bottles.

"What's up?" Jude said, trotting across the road towards them. All four swung round at the sound of her voice. Even the baby leaned forward and craned around the hood of its pushchair.

"The Post Office is shut," said the young woman. "Till they can get someone out to open it."

"Is Jackie all right?" said Jude. Jackie had been there all day, every day that Jude had been in Wigtown.

The young woman narrowed her eyes and said nothing.

"It's okay," said one of the velour women. "She's at Lowell's, working." She turned to Jude. "Jackie's collapsed."

"If you must know," the young woman added, with puzzling belligerence.

"Collapsed? Inside?"

"Last night," said the man. "She's in the

hospital in Dumfries. Typical government outfit. No one here to take over. It's my pension day."

"What time last night?" said Jude. She wasn't heartless, and she liked Jackie, but the fact remained that *someone* was out in that fog and they hurried away from her when she hailed them. And *someone* had been at her cottage with the note. And Jackie was one of the only three people who had heard her talking about the dead. *Archie and Etta and them.*

"Half six," said the other velour woman. "Why?"

"Just that I was in the shop at six o'clock when she was closing."

"And was she — ?"

"She was fine."

"Aye well, she barely made it home before she went down," the young woman said.

"Poor thing," said Jude. "What ward is she in, do you know? For a card?"

They all unbent a little at that, her proving that she might be from London but she knew how to behave.

"HDU," said the young woman. "Sedated."

Jude nodded, shared a solemn look, and then carried on towards the bookshop, thinking.

Lowell was there already, seated at the computer, with a catalogue open and the phone crooked against his shoulder.

"Have you heard the news?" Jude said. Lowell put the phone on speaker, unleashing call-centre music, and set it down. "Jackie at the Post Office has been rushed into hospital. HDU. High dependency unit," she added, as he blinked at her. "One down from Intensive Care. That's not good."

"And so it begins," Lowell said. "We're all the same age. When one's peers begin to drop from their perches . . ."

Jude ignored him. "Where does she live?"

"Hm? Oh, right here in Wigtown. Seaview, off Harbour Road." It was the southeastern tip of the town.

"And she doesn't drive, does she?" Jude said. "She walks in and out?"

"We're always hearing about the benefits of exercise. But a woman in her sixties working hard all day and walking home in that nasty fog . . ."

Jude had stopped listening. There was no way Jackie could have made it up to Kirk Cottage and back to Harbour Road between six and half past. Not even on a mild summer evening when she could stride out with a following wind, and certainly not on a

298

night like last night, where you had to feel your way. It couldn't have been her who put the warning letter through Jude's door. That left . . .

"Eddy," Lowell was saying.

"What?"

"I was worried about her last night. She locked herself away and wouldn't talk to me. Not even to assure me she was well."

"She probably had her earphones on," said Jude. "She probably didn't hear you."

"She heard me," Lowell said, rather grimly for him. "When I threatened to break the door down she finally relented. I've no idea what she was doing in there."

Jude nodded absently and then let his words in. "In where?" she said. None of the attic rooms had locks. It had worried her at first until she'd taken a long hard look at Lowell, blinking mildly behind his spectacles and apologising for passing her on the stairs.

"She was in the carsy," said Lowell. "I told you. Locked in the bathroom with the water running."

"For God's sake, Lowell!" said Jude. "She was having a bath. Of course she didn't want to talk to you through the door."

"The *downstairs* carsy," Lowell said. "Are you listening? There *is* no bath. And yet she used every scrap of hot water. I could hear the tank belching and glugging — absolutely empty. I worried for the boiler."

Jude thought about it for a minute. If Eddy wore a silicone belly next to her skin all day and maybe at night, she would have to wash it sometimes. But why she didn't pick a time when Lowell was out was a mystery. Then again, she might not have foreseen him banging on a locked bathroom door and demanding to be let in. She had a dismissive remark upon her lips when she thought the better of it.

"What time was this?" she said.

"Once you'd gone," said Lowell. "About half an hour after you went home. Why?"

Because, thought Jude, if she had gone home without getting lost, she would have been safely inside by then and, if Eddy had climbed out the bathroom window and come to leave a note, Jude would have found it this morning.

But why would Eddy care about Todd and the rest — *Etta and Archie and them.* The *them* she now knew was Norma Oughton and Elspeth Day. How would she even know their names to write on the note?

"No reason," she said. "And as to what she was up to, do you really want to know? She could have been waxing her legs, waxing anything really. Pore strips?"

"What are — ?" said Lowell. Then he held up a hand. "Don't tell me. Well well, yes, I see. Dear me. I should probably apologise to her then for scolding her."

"Or just leave it," Jude said. "Least said soonest mended?"

"Indeed," Lowell said. "Let peace descend."

Jude smiled, offered to make coffee, and was half turned away before his words hit her.

Let there be light," she said, turning back.

Lowell pushed his glasses up his head and looked at her from under a wrinkled brow. "One would never argue with that sentiment, my dear," he said, "but I'm not sure I quite understand the force of it here and now."

"What *is* that?" said Jude. "It's not a . . . I mean, you're not saying, *Oh go on, let there be light, will you, just this once?*"

"Hah!" said Lowell. "No indeed. No indeed. *God save the queen* isn't *God? Save the queen, won't you, old chap?* No, it's not a command — how very perspicacious of you. It's a relic of an earlier time when English was rather better off for grammar than it is these days. It's a subjunctive, my dear."

"Uh-huh."

301

"Expressing wishes or desires or hopes or
—"

"Oh, right!" said Jude. "Yeah, that's right, isn't it? It's like, I *hope* God saves the queen. I *hope* there's some light. Got it." But it wasn't firmly embedded. She had to go quickly to the kettle corner, fill it under the tap, and stay out of Lowell's way while it boiled, thinking it through.

The note. *Let the dead rest,* she decided, might not be an order at all. It might be a hope. It might have been someone telling her to keep digging, so that those who were resting ill could eventually rest easy. In fact, that made a lot more sense. Why would anyone warn her off and at the same time tell her the names she was trying to find out?

She poured water into the mugs, turning sharply away as the sour hit of the coffee granules reached her nose. She would have to do something about this kettle and jar of Nescafé if she really was going to stay here. On the heels of that thought, all the reality she had pushed back came flooding in again and she was struck still, standing there like a stone in the dark corridor.

What was she doing? What was she *thinking*? The last thing she should do was attract the attention of someone who might want her to leave this perfect hiding place. If the note was a warning, she should heed it. If the note was an invitation to poke around in a dormant nest of adders, she should ignore it. The only reason she should be looking at gravestones at all was to find that elusive young woman, born around the same time as her and dying before she had worked or signed on for benefits or got a driver's licence or done anything that would get in the way of Jude becoming her, staying in Wigtown, and starting over.

She would fill the bookshelves of her cottage with all Todd's volumes, just for fun, just because he had eclectic tastes and a way with words. It didn't have to be connected to anything, or mean anything, or put her in any danger. She told herself that as she went into the dead room for the morning. Lowell was on the desk and she was determined to make a proper dent in the mountain today.

She had a false alarm with a bag full of hardbacks from the early eighties. They looked like books you'd want to read before you die — *David Copperfield, The Great Gatsby, The Count of Monte Cristo* — but they had the stickers she had come to loathe, like barnacles after all these years. And also in the bag were knitting patterns for babies' bootees and bonnets and *People's Friend* annuals for ten years stopping in 1983. Not T. Jolly's taste at all.

They were kitsch enough to find a market in a city, she thought, flipping through them. They would make great toilet books in a boutique hotel run by people who thought they'd invented irony. Maureen would be able to sell the knitting patterns, certainly. She dished the bag's contents out between her three towers and carried on, telling herself she was *letting them rest,* knowing she wasn't, really.

TWENTY

By lunchtime, she had turned the canyon into a wide valley, emptying and dispersing seventeen bags, emptying and flattening twenty boxes. Down and down she went from *Deathly Hallows* to the *Philosopher's Stone.* She hoped poor J.K. didn't poke around secondhand bookshops these days, because they would hurt her heart and it wasn't a true reflection. Harry was loved more than anyone else in the land, except maybe Jesus and Kate.

One of the boxes had a very old mouse nest in it, all the books in one corner nibbled to a kind of dry froth and the whole thing reeking of urine and rattling with desiccated pellets when she moved it.

"Stand back," she said, emerging with it at arm's length. "Eddy, get the door!"

Eddy, who had been sitting almost horizontally in Lowell's chair with her legs stuck straight out and her chin on her chest, leapt up and sprinted along the hall.

"Garden door, Eddy," Jude said. "Gawd, what a stink when it shifts."

"What *is* it?" said Eddy, trotting back again. She scooted ahead of Jude to the back of Coasters and Key Rings, reached up, took the garden-door key down from above the doorframe, and opened it.

"It's what landlords call 'evidence of rodent activity'," Jude said. "Ugh." She put the box down on the small patch of concrete right outside and turned away, wiping her hands. "I'll take it down to the wheeliebin after lunch. If I do it now I'll lose my appetite." Then she gave Eddy a smile. She couldn't help it. "Good thing you knew where the key was. I don't remember telling you."

Eddy looked blankly at her, not scowling but without even a wisp of a smile. "Dad told me," she said.

"Funny," said Jude. "I kept meaning to tell *him* where I put it, but I forgot."

"Lucky guess," said Eddy. "Why are you being such a bitch?"

"Speak your mind, why don't you," said Jude. "Because you won't tell me why you were in the garden that first day."

"I wasn't —"

"I covered for you with Lowell about last night."

"What are you talking about?"

"I told him you were waxing your legs or something."

"So? What do you mean 'covered for me'? I was . . . doing my hair. And texting."

She looked scornful and completely calm and actually now that Jude took a closer look at her hair it did look lovely, shining like a beetle's back.

"So you didn't jump out the window and go wandering?"

"Jump?" said Eddy, pointing at her belly with both hands, like a rapper. "No I didn't 'jump'. Why the hell would I? Lowell would drive me anywhere I wanted to go. What are you *on* about?"

Jude took a long time to decide, but in the end she locked the back door again, saying to Eddy, "I've got to trust someone and God help me, it looks like it's you." She shouted upstairs, "We're going out for lunch!"

They both heard Lowell's muffled reply from somewhere on the second floor and heard the old house creak as he began to move.

"Laters!" Eddy shouted, and they hurried towards the front door. "That sounds tons

better in your accent than mine. No one
Northern Irish is cool. God, it's brilliant to
see the sun!" she went on as they emerged.
"Where we going?"

Jude smiled at the girl's instant lift in
spirits, then she put her face up and let the
dishwater sunshine lighten her own eyelids.
"Liam Neeson's cool," she said. "Picnic
down by the harbour?"

"He's bloody ancient," said Eddy. "He's
Lowell's age. You shouldn't give up so easy,
Jude. If you did a bit of work and got some
different clothes, you could totally get
someone great."

Jude only laughed. Then, hurrying to
catch up with Eddy — who was sailing
along no matter what she'd said about
jumping — she put a hand on her arm.
"Cool it when we go past the Post Office,
all right? Jackie's really ill in hospital and
we don't want to look unfeeling."

"Who to?" said Eddy. "It's shut. And how
do you know anyway? How do you know so
much about everyone? You're like a spy or
something. God, I wish there was a chipper.
Do you think the café round the top road'll
do chips to carry out?"

They didn't, but they did sandwiches and
chocolate and cans of Sprite, and the sun,
at the height of its short arc, had a trace of

mild warmth about it that the breeze couldn't quite blow away. So, as they larked down the harbour road towards the picnic tables, Jude felt a lightness she almost didn't recognise. Not since Max dropped his trio of bombshells — girlfriend, pregnant, over — had she looked forward to telling another person her worries and having them soothed away.

That was part of the problem, she'd realised, once it was too late. All *her* friends were *their* friends, mostly from the ambulance depot, and so they went with Max when the time came to choose. Her own friends? She had let them go, the girls' nights turning to lunches and then to emails and then to Christmas cards as she made her nest and shared it with Max. *You're my best friend,* she used to say. And he smiled and ruffled her hair. It only occurred to her during the divorce that he had never replied.

"Bloody seagulls!" Eddy said, looking at the splotched picnic benches when they arrived. It wasn't what Jude had imagined. A *harbour* to her meant Southend or Margate: bustle and boat-trips, vendors of tourist tat. Here there was a wooden jetty, a tarmac car park edged with more of the high bracken, and these picnic benches. "Rip that bag and we'll sit on half each," Eddy said.

They settled themselves side by side, both facing the water. The tide that rolled quietly in and out of the bay was at its gentle highest, and the water lapped and slopped against the wooden bracings while the few small boats not yet taken out for winter tugged at their moorings and seesawed on the dips and swells.

"I'll puke if I watch that anymore," Eddy said after a few bites. She rose and resettled herself, facing in towards the fields, staring across the table at Jude. "Right then," she said. "Shoot."

"Something's going on," Jude said.

"No shit," said Eddy, "but we agreed we wouldn't talk about it."

"I don't mean with you or me," Jude said. "Something else."

She put her sandwich down on its wrapper. It was making her feel heavy in her heart, the way a lot of things about Wigtown seemed to. It was a place from the past. Instant coffee in polystyrene cups and these tuna sandwiches, made from sliced bread scraped with margarine. And for every middle-aged woman in a velour tracksuit with a water bottle, there was another one with a tartan shopping trolley and a plastic rain bonnet. The men at the bowling club wore shirts and ties, and the children at the primary school played hopscotch. What with finding another *Valley of the Dolls* or *Little Red Hen* every day, altogether too much about the place took her back to when she was a child and seemed to make that lost time so close that, perhaps if she tried hard, she could jump tracks and end up somewhere that wasn't here and now. She could keep up with her girlfriends, stick with the exposure therapy, or make it so she never needed the bloody exposure therapy. She could ignore Max that night in that bar when he kept looking over and smiling. And she could tell her parents what no competent adult should ever need to be told: don't sleep in a closed garage with your engine running. If she had done all of that, she would be single and surrounded with pals, or happily married to someone else, taking him round to tea at her mum's every Sunday. She wouldn't be sitting on a plastic bag on a picnic bench covered in seagull shit, about to be mocked by a teenage headcase like Eddy. But then she flashed on Lowell's face and his voice saying *It's a subjunctive, my dear,* and she couldn't help smiling.

"I had an anonymous note shoved through my letterbox last night," she said. "I wondered if maybe you had put it there."

"Nope," said Eddy. "I'll tell you stuff to

311

your face: you should grow your hair and get some highlights in it, and you wear your jumpers too long." She winked, but something in Jude's expression got to her and, after clearing her throat, she started listening.

"It said *Let the dead rest.*"

"But that's just kids. That's just someone yanking your chain, isn't it? Cos you live in a graveyard."

"I don't think so," Jude said. "Because then it gave names. Five names of dead people. And three of them were names that had come up before. Written in books at the shop."

"What do you mean *written in books*? You mean like voodoo?"

"What?" said Jude. "I'm serious. Someone — Todd Jolly, who lived in my cottage — was recording the names of people who died. There were four and then he was the last one."

"Of course he was last!" Eddy said. "It's like that hundred books, isn't it? He's hardly going to write more names after he's dead."

"But here's the clincher. Whoever wrote the note last night went round the graves too. They left footprints in the frosty grass."

Eddy had grown slack-jawed as she listened. Jude could see a half-chewed bite of sandwich in her cheek. She washed it down with a painful-looking gulp of Sprite and then answered.

"Of course they went round the graves," she said. "They had to, to get names to write down to yank your chain. And of course they left footprints. It's when someone's flitting about a graveyard without leaving footprints that you have to worry."

"That's —" Jude began and then blinked. "Shit, that's true."

"It's quite funny, really," said Eddy. "Like some kind of neighbourhood watch committee! I don't blame you for thinking it was me. I might have done it if I'd thought of it."

"Okay," Jude said. "Okay. I admit, I've made fool of myself."

"You're under a lot of stress," Eddy said.

"But when I mentioned it to Jackie, she pretty much warned me off. And then she collapsed. The same day."

"Mentioned what? If you only found out late last night when you went home from Jamaica House, how'd she even know?"

"I mentioned two of the names — Etta Bell and Archie Patterstone — when I stopped in at the shop at teatime. And she definitely knows something." Jude sat ruminating for a moment about how best to explain it to Eddy. It was real; she knew it was. But it was a delicate thread and Eddy could break it with one shout of her scoffing laughter. Jude pulled the frilly edge of a lettuce leaf and it slid out of her sandwich, slick with dressing, wilted dark where the oil had got in. She let it drop and wiped her fingers.

"Etta and Archie and them are resting easy," she said, and arched her eyebrows. "That's what Jackie said to me."

"Resting easy?" Eddy echoed and Jude saw that her interest was hooked. She wasn't a stupid kid, not by any means. "And then the note said *let the dead rest* too?"

Jude nodded. "But she *really* didn't have time. She shut the shop at six and she was at home away down that way somewhere at half past and collapsed as soon as she got in the door."

Eddy looked over at where Jude was pointing and then back towards the town. "Half an hour?" she said. "Yeah, that's pretty tight. That would totally make you collapse if you'd legged it there and back, eh?" She had finished her sandwich and now she screwed up the paper, looked around, and threw it at the bin, missing. "Come on! Get that sarnie down you and let's time it."

314

"It was foggy."

"Yeah, but she was born here. I bet anyone who belonged here could trot about just fine in a fog or that."

Jude remembered the footsteps hurrying away from her last night. "Okay, but actually, Eddy, before we go chasing off? That's not the bit I was thinking of. *Etta and Archie and them are resting easy. Resting* is only part of the puzzle, you see?"

Eddy finished her Sprite and burped, getting through *doh, ray, mee* before it ran out. "Pardon," she said. And then went on in a singsong voice, counting the words off on her fingers. "Resting. Easy. Etta. Archie." She stopped, crooked her head to one side and gave Jude a look. "Wait a minute," she said. "And who? Etta and Archie and *who*?"

"Right," said Jude. "Exactly. Now, I know this was a long time ago and I know they'd all be dead now anyway. But there's two things I know for sure. Auntie Lorna — Jackie's Auntie Lorna — was ninety-nine and she went into a nursing home."

"The one Lowell's dad made him work in?"

"I don't know. But she went into the nursing home and died pretty much overnight. And Todd Jolly died at home. He left his cottage to Dr. Glen in gratitude for all the care and help and things that meant he never *had* to go into the nursing home. And he kept notes about who died. He wrote in his books. They started like reviews, but then they . . . changed into something else."

Eddy was sparking now. Her eyes darted from side to side and she played a little tune with her tongue and her bottom lip. "Bloody hell," she said. "I knew there was something weird about this place. So you think everybody put their oldsters in this home to make sure they didn't rip through the inheritance? I wonder if it's still open." She cast her eyes at Jude's half-eaten sandwich and wilted lettuce leaf lying on top of it. "Are you eating that or can we get going?"

"That's her house," said Eddy when they turned the corner onto a row of semis. One of the doors was open, a woman in slippers leaning against the doorjamb enjoying a cigarette and another standing on the step.

"How do you know?"

"Because I'm from a village," she said. "Hey!" she shouted. "Any news?"

Both women turned to look. "Who's asking?" the smoking woman shouted back. She stubbed out her cigarette on the harled wall of the cottage, leaving a black smear there, and threw the stub into the flowers.

"Are you one of Billy's girls come over as quick as that?"

"What's she on about?" muttered Jude.

"Billy?" said Eddy. *"Come over?* Shut up and follow my lead, Jude." She opened the gate and strode up the path. "Aye, I am," she said. "Is he in? Or is he at the hospital?"

"Christ, how many years has it been since you saw him?" said the woman. "If he was fit to be at the hospital why would I be here, wiping his arse for minimum wage? This is emergency care on top of my regular shift, you know."

That was when Jude noticed that as well as her slippers she wore a nylon tabard and had a name badge pinned to her chest.

"Well, aren't you a fucking bitch?" Eddy said. "He's expecting us."

"You think I'm daft?" said the woman. "Why would he be expecting *you*?"

"Why wouldn't he?" said Eddy, squaring up to her.

"Because I know who you are now I get a right look at you," she said. "Both of you. You're nothing to Billy at all."

"Now, now," said the other woman, with a chiding note in her voice.

But the care worker sailed on. "You're the pair that have shacked up with the Glen one. Maureen Bell's my cousin, by the way.

317

I ken all about you."

"And I'm finding out more about you every time you open your mouth," Eddy said. She shouldered past the woman with her hand raised to block any more talk.

Jude scuttled after her, marvelling.

Thankfully, there were so many visitors inside and all of them talking that it seemed unlikely the man of the house had heard his care worker's words. At least six women were either sitting around on hard dining chairs or bustling back and forth from the kitchen with tea things.

Billy himself was in the main living room in a hospital bed with a drip and a catheter bag on one side, two tanks of oxygen on the other. He was a terrible greyish-yellow colour, but he was all there. Jude knew that as soon as he turned his head and looked at Eddy and her. She saw the lift of helpless hope in his eyes and then the swift drop.

Jude squeezed Eddy's hand, willing her for once not to say anything from her usual menu. But Eddy surprised her. Surprised them all.

"Sorry to disturb you, Mr. McLennan," she said. "We were just coming to ask after Jackie. We're not wanting to be bothering you."

"Oh!" said the old man, lifting his head

from the pillow just a shade before he ran out of energy. "Listen to that now, will you? And who might you be?" There was a thick layer of Galloway in his voice, but the sound of Belfast lay underneath it like a seam of iron.

Eddy played up her own accent even more as she answered him. "Sure, I'm Lowell Glen's daughter, sir. I'm the big scandal of Wigtown, with the state of me, see. Had you not heard?"

The old man's face cracked into a smile, his eyes swimming. "Aye, Jackie was telling me." He turned to Jude. "And you'll be the girlfriend, are you?" Eddy cackled and then smothered it. "You're surely young? But look at that. Jackie and me had forty-odd good years till this morning." He turned away and groped around on his bedspread until the nearest of the women in the dining chairs took his hand. She had red-rimmed eyes and looked exhausted.

"Oh, Dad," she said. "Don't lose hope. Come on, eh?"

"I wonder," Eddy said, "Mr. McLennan, can I have a wee word with you? Can *we*? Jackie . . . see now, the thing is that Jackie told Jude here something in confidence yesterday, and we've sort of been left with it hanging. We don't want to bother you at all,

319

but can we just have one wee quiet word?"

His daughter was frowning and she gave her dad an uncertain look.

"*You* can stay, of course," Eddy said to her. Clever psychology, Jude thought. It was enough to get the woman on her feet and backing away politely.

"Right," she said. "Ladies? Fag break in the back garden. Come on. You've got five minutes," she told Jude. "And only because I know my mum would never have taken ill if there wasn't something really badly wrong." She dropped a kiss on her father's head. "Don't upset him," she said to Eddy, and then she herded the other women out ahead of her and closed the door.

Eddy sat down on one side of the high bed and left Jude the other. The old man reached out a hand to each and held tight. His skin was thin and bruised from needles, but his grip was firm. "I can't do without her," he said. "I don't mean for the nursing. It's not fair."

"Forty years, eh?" said Eddy.

"She deserves time once I'm gone," he said. "She's been a slave since I took bad. Never a night out. Never a weekend away. This is the wrong way on."

"She'll have her time," said Eddy. "You and her'll have your wee golden sunset and then she'll be dying her hair and away to Vegas with her pals and you'll be that jealous you'll haunt her."

Jude cast a wary at eye at the old man — it was the strangest comfort she'd ever heard — but he was laughing. Of course, Eddy had experience talking to people at the end. She'd have learned better than platitudes with her mother.

"So what happened, Mr. McLennan?" Eddy said.

"Billy," he told her. "She came in from her work, got me fed and changed, but I knew something was troubling her. She was quiet."

"Is that odd?" said Eddy.

Jude smothered a laugh. "She's never met Jackie," she said to Billy. Then, "Yes, Eddy, it's very odd. Billy, was she in at the usual time? Was she out of breath?"

"Wee bit early if anything," he said.

Eddy flashed Jude a look. Jackie didn't leave the note then.

"And she didn't say anything?" Eddy asked.

"Not to me," Billy said. "She phoned someone, though."

"Did you overhear the phone call?" said Jude.

Billy shook his head. "She went out in the

321

garden."

"In all that manky fog?" Eddy said. "*That's* odd."

"And all I heard was her raised voice. I couldn't make out the words. What's this about, girls?"

Jude and Eddy glanced at each other.

"It's hard to know," Jude said. "It started a long time ago and we're only catching the echoes."

"Where's her phone?" Eddy said. "We can look at the call log."

"Oh, you're a wee smarty," said Billy. It sounded like an insult to Jude's ears but it got Eddy beaming. "Aye, it was in her pocket like always but they brought her stuff back from Casualty in a bag last night. It'll be in the front bedroom there. That's just a dumping ground for my bottles and whatever these days." He lifted his head and raised his voice. "Hey? Are you through there? Can you bring me Jack's bag from last night?"

"Who are you talk — ?" said Eddy, then she sprang to her feet and made a dive for a connecting door. The smoking woman in the tabard had a thick blue plastic bag in one hand and a mobile in the other. She dropped the phone and held the bag out.

"Everything's in here," she said. "I was

just checking."

Jude struggled to keep up with the girl on the way back into the village. "Are you timing it?" she said.

"No, I'm just that mad with myself. I never even stopped to think where that sly bitch went once we were in. Maureen Bell's *cousin*, Jude! Etta Bell's *something*, for sure. And she cleared the call log on Jackie's phone because we practically told her to! What a pair of morons."

"Well, she didn't strike me as a very helpful person anyway you slice her," Jude said. "And you kind of put her back up, you know, calling her a fucking bitch like that."

Eddy blew a raspberry. "So you think it might just be a great big coincidence then?"

"I talk to Jackie about Etta and Archie; she collapses; someone warns me off Etta, Archie, and three more; and we find out Jackie spoke to someone, but one of Etta's relatives tries to hide who? Coincidence? Ah no, Eddy, I don't think so."

They had arrived at the bookshop. Eddy rested her bottom on the windowsill of Spinning Yarns and splayed her feet. "Christ, I'm sick of lugging this around," she said, lacing her hands under her belly. "And I don't believe in coincidences anyway." She hauled herself to her feet again. "Let's lay it all out for Lowell and see what he says."

"Eddy, this is moving kind of fast, don't you think?" said Jude. "We — Shouldn't we . . . think it through? Before we say anything? To anyone?"

"Lowell?" Eddy said and opened the door.

He leapt to his feet when he saw them. Two of the shallow drawers were open but, quick as a fish, he slid the picture he'd been looking at into one, pushed both closed, and leaned against them.

"Nice picnic?" he said.

"Not so's you notice," Jude said. "We stopped in to see Jackie's husband. He thinks she'll die and it's breaking him."

"Poor Bill," Lowell said. "Oh my! He'd never cope on his own. Even with all the nurses and carers. He'd have to go into a home. Oh poor Jackie! I spoke to her yesterday, you know."

Eddy said nothing but Jude managed, "Really?"

"Yes," said Lowell. "She phoned me to check if I really wanted the card for the cottage taken down."

"You never mentioned that," said Jude. "And I took the card down. That's why — You never said any of this."

"Don't be offended, my dear. Jackie is a

very conscientious postmistress. She let you take it down but she checked with me before she destroyed it, you see?"

"Hey, Dad," Eddy said, "if Billy does go into a home, will it be the same one you worked in? Is it still open?"

"Hm?" Lowell said, blinking as he tried to split his attention between them. "Good heavens no, that place closed millennia ago. Just after I left, actually." His eyes came to rest on Jude. "Are you quite well, my dear? You look pale?"

"Period," said Eddy. "She's going home."

"Oh um, golly," said Lowell.

"I'll chum you," said Eddy to Jude. "Exercise'll do us good."

Before Lowell could work out that they had just walked the mile from the McLennans' cottage, she grabbed Jude's hand and pulled her out the door.

TWENTY-ONE

"If your dad punished you for not doing medicine by making you empty bed pans," Eddy said, "would that piss you off? It would piss me off."

"Are you saying what I think you're saying?" Jude asked her. "You think your dad, my friend Lowell, was bumping people off in the home and his dad knew and covered it up? And Todd Jolly knew and bribed the doctor into making sure he never ended up in there?"

"And Mrs. Hewston knew too," said Eddy. "That's why she's so down on him. And fuck, yeah! This always bugged me. That's why she gets to stay there even though she's a pain in the arse and he could chuck her out."

"But Lowell?" said Jude. "Dear me, yes, quite, oh golly *Lowell*?"

They turned a corner out of the sunshine, which was already beginning to lose what little strength it had had that morning. Jude shivered.

"Although," she said, "there is the creepy porn collection. You might be right about that, Eddy."

"Creepy but harmless," Eddy said.

"And living all alone in the house he was born in."

"That sounds like your classic serial killer, right enough," Eddy said. "But he had friends. He had . . . we've seen the pictures of that summer!"

"And one by one they all left," Jude said beginning to nod as she caught up. "And your mum kept you away from him all those years, even when being married to Dave Preston went wrong."

"But she sent me back to him again!" Eddy said. "And I think you're forgetting something, aren't you? He's not my dad! My mum lied about when my birthday was so I'd . . . wait a minute. Wait a minute." She stopped talking and stopped walking too, ten feet from the turn into the cemetery lane.

Jude put a hand in the small of her back and pushed. "Keep it moving," she said. "It's brass monkeys out here."

"If he's not my dad — and he can't be — she might send me back to a kind man she slept with once, especially if he could help me track down my real dad. But she'd hardly send me back to a psycho she slept with once, would she?"

"Unless she sent you back to bust him," Jude said. "You told me she was going on about something wrong she'd done. On her last night? She'd done something terrible? Maybe she meant keeping quiet about Lowell."

Eddy said nothing and after the silence had gone on for a while, when they were almost at the gates, Jude peeked past the curtain of hair. It was soot black, blacker than death and midnight in the low light. Inside it, Eddy's face was candle white.

"That's right," she said, and her voice was tiny. "That actually makes sense, if you must know." She reached for Jude's hand as they entered the graveyard. "She said she couldn't pass over with it on her conscience."

"*It* what?" said Jude.

But Eddy only shrugged. "She was scared. *What if we all meet up?* That's what she said. I thought it was the morphine. The nurse said it was the morphine." Eddy sniffed and came out of her memory. "Jesus fucking Christ, Jude. Seriously, how can you live here?"

And indeed the cemetery did look particularly bleak that afternoon, a very different place from Jude's morning memory of blue sky and sparkling, frost-tipped grass.

"I can't," she said. "Of course, I can't live here now. Not after that note. Know what I mean? Better safe than sorry."

"Right!" said Eddy, catching on without a hitch. "And it's different now I know you, isn't it? I was a right cow chucking you out, but that was when you were a stranger. Now I know you, I'm dying to get you back round to Jamaica. Hey, maybe I even did the note thing — you know, to persuade you? Maybe I *did* jump out the window and haul my fat arse round here to freak you out."

"Let's not complicate it," Jude said, and Eddy blew another raspberry at her.

Then she folded her lips in, drying them, and turned serious. "Thanks," she said. "You really think Lowell might be dodgy as fuck and you're coming back anyway?"

"Haven't got much choice," said Jude. "You know too much. You could make one phone call and I'd be toast."

"Course," said Eddy. "Duh. I've got something on you, so you've got to do what I say. Back scratching like we said, yeah?" Her eyes were shining.

"It's not just that," Jude said. "Sorry." She shivered again. In the shadow of the church it was even colder, not just from the chill in the air, but as though cold was seeping up from the ground and leaching out of the dark stone beside them. "It's that I really do want to find out what's going on. Something is. Jackie knows and the strain of it's done her in. And you shouldn't be on your own. You're too young and too —"

"I'm a shit-ton tougher than you, pal," Eddy said.

"You're not even twenty and I'm forty," Jude said.

"And you've spent the extra twenty years in a . . . *wooo* . . . library," Eddy said, making ghost hands.

"Don't kid yourself," Jude said, in her best south-London. "You get rougher homeless in a London library than you'll have seen in Derry, gel."

"Oh right," Eddy said. "Yeah, we wouldn't know the meaning of 'trouble' in Ulster."

Jude rolled her eyes and shook her head. "All right, have the last word. I'm mature enough to let it go. You've said thank you and I'll say you're welcome."

Eddy smirked but she didn't start another round. Instead, she sniffed and squeezed her eyes tight to get rid of the sheen of tears.

"So where's these graves then?" she said. "We need to take a pic so we can study them up when you're not staying here anymore."

Jude led her around and waited while Eddy snapped each of them. Archibald Patterstone, Henrietta Bell, Todd Jolly, Elspeth Day, and Norma Oughton. She scrolled through the photographs as Jude was opening the cottage door.

"Tell you one thing for nothing," Eddy said. "It wasn't kids. The note, I mean."

"How do you know?" said Jude. She was looking round at the living room. She hadn't made much of a mark in here, but she would be sorry to leave Todd's shipshape kitchen and she was filled with a kind of blank, dead feeling inside to think of leaving the upstairs library.

"Because," Eddy said, "if it was kids going round collecting the names and writing them down, right? They'd have written Archibald and Elspeth. And definitely Henrietta. It was someone who remembers them who wrote that note to you."

"My God, you're right!" Jude said. "Elsie and Etta and Archie. It's got to be someone old enough to have known them."

"And at least we know *that* bit wasn't Lowell," Eddy said. "I was with him right from teatime to bedtime."

"What about when you were waxing?"

"He was at the door every two minutes," Eddy said. "He wouldn't leave me in peace. And I wasn't waxing. I was just having a wash and that. Not like anyone's going to see any bit of me that grows hair anytime soon, is it?"

"What? Liam and Terry aren't coming to the birth?" Jude said.

But Eddy only snorted and told her to start packing.

She really wanted to take the books and tried for a quite a while to convince Eddy it made sense.

"There are clues in them," she said. "I found the start of it in them."

"So take the ones with the clues in," Eddy said. "What's that, like three?"

"It's hard to explain," Jude said. "It's all of them."

"It can't be," said Eddy. "Get a grip."

So Jude took the copies with the long reviews in the back and left the rest. She took O. Douglas even though they were tainted now. If Lowell was what they suspected him of being, then every memory was stained. The first visit last summer when he popped his head round the door to share her joy and certainly every moment since she came back and he showed her *The Day of Small Things* he'd been saving for her. What had she been thinking? Going round to a stranger's house and sleeping in his bed? She must have been crazy.

"What?" said Eddy.

Jude had laughed out loud. They had phoned for a taxi from Newton Stewart and they were sitting in the living room waiting for it to arrive, surrounded by boxes of perishable food from the fridge and binbags full of Jude's clothes. She had her stash in a tower on her lap. Douglas, the downed plane, the Rushdie, the Allingham, and the old cloth *Rebecca.*

"I just can't believe it," she said. "I cannot believe that man could do harm to a living soul. Can you? Really?"

"Nope," said Eddy. "Maybe . . . Maybe he knew who it was, though. At the nursing home. Maybe he covered something up and my mum covered for him. Christ, I wish she was still here so I could just ask her."

They both fell silent. One thing Jude had learned after her parents' death, in the first few horrendous weeks following it, was the kindness of silence.

If she'd had someone who understood and would sit quietly, shoulders touching, and let her feel her feelings, she wouldn't have ended up back round at her old house the night of the funeral, looking for comfort in the place she'd found it all those married years.

But all she'd had was people commenting under the online *Standard* article, sniggering like idiots. And then the neighbours asking if there was anything they could do or telling her they'd pray for her and so, without even deciding to, all of a sudden she was opening the wardrobe door and standing looking down at the back of Max's head hanging over the side of the bed, keeping his airways clear. She wanted to slap him awake. To open his eyes with her fingers and make him see her. She didn't get quite that far.

The baby had been crying when Raminder opened the front door. Jude heard the thin, high wails before she even heard the latch.

"Max!" She'd sounded a little bit anxious but happy underneath. "All hands on deck, sweetheart! Jade needs a feed and a bum change and I'm busting for a pee!"

Jude was frozen in place. Max snored steadily.

"Max?" Raminder called up. "Come on, love. This isn't funny. Listen to her! Are you

334

in the shower? Max, for God's sake, will you — Are you okay?"

Jude didn't have time to get back to the wardrobe — thankfully, as it turned out. She withdrew into the deep shadow between the open door and the bedroom wall as Raminder came up the stairs, leaving the baby's cries behind her.

"Max, for God —" she said, striding into the bedroom. She stopped dead, a foot from the bed where Max was now snoring harder than ever, gurgling snorts that filled the air of the small room with the belch stink of beer and the reek of whisky. She was so close that Jude could see individual stray hairs, mussed out of her ponytail, silhouetted against the light of the bedside lamp. They were quivering.

"You promised," Raminder said. "Wet the baby's head. One drink. You promised me."

Max snored so loudly it sounded like a snarl and Raminder spun away, into the tiny en suite bathroom. Jude could hear her opening and shutting drawers, thumping and rustling, while she peed. Jude had done it herself, sitting on the loo and reaching over to the sink to the little cupboard, putting new toiletries away, tidying, packing like Raminder was doing now. The toilet flushed and when she came out she was carrying a little drawstring bag. If she had looked over she would have seen Jude standing there, but she was busy. She got a case out of the wardrobe, threw it down on the bed beside Max and dropped the drawstring bag in it. Downstairs the baby's cries went up in pitch.

"Mummy's coming," Raminder said, under her breath. She went back and forward twice from the chest of drawers with underclothes and pyjamas, once to the wardrobe for jeans and shirts and then she zipped the case shut and stalked out of the door without a glance at the bed.

Jude only had to stand there for another minute and she'd be clear, but she heard the first sob wrench itself from Raminder's throat and found her feet moving.

The banging on the cottage door brought both of them back, Eddy starting as violently as Jude.

"Taxi!" said a woman's voice. And then, "Is this it?" surveying the bags when Jude opened up.

"No!" Jude said. "Sorry. Start the metre if you like, but I've got more I want to take." She ignored Eddy's snort and ran back upstairs. She had no idea why, but she *knew* she needed the books. Not the natural history collection or the reference books, but all those book club choices with the notes in the back. It took three trips for her to carry them, both Eddy and the taxi driver rolling their eyes and neither offering to help.

"I can't explain it," she said, when they were underway at last. "I just know the answer is there somewhere."

"Like in a secret code or something?" said Eddy.

Jude shushed her but the driver wasn't listening. "No, of course not," she said. "There's notes, but no one was ever meant to read them. They're like a diary."

"I never understood the point of a diary if no one's meant to read it," Eddy said. "You don't need to tell yourself, do you? You were there. Know what I mean? I reckon everybody that writes a diary must basically hope someone's going to read it one day."

"Not at all," said Jude. "Todd Jolly's notes were private jokes between him and him." Then she stopped.

"What?" said Eddy.

"I don't know," said Jude. "Something's bothering me."

"This right?" said the taxi driver. Jude looked out and saw that they were on the corner of Lightlands Terrace, Jamaica House almost in view. "All the way from Newton

Stewart for this?"

"Oh, shut up your moaning," Eddy said. "There's a minimum fare, isn't there? Right, well, there you go. Pay her, Jude. I'm nipping in fast, cos I'm busting."

Her words brought Raminder back and Jude was lost again as they rolled up the side drive and parked at the front door. She paid the driver the modest minimum tariff and doubled it with a tip, then unloaded the bags and boxes by herself, without help. Eddy had not reappeared.

She was standing looking at the pile of luggage, wondering whether to take it round in loads or try to find the front door key when she heard a familiar voice and her heart sank.

"It's like Paddington Station round here today." Mrs. Hewston was crossing the side lawn in her slippers with a half apron on top of her skirt and her sleeves rolled to the elbow. "I was at my kitchen sink, peeling spuds," she said. "Was that a taxi? I thought you liked Digger's Cottage."

"I do," said Jude. "I'm just moving in to be here for Eddy." She looked at the piles of books around her feet on the marble step and knew how unlikely it seemed.

"Is she near her time?" said Mrs. Hewston. "My goodness me, like mother like

338

daughter, eh? But she'll be away to the hospital when it comes, won't she?" Jude nodded. "It's a filthy time of year to be having a baby, if you ask me," said Mrs. Hewston. "Rotten time for getting nappies dry. It's like winter weddings. What are you supposed to do for flowers in your bouquet?"

Mrs. Hewston, thought Jude, seemed to live in a time warp where there were no such things as Pampers or global markets.

"Have you heard the news?" Jude said. Her head was reeling with suspicions of Lowell and half-formed notions of what might have happened here years ago, and all of a sudden, Mrs. Hewston, loyal to the doctor, scathing about his son, seemed like someone with good radar. *If* they were right. *If* the monstrous idea could possibly be right.

"About Jackie Mac?" said Mrs. Hewston. "Yes, terrible." She pressed a hand to her chest. Her fingers were raw and pink-looking, as if she'd peeled the spuds in cold water.

"But she's in the best place," said Jude.

"Well, you say that, but it's different these days. It's all about not getting sued these days. Nursing and medicine isn't what it was. And if it's a stroke she's had, maybe it's best she doesn't linger."

Jude didn't know where to start. Mrs. Hewston had no idea whether it was a stroke or what it was. No one did. As quick as that, she changed her mind back again. She was just a daft old bat who lived half in the past and half in a dream world.

They both turned as the front door, creaking and yawning, was dragged open.

"Sorry," said Eddy. "I didn't mean to — Oh."

"Hello to you too," said Mrs. Hewston. "It's nice to see that door open. When the doctor was alive that door was never closed. The vestibule floor was polished with linseed oil and there were fresh flowers in a vase on the hallstand every day of the year."

"Polish it himself, did he?" said Eddy. "What a guy! And he did the flower arranging too?"

Mrs. Hewston ignored her. "But now look at it. The brasses not even shined and — Oh! Oh!" She pointed with a shaking finger. Jude followed her gaze with real alarm and then let out a huff of relief when she saw what had caused the problem. On the hallstand, in the vestibule, was a glass vase brown with old algae and completely dry, a few dead twigs sticking up in it. Mrs. Hewston tutted at it and then left them.

"That's a bit scruffy," said Jude. "I'll clear

it away."

"Or you could leave it," Eddy said. "Kind of just . . . leave it and sit and do some relaxation instead. It'd be a start. I'll help you."

Jude's breath was knocked out of her. She stared at Eddy for a minute or two until the girl's eyes were wide with worry. "Thanks," she said. "That means a lot, really. But one thing at a time, eh?"

She moved her bags and books into the hallway in relays. The bright start to the day had run out and clouds were rolling in across the water, a haze under them telling her they were dropping rain out there in the bay and their purplish colour, weighty and threatening, telling her they wouldn't be empty by the time they got to the coast.

It was beginning to feel normal to be able to look out for miles and see the weather long before it reached her. She could imagine getting used to it, becoming one of those people who found London cramped and confusing; becoming someone who, like Mrs. Glen, could keep fresh flowers in the house every day of the year. Once her belongings were under cover, she took the vaseful of Lowell's failure into the kitchen where Eddy was waiting.

"Be fair," she said. "This must have been

341

sitting there for —"

"Months," said Eddy. "That's forsythia. It's out in the spring." She picked a little twist of something dead off one of the branches and rubbed it to crumbs between her fingers.

"Well, aren't you full of surprises today!" Jude said.

"Nah, it was Mum's favourite," Eddy said. "One of them."

Jude set the vase down amongst the bills and batteries that littered the top of the long dresser and rubbed her hands on her jeans.

"If we're serious about suspecting Lowell and I'm serious that there's a clue somewhere in all those books," she said, "I better get them out of sight before he comes home."

"Put them up in my bit," said Eddy. "He never comes up there. I told him I wander about naked and he nearly poked his eye in with his fountain pen just thinking about it."

"Smart," said Jude. "Okay, I will then."

She had only spent a few days in these rooms, but that was long enough. Seeing them again, with Eddy's magazines lying around and Eddy's shoes kicked off at the top of the stairs, made her feel as if she'd cleaned a toilet with her bare hands and now she was licking her fingers. And Eddy's kindness had sent the portcullis rattling up so high she couldn't reach it to bring it down again.

"I'm not here. I'm not —" she began. Then she sighed. "Except I am."

It was crazy. She knew that. It was crazy to feel sick because there were shoes on the floor of a flat she'd slept in last week. Like it was crazy to move to Cataloguing, bored senseless but surrounded by clean new books and away from the readers with their snot and chocolate. It was crazy to say she wouldn't have children because snot and chocolate weren't the half of it. She knew no one blamed Max for what happened. Poor Max. What could he do when his wife was crazy?

When she was finished ferrying the books upstairs, she took her clothes and toilet things into one of the first-floor bedrooms. Then, wondering, she went back to the kitchen.

"Do you want me to sleep up top with you?" she said. "I could make up a kind of whatsit with sofa cushions." They stared at each other.

"Are we really serious?" said Eddy. "We're really saying Lowell abused his position at the care home. That his dad knew. That

343

Mrs. Hewston knows. That Jackie collapsed when you brought the memories back?"

Jude sank into one of the kitchen chairs. Carting boxes up and down was part of it, but really she felt bowed under the weight of too many mysteries, too many switchback changes.

"There's too much . . ." she said, and Eddy shouted with laughter. It was a sound, Jude thought, she had picked up from Lowell in the time she'd been here.

"You're telling me!" Eddy said. "There's my shit and your shit and then there's all this shit! Where are we supposed to start, eh?"

"We don't need to start with my —"

"Shit," said Eddy.

"— because there's nothing to do except sit tight and see what happens."

"You're a machine," Eddy said. "I couldn't do that if you paid me." She put a mug of tea on the table in front of Jude and opened a packet of biscuits, sawing through the wrapper with the breadknife.

"And you've dealt with your . . . situation, haven't you?"

"How'd you mean?" Eddy said. "Oh, telling him about Liam and Terry, like? Well, sure, but that's only half of it, isn't it? That's only the future. There's still the past. Fuckadoodledoo is there ever the past." She took a biscuit out of the packet, dipped it in her tea for longer than Jude thought was feasible and then held it over her open mouth until the soggy half moon sloughed off and dropped. She closed her lips with a smack. "But I'm on it. I nicked his toothbrush," she said. "Sent away for a DNA test. That's my way, see? Rip off the plaster and see what's under there."

"But I thought you were sure he wasn't?" Jude said.

Eddy dropped her eyes to her cup and a new biscuit. "I am. I don't see how he can be. Cos of the dates. She'd never lie about my star sign and birth date. All that woo woo. Birthstones are crystals, man. Powerful stuff. Burying them at the foot —" She stopped.

"What?"

"Nothing. Getting myself mixed up. It's liver and lights you bury, right? Full moon, for a bumper crop. So, like I was saying, I've dealt with it. When the DNA comes back, I can either tell him and skedaddle or not tell him and stay."

"And wonder forever who your real dad is?"

"Unless the other shit we've still got to work out explains it all," Eddy said. "If he's a loony, that's why she kept me away. If someone else from that summer is my real dad, that's why she sent me back. She told me I was his so he'd take me in. Or, she sent me back to bring something to light that she'd left hidden."

"So where do we start? What do we think? What do we know?" said Jude. "What are the uncontested facts?"

Eddy opened the drawer in the kitchen table — the knife drawer it was called, although it contained napkins and a corkscrew and a little dust pan and brush for sweeping away crumbs in between courses. It also contained a pad of paper Lowell used for working out knotty crossword clues, and Eddy drew that out and turned over to a fresh sheet.

"Shoot," she said.

"I received an anonymous note," said Jude, "tying together the deaths of Todd, Archie, Etta, Norma, and Elsie. Todd Jolly put his wife in a home — the home Lowell worked at? Let's find out — and was very keen not to follow her. Auntie Lorna McLennan died two weeks after going into a home. Again, *the* home? Let's find out. Mrs. Hewston has some kind of hold over Lowell, and Todd wrote in one of his books *I will tell Dr. Glen enough is enough.* Then

346

Lowell left the home and Dr. Glen retired and took an interest in the bookshop, a place he'd always hated and disapproved of. He organised the Fiction rooms, you know."

Eddy caught up and stopped writing, then bent over again and added a thick blot like a bullet point beside each of the lines. "Jesus," she said. "When you write it all down like that, it's pretty bad, eh?"

"And in the present day. Jackie warned me off face-to-face. Someone warned me off in a note. But it wasn't Lowell or Jackie. But Jackie did speak to Lowell before she collapsed. Did she speak to someone else? We don't know because someone related to Etta Bell stopped us finding out."

Eddy turned over a page, scribbled a little more, and then threw the pen down. "This is too hard to organise," she said.

"We need lists," said Jude. "We need a timeline. What happened when."

"Right," said Eddy. "Names and dates. On it." She pulled her phone out of the capacious pocket of the afghan coat and started clicking.

"Archibald Patterstone, 21st of June, 1984," she said, scribbling. "Here, Jude, read these out to me, will you?"

Jude clicked through the pictures and read off the names and dates ending with Henrietta Bell who had died only weeks before Todd himself. "But Todd didn't die in the nursing home, did he?"

"And the rest did?" said Eddy.

"Presumably," Jude said. "And we can surely find out. I mean, there must be relatives of them all still around. Some of them anyway."

"I can go round and ask Billy," Eddy said. "It'll be easy to get him talking about family at a time like this. I'll go tomorrow."

"And I'll ask Maureen from the Cancer!" said Jude. "Maureen *Bell.* If I slip round and see her when someone's collapsed, I'm sure I could get the conversation onto going suddenly or lingering. Who she knew that popped their clogs different ways."

"You'll be a right wee ray of sunshine," Eddy said. "But you'll have to hoof it, cos it's nearly five now."

TWENTY-TWO

Those purple clouds had arrived and the wind dropped as soon as they reached Wigtown, leaving the clouds there driving cold spikes of rain straight down at the ground, battering flat the last of the flowers in Lowell's garden, making Jude hunch over under her hood as she hurried through the empty streets.

She fell into the charity shop, gasping and shaking herself. Maureen was counting up the change, with a bundle of notes already sorted and bound with a rubber band.

"Ocht!" she said. "Whatever you're after, you can take it and owe me till tomorrow."

Jude pushed her hood back and used the edges of her hands like windscreen wipers to sweep the worst of the weather from her face. "Lowell's got the car in town with him," she said. "He could give you a lift home, if I shout over."

Maureen narrowed her eyes. "I live upstairs," she said. "I thought you knew that. So, how can I help you?"

"Eddy said there was a jigsaw puzzle," said Jude, spying a row of them on a high shelf behind the counter and thinking it was a safe bet. "Oh, what did she say it was of? I'll remember if I take a look."

"Lowell's daughter Eddy?" said Maureen. "She's never been over the door. Try again, you're on your last go."

Jude felt her colour change and didn't even try to hide it. "Caught me," she said. "Okay. Did you hear about Jackie?"

Maureen's face grew pained and she shook her head. "Poor soul. I've been praying all day."

"She always seemed so well," said Jude.

"She takes a lot of heart pills," Maureen said. "But she's years younger than Billy and his lungs are away." She scraped the change into a cotton sack with a bank logo on its side and gave Jude an expectant look. "Is that all you're after then? Telling me about Jackie? I never had you down as a gossip."

"I met your cousin at Jackie's house," Jude said. "She was on an emergency call to see to Billy. *She's* got me down as God knows what."

"You were at the house?" said Maureen

and now she looked very searchingly at Jude, who couldn't blame her. It was impossible to explain. It was just as impossible to start up a casual conversation with someone who was itching to get home after a long day's work, when your first two attempts had been seen through.

"I upset Jackie yesterday," Jude said at last. "But I don't know how. I came round to ask if you could help me work out what it was I said because I can't stop thinking about it."

Maureen put her head on one side, with a small smile. "Well, why didn't you just say that? It'll not have been anything." She put the cloth bag down and leaned her elbows on the counter. Jude moved away from the door and took a couple of steps towards her.

"We were talking about her Auntie Lorna, because I found one of her old books in the shop."

"O-ho!" said Maureen. "Still trying to move the mountain, are you?"

"And I asked about another couple of names I'd come across and she didn't seem to want to remember them."

"Oh?"

"One of them was Henrietta Bell. I wondered if she was a relation of yours."

"Distant," said Maureen. "Some kind of

351

cousin. What about her?"

"Well, this is going to sound mad but, before she died, was she in a nursing home or old people's home or anything, or was she still in her — Maureen? What is it?"

"Oh no!" Maureen said. She wasn't leaning on the counter now. She had stood up as straight as a tin soldier and was glaring at Jude. "No way. Not this. Where'd this come from?"

"Maureen, I don't know what you mean. I just wanted to ask about Archie and Etta and —"

"Aye, aye, Norma Oughton and Elsie Day. Now, listen to me, that was a terrible time and it's behind us. So leave it there."

"I don't know what you mean," said Jude. "I'm just asking a simple —"

"Out!" Maureen said. "Go on. Get out. Why are you stirring this up again? Who are you really? A journalist? A muckraker? If I Google you, what will I find, eh? And what's your whole name anyway? You've come slinking in here, getting round us all, and what do we really know about you?"

Jude had her hand on the door to leave before half of this was said. Her heart was thrumming and she knew she was pale, but still she stopped with the door half open. "Maureen, I'm sorry," she said. "And I'm worried. I don't understand what's going on, but I'm worried for all of you."

"Are you threatening me?" Maureen said.

"No!" said Jude. "But I'll tell you this: someone threatened me last night. Someone put an anonymous note through my door."

"And you're accusing me?"

"No! For God's sake. I'm trying to warn you."

"Out!" said Maureen, louder. "Get back to London where you belong."

Jude stumbled outside and started to run back to Jamaica House, her hood down and her jacket unzipped, feeling the cold rain sting her eyes and the hot tears prick at them. She was streaming with water, her hair plastered in cold hanks to the sides of her face when she got there, bursting in at the kitchen door, not noticing Lowell until she had started talking.

"It's real!" she began and then stopped.

"No shit, it's real," said Eddy. "Look, don't go nuts, okay? I told you what I'm like. Rip off the plaster and worry about it later. I did tell you, didn't I?"

"What do you mean?" said Jude.

"I thought of something." Eddy nodded at Lowell. "So I just out and asked him."

Jude blinked the rain out of her eyes and stared at Lowell, expecting to see anger or perhaps a wry amusement there, but his face was more solemn than she had ever seen it.

"It's about the photographs," Eddy said. "You know how I said they were creepy but harmless? Well, I thought of a way they could be creepy and anything *but* harmless. So I asked him. I asked if any of his rare Victorian 'figure studies' were . . . old people that he worked with."

"Oh God," said Jude. "They're not, are they?"

"Tell Jude what you told me, Lowell," said Eddy. "He just said this the minute before you walked in."

"I didn't mean to be so mysterious that I worried you," he said. "It's just that some people find my pictures . . . upsetting."

"Tell Jude what you just told me," said Eddy grimly.

"My dear child, don't distress yourself," Lowell said. He turned to Jude. "I told young Eddy here that some of the photographs are of the elderly, some children, some adults, and some are a mixture."

Jude sat down, dropped like a coal sack into a chair, and stared at him. "A mixture?" she said. "The elderly?" She turned to Eddy, who had tears in her eyes.

"See?" said Eddy. "It's a motive. His dad

knew and the relatives knew and everyone covered it up. Well, you would, wouldn't you?"

"My dears," said Lowell. "What are you talking about? I assure you I've been most discreet about my collection."

"But you're not just a collector, are you?" said Jude. "You're a photographer. You took pictures in the care home, when you worked there. You took pictures of Mrs. Jolly, and Todd knew."

"What?" said Lowell. "Of course, I didn't. Why would I? No, my dears, that particular custom had fallen quite out of favour long before my time."

"Custom?" said Jude, her voice rising. *"Custom?"*

"Tradition, fashion," said Lowell. "Call it what you will. It was in its heyday when photography was still very young." He smiled at them both. "Itinerant photographers had their rounds like publishers' reps today. I know a little about all that. Once upon a time, LG Books was going to be much more than the glue factory for old nags it turned into. Well, and so if dear old Grandma or little Lizzie or poor baby George popped off before the chap came with his Box Brownie . . . I mean to say, needs must. 'In Memoriam' photography, it's called."

"Wh—Wha—?" Jude asked, then took an extra breath. "You're saying you collect pictures of dead people in their coffins?"

"Not necessarily in coffins," said Lowell. "They posed them, rather ingeniously. Sometimes in family groups."

"Dead families?" said Jude. "Whole families?"

"Not dead families," Lowell said. "Just families with one of them appearing for the last time."

"Oh. My. God," Eddy said.

"And because the families didn't make a point of recording the harsh fact — made a point, rather, of trying to *hide* the fact — for a long time the photographs passed as normal portraits, you see. And the poor child standing there covered in powder and paint would just be thought of as not particularly photogenic."

"Fuck-a-duck!" said Eddy.

"Or so one might have expected," said Lowell darkly. "But it's usually the reverse. The first one among my collection, that is to say, the first one among my photographic collection that I successfully identified as 'In Memoriam' was a group portrait that had always troubled me. It was a couple with a teenaged child, and the couple —

merchant-class, lots of whiskers and ruffles — looked like ghosts. Rather indistinct and not quite there."

"The poor kid!" said Eddy. "No way that was her idea!"

"She, on the other hand, was crystal-clear and sharp-edged, staring straight out of the picture."

"She must have been freaked! No bloody wonder she was staring!" Eddy said, but Jude had taken a few steps ahead of her.

"Oh no," she said.

"What?" said Eddy.

"Indeed," said Lowell, nodding. "Exposure times were lengthy and during this one, the parents had moved. Perhaps they were shaking with emotion. The child, on the other hand, was perfectly still and therefore in focus."

"Oh, shit!" said Eddy. "That's *wrong*!"

"Exactly my point, my dear child," Lowell said. "It's an inversion of nature. The dead should be gone and the living remain."

"You said that to me once before," Jude said. "But I didn't know why."

"And so I collect them and take them out of circulation, away from prying eyes and the digital Sodom and Gomorrah, where they would be clicked on and sniggered at.

But I'm sorry I kept it a secret from *you* two."

Eddy and Jude exchanged a glance.

"S'all right," Eddy said.

"I'm glad now everything is out in the open," Lowell said. "It's my vocation and it's come to seem like my duty, but I don't speak of it for fear of shocking people, as I see from your faces that I have shocked you. I am truly sorry."

"Dad," Eddy said, "we thought you'd abused five old people in the nursing home and killed them to cover it up. So, you know, we kind of forgive you."

TWENTY-THREE

"I've never so much as shot a pop gun at a sparrow!" Lowell said. He shook his head and muttered at them for a while and then roused himself. "Jude, my dearest, you need to change and have a hot drink. I'll make cocoa while you go and get into a dressing gown, and then let's talk this over, shall we?"

Jude shot a look at Eddy.

"She is quite safe, my dear," Lowell said. "I admit I'm surprised to be accused of several brutal murders, but she is a teenager, and I believe teenagers have regularly charged their fathers with as much and more. Still." He gave them both a stern look over the tops of his spectacles then turned away.

"I worked in the nursing home," he began, a few minutes later when Jude was back in a tartan dressing gown and woolen socks, scratchy but warm on her numb feet. She had a towel wound round her head and had

wiped her make-up off roughly, leaving her
face tingling.

"My father wanted to punish me for the
snub of my neglecting medicine. But, one!
That was when I was a boy. When I was at
school. Dear me, how could he compel me
to take a job at a nursing home when I was
a grown man with my mother's money and
my bookshop to run? It makes no sense.
What were you thinking?"

"I said we needed a timeline," Eddy said,
sulkily.

"And, two! I worked in the kitchens, chopping carrots and scrubbing out pots. I didn't
have anything to do with the old people.
Good heavens, I've no aptitude for anything
of that nature. And Lord knows I could
never pass any of the certificates."

"We met Billy McLennan's care assistant
and she's worse than you," Eddy said.

"And, finally, three! The five people Eddy
named all died at home."

Eddy drew a breath to quibble again and
then said, "Oh."

"Why aren't you angrier?" Jude said.

He gave her a smile that crinkled up his
eyes. "I find you impossible to be cross with
when you're wearing my dressing gown," he
said. "And also, dear me, it's our old friend
the grain of truth again." He brought a

360

perilously full mug of cocoa over to her and set it down gently. "There was a bit of a scandal, you see. Dear me, yes. I mean, it was averted —"

"Hushed up, more like," Eddy said.

"But there was talk. Of course, this was long before Harold Shipman."

"Who?" said Eddy.

Lowell tutted and nodded at her phone lying on the kitchen table. Eddy tutted back at him, but she grabbed it and her thumbs started flying over the keys.

"My father was a terrible father but a wonderful doctor," Lowell said. "He was ready to retire, but there were a few old patients he didn't want to see swept up into the new wave of appointments and care teams. He hung on until they were gone. And of course it was a single-handed practice, and he signed the death certificates." Lowell gave them a significant look. "You would have seen what else they all have in common, wouldn't you?"

Jude shook her head.

"Well, my dear, of course, they were buried. No cremations. So one signature was all that was needed."

"What are you saying?" Jude asked him.

She had barely started her cocoa, but Lowell drained his and went to the dresser for the bottle of malt whisky and two glasses.

"Jesus Christ!" said Eddy, still staring at her phone. "Is this for real? This guy was a doctor and he murdered like hundreds of people!"

"And of course the *other* thing they all had in common is that they were widows or widowers or single. They lived alone with no one who'd want them to linger."

"So your dad offed a pile of oldsters and covered it up," Eddy said. "Like that Shipman did too."

"No," Lowell said. "But he was accused of it. He was accused by the family of Lorna McLennan."

"But Lorna McLennan was in the nursing home," said Jude. "It caused a family feud."

"Indeed it did," said Lowell. "The faction who wanted her left in her little flat blamed the care home staff."

"That would be Jackie," Jude said. "She told me."

Lowell nodded. "And the faction who had pushed for her to be in the home blamed my father. Both sides wanted a post-mortem to shut the other side up. They knocked off before it got quite that far, but by then the talk had started and there was no stopping it. Lorna's family, unable to blame the home or to accept responsibility themselves,

362

needed a whipping boy."

"Shower of shitbags turned round and bit him," said Eddy, like a glossary.

"He was horrified," Lowell said. "He threatened to recant every death certificate he had signed for a burial in the whole of the time he practised here. It was too bad if the bodies had been cremated, of course, but he threatened to rescind every other one and have all the dearly departed exhumed and autopsied. It was a dreadful time. Such a stain on . . . Well, I daresay that's terribly old-fashioned."

"How many did they dig up?" asked Eddy. "You'd have been right in there, snapping away."

"I am interested in the history of grief and its changing —"

"Oh blah blah blah," said Eddy. "How many?"

"None," Lowell said. "He changed his mind. Instead he retired, moved away, never visited the town again, and could barely speak its name."

"Holy shite!" said Eddy. "He called their bluff, didn't he?"

"That is what I concluded," said Lowell, sounding weary. "I think one of the sets of relatives knew that a post-mortem would raise, dear me, yes, awkward questions for them, and begged my father not to go ahead with his threat."

"And whoever it was," Eddy said, "Jackie phoned them last night and then they went round to Jude's and put the note in her door?"

"Note?" said Lowell, springing upright in his seat like a stepped-on rake. "What note? Show me."

Jude groaned, catching hold at last of what had been tickling her. "I was right!" she said. "I should have brought all the books. I left it behind."

"What note?" asked Lowell, sounding very stern.

"Someone pushed it through my door last night," Jude said. "But I've left it in Macaulay's essays. In the cottage. I'll go and get it tomorrow. Eddy, I *told* you I needed all the books."

"And what did it say?" Lowell demanded. "Describe it."

"Well," Jude began, "it was cheap pape—"

Eddy gave a long low snort that made her cough. "If you had a phone you could have taken a picture," she said. "Get a bloody phone! Get a dealer's burner if you don't want to register, but for Christ's sake!"

"Cheap paper," Jude said again, "sticky red biro — you know what I mean? Dark blobs?" Lowell nodded and Eddy rolled her eyes. "And it said, *Let the dead rest.* And then listed their names, like they'd signed it: Etta, Archie, Elsie, Norma, and Todd."

"In that order?" said Lowell.

Jude squeezed her eyes shut. "Norma, Elsie, Archie, Etta, Todd."

"You're sure?" said Lowell. Jude mouthed the names over to herself again and then nodded. "Because what I'm thinking is that whoever sent the note would put the most salient name first, do you see?"

"No" said Eddy. "What's *salient* mean?"

"Norma Oughton," said Jude. "Are there Oughtons still around?"

"Oh yes," said Lowell. "I should say there are. The Oughtons own a dairy farm over towards Monreith. Frank and Peter, the two brothers, run it between them. But when old Frank died he left his wife Norma in charge and she made a good age."

"Ninety," said Eddy, who was studying her phone.

"The brothers were itching to modernise, but the old lady stuck with the way her dear husband used to do things."

"You're not seriously suggesting . . . ?" said Jude. "Seriously? Two men would kill their mum to get . . ."

"An automated milking parlour," said

365

Eddy. Then blew a raspberry at their looks. "I went to a lot of Young Farmers' barbecues for the free cider."

"And does Jackie know them?" Jude said. "Would she have been likely to phone them yesterday and warn them that I was sniffing around?"

"Jackie knows everybody," said Lowell. "Well, e*verybody* knows everybody, dear me, yes, but I think Jackie was a bit of a childhood sweetheart of Frank Oughton, in our schooldays. Young Farmers' barbecues and all that, dear child, as you say."

"So, let me think this through," Jude said. "That would mean . . ."

Eddy, impatient, interrupted her. "You freak out Jackie, she phones up Frank and freaks him out too. He freaks her back. She goes home and collapses. He comes into town and puts a note through your door."

"But I heard someone walking," Jude said. "Not in a car."

"Well, he'd stash his car in case anyone saw it, wouldn't he?" said Eddy.

"And I think it was a woman," said Jude.

"High heels?" Eddy said. "Maybe he was in disguise."

"No, not high heels. It sounded like wellingtons, but small feet."

"But wellies!" Eddy said. "That's pretty

much a farmer's dress code, isn't it? What size are the Oughtons, Dad?"

"Wiry," Lowell said. "Not tall. And besides, there are wives. I remember one of the Oughton wives being rabid to get out of a cottage and into the farmhouse. The old lady wasn't cold before they cleared it and got the decorators in."

"Shite!" said Eddy. She threw her phone down and ran her hands through her hair. Distracted as Jude was, she still noticed the heavy silk of it spilling over the girl's hands and flowing down. "Forget it," she said. "It makes no odds that Norma-Oh was first on the note. I just checked the engraving on the headstones and that's the order they died in. Norma to Todd. The end." She sighed. "Can I have one sip of whisky? God, never mind! The face on you." She sighed again. "Why do you think Lorna McLennan's name's not mentioned?"

"Good question," said Jude. "I never noticed before because I'm working from Todd's notes, and they stopped when he stopped. Obviously."

"One hundred reviews to write before you die," said Eddy.

"What do you mean, *Todd's notes*?" said Lowell.

"I'll bring the books down and show you,"

Jude said. "Todd Jolly wrote reading notes in his book club selections and they morphed into a sort of diary. But it stopped before Miss McLennan, of course."

"And then with her death, everything stopped," Lowell said. "The end of an era. No more Dr. Glen in Wigtown." He took a long swallow of his whisky. "It was a terrible time. My father in an interview room in Newton Stewart, answering questions. Oh yes, it got that far. Lorna's family said he made an unscheduled visit the day she died. It was mischievous nonsense, but he was ashamed. He had nothing whatsoever to be ashamed of, but still he was ashamed."

"How did it get sorted out?" said Eddy. "If it got as far as the cops, the families backing out would make no odds."

"Mrs. Hewston gave him his alibi," Lowell said.

"Ahhhhh," said Jude. "That explains a lot."

"Were they having a roll in the hay?" said Eddy. "Your dad and Mrs. H.?"

"They were doing a stock take of the dispensary," Lowell said. "My dear child, life is so very much less action-packed than you seem to be expecting. I hope you don't find it dull as the years begin to roll by."

If he had known what was in store in the

days to come, if anyone of them had known even a fraction of it, he wouldn't have spoken so lightly of dullness, as though dullness were not welcome. When quiet days came again, it would be a long time before anyone found them unrewarding.

TWENTY-FOUR

They weren't exactly dreams. Jude was only half asleep while memories and visions rose and fell in her, twisting together and then unravelling. The photograph she had never seen of the still child and her trembling parents became the photograph of the dark Miranda, head thrown back and cherry-red mouth wide with laughter, her little friend against the light, glowing. Then Miranda became Raminder, lying on the floor while the baby cried, and Lowell's voice said, *The dead are lost and the living remain.*

She felt someone touch her hand. Max used to kiss her head when he went out on an early shift at five o'clock or came off a backshift at one. And she would kiss his when she slipped out of bed quietly the next morning to let him sleep. No one had ever woken her before by touching her hand.

She opened her eyes to see Lowell at her bedside, in his dressing gown with the striped collar of his pyjamas sticking up and his hair snarled into a nest.

"I'm going out," he said. "I didn't want to upset Eddy."

Jude took her hand away and sat up. "Going out where?" she whispered.

"The cottage," said Lowell. "Kirk Cottage is —" And then he astonished her by putting his arms around her shoulders and pressing her tightly to him. She could feel the grizzled grey hair on his chest scraping a section of her cheek and the incredible softness of his flannel pyjamas, like down, against the rest of it. And she could smell the staleness of his dressing gown and a hint of mothballs. She struggled free and stared at him.

"The cottage is on fire," he said. "The fire station rang me."

"My cottage?" said Jude, still not quite awake. "Jolly's Cottage?"

"Thank God you're here," Lowell said, and pressed her to him again.

"I switched everything off," said Jude, her voice muffled. "And I haven't lit the fire."

"Thank God," Lowell said again. "I couldn't have borne it."

"I'm coming," Jude said, pushing him away and sweeping back the bedclothes.

"No," said Lowell. "I need you to take

care of Eddy and . . . Well, dear me, my dear, yes indeed, you see, the police are bound to be there."

Jude froze with her legs half out of the bed. "Eddy told you?"

"She didn't need to," Lowell said. "And I don't know any details, nor do I want to. I trust you."

"But you know I don't want to run into cops."

"Eddy thinks everyone over twenty-five is a pensioner," said Lowell. "She thinks it no stranger that you don't possess a mobile phone than that I don't. But I know better."

"So why do you trust me?" said Jude.

"Because I have never known an O. Douglas admirer to be a scoundrel," Lowell told her with a smile. "Now, go to sleep. I'll come back as soon as I can. And don't upset Eddy, please, will you?"

Jude lay in the dark after he had gone with a swarm of unruly thoughts filling her head, deafening her. There was relief that he hadn't gone upstairs and found his "grand-child" hanging on a hook by its shoulder straps on the back of Eddy's bedroom door. There was the question of what he meant *by couldn't have borne it.* Was it possible? Was it welcome? And there was cold hard reality nudging at her too. The end of the fairy tale. The police were at the cottage where she'd been living. And if it wasn't that, it would be something else soon enough. A slip and fall and trip to Casualty. A traffic stop for a missing headlight.

She pushed that thought away, put it behind a door, turned the key, and swallowed it. She couldn't let herself think about that now. And it was easy. More than anything, her brain was filled with images of the cottage: those shelves and nooks in the headboard; the tiles on the coffee table; the handmade rack behind the kitchen door for everything from Clingfilm to clothes-pegs. She could see them all in sunlight and lamplight and couldn't bear the thought of them disappearing under a cloud of smoke that was more like fog and hid footsteps no matter how fast she ran and how loud she shouted, the other person always managing to stay ahead of her, shrouded by that curtain of grey.

Then Raminder was there, rummaging, just out of sight, taking bottles and blister packs of pills out of Jude's bathroom cabinet and filling her suitcase with them, packing them in and shaking the case to make more room, while Jude was crouched by the bed, flicking and flicking a plastic Bic lighter at the edge of the bedclothes, whispering, *Turn over. Max! Turn over!* But the back of Max's head, his hair snarled up from sleep, was too heavy for her to shift. It wasn't his real head. It was monstrous, bloated and spongy, strapped on to his skull and weighing him down. *Max!* she whispered, terrified that Raminder would hear her, or finish packing the pills and come in and see her. *Max! Wake up. Turn over.*

"Jude, wake up! What the bloody hell's going on? Where's Lowell?"

Eddy opened the curtains, sending the brass rings screeching along the pole and letting a slice of cold light fall across Jude's face. She put an arm up to hide her eyes and groaned.

"He had to go," she said, her dry throat clicking as she swallowed. "There's been a fire."

"Jesus Christ? At the *shop*? All those books! The whole town'll be gone. He should have had sprinklers. Why didn't you wake me?"

Jude waited until she ran out of steam and then told her.

"The cottage," she said. "He didn't want you upset." She felt the bed springs drop as Eddy sat down.

"Oh my God!" she said. "Someone tried to kill you. No one knew you were here

374

except Lowell and me. Jude, someone tried to burn you to death!"

"And Mrs. Hewston," said Jude, getting up. "She knew too." She went to the window to tidy the mess Eddy had made of the curtains and was standing in full view when a white estate car with an orange light on top turned into the side drive and approached the house.

"Who's that?" said Eddy, sidling up beside her. On her other side, Jude caught a flash of movement: Mrs. Hewston's garden gate opening and shutting and the high fronds of the asparagus bed swishing as she passed through.

"Oh Jesus," Eddy said. "The jungle drums have been on the go then."

They could hear Lowell in the kitchen when they were halfway downstairs, the cutlery drawer sticking as he tried to open it, spoons and forks clashing until it came free, and the sound of the kettle. There were voices too, but they quieted as Jude and Eddy entered.

The visitors were firemen, one in his uniform, minus the outer layer, and one in civvies with just a regulation body-warmer on, holding a clipboard.

"How bad is it?" said Jude. Lowell looked ten years older, grey and shaking. Eddy went over and hugged him hard, reaching up and smoothing his hair back. She must be pretty sure of the weight and texture of that strap-on belly, Jude thought. But Lowell, at least at this moment, was too distracted to register anything so subtle. He barely reacted to her touch at all.

"The porch is gone," he said. "And there's smoke damage and water damage and the roof looks . . . poor little house." He took a ragged breath that was almost a sob.

Jude felt a wave of nausea; the thought of the cottage soaked and ruined was more than she could stand. To distract herself, she asked a question. "The porch? Where did it start?"

One of the fireman, the older one with the clipboard, glanced at Lowell and he nodded grimly.

"In the letterbox," the man said. He had such a strong local accent that Jude struggled briefly. Litter box? Then she gasped. "Aye," the man went on. "Crumpled newspaper and a firelighter. You were lucky, hen."

"Well, but I'd have been okay, wouldn't I?" said Jude. "If it's just the porch."

The fireman's eyes hardened as he looked over at Lowell, who was spooning tea into the big pot, shaking so much that little scraps of loose leaves dropped from the spoon and sprinkled the worktop.

"Dad?" said Eddy, peering up into his face. "Sit down and let me. You're making a bloody mess."

"No smoke alarms," said the fireman. "No upstairs exits. That suite's too old to pass fire regs. There's no way that house was fit to rent out."

"It wasn't rented," said Jude, coldly. "I was Mr. Glen's guest and I'm not the suing type, so you can just calm down."

"Yeah," Eddy said. "You can see he's upset. Stop being such an old sweetie-wife. Hey!" she said, turning towards the back door. "Speaking of which, where's Mrs. H.? She was on her way over."

"So," Jude said. "Arson, eh? And you're an investigator, aren't you? What happens now?"

"We're not here to share information," said the clipboard man. "I offered Mr. Glen a lift home as a courtesy since he wasn't fit to drive, but we'll pass on the tea."

Eddy poured water from the kettle into the pot and swirled it round.

"I said we'll pass on the tea," the man repeated.

"You're not the only one with a mouth," Eddy said, and Jude saw the other fireman, the one dirty and smoky from actual firefighting, suppress a grin.

His boss stood and placed his chair under the table with a kind of fussy efficiency.

"I'll stop on," said the sitting man. "I'm off shift now. I'll get Sandy to come round and pick me up when I've had a cuppa."

His boss left without another word, picking over his keys and ignoring Eddy, who followed him.

"I'm not seeing you off the premises," she said, "so don't get all humpty. I'm just checking out for our neighbour, see what's happened to her.

"Well," she said, when she returned. "That's a mystery. No sign of her. Do you want some toast, Dad? And how about — ?" She turned. "Do you eat burnt food like toast? There's cornflakes if not."

The fireman chuckled. "Toast would be grand," he said. "Sandy was right. You're a wee belter, aren't you? You've got your hands full, Low!"

"Who's Sandy?" said Eddy, scowling either from natural bent or because she didn't know she was being complimented.

"My wife. Met you yesterday at Billy McLennan's." He took a slurp of his tea. "That was a terrible thing and now this. What next, eh?"

"Don't tell me you're married to that

378

bitch of a care worker," said Eddy.

"Thankfully — given your complete lack of diplomacy, dear child — no," said Lowell. He was beginning to revive and he turned with a look of interest as Eddy pushed two rough slices into the toaster and sent them down. "This is Frank Oughton."

Jude managed to keep her face neutral and Frank was facing away from Eddy, so he didn't see her jaw dropping.

"Frank and Peter are volunteer firemen," Lowell went on.

"Do you take it in turns?" Eddy said. "It'd be kind of shite if you both died in a fire you went to together."

"Too many films," said Lowell, at Frank's look. "Blame Bruce Willis."

"So," Frank said. "Who's behind this then? Who've you pissed off, Lowell? Or is it you . . . ?" He turned to Jude.

"Judith. Judith Crowther."

Lowell frowned, just a flicker, and then smoothed his brow again. "I've been wracking my brains," he said. "The cottage lay empty for aeons, so it's not a disgruntled tenant. And Judith's new here and didn't take anyone's job or anything of that nature, dear me, no, so it's rather hard to see a personal motive."

"And you've not left someone hacked off

with you down in London?" Frank said, still looking at Jude.

"Here!" said Eddy. "Isn't this that other bloke's job? What's it to you?" She probably thought she was helping.

"I'm a librarian," Jude said. "We don't make enemies, not now you're allowed to talk."

"Barbarianism," said Lowell.

"So it's not a running away type of thing?" Frank said. "No one looking for you? And no trouble since you got here?"

Jude gave him a smile as she shook her head. "I'm helping Lowell with a big overhaul of his cataloguing system, getting the stock online and reorganising. He answered my advert in the *Bookseller*. It's a trade magazine."

"Yeah," said Eddy. "A real page-turner."

"And the worst I've had since I got here's a few sideways looks because of the accent. Couple of digs about London."

"Aye, well," said Frank, as if that was to be expected.

"It'll be kids," Eddy said. "We always blame the Troubles for the wee shites kids are with the matches and the fireworks, but if they're just as bad here it's nothing to do with it, eh no?"

"Wigtown's not had kids like that these

last few years," said Frank. "The Powells were wild in their day, but they've scattered."

"You know what I think," Lowell said. "I think someone noticed the sign had gone from the Post Office and thought the cottage had been abandoned. Kids, as you say, dear child. They can't possibly have realized someone was living there."

"The sign?" said Frank. "The For Rent sign that doesn't exist, seeing as you're not a landlord of a substandard cottage, Low?" He stood up and flapped a weary hand. "Don't look so worried. I'll not say anything. He can rake his own muck if he wants to. Thanks for the tea."

"Don't you want to phone your wife?" Jude asked him. "Get a lift."

"I'll walk," said Frank. "Chance of a smoke with no one nagging me. Aye," he added, "I know." They watched him through the kitchen window, lighting a cigarette before he shrugged into the bright yellow waterproof he had left outside the door. They were silent until he was gone.

"We fooled him," Eddy said.

"Thanks for your help," said Jude, dryly. Lowell gave her an absent smile and Eddy scowled.

"I don't believe Frank Oughton wrote that

note," Lowell said. "And he and Peter are as thick as thieves."

"I'm really sorry about the cottage," said Jude.

"Tush," Lowell replied. "It could have been so much worse."

Even as he spoke, the knock came at the front door that would make it so, would push peace and happiness further away than ever from them all.

Eddy answered it. She went swishing away along the passage to the front door with the chiffon of Miranda's peignoir billowing out behind her. The fleece pyjamas underneath spoiled the effect, but the pale yellow silk was beautiful against her hair.

"I don't know where she gets the energy," Lowell murmured when she was gone, and Jude made a mental note to remind Eddy to act a little tired now and then.

Her footsteps were even faster as she returned, flying along the thin carpet strip. "Judith!" she called out. "Father!"

Lowell and Jude sat up and stared at one another.

"Cop," said Jude, under her breath. "Bet you."

TWENTY-FIVE

When she looked back, it was only an hour, if that.

Eddy, who had been questioned by police before, took the whole thing in her stride.

"I'll wait upstairs in my flat till you're ready for me," she said. "And here." She took the back off her phone, took the battery out and gave the phone to the younger of the two policemen, young enough to blush at the implied insult. His boss, a woman in her forties, gave Eddy a knowing look out of narrowed eyes.

"What makes you think we need to speak to you? Miss — ?"

"Glen," said Eddy. "Miz. I can alibi them. Lowell and Judith and me were together all night. Nobody went round to the cottage to set it on fire. Like for the insurance or that."

The policewoman — a sergeant, Jude thought, although the Scottish uniforms were unfamiliar — gave Eddy her phone battery back and turned away.

"Suit yourself," Eddy said. "I'm having a bath, Father dear. Will I leave the water in?"

"Um, well, I mean, if we're finished before it's cold," said Lowell.

"I'll whistle down when I'm done," Eddy said, "and then you can just tell them to stuff it. Unless they arrest you or offer to chip in on your water bill."

And so the sergeant was good and angry when she took Jude into the drawing room on her own and opened a notebook.

Jude chose a comfortable-looking velvet armchair near the empty fireplace, surprised when she sat by how unyielding it was, despite the deep buttoning and the dome of the seat. It had to be horsehair, she decided, and put her hands to her sides to feel for bristles poking through.

She had never spent any time in this room. None of them had, gracious as it was. Jude wondered, looking round, if it had been used since Mrs. Glen had died all those years ago. The ornaments on the high mantelpiece were delicate white china, touched here and there with gold, probably valuable since they looked too old to have been made in a factory. No doubt it had a name, although Jude didn't know it, and she could imagine Mrs. Glen in the fifties

384

telling a maid to be careful with her Such-and-Such when the girl washed it as part of the spring cleaning. Life must have been simpler then, when you'd tell a girl to beat the carpets and you'd go out for a walk to escape the dust while it was done. Even if you were the girl, it had to be simpler than the life Jude was leading.

"Right then, Miss — ?" said the sergeant, sitting down with her own startled look at how hard the chair was when she got there.

"Crowther," said Jude.

"Judith?" the sergeant said. "And is it Miss?"

"It is Miss," said Jude, expecting the woman to approve, surprised by the twist of her mouth.

"I'd have put you down as married," she said. "There's a different look."

"How can there be?" Jude said. "I mean, that's interesting."

"Hard to explain," said the cop. "A lot of detective instinct is hard to explain. It's a right pain in court."

"It must be," said Jude. Then she heard her own sycophantic voice and thought the cop would know she was trying to ingratiate herself. What would Eddy say? "*Are* you a detective, then?" She was rewarded with a quick frown.

"Right, Miss Crowther." The voice was more clipped now. "Address?"

"Here, now," Jude said. "Since the cottage isn't exactly —"

"Permanent address," said the sergeant.

Jude rattled off her parents' house number and street, the postcode she'd learned as a child. They wouldn't check. They had no reason to.

"And you've been here how long?"

"Just over a week," said Jude. "Working for Lowell. Mr. Glen."

"Oh, we know Lowell," she said. "He's an old friend of the D&G constabulary, is Lowland Glen. Although he's been living quietly this last while."

Jude said nothing. Was she harking back to the summer of love, 1994, the time Eddy would so dearly like to learn more of?

"Although . . ." the cop said. "Maybe he's starting up again."

Jude shook her head. "I'm a librarian and Eddy's his daughter," she said. "We're not exactly setting the rafters ringing. Eddy's mum was one of the ones who used to hang out here, you know. Back when Lowell had a houseful."

"Aye, so I heard," said the cop. "And she has a look of her."

"So, was it really wild?" Jude said. "It's

hard to imagine."

"We never got the chance to find out," said the copper. "They all kept their noses clean, kept it on the premises, and the only neighbour" — she jerked her head — "never complained officially about the noise, so we never got a chance to come in and see what they were up to."

"Frustrating for you," said Jude, but she had gone too far and the woman's eyes narrowed.

"Let's get back to business," she said. "Any enemies?"

Jude felt her face freeze. Raminder had an unknown number of brothers and sisters, plenty of them in the only photo Jude had ever seen, although some might have been cousins.

"Something bothering you?" the cop asked.

"Just made it seem real, you asking that," Jude said. "I was feeling guilty, thinking I'd left something on and destroyed Lowell's lovely little house and then, when the fireman said about the letterbox, I was feeling lucky — understatement! I was feeling sick with relief that I wasn't in there. I never even thought of it being about me until right there. I — Sorry." She put her head down between her knees to buy herself time, tense, waiting to see if her story had gone over.

"Really?" The woman's voice was dry. "That wasn't the first thing that occurred to you?"

"Of course not," said Jude, sitting up again. "I mean, it's like something off a film."

"Huh." Jude thought she saw a drop in the woman's shoulders. "Now that's interesting. See, I'd have said coming from London you'd be more alert for crime. But I suppose a crime like that — targeted arson — that's the kind of thing that comes easier in a wee place like Wigtown. Know what I mean?"

"Not really," said Jude.

"Big city — everyone's a stranger. And if nobody knows your secrets there's no point trying to get rid of someone to stop them spilling."

Jude couldn't have helped her eyes widening even if she'd tried, and so it was just as well that it fit the bill. "So you really don't think it was just kids being bad?" she said. "You think someone's got a grudge against Lowell? And I just got in the way?"

"Lowell, the church, Todd Jolly . . ."

"Todd *Jolly*?" said Jude. "He's been dead thirty years."

"Ach, it's not a proper grudge till it gets down a generation or two," said the woman. "And you're dead right, by the way. It was thirty years past just in the spring there. You've got yourself up to speed nice and quick, eh?" She winked at Jude and grinned at the effect of her wink.

This was why Max never liked cops, Jude thought. They ran up against each other most days at work, going out to accidents and sudden deaths, and Jude thought they'd be natural allies. But Max changed pubs when the one nearest the ambulance depot turned into a coppers' haunt thanks to the new offices being built. Their old pub — the Bobbies' it was called for the years it had done service to police coming off their shift — was too far away.

"They're *never* off their shift," Max had said. It had taken a while for her to work out the problem, but in the end it came back to drink, like everything. He had told her when they were dancing at Allan's retirement do. Everyone else was shaking their tail feathers since it was a fast song, but Max could only drape his arms over Jude's shoulders and shuffle around the floor.

"Go home after this, eh love?" he'd mumbled into her hair. "Place is crawling with bloody filth." She hadn't understood, had looked around at the sparkling black and silver décor of the function room. "That fat one with the pint in his hand. He's got a lip on him. I can't be arsed with him. Dunno why Allan invited them all."

Jude looked over at the man with the pint, an off-duty cop as clear as if he'd a sign above him. He was standing with his legs spread wide and surveying the room with a smile on his face, switching his gaze from corner to corner like a metronome. When he caught Jude's eye, he came over.

"Day off tomorrow, Maximilian?" he said, a rich chuckle bubbling just under his words.

"No," said Max.

"Shame you've got leave so early then," the man said. "Still, you've managed to get a whole night's partying in in half the time, eh?" He threw a look at Jude. "Let us know if you need a hand, love," he said. "When your taxi gets here."

"I'm driving," Jude said.

"Are you?" said the fat man, still grinning. He glanced over at the table where her bag and cardigan were sitting. "You just leaving that nice big glass of Chardonnay for some-one else, are you? That's very generous. You're like your husband. I see him buying drinks that turn out to be for other people all the time."

Jude had driven home in burning silence, making up retorts, while Max snored with his face against the window, a line of drool joining his chin to his tie. A silk tie, ruined. She'd thrown it out in the morning.

She had been quiet too long. This copper was looking more amused than ever.

"You think someone's sending a message?" Jude asked. "Like the Wigtown mafia or someone?"

Annoyance was better than amusement, and the woman was pretty annoyed to have a Londoner laugh at her little town, at the possibility of crime there. She retreated into routine questions: had Jude seen anyone hanging around, had she heard any noises at night. Jude kept quiet about the footsteps in the fog and the footprints in the grass, and when five more minutes had passed, it was over.

"Right-oh," the cop said. "Phone?"

Jude gave the number of Lowell's landline and the woman looked annoyed. She added the shop number and the cop went as far as to lift her pen from her little notebook and look over.

"Are you deliberately refusing to give me your mobile number, hen?"

"I haven't got one," said Jude. "They're not compulsory."

Again the copper's eyes narrowed but she said no more, just stood and walked out, leaving Jude sitting there.

She heard Eddy clattering downstairs as soon as the kitchen door closed.

"Christ on a bed of rice!" she said. "I was sitting halfway up, like whatsisface. I heard everything. What a prize bitch *she* is."

"Christopher Robin," said Jude. "You were right about a mobile, by the way. She looked at me like I was a space alien."

As if to cement Eddy's triumph, her phone rang at that very moment and she cackled with glee as she fished it out of her pocket. She had bathed and dressed and was wearing a long cardigan of Lowell's like a dress, nothing but her wrinkly ribbed tights underneath. She had Birkenstocks on her feet and a towel round her shoulders while her hair dried. She looked about fifteen, despite the belly. She glanced down at her phone and then wheeled around, turning her back on Jude so fast that her wet rats' tails of hair flew out like blue-black sunrays.

She touches that up, Jude thought, and felt a shift inside her. It was partly something she couldn't put her finger on and partly, of course (what else?), Raminder. Raminder was more and more in her head; the dream getting to be nightly, the picture there behind her eyelids, whenever she closed them.

"What is it?" said Eddy, turning back.

Jude looked up. Maybe it was that blue-black hair and the cold blue light in this room — no wonder Lowell never used it — but Eddy's face looked whiter than Jude had ever seen it.

"Never mind me," she said. "What's wrong with *you*? Who was that?"

"No one," said Eddy. "Ex-boyfriend. A ghost. Jude, what *is* it?"

"Just memories," said Jude. "I don't want to talk about it." But that was a lie and Eddy knew it. Jude tried again. "I don't trust you not to tell Lowell."

"Me?" said Eddy. "I'm like a bank vault. Why are you looking at me like that?"

"It's your hair," Jude said. "Your black hair. It reminds me of someone."

"I've seen the photos," Eddy said. "In the news. But hers was straightened. Mine comes out my head like this." She tossed it this way and that again. It was so fine it was drying already.

"She fell." Jude blurted the words out. "She was crying. And she was carrying a suitcase. She tripped at the top of the stairs."

"Raminder," said Eddy.

"I didn't push her," Jude said. "I went out onto the landing to . . . talk to her, I think. Help her. Like, drive her somewhere or help with the baby. The baby was down at the front door in her pram, bawling her eyes out, and Raminder was crying. So I went out onto the landing and she heard me and turned round and then she just tripped. She went down like . . ." Jude put her head between her knees for the second time in half an hour. The cool blue room had started to darken from each side, turning to grey as her eyes lost focus and all the blood left her head to puddle under her feet.

"Where was *he*?" said Eddy. "Cos the news said —"

"Passed out drunk," said Jude, into the tent of her skirt. "That's why Raminder was leaving. That's why she was crying."

"So she didn't find you together?" said Eddy. "Cos the news said —"

"She didn't know I was there until I went out onto the landing," said Jude and sat up and back, feeling the hard mounds of the button-back chair behind her, feeling at last the stiff end of one of the horse hairs she knew would be there somewhere. It dug into the back of her head and she let it keep pricking at her, drove her head back harder to see if it would break her skin, but instead she felt it buckle. "I was hiding behind the bedroom door," she said, "like someone from a French farce."

"What, starkers?"

"No! I wasn't in bed with him!" Jude said. "He didn't know I was there either. I hid — Jesus, this should be funny! When I heard him coming in, I hid in the wardrobe and then when he passed out, like he always did, I came out and I was standing there looking at him when she came in the front door. I didn't have time to get back in again."

"Thank God for that, eh? If she packed her stuff."

"So I was just standing there. Behind the bedroom door."

"And then you followed her," said Eddy. "And you saw her fall."

"I never touched her," Jude said. "She turned and tripped and she went down, slid and tumbled and slid again. Right to the bottom. She was face-down. All that black hair like a sheet, I couldn't see her face. She was kind of — Sometimes people fall and you know something's broken from the angles, right? But it wasn't like that. Her legs were straight and her feet were sort of still up on the bottom step and her arms were straight out down by her sides from the way she'd slid, you know? I couldn't see her face."

"Could you hear her breathing?" said Eddy.

"I couldn't hear *anything,*" said Jude, "with the noise of the baby."

"Oh, yeah," Eddy said. "I forgot the baby. Poor wee mite, eh?" She put a hand on the top of her belly and held it there, looking at Jude with not a single twinkle in her eye. "And then you dialled 999," she said. "Just like anyone would. You did the right thing. Just like any other good person. Didn't you?"

TWENTY-SIX

"Oh my dears!" Lowell had opened the
door so quietly that neither one of them had
time to compose her face. "Those *ruddy*
police!"

"Steady on, Dad," said Eddy, with a shaky
laugh. "Mind your language."

"They let *me* off comparatively lightly,"
he said, "thanks to the fact that the house
was empty and it's not insured."

"It's not insured?" said Jude. "Oh Lowell.
I'm so sorry. If only I hadn't come and
started kicking up dust."

He shushed her, flapping his hands as
though he were swimming doggy paddle.
"Truth will come to light," he said. " 'Murder cannot be hid long.' "

"What?" said Eddy. "What murder?"

"Oh my *dears*! I should be shot."

"It's just an expression, Eddy," said Jude.
"A quotation. From . . ."

"The Merchant of Venice," said Lowell.

"Who?"

"What do we do now?" Jude said.

"We get back into the cottage and purloin the letter for one thing," said Lowell.

"Which, if you'd put it in your bag or your back pocket instead of in some old book where you'd completely forget it *was,* we'd already have it," Eddy offered.

"I just hope, dear me, yes, that the fire investigator doesn't find it first."

"Oh yeah, like the fire investigator's going to go snooping through a pile of manky old books looking for clues to a fire that started downstairs. Why would he? Why would anyone? Who puts stuff that matters in a book deliberately, instead of like bus tickets or that to keep your place?"

Jude leapt up from the button-backed chair. "Eddy, you're a genius," she said.

"I try," Eddy said. "How come this time though?"

"I *knew* there was something," Jude said. "I knew there was some reason I wanted to bring the book club books. I've got it. Lowell, where can we spread them out?"

"Dining room," Lowell said, striding out and across the hall, into another of the unused parts of Jamaica House. It was dancing with dust motes and sad in the daylight, its dark wood and rich colours much more suited for lamp-lit evenings.

"Christ Almighty, when's the funeral?" said Eddy, looking around.

Jude clicked on the electric light hanging low over the long table. "Perfect," she said. "Eddy, we'll run up and down and you unpack them."

"Right," Jude said, twenty minutes later. "Three book clubs, like you said, Lowell." She picked up the nearest volume. "First, the one he joined himself when his wife was still alive. He didn't write anything on any of these because he didn't need to; he had someone to talk to. But then there's the next one — the one his daughter Angela got him. He wrote wonderful little reviews in them. Witty, pithy, clever little summaries. I think I fell in love with Todd Jolly because he gave *Rosemary's Baby* the one-word review *Blimey!*"

Eddy rolled her eyes. Lowell shouted with laughter.

"But I'm not entirely sure I quite see, my dear," he added mildly.

Jude opened *Black Narcissus* to the endpaper. "*Brilliant but I bet the tourist board hates him.* See the thing about these is — and this is the lightbulb you turned on, Eddy — it never occurred to him that anyone would ever read them. These were his little jokes with himself, part of the pleasure of reading, along with building his shelves and all the rest of it. He never meant anyone to see these. But then something happens."

She took the volume of *Lolita,* which had put itself under her hand, and opened it.

"A *third* book club. One hundred books to read before you die. He's thinking about death, you see. And he's old now; his friends are starting to go and he's seen it happen that a house is cleared and people go through a person's belongings. He knows that someone will see his words once he's gone. He *means* someone to see his words. In one way it destroys his writing — there's no playfulness, no little jokes. But what there is . . . is messages. He's writing down what someone needs to know. *Archie Patterstone is dead. Etta Bell is fading fast. I will tell Dr. Glen enough is enough. This plain man is sick of the world tonight.*"

"What *are* you on about?"

"He knew what was happening," Lowell said.

"But what *was* happening?" Eddy said.

"Frank and Pete Oughton wanted the farm," said Jude. "What about the rest of them, Lowell?"

"Elsie's daughter moved into her house,"

said Lowell. "As far as I remember. I can't tell you anything about Etta Bell, though. And Archie Patterstone was a lifelong bachelor."

"I don't suppose you can remember what happened to his estate?" Jude asked.

"*Estate* is rather a grand word for it," Lowell told her. "He lived in the pensioners' cottages. Can't have left much beyond his Post Office savings and his —"

"What?" said Jude.

"Well, dear me, this might sound silly, but his allotment."

"For growing prize leeks?" said Eddy. "Or does *allotment* mean something else here?"

"I know, I know, it *does* sound silly. Good heavens, how could it fail to? But two things. Archie Patterstone worked on that soil for decades. It was like caviar. And I've just remembered who inherited it." He paused. "Bill McLennan."

"So what?" said Eddy.

"Billy McLennan," Jude said, "whose wife was so angry when I started snooping."

"What?" said Eddy.

"Jackie didn't want Auntie Lorna in the nursing home. Cared for and looked after and using up all her money."

"This is pretty wackadoo, Jude," said Eddy.

"Look, we already thought someone had done it, didn't we? Someone freaked out when the doctor started threatening exhumations. So all we're saying now is that it happened more than once. The Oughtons offed the old lady for the farm. The Days offed Elsie for the house. Bill offed Archie for his allotment. The Bells . . . Maureen was rattled when I asked, and her cousin deleted Jackie's call log."

"And you think Todd Jolly saw what a doctor missed and he left hints in his books?"

"At least hints," said Jude. "If we're lucky, proof! He was certainly writing in the hundred-books volumes all through the time these people were dying. Eddy, what are the dates again?"

"I still think this is major nutso," said Eddy, "but . . . December 1983 to May 1985," she said. "That's like fifty books!"

"Eighteen," corrected Lowell. "Dear me. Late '83 to early '85, eh? Well well."

"What?" said Jude.

"Let's hope nothing," he said, not quite meeting her eye.

"Rip it off," said Eddy, understanding the emotion he was feeling, even if she couldn't guess at its source. "Just grab one corner and rip it off, Dad. It's the only way."

Lowell looked at her at first unseeingly and then with a small smile. "Do you have any idea, my dear child, that you make my heart leap like a salmon every time you say that word? Of course you don't, and that is part of the wonder. Now see here, Jude and I are going to be mining the book mountain in the dead room all day. I want you to come with us. I think we should stick together."

Eddy regarded him steadily. "I can't bloody stand salmon," she said. "Too pink and too greasy."

It was more than twice as fast with two of them, somehow, and Jude was forced to admit that, in spite of all of his vagueness and the way he pattered about, when it came to shifting books, Lowland Glen was the equal of any librarian she had ever known. He was big, for a start, and could move twelve paperbacks at a time, six in each splayed hand, if he lined them up well. And he didn't stop to leaf through what he was unpacking. So he kept Jude up to the mark. Between them they got into a rhythm of stripping back the plastic of the carrier bag or untwisting the dovetailed flaps of a cardboard box, assessing what was in there, and then Lowell would clear the chaff away while Jude delivered the wheat to Eddy.

"But some of the hundred-books books don't even have his name in them," Jude said. "I only know them from the book club stickers."

"Just keep everything," said Lowell. "Whittling down is a great deal easier than whittling up."

The corridor was in danger of closing completely and Lowell decided not to open the shop, told Eddy not to put lights on in the upstairs rooms, if she wandered there in between deliveries. She didn't wander, but she did complain about being bored and asked them to talk to her, standing in the dead room door with her Birkenstocks kicked off and her feet in padded posting bags to keep them warm.

"How can you be bored?" Jude said. "There are eighty thousand books out there."

"And what of the dreaded device?" asked Lowell, pushing his spectacles up his head and smiling at her.

"It's off," said Eddy. "I thought you'd be happy."

"Off because of that phone call?" said Jude, but Eddy only scowled at her and shuffled away, little pockets of the bubble wrap in her makeshift shoes snapping with every step.

"Todd!" Lowell sang out. Jude crowded in beside him to see.

"BCA, BCA, BCA," said Lowell. "Ah, 'One Hundred Books to Read Before You Die,' number 45: *Ulysses.*"

"God almighty," said Jude. "They should have made it 99 with just one after it, so you could die happy. Will I get that other *Ulysses* back from Eddy now? Now we know it's not his?"

Lowell looked down at her through his spectacles, clouded with dirt and slightly steamed up from his exertions. "Let's leave it," he said. "I'm interested in the duplicate copies. I'm sure some of the other book club members were as elderly as Todd himself. Who knows? Perhaps we'll find another diarist among them." He looked back at the book in his hand. "Anyway, 45 is well within our range. Number 34 was 1982's Christmas pick. You do the honours."

He handed the book to Jude and then, to her astonishment he put his arm casually around her shoulder while she opened it. It might have been partly to help him rest and it would have been more welcome if he hadn't been so hot; hot enough to warm every layer of outfit from shirt, through musty cardigan, through elderly hairy jacket, so that she got fresh sweat and stale sweat and ancient sweat all mixed in. But she leaned into him anyway and was even more astonished when he dropped a kiss on top of her head.

She turned the book towards the light, the single naked bulb in the centre of the room, and read.

He's either a genius or a madman, Todd Jolly had written. *It's like dancing to jazz music, reading this.*

"Wonderful!" Lowell said. "I had no idea these notes were here. What must you think of me?"

He took his arm way and plunged into the box for another. "Number 46!" he announced. Then he threw back his head and shouted. "You're missing the best bit, dear child."

There was silence from outside and then Eddy's voice shouting back, "I'll cope."

"Number 46," said Lowell again. *"The Wind in the Willows."*

"A reward after *Ulysses*," Jude said.

"Seems like a kid's book," Lowell read. *"Not so much to it as Animal Farm and a gey sight too English to bring back memories of my boyhood.* That's all he wrote at first, but look."

Jude peered over his arm and read what was written in Todd's firm handwriting.

"This was when Norma Oughton died. They said she was worn out. She was nothing of the sort. M. told me N. didn't think much of U. and I phoned her up and we agreed about it and had a good laugh. We talked for half an hour and only rang off because I was tired. I was tired. She was fine. She had years left in her."

"Who's M.?" said Lowell.

"I have no idea," said Jude. "It's come up before, though." She read it over. *"This was when Norma Oughton died,"* she repeated. "You see what it means, don't you?"

Lowell nodded. "He went back later — possibly much later — and added that. Different pen too."

"I'll deliver them to Eddy," Jude said. "Keep digging." She took both books and picked her way out of the room towards Lowell's desk. "Here's two mor—"

Eddy was sitting there, turned away and whispering fiercely into her phone.

"Eddy?"

The girl shrieked loud enough to bring Lowell stumbling from the dead room, crashing into one of Jude's towers and sending the books, so carefully sorted, in an avalanche across the floor.

"Jesus Christ!" Eddy said. "What the fuck, Jude?"

"Darling girl, what's wrong?" Lowell demanded.

"Nothing!" said Eddy "Fuck sake. Calm down, Da—" She bit off the word and snapped her gaze back to the phone. She lifted it and spoke in a hissing whisper. "Now see what you've done? Leave me alone!" She killed the call, pressing her thumb down as if she was trying to choke the life out of her phone.

"Who was that?" said Lowell. "Are you sure you're —"

"No one," said Eddy. "A friend."

"A friend who needs to leave you alone?" Jude said.

"I bloody wish *you'd* leave me alone. Both of you."

"In that case," said Lowell, "Jude, come and see what I've found now."

He hadn't noticed the bitten off *dad* while the line was open. Jude had.

"One minute," she said. And when he had gone she spoke in a low voice. "Are you in trouble?"

Eddy pointed at her stomach and said, "Duh! No, I'm not. If everyone would stop freaking out. I'm not, but yeah, I might be. As it happens."

"Tell me," said Jude. "I'm here for you."

"Yeah, right," said Eddy. "*You'll* be there

408

for me if I get dragged off to the cop shop. You'll be right there bailing me out, eh?"

"I think that's on films," Jude said. "Bailing people out of jails. But I take your point."

"I take your point," said Eddy in a mincing singsong, mocking her. "In other words, I'm on my own."

"Eddy, for God's sake, how can you say that?" Jude jabbed a finger towards the dead room. "That man loves you. Instantly. Unconditionally. You pop up out of nowhere — *I'm your daughter, here's your grandkid, oh wait, no grandkid after all* — and all he does is *love* you."

"It probably helps that he thinks he's my dad, yeah?" Jude said nothing. "And about the grandkid, I'm kind of rethinking the whole Liam and Terry angle again, so I hope you're right."

Jude gave her a stunned look. Did *rethinking the angle* mean coming clean? If Eddy came clean about her own secrets, would she still keep Jude's? Before she could think of a way to ask, Lowell called for her.

"I've found his *Godfather*!"

"Go back to your clues, Nancy Drew," Eddy said.

In the back of *The Godfather* (49) Todd had written, *Should have read it before I saw* the film. *I couldn't get that that daft voice out of my head.* Then later: *Elsie Day is gone. I mind her skipping in the playground with her skirt flying up and her wee navy-blue knickers. Dead from renal failure. She was still dancing at the bowling club on Christmas Eve. She winked at me.* Later still, and this time with a shaking hand, he had added: *Number two.*

"Then came Archie," Jude said. "Written about in *On the Beach*. And *Lolita* was only six months later, and Etta Bell was already fading. That's what he wrote. *Fading fast.*"

"I wish this book club advertised the next volume in the current one," Lowell said. "Then at least we'd know what we were looking for."

Jude clicked her fingers. "Keep rummaging." She backed out of the room and squeezed along the corridor. They had given up all pretence of organising the books now as they threw them over their shoulders. The mess should have appalled her, should have made every inch of her skin crawl, should have made her throat feel felt-lined. In fact, as she edged past them, they barely registered. Perhaps like a very small pebble under the instep in her shoe.

The girl was gone.

Jude listened at the toilet door and then

knocked softly.

"Eddy?" she said. "You okay, love?"

There was only silence and when Jude turned the handle and entered, the tiny room was empty and the cistern quiet.

"Eddy?" she shouted up the stairs, listening. The whole house was still.

She looked along the passage towards where Lowell was working and hesitated. If Eddy wanted to run, she should be allowed to run. She was over eighteen. But Lowell thought she was eight months pregnant. Jude took a step towards him and then breathed out a huff of relief as she heard the garden door open. A moment later, Eddy appeared from Coasters and Key Rings, stepping quietly, looking the other way, towards where she thought Lowell and Jude were both working. When she heard the noise of books being moved in the dead room, she breathed out and trotted along the side passage.

"Been out for a breath of fresh?" Jude asked and then felt rotten as Eddy jumped in the air and, swinging round, turned her ankle. She was carrying something and, from instinct at the fright, she had put it up like a weapon. Jude frowned. "What the hell?"

Eddy was brandishing one of the spoons

411

from the kitchen alcove, a tablespoon that usually sat in the coffee jar, making everyone tip too many of the bitter granules into their mugs, making the bad coffee even worse. Jude stared at it. It was caked in mud, as was the hand Eddy held it in.

"What are you up to?" Jude said.

"Nothing," said Eddy. "I was . . . burying a mouse." Jude blinked. "A little mouse had died, through there. I buried it in the garden."

"Of course you did," Jude said. "That sounds just like you, right enough." She knew from Eddy's face, tight like she'd pulled a drawstring, that there was no point asking more, and she walked away. Then a thought struck her and she turned back. "Is this anything to do with why you were in the garden that first day?"

"How many *times* do I have to *tell* you!" said Eddy. She brushed past Jude and went into the toilet, slamming the door and locking it.

"Lowell wants you to Google the hundred-books book club," Jude shouted over the sound of the hot water running. "See if you can find a list of what they published when. It's a long shot. And look on your phone and remind us when Etta Bell died, will you?"

"I can't hear you!" Eddy shouted back, and turned the cold tap on.

They never found the last one. By teatime, filthy and exhausted, surrounded by the litter of a take-away lunch, they had blasted through the whole of the dead room. There were multiple copies of *Ulysses* (45) and several *Wind in the Willows* (46) and more *Godfather*s (49), but not a single book with Todd Jolly's name in it that recorded Etta's death. The latest one they found was too early. It was March 1985's *To The Lighthouse* (61), Todd's verdict: *Doesn't know she's born* and his diary entry: *M. apologised for this one. Said there's a great story coming next month but wouldn't tell me what it was. I asked after Etta. M. said she can't keep anything down. It'll only be days. Sometimes folk can't see what's right in front of them.*

"Who's M.?" said Lowell again.

"Maureen?" said Jude. "Was Maureen a friend of Todd's?"

"Maybe it's someone from the book club. It was before the infernal Internet, after all. Perhaps the book club rep was available on the phone."

"You know what's strange?" said Jude. "Speaking of the book club? We never found a single slip, or covering letter or bill or anything in any of these book club books, did we? If it wasn't for the stickers, we wouldn't know a thing about it."

"Moira," said Lowell. "There's a Moira in the case. Peter Oughton's wife."

"Pretty tenuous," Jude said. "And I'm sure there's something . . .dates and books and notes and names and dates and . . . Oh, Todd! Why didn't you just say what you meant?"

Lowell heaved a sigh up from below the floorboards and rubbed his hands over his face, leaving it streaked with dirt.

"Perhaps he had a very good reason," he said. "In fact, I think I *know* he had a very good reason. And I think I know what it was too. My dear, there's something I need to tell you."

"Oh God, Lowell," said Jude. "If you only knew the things I should tell you and haven't." She saw him look at her with a spark of interest. "Will we just leave it? Will we shut this door and pull a curtain over it and pretend none of it happened? Will we just start from here and be happy?"

They sat in the gloom of the single lightbulb, both on stacks of books, staring at one another. Lowell took a breath to speak and Jude knew from his face that he was going to agree. She wondered if she could follow through with it. Could she really forget those five names?

"Fuck a duck and stuff it with muck!" Eddy's voice carried through the quiet air and made both of them laugh. They heard her footsteps, the padded envelopes slipping and popping as she hurried towards them. She stopped short in the doorway.

"Jesus wept," she said. "What a bloody mess!"

"What is it?" asked Jude.

Eddy grinned and waved her phone. "I got an email back," she said. "I paid extra for the quickest service." She turned to Lowell. "You're my dad."

"Yes . . ." Lowell said, but Jude could feel her eyes growing wide as her mind started to whir.

"Yeah, but —" Eddy said. "I — Okay, I maybe should have told you this, but I didn't think you were. I didn't think you could be. So I nicked your toothbrush and sent it away for a paternity test, and you are."

"Whose toothbrush have I been using?" said Lowell. "The red one." Eddy grimaced. Then Lowell seemed to catch up with her words. "You didn't think — You came here to trick me?"

"No!" Eddy said. "It was after I got here.

415

I wasn't born in June, Dad. I was born in April. I wasn't born nine months after OJ night, see?"

"How can you not know when you were born?" said Lowell, blinking. He rubbed his face again.

Eddy turned a beseeching look on Jude. Jude thought about the horoscopes and the birthstones and the reluctance of Miranda to get involved with social services, her inability to procure a passport and move to the west of Ireland. "It's a long story," she said. "And I've got another one, actually."

"So have I," said Lowell. "As I was just saying, dearest. Dear me, yes, I think I do anyway. Let's go round to Jamaica. Three hot baths and a pot of tea."

"But we're taking the books," said Jude. "All the hundred-books books. They've got a story to tell too."

TWENTY-SEVEN

"Oh great!" said Eddy as they climbed out of the car. Mrs. Hewston was on the move. They could see her torchlight bobbing as she trotted over the grass, the raindrops caught in its beam like fireflies.

"Go in, dear child," said Lowell. "Don't catch cold. And, darling, if you could fetch the golf umbrella from the stand there and hold it over me, I'll carry the boxes."

"Darling!" said Eddy and went into the house hooting with laughter. Jude kept her grin in check as she pulled the umbrella free from the tangle of fishing rods and walking sticks jammed in beside it and hid her face under it as she went back out again.

"Having another run at it, Mrs. Hewston?" she said, as she drew up beside Lowell again. "We saw you this morning."

Mrs. Hewston stopped short. She was holding a small collapsible brolly, one of the ones that fits in a handbag but isn't robust enough for anything more than a gentle shower. Indeed, this one had a crooked spoke, so some of the rain was dripping onto Mrs. Hewston's shoulder.

"I turned back," she said. "This morning. I remembered I'd left the grill on."

"Good thing," Jude said. "Can't be too careful. I suppose you've heard what happened at Jolly's Cottage?"

"I did!" said the woman. "I'm just relieved to see you're all right."

Jude frowned at her. "You knew I was all right, Mrs. H.," she said. "We met the night before. You knew I was staying here."

Mrs. Hewston gave a laugh with more bravery in it than amusement. "Old age, hen. It comes to us all and it doesn't come itself. That had flown right out of my mind when I heard in the Co-op this morning about the fire."

"So what did you come to tell us?" said Jude. "Or ask us?"

"Oh!" said Mrs. Hewston. "There I go again. I'll need a minder soon. Well, I was looking out for you, you see, to tell you this: Jackie McLennan is much better. Maureen told me. And so I was looking out for you, as I say. And I need to tell you: men came."

"Yes," said Lowell. "Thank you, Mrs. Hewston. Those were firemen, bringing me home from Kirk Cottage. But thank you."

"No, no, no, no," Mrs. Hewston said. "Not them! I mean later. I was looking out later and two men came. Drove right up the drive and got out, banged on the door, and looked in the windows. Walked right round the house."

"Really?" said Lowell. "How distressing for you. They were probably police, or perhaps fire investigators."

"They didn't look like police," Mrs. Hewston said. Jude was suddenly aware of a movement. Eddy was standing in the shadows of the vestibule, hidden behind the porch light. "They certainly weren't Stranraer police." She dropped her voice as she went on, "I don't mean anything by this, but one of them was very dark."

"Jesus Christ!" said Eddy.

"You know I don't care to hear His name taken in vain, dear," said Mrs. Hewston.

"Aye, well, He was probably quite 'dark' too," Eddy said.

"Thank you," said Lowell, putting a hand on Mrs. Hewston's shoulder and turning her a little to face back towards her cottage. "Thank you for the information. You're a good neighbour."

"I try," she said. "I don't like to stick my nose in, but I —"

419

The end of it was lost under peals of laughter from Eddy. Jude shushed her but, when she turned back, Mrs. Hewston was well away over the lawns, her torch beam quivering with indignation. Jude, in spite of everything, felt a small tug of tenderness towards her. She really was old and getting wandered. Then something struck her.

"Mrs. H.!" she shouted.

The woman turned. "Mrs. Hewston, hen. Not to criticise you, but I don't care for nicknames."

"What was it you came to tell us this morning?" Jude shouted.

"What?"

"This morning when you turned back because the grill was on? What was it you wanted to say?"

"I told you!" she shouted. "About Jackie. And the strange men. And to say I was so sorry to hear about the fire."

"But that was after —" Jude began. Then she saw the way the rain was soaking the woman's shoulder, the way it dripped off the buckled umbrella, and she waved a hand. "Never mind," she shouted. "On you go."

Lowell had started moving books, doing without the golf umbrella. Jude stood staring until the torchlight winked out and one

420

of the small back windows of the bungalow lit up instead. Mrs. Hewston was safely home for the night.

"Poor old girl," she said to Lowell as he came back, empty-handed and puffing.

"You're a very kind woman," he said.

"She's completely losing it," said Jude. "She doesn't even know what time of day it is." She shivered and Lowell took hold of her hand, slamming down the boot with the other.

"I'll get the rest of this later," he said. "Let's go in."

They heard Eddy crying when they were halfway through the little pantry connecting the kitchen to the front parts of the house. Lowell dropped Jude's hand and bolted through the door.

"I'm all right," Eddy said, swiping viciously at her tears. She sniffed deeply and spat into the sink. "Yuck, sorry."

"My dearest, dearest child," said Lowell, striding over and wrapping her in his arms. "What's wrong, my little one? Tell me."

"Nothing," she said. "I'm happy. I'm happy you're my dad even though I don't see how you can be." She leaned against him, sobbing.

"Well, shush then," said Lowell. "Dry your tears."

Eddy sniffed again and then made a gagging noise. "Fucking hell, Dad, your jacket honks. You need to send every stitch you own to get cleaned, and I don't know what you use for deodorant but it's not working."

"You are a wretch and an urchin," said Lowell, but he was still patting her back. "If I had spoken to my father that way he'd have hit me with his slipper."

"Aye well, I've smelt your slippers too and they'll need to be taken to the special bit of the dump and signed for."

Jude had to turn away until she brought her face back under control.

"I'm not at all in favour of this modern fad of washing oneself to a sliver," Lowell said. "It's unhealthy. I suspect it's American."

"Well, I'm in favour and Jude's in favour," Eddy said, "so you're outnumbered. Tough shit and put a shower in." She pulled away from him, yanked a long bolt of paper towel from the rack and blew her nose enormously. "And speaking about your dad," she said. "Do you want to go first? We're all coming clean, aren't we?"

Lowell stared at her for a moment and then sank into a chair. "I don't know why you pretend to be such a churl," he said. "Anyone as perspicacious as you must have brains somewhere."

"Perspicacious," Eddy repeated. "I literally have never heard that word in my life."

"Well, anyway, I shall go first," Lowell said. After a sigh he went on. "It's the dates. Norma Oughton to Todd Jolly. Late 1983 to early 1985. As soon as you said the dates, my dear, I started to wonder." He broke off and looked around himself and although he said nothing, Jude interpreted the look correctly.

"Glass of wine?" she said.

"At least," said Lowell. "Might take whisky."

"I'd kill for a voddy and Sprite," said Eddy. "Even just the Sprite. I'm definitely coming with you to Tesco next time."

Jude opened the dresser cupboard and took out a bottle of red. Then she took down two of the good dusty glasses from the open shelves above and set the lot in front of Lowell with the corkscrew.

He was still staring at the dresser.

"Who moved the vase?" he said, nodding at it.

Jude followed his gaze and then frowned at Eddy.

"It's there for Jude," Eddy said. "It's

therapy. Look, I didn't think it mattered. It must have been sitting there for months."

"It's been sitting there for years," Lowell said. "Your mother cut that forsythia before she left."

"You've had dead flowers in your front lobby for *twenty years*?" said Jude. "Why?"

"It started as an act of faith," said Lowell. "I believed she'd come back, and I left it for her. And then . . . well, dear me, the days go by. And then the years and then all of a sudden one is old. I can almost understand it when I think of it that way. Not the flowers. I'm thinking of the thing I must tell you."

"We won't judge," said Jude. "God knows, we're in no position to."

"Speak for yourself," said Eddy, inevitably.

"It's the dates," Lowell said again, ignoring her. "Norma Oughton died about six weeks after my mother."

"So?" said Eddy. "I mean, sorry about your mum, but it was a while ago. So . . . so?"

"I think my father killed them," Lowell said, simply. "We were clutching at straws blaming the relatives. I think as long as my mother was alive he kept up the façade of . . . whatever it was, but as soon as she was gone he couldn't get away quick

424

enough. He had a handful of old patients. A Norfolk handful, counting Lorna McLennan, and since he couldn't see his way clear to retiring before they were gone, he helped them get gone sooner. Killed them, signed their death certificates, and went to their funerals."

"But . . ." Jude took a deep swallow of red wine. It was rich and full-tasting with a bite at its back, making her think of blood, warm and metallic. She shuddered but took another swallow anyway. "But he threatened to ask for exhumations."

"Double bluff," said Eddy. "Classic."

"And he didn't kill Lorna," Jude insisted. "He had an alibi."

"Ah yes, Mrs. Hewston," Lowell said. "Well, if providing an alibi bags a free cottage for life, then providing a false alibi certainly should, shouldn't it?"

"Why would she do that?" Jude said. "Why would she lie for your dad?" But as soon as she asked the question, the answer was clear.

"She adored him," said Lowell. "Even if she found out something like that about him, I can imagine that she wouldn't want him brought low. Oh yes, I can easily imagine that."

"Yeah, but if you're right," Eddy said,

"and I'm not saying you are — but if you're right, who left that anonymous note for Jude? And who did Jackie phone?"

"The phone call was irrelevant. She has daughters and sisters and you women are always ringing one another up about something. Usually," he added with a look at Jude.

"But who set the fire?" asked Eddy.

"I don't know," said Lowell. "I don't understand the details, but it makes sense of one fact that's never made any sense before: My father died a very unhappy man. His last years were haunted."

"But that's not right," Jude said. "If he was racked with remorse when he started it, why would he carry on? It was over the course of better than a year, remember?"

"I didn't say it was remorse," said Lowell. "I think he was haunted by the spectre of being reported and shamed. It was fear."

"It might have been both," said Jude. "They're a killer combination if you get the mix just right. I should know." She was scared almost every minute of every day, and guilty for being scared instead of just being sorry. And in the few moments she felt neither — in the moments she felt happy — the guilt just gathered strength to hit her harder on its return.

Lowell was looking at her not with his dim, scattered look and not with his rueful look, the one he kept for the modern world and Eddy's language. He was regarding her with a very steady and affectionate gaze, as though nothing she could say could shock him. She didn't believe it, but that only spurred her on. If she had to lose him, the sooner the better, before she could get used to having him. Before the loss would wound her. Rip off the plaster, as Eddy said.

Another gulp of wine and she was down to the sediment, black flakes sticking to her tongue.

"You know about my parents," she said. "And you know about my husband. But you don't know about my husband's new wife and their baby."

"Except yeah he does, cos I told him," Eddy said.

"Devastating for you," said Lowell.

"But I never told about the night of the funeral," Eddy added.

"Only because you haven't had a chance yet!" said Jude, but she smiled to show she wasn't angry. In fact, she wished he *did* know, then she wouldn't have to say it. She fixed her gaze on the tabletop and spoke quickly, describing how she hid in the cupboard, Max passing out, Raminder's arrival, standing behind the door in the shadows with her heart banging at the base of her throat, Raminder's sobs and her flight. And the moment she tripped, that slow-motion moment when it seemed impossible that she could fall too fast for Jude to catch her, because she was falling so slowly and Jude reached out so quick, like a lizard's tongue, but all she managed to do was put the tip of her middle finger on the fluttering end of Raminder's scarf, feeling the slide of chiffon before it followed her plunge, down and down, and then settled softly on her back as she lay so still at the bottom.

"And the baby was screaming and screaming. I looked into her pram and her face was bright red and her eyes were shut and her little mouth was wide open. She was yelling and waving her fists, kicking her legs. I put my hand on her to try to comfort her and maybe if she had quieted, I'd have been able to think, but she . . . she hated me! She screamed even louder, even higher, and she went rigid! She arched her back right off the pram, like she was trying to buck my hand off her. I was . . . it sounds stupid, but I was scared. I didn't know what to do."

"So you phoned 999," said Eddy. "Didn't you?"

"Of course you did," Lowell said.

"Yeah but . . . Okay, I'm just going to tell you and if you want me to go, I'll go."

"I can't imagine anything you could say that would make me want you to go," said Lowell.

Eddy snorted. "Get a room."

"I dialled 999," said Jude. "But I used Raminder's phone. Because I'd already decided I needed to get out of there. And I knew if I used my phone, they'd know. She had hers in her hand when she fell and it was still in her hand. I took it from her. Her hand was warm, but limp. She wasn't gripping it. I took it and I dialled and they say . . . 'which service?' and you're supposed to say ambulance or police or fire, I think. But this woman said 'which service?' and I said . . . I said . . . I said . . ."

She squeezed her eyes shut and remembered. The absolute stillness of Raminder on the floor, with her feet up on the second step and her hair covering her face and spilling out in a pool around her head. And the sound of the baby, screaming as if someone was torturing her, and the feel of Raminder's phone in her hand, the smell of Raminder's perfume — something light and sweet — clinging to it, and then her own voice saying it.

He pushed me.

"And then I wiped the phone and put it back in her hand and I stood up and went out, and I left the door open and I walked away. I could hear the baby until I turned the corner onto the main road. But I kept walking and I walked all the way to the tube and took the tube to the station, and when I got to the station I got a train and I came here. So that's what I did. I left a baby alone in a house with one passed out and one dead. She tripped and yet I said, 'he pushed me,' and Max wouldn't remember what happened because he never does. I used her phone and I said, 'he pushed me.' "

"Well, my dear," said Lowell, "from what you've told us, I'd say he did."

"Don't be kind to me," said Jude. "I'll start crying and I'll never stop."

"Can I say something?" said Eddy. "It might count as kind, but it's true, and I think you should know."

Jude nodded.

"She wasn't dead."

Jude felt a wave of something she couldn't name spread through her body, starting at her stomach, flooding in both directions, leaving her ringing from head to toe.

"Are you going to faint?" said Lowell, half standing.

"She was knocked out," Eddy said. "But she's fine now. And the baby's fine too."

"But —" Jude began. "But I saw the headlines. They said 'tragic' and there were so many hits and you told me everyone's looking for me."

"Oh, yeah, that's true too," said Eddy. "They knew you were there. One of the downstairs neighbours saw you leave the house. Jesus, Jude. If you'd Googled it like any normal person . . ."

"One of the . . . I didn't even *know* those neighbours. Never so much as glimpsed them from one year's end to the next. Never heard a peep out of any of them."

"Yeah, well, they knew you," Eddy said. "This one did anyway. You know the sort — 'didn't think much to the Muslim moving in.' That's a quote he gave to the *Sun.*"

"She's a Sikh," said Jude.

"Well, anyway, he was looking out and saw you running away and heard the baby crying. So he called the cops and said there was a suspicious person — wait for it — who had come to live in the street and she'd just chased away the resident of the house *and* she was neglecting her child!"

"Wow," said Jude.

"Yeah, so you're wanted, but as a witness, Jude. Not as a suspect. Just to corroborate,

431

you know."

"Corroborate what?" said Jude. "I thought you said they were all okay."

"No," said Eddy. "I said *she's* okay and the *baby's* okay. He's dead, though."

TWENTY-EIGHT

Jude drank another whole glass of wine, sipping steadily at it until it was gone.

"How did he die?" she said, although she was sure she knew.

"Aspirated emesis,' " Eddy replied. "Whatever that means."

Jude blinked at her, the blinks as steady as the sips had been, and then shook herself. "Look, never mind this right now," she said. "Obviously, I'll get in touch. I'll phone Raminder or something, but forget it for now. We've got more important things to think about. Lowell, what are you going to do? If it weren't for the fire, I'd say let sleep —"

"Eh, excuse me?" said Eddy, waving a hand in Jude's face. "I think you're forgetting something, aren't you? Never mind your dead ex-husband and never mind *his* dead dad and five old people who'd be well dead now anyway. I've just found out I don't know when I was born, remember?

I've just found out that for nineteen years I've basically not known who I am."

"You were born in April," Jude said. "Aries with a diamond birthstone, not Cancer with a pearl. In other words, you were three months early and you were conceived on October the third. OJ day."

"Don't mind me," said Lowell. "I'll just sit here quietly while you discuss my child's conception." He had never sounded more like Eddy.

"But why did she keep quiet about Dad right till the end?" said Eddy.

"You might never know," Jude said. "You might have to just —"

"Eighteen," Lowell said suddenly.

"Eighteen what?" said Eddy.

"My dear child, I know you think you're finished with school, but I'm going to put my foot down. You are not a stupid girl, but you are pitifully uneducated."

"None taken," said Eddy. "Jeez."

"You are not nineteen," Lowell said. "You are only eighteen. If you were conceived, as you two so baldly stated, on the third of October 1995 and born in either the April or June of 1996, then you are only eighteen."

"But I'm not!" said Eddy. "I had my eighteenth when Mum was still well. We had a party. I got legally hammered. And then for my nineteenth we had a picnic in her hospital room. I'm nineteen."

"You can't be," Lowell said. "Miranda must have lost track somewhere along the line. Sometime in her travelling years."

"Oh," said Eddy, in a sort of small cry. She looked down at the swell of her belly, put both hands on it at its widest point, and burst into tears.

"What?" said Jude. "What is it?"

"Is it starting?" said Lowell, shooting to his feet.

"I was seventeen," said Eddy, through sobs. "I was too young!"

"People are different at different ages," said Jude, taking one of Eddy's hands and patting it.

"No," said Eddy. "I was too young for it to be legal."

"What are you talking about?" Jude said. She was still clutching Eddy's hand but she had stopped patting.

"I told you!" Eddy said. "I —" She broke off and let out a piercing yell, scrambling out of her seat, pointing at the blackness outside the kitchen window.

Before Lowell or Jude could do more than whip their heads round, the back door burst open and heavy feet, running fast, pounded along the corridor. Lowell leapt up, grabbed Jude and Eddy, and drew them into his arms, backing towards the dresser.

"Never mind me!" Jude said. "Get her away!"

Two men appeared round the corner of the kitchen doorway as Lowell and Eddy made a run for the front of the house. They were dressed in black leather jackets and black jeans and wore heavy boots with rounded toes and long rows of lacing. The sort of boots that might have steel toecaps in them. Jude reached behind her and groped on the dresser top. Her hand found the vase full of dead forsythia and she flung it wildly at them.

One of them, the larger one, screamed and threw himself in front of the other, shielding them both. The vase broke harmlessly against the stiff leather of his jacket and fell, shattering as it hit the floor.

"Who the feck are you? Fecking psycho!" he said in an Irish accent thick enough to block a chimney.

Jude's mind raced wildly around Raminder contracting Irish hit men or Lowell's father, unbeknownst to himself, killing some member of an IRA gang, undercover in Galloway during the Troubles. Then she came back down to somewhere more like

436

reality, some connection much more likely.

"Which one of you two thugs is Dave Preston?" she said. "And what do you want with her? You've no legal rights to anything, you know."

"Look at the state of his jacket!" said the little one. He was pale with very black stubble to match the very black eyelashes ringing his ice-blue eyes. Jude took them in because they were so wide, staring at her in disbelief.

"And who's Dave Preston?" asked the large one. "Has she got a lawyer? Because we can get a lawyer."

"And as for no legal rights," said the little dark one, "we've got a signed agreement. And before you start lying, we saw her, sitting here bold as brass, the wee shite that she is."

"Who *are* you?" said Jude.

"Oh, aye, I'm sure she's kept us quiet," said the large one. "I'm Terry Ennis and this Liam Doyle and we are the fathers of the unborn baby that wee menace has kidnapped, aren't we?"

Jude tried to speak but felt her breath leave her as though she'd been punched. She took a beat and tried again. "Liam and Terry?" she said.

A muffled voice came from just behind

the pantry door. "I didn't keep you quiet. I told them all about you." Eddy opened the door and came sidling in, Lowell behind her with a protective hand on her shoulder. "Eventually."

"It's true?" said Jude. "I mean, it's real? I thought . . . Eddy, I thought you made up 'Liam and Terry' for something to tell your dad for why you were going to go away and come back without a baby."

"What did you think I was going to do with it?" Eddy said.

"Sell it to the highest bidder!" said Liam on a rising note. "We don't even know if it's a boy or a girl because we wanted the surprise. So our child would be out there in Phoenix or Kiev or somewhere and we wouldn't even know if we were looking for a son or a daughter."

"I didn't think you were going to do *anything* with it," Jude said. "I didn't think it was real. I thought you'd bought a foam belly off the Internet to get sympathy when you turned up here."

Eddy stared at her. "Why would you think that?"

"Because you locked yourself in the bathroom and freaked out when Lowell disturbed you, for one thing," Jude said.

"I was doing my roots!" said Eddy. "I

438

freaked out because he gave me a fright and I got the stuff in my eyes! And anyway, I showed you!"

"Not the edges," said Jude. "I thought it was fake."

Eddy walked over to where Jude stood and took her hand. She placed it high on the mound of her stomach. "That's real enough, isn't it?" she said. "Poor wee mite, it's all upset."

Jude had heard it called kicking and heard it described as fluttering, but inside Eddy was a commotion more like a tiny person moving furniture. She felt bumps and jabs and almost took her hand away at the oddness of it.

Eddy turned to the men. "I'm sorry," she said. "My mum died."

"Oh," said Liam. "I'm sorry."

"And she told me, on her deathbed, that this was my dad I'd never met," Eddy jerked her head up to indicate Lowell, who had walked with her and was still standing behind her, gripping her shoulders. "So I just kind of took off. I wasn't really thinking. I was coming back, honest."

"Let's all sit down, shall we?" Lowell said. "Gentlemen? Would you care for a glass of wine or perhaps a cup of tea?"

"Tea would be grand," said Terry, crunching his way towards the table through broken glass. Lowell frowned at it but said nothing.

"So you found out where I was and got the next boat?" Eddy said.

"Flight," said Liam. "Eddy, we're really sorry about your mum and we're really glad about your dad." He smiled at Lowell. "But you've got to understand our position. You just disappeared."

"I signed a contract!" Eddy said.

"Ach, it's hardly worth the paper it's written on," said Terry. "I mean, it records intent, but the law's a bitch. If you had changed your mind . . ."

"As it happens," Lowell said. "The contract is void. And even if it weren't, I would be taking personal responsibility for refunding whatever payment you made to my daughter in order to render it void."

Liam's ice-blue eyes filled with tears and his nose began to turn pink. Terry put his chin in the air and gave a mirthless laugh. "Got it," he said.

"Lowell," said Jude.

"Dad, what the fuck are you doing?" Eddy said. "I'm too young for a baby! And it's not fair on them."

Lowell blinked and frowned, then smacked his hand down on the tabletop.

"Good Lord above, what do you take me for?" he demanded. "Good heavens, I didn't mean to snatch the child from its parents. Dear me, dear me, dear me. Not at all. I simply don't approve of a monetary element being part of family life. And since Eddy was too young to sign the contract, which is therefore null and void anyway, I don't see why there should be grubby commerce associated with my grandchild. It will be my grandchild, chaps, whether you like it or not. I don't have enough family to let any members of it slip through my fingers. I shall repay whatever you gave Eddy and I shall expect visits."

"She wasn't too young," Terry said. "She was eighteen."

"She was seventeen," said Lowell. "She's eighteen now."

"I really don't think that's right," Eddy said. "I would know." She glanced at Liam and Terry, who were nursing the steaming mugs Jude had just handed to them. "We're having a bit of a . . . I don't even know what you'd call it."

"I've thought of something," Jude said. "When was OJ arrested? Because we've all been placing a lot of weight on OJ night — the third of October, 1995 — but there were two OJ nights, weren't there? The verdict and the big chase. I mean, look how mixed up Mrs. Hewston was, thinking you were in America, Lowell, when you were in Plymouth and thinking . . ." When she thought about it for more than a second, though, she could make no sense at all of what Mrs. Hewston said about the last time she'd seen Miranda, busy in the asparagus bed.

"OJ Simpson?" said Liam. "Why are we talking about OJ Simpson?"

"The last time I saw Eddy's mother was the night the verdict was given," Lowell said. "It was the first and last . . . ahem."

"And she planted an asparagus bed and disappeared for ever," said Jude.

"Ha!" said Eddy, looking at her phone. She put her hand on her belly. "Sorry, little darling," she said. "You've proper upset it, you know," she told Liam and Terry with a sideways look. "It never usually goes apeshit when I talk."

"Ha, what?" Jude said.

"The chase through Los Angeles," Eddy read from her screen, "was on June the seventeenth. There you go. June the seventeenth, 1994, I was conceived. OJ night number one."

"Then you'd be twenty-one," said Lowell. "And I didn't even meet Miranda until June the twenty-first that year."

"Are you absolutely sure?" said Jude. "Were you at least on a trip, or coming home then? Because Mrs. Hewston thinks you were mixed up in trouble. Were you in California in the early summer of 1994?"

"I'm not twenty-one," said Eddy. "No *way* I've missed my twenty-first birthday."

"And what about the asparagus bed?" said Liam. "Is that an expression for something filthy we've never heard? I thought I knew them all."

"Wrong time of year for asparagus," said Lowell. "And I've never been to California. I've been to Texas. In fact —"

"I'll go to California with you," said Eddy. "Once I've got my figure back."

"And yes, I'm sure," Lowell said to Jude. "Miranda and Inez and Tommy and Gary came for the Solstice. I'm hardly likely to forget. They stayed all summer and then they left one by one, the last — your mother, Eddy — in the spring of '95. I came home in late April and they'd gone, leaving most of their things and a beautiful asparagus bed behind them. It's not a euphemism," he added, turning to Liam. "I have a splendid garden, even if I say so myself. I'll show you round in the morning. I mean, dear me, I'm assuming you're staying. You're practically family after all, and it's getting late."

"Home from where?" said Jude.

"Dallas," Lowell told her. "A book fair. I remember flying home, happier than I had ever felt in my life. I was oblivious to what was going on around me, completely wrapped up in what was waiting for me back here at Jamaica. And then I arrived and what was waiting for me was nothing. An empty house, no explanation. Silly old fool, to think someone so young would be interested in me. I should have known better. I should certainly know better now." He didn't look at Jude as he spoke. He was rigid with the effort of not looking.

Eddy, in another gesture she seemed to have learned from Lowell over the last few days, put her head in her hands and rubbed her face hard. When she looked up again, her mascara was smeared up to her eyebrows and down to her cheeks, which, along with the white face following all the upsets, made her look more Gothic than ever, with her sheet of black hair falling straight from her prominent parting.

"What is going *on*?" she said. "I was fine with a mum and no dad. It's not that unusual. Now, I just don't know from one minute to the next. Maybe the toothbrush lab's no good. Cost enough, mind you."

"I think they're pretty accurate," said

Liam. "They'd get sued if they weren't. And we looked into it, you know, for after, for if it doesn't look enough like one of us to say for sure. Not that we care — that's the whole point, but in case there was ever a bone marrow or a kidney type situation."

"Jesus, it's not even born yet and you're after its kidney!" said Eddy.

"I think he meant in case the child ever needed one," said Jude. "Right guys?"

"So," said Terry, well-used to ignoring Eddy, "have I got this right? You slept with her mum one night only and you're definitely her dad — passed the paternity test and everything — but that would make her born when she wasn't born?"

"Sitting. Right. Here," said Eddy.

"Jaysis Gawd," said Liam. "Are you serious? This is your big mystery? It's like that old riddle about the surgeon. How long have youse all been scratching your heads when it's right in front of you?"

Lowell frowned and Eddy scowled, but Jude thought she could feel a glimmer of something, far off but getting closer, like a heat shine on a long straight road.

Liam said, "If she's nineteen — and she should know — and you're her dad by a DNA test, but you didn't sleep with Miranda until it was too late . . . it's obvious."

445

He turned to Eddy. "Your mum's not your mum, is she?"

The heat shimmer was gone. In its place were letters three feet tall, laid out in front of Jude, spelling the answer to the question she hadn't even asked. The answer to a hundred little questions she hadn't even realised were nipping at her.

Eddy said nothing, just sat as still as death. A girl in the family portrait looking out into the future, sharp and true, while around her, her parents were blurred, half lost and unknowable.

"It explains a lot," Jude said gently. "It explains what your mum was so sorry about, while she was dying. And it explains why she kept you away and then sent you back here. It explains the problem with your birth certificate, Eddy."

"Wait, hang on," said Liam. "You can't fake a birth certificate."

Then Eddy spoke. "Yeah, you can," she said glumly. "If you're a traveller in Ireland and you roll up with a baby you haven't got round to registering yet, nobody puts you in jail for it. I've seen it, in the Community, loads of times. People having kids on their own and only getting it registered when they need the doctor."

"But Eddy, I don't think Miranda faked

your birth certificate," Jude said. "I don't think you've got one. Didn't you always say she got bolshy if something official was going on? And she never took you west to the coast because to get into Ireland you need a passport, and to get a passport you need your papers?"

"How can I not have a birth certificate?" Eddy said. "I mean, sure, yeah, I couldn't find it, but I thought she'd lost it and I'd get a copy. This can't be right. Mum freaked about forms because she didn't like official stuff. Didn't like Social Services and nosy parkers. Cos she'd been in the system herself. That's all."

"That much is true," Lowell said. "Miranda was rather down on officialdom even before you were born, Eddy. As you said, she had spent time in a children's home and I think she had no great faith in social workers and whatnot."

"But the main thing," Jude said, "is it makes sense of the night you were born."

Eddy turned slowly to face her as if she had string tied to her chin. "The night . . . ?"

Jude nodded. "Mrs. Hewston isn't as addled as we think," she said. "You really were born right here at Jamaica House, like she said. But it was in the spring, when Miranda put forsythia branches in the vase

447

in the porch and planted an asparagus bed. When Mrs. Hewston had her windows open to let the scent of the flowers drift in. And when Lowell was in Dallas."

"Oh my word!" Lowell said. "And Mrs. Hewston was glued to the news."

"Right," said Eddy. "OJ. *October.*"

"No," said Jude. "She never said OJ, did she? We added that bit. Eddy, what day did Miranda say was your birthday?"

"April the nineteenth," Eddy said.

"Google it," said Jude, nodding at Eddy's phone.

"There's no need," Lowell said. "I remember."

But Eddy's thumbs moved faster than he spoke. "It says some guy called Timothy McVeigh blew up a place in Oklahoma."

"That's actually pretty near Dallas," Jude said. "Mrs. Hewston wasn't *too* crazy to worry, in a funny sort of way."

"So . . . I really *am* Miranda's?" Eddy said, her face screwed up in an effort to understand. "Dad, you must have forgotten. Maybe a party. You were smoking everything you could lay your hands on, pretty much, weren't you? Dad?" Lowell stared at her but said nothing. "And I *look* like her," Eddy insisted. "Everyone says so."

"No," said Jude. "You remind everyone

here of your mum — that's true. But you don't look like Miranda except for your black hair."

"It's dyed," Eddy said. "It's no colour at all, really."

"Oh!" said Lowell, softly. "Why didn't she tell me?"

"What's this now?" said Liam.

"Maybe she didn't know," said Jude. "That does happen."

"But she was tiny!" Lowell had stood up and was walking towards the door to the dining room. "I showed you."

"Who was tiny?" Terry said.

"*I* was tiny, Mum said," Eddy shouted after Lowell. Then she slumped back in her chair. "Can I still call her that?"

"Of course," said Jude. "DNA doesn't matter if she looked after you her whole life and loved you." But as she said it, her mind flashed on a gold lipstick tube stuffed into the shriveled elastic strap of a vanity mirror for twenty years.

Lowell was back, carrying one of the albums full of photographs and also a heavy silver frame. "What did you say?" he asked Eddy.

"Mum said I was tiny," Eddy repeated. "She said I was like a fairy. She called me her little changeling."

"Did she indeed?" said Lowell, sitting. "I recognised you as soon as you stepped into LG on that first day, you know. And then I convinced myself I was wrong. I told myself you looked like my mother." He turned the silver frame to show them all. The woman in the photograph was as fine-boned as Eddy and as pale, but she had a swan-neck and a graceful jaw, deep-set hooded eyes, completely different from Eddy's flattish oval, her little nose the only sharp thing on her face.

Lowell opened the album to the photograph Jude knew he would, the last one of Miranda and her friend, Inez. Small, pale, lost Inez, who everyone forgot to mention because beside the other girl she simply faded until she had all but disappeared from view.

This time, looking at her, Jude didn't know how she could have missed it. They were identical apart from the hair: Inez's a dazzling veil against the window and Eddy's the same soft, draping sheet but dyed the impossible black that Jude kicked herself for not seeing through before now. They had the same slightly twisted little nose, the fine collarbones and tiny wrists. Inez's breasts were high and round and her stomach flat behind a cheesecloth shirt, but the legs below it in their jeans were Eddy's pipe-cleaner legs as plain as day.

"That's your mother," Lowell said. "Her name is Inez Cato and I loved her. She broke my heart when she left, and she's just broken it again today. I have no earthly idea why she would do such a thing as to go and take you with her when she didn't even wan—"

"Don't say that, Lowell," said Jude. "Maybe she didn't know how you felt. Maybe she thought you'd send her away anyway. We can't know what was going on inside her head."

"Not until we find her!" said Eddy. "I mean, I'll always love Mùm — she's my mum! — but if I can find this Inez woman . . . maybe I've got brothers and sisters!"

"Of course she knew I loved her!" Lowell said. "I wanted to marry her. I gave her my mother's ring and she accepted it."

"Did she take it with her?" said Terry. "If she absconded with a family heirloom you might be able to get official help tracing her."

"But you didn't know she was pregnant?" Jude said. "How long were you in Dallas?"

"Less than a month," Lowell said. "If Eddy was born on the nineteenth of April, even if she was early, Inez must have known. I would have noticed. We were, dear me, we were sharing a room."

"It happens," said Jude. "Usually with young girls. How old was she?"

"Twenty," said Lowell. "And I was forty, to save you making calculations. I know it sounds tawdry but I loved her, and I thought she loved me. I thought we were going to live here together and she'd paint and take pictures and I'd potter around in the book-shop and we'd be happy."

"She didn't nick your ring," Eddy said. She hadn't spoken for a moment or two and when she did her voice was gravelly. "*She* didn't nick it. Mum had it. She gave it to me."

"What did you do with it?" said Lowell. Eddy put her hands in her cardigan pockets and balled them up into fists. "Did you sell it to buy your ticket here? Your price is far above rubies, you know," he added gently.

"You sold it once you knew we'd found you," said Liam. "So you could scarper!"

"Talk sense," Eddy said. "That was only today. How could I have sold it already?"

"You're not exactly denying it," Terry countered.

"I was scared!" Eddy said. "All that stuff you said about breach of contract and suing

452

me. I only wanted to see my dad! I was always going to come back in time for the baby. Ask Jude! Before you started in on threatening me, I was totally coming back."

"Sorry," said Terry. "Heightened emotion. We've waited so long."

"Lucky little baby this, isn't it?" said Eddy, with tears in her eyes. "Two dads besotted with it, and a granddad. Not like me, eh? My mum just abandoned me with her pal and my dad just wants his precious diamond ring back." She took one hand out of her pocket and threw it at Lowell. "Here!" she spat.

He caught it in one hand and then opened his palm and regarded it calmly. It was a heavy, old-fashioned setting, as crusty as a barnacle and tarnished with dirt.

"Eddy, that's not fair," Jude said. "He just said he'd rather have you."

"No he didn't. He said some guff about rubies that could mean anything," Eddy said. "And don't blame Mum either. She gave it to me the night before she died and she told me if I went to Lowland Glen, to bury it in the garden. She probably meant here at the house, eh? But I didn't know your name was the same as the shop, did I? So I buried it in the garden at the back of LG."

453

"*That's* what you were doing that first day!" said Jude.

"Yes. Fuck's sake. Happy now?' Eddy said. "And then I dug it up today. Because . . ." She flashed a look at Liam. "All right, shoot me! I was *scared.*"

"Did she say why she wanted you to bury it?" Jude said.

"She was always burying something somewhere," said Eddy. "Leather boots and dead things and sacral stones. I thought it was because it was my birthstone and this was going to be my home. I — I — I can't take any more."

"Of course you can't, you poor love," said Jude, standing. "You need a hot bath and some soup in bed and a good night's sleep. You need to put all of this out of your mind and let us see to it. We all care about you very much. And we'll sort it out. It'll be better in the morning."

Eddy had started listening with a wry look, but the tug of comfort was too much for her and she was on her feet, nodding, by the time Jude was done.

"Shall I run your bath?" Jude said. Eddy shook her head. "Well, I'll warm some pyjamas round a bottle. Shout down when you're ready for them."

Eddy looked around the four of them, as

454

if trying to think what to say, then gave up and trailed out of the room.

"Is a hot bath safe?" said Terry.

"It's essential," Jude told him. "She's not a vessel, she's a person." Then she reached out and took the ring from Lowell.

"My dear," said Lowell, "why on earth would Miranda tell Eddy to bury Inez's ring in my garden?" But Jude thought he wasn't really asking. She thought somewhere, deep down inside, he already knew.

"She meant to bring the baby back to you," Jude said. "That's why she made the trip here in the autumn of 1995 and slept with you. So that, a few years later, she could roll up with a kid about the right age and you'd believe her. But then she married that rotten Dave, and by the time she left him she didn't trust men anymore. So she never returned."

"But the ring?" said Lowell. "Why did Inez give Miranda her ring? And where is she?"

"Oh, Lowell," said Jude. "Ten years you said one end of that bloody asparagus bed was giving you bumper crops and the other end was only so-so. You couldn't get that just from burying a placenta, could you?"

TWENTY-NINE

Jude knew the jig was up. A police tent draws the press like jam draws wasps, and by lunchtime the next day there were two outside broadcast vans and a clutch of print reporters gathered beside Lowell's garden wall.

Even without the incidentals — the pregnant teenager and the two waiting dads living in the house; the mysterious London stranger who seemed to have unearthed it all somehow; and the fire in a graveyard, difficult to connect in any sensible way but irresistibly creepy — even without all of that, an exhumation was big news. The worst thing was that they'd got hold of Lowell's hobby. Someone he had outbid at an auction told the press that Lowland Glen collected corpse portraits, and the headline writers went into orbit. The one comfort was that, unbelievably, Mrs. Hewston kept out of it.

Only that saved Eddy from a meltdown. Lowell and Jude told her together, as gently as they could, the next morning, but her breathing grew fast and shallow as she listened and by the time Lowell had finished speaking, hot tears were spilling down her cheeks and she was shouting.

"Miranda killed her?" she blared, sitting up in her bed with the covers pushed to her waist. Jude wondered how she could ever have doubted the pregnancy. In the thin nightie the massive swell of Eddy's stomach seemed to pulse. "She's dead? She killed her and *stole* me?"

"Your mother —" Lowell began.

"She's not my mother!" Eddy screamed, high as a train whistle.

Hovering at her bedroom door, Terry cleared his throat. "You should try and stay calm," he managed to get out before Lowell wheeled round and marched over to him.

"You" — he poked a finger into Terry's chest — "might think you bought my daughter, but you are mistaken. She will shout and swear as much as she needs to while learning this news and if you don't like it you can jolly well lump it."

"Fucking hell, Dad," said Eddy.

"Good girl," said Lowell, coming back. "That's more like it." He resettled himself

457

on the edge of Eddy's bed and took her hand.

Jude took her other one, ice-cold with shock, and squeezed it.

"I meant Inez," Lowell said. "I have many, many things to tell you about Inez, when you're ready."

"But why did she do it?" Eddy said. "If Mum had *loved* you — if she had wanted to get rid of Inez to *get* you — that would be nearly . . . but why did she do it?"

She was so very far from ready. Miranda was her mother, and it was Miranda's motives and actions that were filling her head. Jude supposed there would be a stage when she realised what she had lost with Inez's death. She hoped there wouldn't be a time when she realised what a close call it was — how easy it would have been for Miranda simply to kill them both; snuff the life out of the baby and bury her too. And the more Jude thought about it, the more the idea gathered a head of steam. Miranda had risked a lot over the years to keep Eddy. There had to be a reason.

"We don't know that she did anything," Jude found herself saying. "We don't actually know if Inez is dead — we need to wait and see what happens out there. And even if she is, we don't know why she died.

Maybe Miranda did no more than hide her body and take you."

Eddy blinked once or twice and then lay back against her pillows. "That does make tons more sense," she said. "If Inez died and Miranda told people, I'd have ended up in care, wouldn't I? I'd have ended up in a children's home, Social Services and all that. She'd have done a lot to stop that happening."

"At great personal risk to herself, I might add," said Lowell. "She loved you."

Eddy nodded. "You know when she came back, Dad? In the October? Did she ask you about moving away?" She searched Lowell's face hungrily. "Cos you know what occurred to me? She couldn't live here, knowing that Inez was . . . could she? She'd go ape. Did she try to persuade you to move but you said no and she couldn't explain why and so she was kind of stuck? Did she?"

"Um, dear me," said Lowell. "It was one evening and it was years ago. I can't honestly remember anything like that."

"I bet she did," Eddy said. "That's it. She tried to save Inez but she failed, and she didn't want me to go into care so she did the only thing she could, and then she tried to wangle it all so her and you and me would all live together somewhere, but it

459

was a no-go. I'm not blaming you, Dad. You didn't know."

"Thank you," Lowell said and managed not to sound too dry.

"Now get lost so's I can get up and dressed."

Jude and Lowell walked in silence down the first flight of stairs. On the bedroom landing, Jude took his hand, raised it to her lips, and kissed it.

"It's just a defence mechanism, all that," she said. "It'll stand her in good stead."

"Oh quite quite," said Lowell. "I'm here for her to rail at and get it out of her system. Much better than being angry with poor Miranda, really."

"I'm just praying she doesn't go over it and over it," Jude said. "Or pretty soon she'll wonder why Miranda didn't get help while Inez was still alive. Why she didn't call a doctor when she knew about the labour."

"Dear me, dear me," said Lowell.

"Unless Inez didn't tell her."

Lowell shook his head. "They were inseparable," he said. "I can't believe that."

"So . . . no way Miranda would have harmed her then?"

Lowell was quiet for a moment. "If it were the other way around," he began, "Inez wouldn't have harmed Miranda. Or a flea, come to that." He made a sound somewhere between a sigh and a sob and then said. "Forgive me. But Miranda was a woman of great passions and appetites. She flew into rages as easily as she was transported into raptures. If she discovered that Inez had a secret, that Inez and I had kept Miranda out when she thought she was the centre of our little band here . . ."

"Let's see what the doctor says," Jude murmured.

They stepped over the landing and into Lowell's bedroom, which had a side window. Down at the edge of the garden the white tent billowed and snapped in the wind and, as they watched, someone inside it poked at the sagging roof to spill the rain gathered there. Then, realising that the hubbub of the reporters had grown louder and realising too that every camera was now trained on the pair them standing there, they drew back. Lowell pulled the shutters roughly over the window and bolted them.

"It won't take long," Jude said. "She can't be too far down, can she? One woman alone doing it all on one night?"

"Miranda was a force of nature," Lowell said. "If she did bury a corpse, it would be deep."

Four of them — Lowell, Jude, Liam, and Terry — were in the kitchen when the knock came. The doctor was a short, broad woman in her fifties, with hair too thin to withstand the drenching she had taken on her way up the garden. It was plastered to her head and rivulets were running down her cheeks and the sides of her nose. The policeman with her had a Gortex jacket on over his suit. He pushed the hood back once they were inside.

"We need to question you, Mr. . . . Glen, isn't it?" the policeman said. "I'm Inspector Begbie and this Ms. Naughton, the forensic specialist from Glasgow."

"Sharon," said the doctor, smiling. "Are you all family?"

"More or less," Lowell said. "Modern family, you know. Dear me, yes, very much so. This is my partner and these are the parents-to-be of my daughter's biological child. She's resting. But I can fetch her."

Give them their due, they caught up without so much as a blink. Sharon smiled at each of them and the inspector took out a notebook and snapped open its elastic strap.

"Full names?" he said. He wrote down TERRY ENNIS and LIAM DOYLE without reacting, but Jude was sure his pencil hovered before he printed JEMIMAH HAMNER. "So," he went on, "you were right enough, Mr. Glen. There is indeed the skeletonised remains of a corpse buried in your garden. Who is she?"

"Definitely a she?" said Lowell. He had drained of colour but his voice sounded steady enough.

"Most definitely a she," the doctor said. "From her size alone I'd have said it but also, her pelvic girdle is detached. She died either giving birth or very shortly afterwards and men tend not to, you know." Even these words were softened by a smile at Liam and Terry.

"And do you know who she is?" the inspector persisted.

Lowell nodded. "Her name is Inez Cato. I've got photographs of her, if they'd help."

"Alive?" said Begbie, and then blushed at revealing he'd heard the gossip.

"Photos would certainly help," said Sharon. "Although DNA would help more."

"She was my daughter's mother," Lowell said. "DNA won't be a problem."

"Your wife?" said Begbie, and Jude wasn't the only one who noticed the change in his voice.

"My fiancée," said Lowell. "She lived here from early summer in 1994 until the following spring and then — so I thought —

she left. In fact, I see she didn't."

"You see?" said Begbie, with another sharp drop in the temperature of his voice. "She 'left' and the baby stayed and it's all news to you, sir, is it?"

"What did she die of?" Jude asked the doctor.

Begbie rumbled but Sharon ignored him. "I can't see any signs of trauma beyond the evidence of childbirth," she said. "Of course, I'll have to have a good look at the cleaned bones for nicks and dents."

"Nicks?" said Liam.

"It's unusual for a fatal stabbing not to leave marks on bone somewhere," Sharon said. "Or for strangulation not to compress at least one vertebra. But there are no breaks, nothing dislocated. If I had to guess, I'd say she died of natural causes — haemorrhage, eclampsia, scepticaemia — childbirth, I suppose you'd say."

"Well, aren't you a wee ray of sunshine," said a voice from the kitchen door. Eddy stood there in another cardigan and tights outfit. "That's set my mind right at rest."

"Perinatal mortality rates are lower in the UK than in any other developed nation in the world," said Sharon. "We even beat Scandinavia because they've got so many elderly prims and not as many teenagers as

464

us. You're doing it at the right time, flower, at least as far as your body's concerned."

"This is all getting a bit too much like a tea party," said Inspector Begbie. "Mr. Glen, perhaps you'd be more comfortable answering these questions at the station?"

"Oh no, I don't think so at all, Inspector," Lowell said. "My family needs me here today, I'm afraid. If you want me at the station you shall jolly well have to arrest me."

"Speaking of tea," said Sharon, and Jude and Liam both leapt up as Eddy lowered herself into the last empty seat.

"There's no need to arrest my dad," she told Begbie. "We know who killed her if she was killed. Or buried her anyway. It was my . . . Shit! It was the woman who brought me up. Miranda Preston. What's that wee word, Jude? For Mum's other name?"

"Née?" said Jude. She was sure Begbie had given her another look when he heard what Eddy called her. And he glanced his notebook. *Jude Hamner* was ringing bells in him somewhere.

"Right," Eddy said. "Miranda Preston, née Daley. She buried my . . . Inez and took me to Northern Ireland. I've been there my whole life until this month — you can check the schools and that, but I don't think I've got a birth certificate. Can I get one?" she

465

asked turning to Lowell.

"And can you give us Ms. Preston's current address?" said Begbie. He was working hard not to react to what he was hearing, but it was stretching him. Sharon didn't even try. She was looking at Eddy with her mouth hanging open.

"You were born here and stolen and came back and . . ."

"He didn't know I existed," said Eddy, jerking her head at Lowell.

"And Ms. Preston's current address?" said Begbie again.

"Scattered in the Garden of Remembrance at Crossnacreevy," Eddy said. "She died."

"I'm so sorry, you wee soul," said Sharon.

But Begbie was looking at Jude. "There's a lot of it about," he said.

By the end of the day, Lowell was exhausted. The team had stayed until dark, working under their tent. Until after dark, actually, the last two hours spent with lights inside, making the white dome glow like something unearthly and malevolent. They had photographed and photographed and then even when Inez was out and wrapped and gone, they stayed, taking soil samples and small pieces of plant root. And snapping the house and drive and bungalow and garden wall from every angle.

Of course, they had to speak to Mrs. Hewston, but they let Lowell go with them as support for her. And they let Jude go with Lowell, fearful of his bad colour and the tremor in his hands, which grew as the long day wore on.

Inside, Mrs. Hewston's bungalow was exactly what Jude would have imagined. Just like Kirk Cottage, it had been fitted out decades earlier and then kept spick and span but never changed. The spongy beige wallpaper in the kitchen, with sepia coffeepots and bunches of grapes, matched the hedgerow kitchen textiles, the curtains and tiebacks still bright but the oven gloves and tea towels faded with washing. Not so much as a teaspoon was out of place. The sink was bare and dry and a spanking white cloth was draped over the taps.

Mrs. Hewston looked around with a slight smirk of pride as Inspector Begbie, a young constable, and the two of them trooped through. She was glad to have her housekeeping displayed this way. A month ago Jude would have loved it. Now it looked like the definition of loneliness. The living room was just as bad. Not a single book to collect dust, thin foam cushions standing up at regular intervals along the back of the sofa, the only sign of life a TV remote by one of the armchairs, the ever-so-slightly less pristine armchair, with a dented seat and a flattened headrest where Mrs. Hewston spent her solitary days.

"Can I get you some tea?" she said, as everyone sat.

"A glass of water perhaps," Lowell said.

Mrs. Hewston ignored him. She only had eyes, and refreshments it seemed, for the inspector.

"You don't mind, Mrs. H., do you?" said Jude, and slipped back through. She filled a glass and returned, setting it down beside Lowell on a coaster instead of the laminate top of the side table, under Mrs. Hewston's watchful eye.

"And can you tell me what you remember about that night?" Begbie was saying. "April the nineteenth, 1995?"

"I remember it as if it was yesterday," Mrs. Hewston said. "It was a beautiful spring evening and I had the windows open to smell the narcissus. I was watching the news from Oklahoma, because Mr. Glen here was just down the road and I was worried about him."

She hadn't said any of that last time, thought Jude. She hadn't mentioned the

468

kind of flowers, or what the disaster was that she was glued to. And Jude hadn't asked. If she'd thought to check what flowers smelled so sweet or what the terrible doings in America were . . . what? The events of the last week, dreadful as they were between Jackie's collapse and the fire, were nothing to do with Miranda, after all.

As Jude thought that, though, she felt something somewhere. She'd read her share of suspense novels and she had heard it described in various ways. Either as a stray hair across the face, unignorable and elusive, or as a shifting inside like sunken objects when the tide turns. She had even heard it described as a half-familiar face seen from a train carriage and gone again before it was pinned down.

But sitting musing like this, she was missing what Mrs. Hewston was saying.

"— would recognise the sound of a newborn baby's cry in my sleep. I was a nurse, you know."

"And yet you didn't attend?" said Inspector Begbie.

"I don't like to push myself in," said Mrs. Hewston.

There it was again. Begbie didn't know the woman and so he only nodded, but it took all Jude's willpower not to snort. She glanced at Lowell, who didn't catch her eye.

"I mean, for all I knew there was a midwife there, wasn't there? Or a doctor. I don't have anything to do with the new surgery. They're not interested in old-timers like me. For all I knew there was a whole team in."

"So . . . you didn't actually see anything?" said Begbie.

"I saw plenty!" said Mrs. Hewston. "I heard a noise close to my house here, and I looked out and saw the Miranda one, the mother of that piece that's fetched up here now, in the garden, busy with her ways."

"You saw her through the window?" said Begbie. "Or you went out?"

"Me?" said Mrs. Hewston. "An old widow woman like me? I did not. I stayed safely inside, but I saw her in the garden through my small bedroom window. She was digging."

"And when you say 'the mother,' " said Begbie, "you mean this woman, don't you?" He held out one of the photographs, unpeeled from behind its sticky plastic in Lowell's album. The glue had dried onto its surface and it looked decades older than it was, yellowed and tatty.

"Wait a minute, till I get my right specs on," said Mrs. Hewston. She fumbled down the side of her chair and brought up a

470

spectacle case. She opened it, polished the glasses inside with the little cloth, and threaded them carefully over her ears. "Let's see now," she said. "Yes, that's her. The tall one with the bushy hair. The wee thing that's come back now doesn't favour her at all."

"She looks like my mother," said Lowell.

"God help her," said Mrs. Hewston and everyone, even the constable who was taking notes, raised their eyes and stared at her.

"And so you never went outside and you never mentioned this to anyone and you never told Mr. Glen when he got home," Inspector Begbie said.

"I keep myself to myself," said Mrs. Hewston, her mouth pinched.

"Yes, you do," said Begbie. "You certainly do. Not so much as a twitched curtain all day while we dug up round your house and the press was at your gate. You're a marvel."

"My *gate*?" said Mrs. Hewston. "If they'd stayed at my gate, I would have been delighted. They were ringing my bell and shouting through my letterbox. You should arrest them for harassment."

"We'll have to see," murmured Begbie. "We've got one or two wee things to be getting on with." Then he rose, excused himself, and left, with the rest of them trailing after him.

When Jude got outside, Begbie was standing just to the side of the tent, gazing back at the bungalow.

"She told me a very different version," Jude said to him. "I think she's forgotten."

Back at the big house she laid it out. "The newborn baby's cry bit was the same," she began, "but what she said to me was that she went out and saw Miranda with a placenta in a bowl, all bloody and streaked — Miranda, I mean — and barefoot."

"She embellishes," Lowell said. "People do, don't they? And she got it wrong. She knew a baby had been born and so when she saw something being buried she guessed at what it was. And got it wrong."

Begbie played a little tune with his fingertips on his stretched cheeks and then shut his lips with a smack. "And is that true about recognising the cry of a newborn?"

"It must be," said Jude. "If she didn't see the placenta or talk to Miranda, then the crying is the only thing in the whole night that would have made her guess about a baby. No one knew Inez was pregnant. Not even Inez, maybe."

"I'll ask my wife," Begbie said. "She's a lactation consultant up at Ayr. But I have to

472

say, my crap-dar's going off like an air-raid siren." Jude smiled. "Oh, by the way," he added. "A couple of things. First, Sharon got back with a prelim. She's washed the bones and says they're pristine. No sign of violence. So I was talking to my wife at lunchtime, Mr. Glen, and she said to me to say to you that if that's right enough, if young Eddy's mother died of eclampsia or some such, that's crucial information when her own time comes. I don't know if it's genetic, but there's a lot we don't understand and it's best to be safe, eh?"

Lowell took it in only slowly, but then he groaned and, clamping one hand on each knee, hauled himself to his feet. "I'll go and break the news," he said. "She's been talking about doulas and pools of water, you know."

"No way," said Begbie.

When Lowell was gone, Jude smiled at Begbie again. "What was the other thing?" she said.

"No flies on you," said the inspector. "Aye, you're right enough. I wanted to tell you on your own. Not sure how things stand between the two of you. Did you know you're on a missing persons list?" Jude shrugged. "I had to call it in when I realised who you were," he said. "Sorry, love. Life doesn't play the game these days for anyone who wants to take off and get lost. Surprised this Miranda managed it twenty years ago, if I'm honest."

"Me too," said Jude. "Didn't Inez have anyone looking for her? No one who missed her?"

"She had someone who missed her right enough," Begbie said, nodding at the chair where Lowell had been sitting. "Anyway, I best be off."

"Thank you," said Jude. "For the heads up," she added at his frown. For not being what I thought policemen were, she really meant. Maybe none of them were the way they had seemed when she had looked at them from Max's side. "Am I . . . I got in the habit of not looking and I can't seem to break it. Am I just a missing person? Or a witness? Do you know?"

"Witness?" said Begbie. "There's no need for a witness. The guilty one's dead. Just like here. Miranda's dead and gone and the case is closed."

Just like Lowell's father too, Jude thought. The guilty one dead and the case closed.

Except *someone* put a note in a door, *someone* shoved papers through a letterbox and lit them, and *someone* upset Jackie enough to make her collapse.

Maybe none of the stories was the way it seemed. Dr. Glen and the old people. Inez and Miranda. Maybe two more guilty ones were alive and well somewhere and counting their blessings. Just like her.

THIRTY

It took her two days to get there. She arrived at half past eleven on Friday morning and the first any of them knew about it was when they heard a baby crying.

They were in the dining room. Lowell and Jude had started trying to organise the hundred-books books. Eddy had drifted in; since Lowell's lecture about the hazards of childbirth, she had been sticking close to him, catching his eye a lot, assuring him she was fine. She had even moved downstairs from her pink and yellow haven to sleep in the adjoining room. Liam and Terry had taken over the attic rooms now, their third occupants in a month after the long empty years. Jude, that first night after Begbie left, ended up in Lowell's bed and had slept ten straight hours there.

"Totally disgusting, by the way," said Eddy. "But fair enough, because Dad would probably pass out if my waters broke. But

476

you'd be okay."

"I think I'd have time to get to you from any door on the landing," Jude said. "Even from downstairs if I was still up."

Eddy shook her head solemnly. "Who knows how quick it might come on?" she said. "Did I tell you Dad's taking a hotel room beside the hospital starting next week, cos of how we're in the back of beyond. And as for the boat!" It was decided. Liam and Terry's child would be born Scottish. They didn't seem to mind. They were already making jokes about wearing kilts to its Christening.

The question of "how quick it could come on" was one of the many things that troubled Jude about that night almost twenty years ago. Dying in childbirth was surely slow. Even if Inez meant to go it alone, wouldn't she finally panic and cry out? And even if Miranda meant to do everything with a cup of raspberry tea and some lavender oil, wouldn't she eventually realise she was out of her depth and get help? The only pictures Jude could bring to mind of women dying alone in childbirth were Victorian and as gruesome as any of Lowell's collection, involving locked doors and shackles and grim-faced wardens determined to see that some wretched girl paid for her sin. When

477

she tried to think of Miranda and Inez in those terms, tried to imagine Miranda locking Inez in a bedroom and ignoring her screams, she felt faint and foolish. They were friends. It couldn't have happened that way.

She was half thinking about it as she sorted books on the Friday morning. Eddy was propped across two armchairs, complaining about her newly swollen ankles. Liam and Terry, who followed Eddy as closely as she followed Lowell, were massaging one each. Jude was trying not to roll her eyes.

When they heard the baby cry, Lowell put a hand out to steady himself and Eddy batted the fathers' hands away. "What the fuck?" she said, suddenly white in the face. "Jesus Christ, see what's happened now? They've disturbed her grave and here she is."

"Eddy," Jude said over her shoulder, making her way to the door, "it's lunchtime. Ghosts haunt at night. And the baby didn't die, you moron. The baby's *you.*"

"Oh yeah," said Eddy, sitting back and lifting her feet again.

"Is it who I think it is, dearest?" said Lowell. And then louder when she didn't answer, "I'm here if you need me."

"I'm fine," Jude called back. She went on her own and opened the inside porch door.

Raminder was standing on the tiled floor of the vestibule with a wailing, wriggling bundle under one arm and a phone in her free hand.

"Hi," said Jude. "You better come in."

"I'm glad you see it that way," Raminder said and, despite everything, Jude felt a surge of emotion to hear the sound of home in her London accent after all those weeks of dry Scottish twigs snapping. "Jade's starving."

She cast her eyes about as they walked along the passageway to the kitchen. Jude could see her appraising the place, the soaring ceilings and deep mouldings, the shabby carpet and dusty picture frames.

"Looks about right," she said. "The *Mail* said he was some kind of corpse collector. Photographs of remains and owned a house in a graveyard. But he didn't know about the woman in the garden?"

"He's not really as — I mean, they can twist anything," said Jude, holding open the kitchen door and stepping back to let Raminder enter. The baby was gasping and grizzling, sure she'd be fed soon now that they were inside.

Raminder shrugged out of her coat and

plumped down in a chair. She lifted her jumper, rootled in a capacious beige bra, and then bent low over the baby until the crying stopped, replaced by soft little snorts and grunts. She sat up and smiled.

"Anyway, I just wanted to say thanks, really," she said.

"For . . . ?" Jude sat down opposite her. She should offer tea, but she didn't know if Raminder could drink hot tea over Jade's head. Anyway, she seemed to have lost the use of her legs.

"For phoning," Raminder said. "Dialling it in. No one sussed out it wasn't me, by the way. It only took them two minutes to get there. Shouldn't get preferential treatment, I suppose, but the truth is, what with it being my number and me being on a crew . . . Yeah, about two minutes."

"But — I mean, you know what I said, right?"

"Oh yeah," said Raminder. "I worked it out eventually."

"I'm not sure I —"

"Police came round the next day. I was still pretty out of it. They asked me what I could remember. I said I tripped and fell. They said they understood I was frightened and would it help to know I wasn't in any danger."

"What?"

"I twigged then. That's what they say to abused wives. They say, 'He's under lock and key, love. He can't hurt you.' Get the woman to make a statement and then they bail the bugger out and he goes straight back round and beats her bloody. Brilliant system."

"How do you *know* all that?" Jude said. "Max never —"

"No!" said Raminder. "Just from us being there getting the poor cow on a stretcher and the cops being there asking questions at the same time. This one time, we were splinting the wife — dislocated shoulder, dislocated jaw — and there's a copper with his notebook out saying, 'Where does he drink, love? What's his local? We can pick him up now and he'll never bother you again.' Little kids in their pyjamas standing there listening to it all. And she goes — through her dislocated jaw — she goes, 'Don't arrest him. We can't afford a babysitter.' "

"So . . ." Jude was trying to piece it together. "The cops prompted you? Told you what I'd said?"

Raminder shook her head and glanced down at the little head burrowing deeper and deeper into her. "The crew came to

481

check up on me. Tom and Bernie, it was. Came shuffling in looking at their feet. And I asked them. I said I couldn't remember what I'd said on the call. *They* told me. And so when the cops came back — no one had said a word about Max at this point, mind — when the cops came back, I said he was angry and drunk and he didn't mean anything by it. Probably didn't even realise I was at the head of the staircase, just pushed past me to get to the bedroom."

"When did you find out he was dead?" Jude said.

"Later that day, once the nurses said it was safe to upset me. Yeah, later that afternoon. My mum was there. And they told me. He'd passed out drunk and choked on his own."

"But why didn't the ambulance crew that came to get you take care of him?" Jude said. "Tom and Bernie."

"Ah yeah, there you've got it," said Raminder. "That's why the police were so keen to get me on record that he'd beaten me about a bit and why Tom and Bernie wanted me to spill. *They never checked the house.* They found me and Jade and took us off and never looked upstairs. They were covering their arses in case I tried to sue them, innit? In case I asked for forty jillion for the loss of my loving husband."

"Tom and Bernie never looked upstairs?" Jude knew ambulancemen. It was second nature to check a premises when they were called out.

"That's their story and they're sticking to it," Raminder said. "Said they were concerned for my safety, what with me being a colleague. If they'd known he was there, they'd never have left him . . . like that, you know?" She paused, chewing her lip. "If you back me up, we're all okay."

"Back you up . . . ?"

"I've told the cops you left before it kicked off between Max and me."

"But one of the neighbours saw me leaving."

"That's right," Raminder said. "I told the cops you left and that's when Max went to bed and pushed past me and I fell down the stairs, just had time to dial 999 and say he shoved me before I passed out. Neighbour hears Jade crying, sees you leaving, bit later sees an ambulance turn up. There's no loose ends."

"You don't seem — I mean, are you okay? You seem okay." In the depths of the house, Jude was aware of the doorbell, but she ignored it. "I mean, he's dead, right? And you loved him."

483

"Must have, innit?" Raminder said, hollowly. "I went against my family, broke up a marriage. If I didn't love him that'd make me a bit of a bitch." She looked down again and this time crunched herself over so she could kiss the side of Jade's head. The baby was lolling, sated already, and Raminder pulled her gently away from her breast, with a soft sound like a small pebble falling into water. Jude took her eyes away after just a glimpse of a dark egg-shaped blotch and a sharp black nipple. Raminder was still smiling. "I can't regret anything I did," she said, "or I'm wishing this little one away."

Jude was speaking before she knew what she would say. "I don't regret anything you did either. Choice between living in London still married to Max and being here? Easy."

Raminder nodded, rhythmically. She looked almost as sleepy as the baby, blinking slowly.

"How did you get here?" Jude asked her. "Did you drive?"

Raminder nodded again. Jade was snoring.

"Do you want to go upstairs and rest?" Jude asked. "First left at the top's a spare. Bathroom's the one with the etched glass."

Raminder got to her feet and pushed her car keys across the table. "Don't suppose you'd slip out and get her changing bag?" she said.

"Course," said Jude. Raminder's words were still ringing in her ears. *They'd never have left him . . . like that, you know.* "Hey, can I ask you something?" she said. Raminder was walking slowly, carrying the sleeping baby like a ticking bomb, Jude thought. "Was that his first slip? Since you two got together?"

Raminder snorted. "You're kidding, aren't you? That was his fourth 'slip.' First time since Jade was born, though."

"I remember that," Jude said. "First time this year, first time this holiday, first time since the last time."

Raminder gave a ghost of a laugh, just a lift of her chin and a single breath. The weariness couldn't all be from her long drive and the broken sleep that comes with a baby.

She knew, Jude thought. She'd been three times round the merry-go-round Jude had been round so *many* times she couldn't count anymore. She definitely knew.

"No regrets," Raminder said, reading her mind. "No complaints. My parents have forgiven me. Well, this one helps." She lifted the baby a little and then let her settle again.

■ ■ ■ ■

Jude was dazed when she walked back into the dining room. Liam and Terry were dusting books now and Eddy was sitting in one of the armchairs in the window staring at her phone. Lowell stood with his back to the fireplace, hands in his pockets, sorting his change. In the two carver chairs at either end of the long sideboard sat Maureen Bell and Jackie MacLennan.

"Hey!" said Jude, rushing over and taking both Jackie's hands. "You look fantastic. But what are you doing out?"

"Out of the hospital or out in the rain?" said Jackie. Her voice was rough and she had bags under her eyes, but she gripped Jude firmly. "Billy told me you'd been round so I asked Mo here if she'd give me a lift. See if we couldn't set things straight somehow."

Maureen shifted in her seat and cleared her throat. "I'm sorry I was a wee bit thon way last time," she said.

Jude managed to smile without her eyebrows rising, but she couldn't forget Maureen's jabbing finger and her voice snapping *Out!* like a dog's bark.

"You've nothing to be sorry for," she said.

"I raked up old hurts."

"It was a terrible time," Maureen said. "We'd always been such a friendly wee town and then suddenly everyone was looking sideways at everyone else."

"Aye well, it was us MacLennans that started it," said Jackie. "That besom putting poor Auntie Lorna in a home. Like kenneling a dog."

"And what with this trouble that's come to you now," Maureen went on, with a glance at Eddy, "I was glad Jack asked me to bring her. Gave me the excuse to say sorry and let's just forget it happened, eh?"

Lowell was frowning deeply. "That's very generous of you both," he said, "but you're not in full possession of the facts."

"Lowell," said Jude, flashing a desperate message at him with her eyes. "They're not facts. They're suppositions. And Maureen and Jackie want to let it drop."

He was going to fall on his sword if she didn't stop him. He was going to tell the world his father was a killer and do no one any good — not the relatives, not himself, not the town that was already reeling.

If she could take what Raminder offered, Jude thought, then Lowell could grab this chance that the two women were holding out to him now.

"Since it was me who opened up the can of worms," she went on, "flying around dropping names, it should be me who gets to close it again."

"My father —" Lowell began.

"If you want to be generous," Jude cut in, "be generous about the cottage. Let the question of who set the fire quietly die."

"I was in HDU," said Jackie.

"I was upstairs with my curtains drawn," said Maureen. "You'll have to take my word for it."

"My dear," said Lowell, "I shouldn't dream of accusing you. I rather like my original idea: that some young scamps took the chance to make mischief."

It was an uneasy truce, but when they left minutes later, Jackie suddenly pale from exertion, they were agreed.

"Our family gets more and more baroque," Lowell said watching them drive away. "Your ex-husband's widow and child tipped us over into soap opera territory anyway, but my father the serial killer? Well, we're squarely in the horror genre now, aren't we."

"If you're not a horror fan," said Terry, "don't join a fecking book club." He finished with the volume he was wiping and added it to the top of a pile.

Jude and Lowell both turned to stare at him.

"What?" Jude asked.

"Well, look," said Terry. "Speaks for itself, doesn't it?"

Jude blinked and gazed down the length of the long dining table at the piles of books laid out like a 3-D chart there.

"Norma, Elsie, Archie, Etta, and Todd," Terry said. "Eddy explained it all and showed us pics of the gravestones. They were all in the book club. And they were all still alive when *Ulysses* was pick of the month. Look. Five copies. Number 45 and they're all alive."

"Then Norma died and by number 48, we're down to four *Mockingbird*s. Four, four, four, and then *bam*! Elsie Day died and there's only three copies of *On the Beach*."

"So *what*?" said Eddy. "God, you're as bad as them! Books, books, books. Of course they stopped getting books. They were *dead*! Even the fucking hundred-books book club's got a clue in the name."

Lowell was shaking his head, the picture of patience. "My dear child," he said. "One doesn't stop getting book club choices, magazine offers, or gas bills merely because one is dead."

"And anyway," Jude said, "isn't it a bit

489

weird for all of them to be in the same book club?"

"Five random old identikit people?" said Eddy. "No."

"And then two," said Terry in a very small voice and with a wary look at Eddy. "Just two copies of *Lolita*. One was Todd's with his name in and his notes in the back, and the other one was probably Etta's."

"You've no need to pander to her, my dear boy," Lowell said. "I shan't let her . . . I hardly know how to express it."

"Dick us about?" suggested Liam.

Eddy, in spite of herself, snorted with laughter.

"And then one," Jude said. "What's the last one?"

"Last we found is two number 61s," said Terry. "Virginia Woolf."

Jude opened one copy of *To the Lighthouse* again and read Todd's words. "*I asked after Etta. M. said she can't keep anything down. It'll only be days. Sometimes folk can't see what's right in front of them.* So we've missed one," she said. "Lowell, didn't you put *any* of the cleared-out books on the shelves? Were they *all* in the dead room?"

"Every one. I didn't want to upset the relatives," he said. "As I told you."

"Seems like smart thinking," said Liam.

"If one of the relatives has started burning down houses they might start bumping off old people again."

"It was my father who did the first round of bumping off," Lowell said. "I assumed Eddy would have told you."

"That's my granddad!" Eddy said. "I didn't want them getting weird about my genes."

"But didn't you say the egg came from a lawyer?" Jude asked.

"Yeah," said Eddy. "Yeah, I did say that. Well, it didn't."

"Was your father still alive in the mid-nineties?" said Liam.

"He wasn't," Lowell said. "But had he been, your inference is quite right. He attended home births quite readily."

"Not like that arse you've got now," Eddy said, missing the point. "I thought I'd had the last load of nagging after Mum — Miranda — died. She was insane about it, Liam. It was her right blind spot. *Get into hospital, Eddy, do what the doctors tell you, Eddy. Promise me if I'm not here you won't listen to anyone in the Community. Promise me you'll get to the maternity wing in Derry. Cross your heart and hope to die.*"

Jude stood up and, giving Lowell's hand a quick squeeze, she left the room, going as fast as she could without alarming them. She took a mackintosh from the coat pegs at the back door and let herself out, sliding on the cobbles and then slopping and skidding over the soaked grass towards the bedraggled asparagus bed, where the white tent had been.

"Knock knock," she said, opening Mrs. Hewston's kitchen door. The television through in the front room snapped off. "Only me," she added, kicking off her clogs and folding her mackintosh over the back of one of the chairs to drip harmlessly on the lino.

Mrs. Hewston was sitting in her upright armchair with her spectacles case clutched in one hand, the remote in the other. "You again!" she said. "I told that inspector everything I know. What do you want?"

"I couldn't work out why you kept the secret," Jude said. "A baby born and stolen away and a body buried in your garden? Why didn't you tell anyone?"

"It was none of my business," said Mrs. Hewston, sitting back a little, not even pretending she didn't know about the body, not even bothering to tell her placenta story now.

"No, that's not it," said Jude. "It was quid pro quo. Miranda wanted the baby. She kept

492

her mouth shut about you, and you kept your mouth shut about her."

"About *what* about me?" said Mrs. Hewston, and Jude could see her chest rising and falling.

"She came to you, didn't she? She asked you for help and you refused to attend."

"Nonsense!"

"You let Inez struggle away on her own and you let her die."

"She should have been in the hospital. I knew nothing about it."

"Of course she should have, but by the time Miranda knew she was in danger, she was too scared to call an ambulance. She thought the courts would take one look at Inez — trying to give birth on her own — and take the baby away."

"And how could anyone blame them!" said Mrs. Hewston. "The girl wasn't fit. None of them were good for anything, lying around the garden playing so-called music and taking those daft pictures with nothing in them."

"But you should have helped her."

"I didn't know it was happening until it was too late," said Mrs. Hewston. Her voice rang with outraged indignation. "First I *knew,* it was too late!"

"But why did you keep quiet?" asked Jude.

"If you weren't at fault, what did you have to gain?"

"It was none of my business," said Mrs. Hewston again, and would say no more.

The rest of the day went past a long way from Jude somehow. She was back in that clouded-glass paperweight again. She could see Liam and Terry taking turns holding Jade, see Raminder flirting with them, and Eddy's wide eyes when she caught sight of one of Raminder's enormous nipples. She could see Lowell at the head of the dinner table looking up and down both sides, beaming.

It was winter and everyone except Eddy was older and sadder than anyone in 1994, but the house was full again, people were in love or falling in love, one baby was passed around, the other kicked and punched and everyone took a turn to feel it, standing with a hand on Eddy's belly, heads cocked and eyes focussed on the distance, like safebreakers. Raminder talked about the ambulance service, telling funny stories. Eddy talked about Jolly's Cottage and the attic rooms, where she should settle. Where the baby would be best when they came over to visit.

"Shame about that bungalow," Liam said.

"No shifting Mrs. H.," said Eddy. "She'll live forever."

Through it all, Jude was silent. Once, in the hothouse at the botanic gardens at Kew she had brushed her hand across a cactus. A proper Desperate Dan cactus. She had brought away hundreds of fine hairs stuck in her skin, transferring to her clothes and back to her skin in new places, one near her eye, one on her lip. For days afterwards she had kept finding those tiny needle-hairs all over her.

They were back now, the ghosts of them, piercing her in fifty different places. Where was the last hundred-books book? Why did Mrs. Hewston keep quiet? Who started the fire?

"You were solemn tonight," Lowell said once they were in their room. Liam and Terry were still up, but Raminder had lain down with Jade and fallen asleep, and Eddy, gravid now, had gone to bed at nine. "Was it the picture?"

Jude shook her head. Lowell had decided to donate his collection to a museum of photography, with the condition that they would not be on open view but only available to scholars by consultation. The brown paper parcels were on the side table in the vestibule ready to go to the Post Office. Jude

495

had only asked to look at one — the still girl and her blurred parents.

"Are you sure?" she had asked Lowell. "She looks so perfect."

"That's the problem," Lowell had said. "That's the clue. Life is so very far from perfect, my dearest. Life is filthy, ludicrous, perplexing chaos."

He emptied his pockets out onto the dressing table and yawned. "Is it hard seeing the little one?" he asked.

"Jade? No. It's not even hard seeing Raminder. Strangely."

"Hmph," Lowell said. He was undressing, laying his clothes over the chair but putting his shirt and underpants in the basket, after Eddy's nagging. He was bathing more too and shaving closely. Catching on quick, really. "I can't say I care for her greatly. She's rather abrasive." Catching on very quick, Jude thought, smiling. Bitching up the new wife was basic boyfriend good manners. She wondered if he had read an article or if Eddy had coached him.

"I'm just a bit done in with it all," she said. Lowell nodded and got calmly into bed beside her in his striped pyjamas, lifting his book and settling his spectacles.

"You should read," he said. "A quiet book is better than a tranquiliser. Young Eddy has

496

been asking for a television in her bedroom, but that's a dreadful idea. I shall select some bedside reading for her instead. Or you can." He nodded at the little pile on her table. O. Douglas, *Rebecca,* the Allingham, *Midnight's Children,* and the downed plane with the rugged chap and his love interest. Jude turned to them. It felt like a year since she laid them beside her bed upstairs in the pink room. They had followed her to Jolly's Cottage, back here to the room across the landing, and finally to Lowell's bed, and she'd never so much as glanced at any of them.

She pulled the whole pile onto her lap. Allingham's *Beckoning Lady* started with a corpse. No good for her tonight. *Rebecca* too, with its lost woman and all its secrets, was far from what she wanted. And O. Douglas was too much the other way. Too sweet and light, too far to bridge from her life to that world. That left the ripping yarn — but it made anguish and disaster seem like such a jape — and so it came down to *Midnight's Children.* She opened it to read the jacket copy and her breath died in her throat. There it was in the fly-leaf. *T. Jolly.* She flipped to the back.

"Gosh, never had you down as one of those," murmured Lowell beside her.

Etta is gone, Todd had written. *M. says heart this time. Her heart was stronger than mine. I'm not going to say anything. I want to end my days here in my own house with my quiet neighbours. But when I'm gone someone should know what happened here and so I'll write it down. She thinks getting rid of us will bring her what she wants, but she's wrong. He doesn't love her.*

"Lowell," Jude said. "You know when Begbie went to interview Mrs. Hewston?"

"Mm?" said Lowell, deep in his book.

"I went out to the kitchen to fetch you a glass of water and I missed the bit when they asked for her full name. They always do that, though, don't they? Ask for your full name."

"Mm."

"What's her name? No one calls her it because . . . Well, I don't know why not, but I don't think I've ever heard it."

"Ahhhhh — what?" said Lowell, putting his book down open on his lap and blinking at her.

"What's Mrs. Hewston's first name? She must have said it to the policeman."

"Ahhh, Marion, I think," said Lowell. Jude said nothing. "Can I go back to reading?"

"Your father didn't kill anyone," Jude said.

"I appreciate your kindness," said Lowell,

498

"but there's no need."

"I'm serious." She put the stack of books on the table and turned to face him, kneeling up half in and half out of the covers. "She killed your father's old patients because she wanted him to retire and run away with her. When he threatened to have them exhumed, she told him. That's why he left and why he never came back and why he was haunted for the rest of his life."

"But why would Mrs. Hewston think my father cared for her in that way?" said Lowell. "He never gave her any indication of it, I'm sure."

"Me too," said Jude. "But her faith has never wavered."

The Plexiglas bubble was gone and the hair-like needles were driven out of her completely. Jude felt as if she was floating high above the earth looking down on them all and could see everything. "She ran a book club. For the community, she said. Really, it was so she could get into everyone's houses. She killed them, Lowell."

Lowell shuddered and put his hand on Jude's knee. "Did she set the fire?" he said.

"Of course she did. I heard her on the street in the fog and she hurried away. She left the note, she set the fire, and then she nearly blew it. The next morning when we came back here with the firemen she was halfway across the lawn to come and cluck about it when she realised she hadn't been to the shop yet and she shouldn't know! She's not as sharp as she was."

"Did Jackie phone her?" Lowell said.

"I suppose so," said Jude. "We can ask."

"And did Jackie guess in '85 and then keep quiet?"

"We can ask that too."

They were silent for a moment and then, "Oh!" Lowell covered his mouth with his hand. "Did she kill Inez?"

"No," Jude said. "No, I believe what she said to me today. It was too late by the time she knew anything. But I could never work out why she would keep the secret. Why she would let Miranda go with the baby and keep quiet. I know now. She didn't want any trouble. She had got away with murder five times and she didn't want police and press sniffing round. This was only ten years later, remember. It's thirty years *now* and she's been hiding in her house since the news broke. Don't tell me that didn't surprise you."

Lowell spent a moment or two thinking hard, his eyes moving back and forward, gathering facts, checking memories, matching questions and answers. Then he clapped his hands, almost crying with relief, whooping with it.

"Shut up!" came Eddy's muffled voice through the wall. "You're disgusting."

Lowell only laughed louder. He jumped out of bed.

"Where are you going?" Jude asked him.

"To phone the police!" he said. "To get this straightened out at last after all these years! To clear my family name." He stopped to kiss Jude once on the head, a rounded smack that was still ringing in her ears when he'd gone.

She had made him so happy. She hadn't even realised he felt guilty, that he *cared* about his family name. She lay back and stared up at the ceiling. Of course it was better that the truth was out. And it was good for Lowell to be able to remember his father again without — what did he call it, a stain? But she was sorry. She had felt they were a better match when he was the son of a killer.

She had even imagined that one day she'd be able to tell him and he'd be able to forgive her. Now, seeing how happy he was to have the weight lifted, she wasn't so sure. Maybe it was hers to take to the grave. Hers and Raminder's, anyway.

If Max had only fallen off the wagon for

the first time, Raminder wouldn't know. But since it was the fourth time, she'd be quite familiar with him dropping onto the bed on his face and letting his head hang down, airways clear. She can't have thought of it when she saw him lying there for the last time, but she'd certainly thought of it since. *No regrets, no complaints,* she'd said. And Tom and Bernie? Of course they checked the house. Of course they saw their old pal Max lying there drunk, with his wife at the bottom of the stairs. And they left him . . . like that.

So it wasn't Jude's fault alone. But it was her hand. She had reached out and turned him over onto his back to look at his face. And then she had walked away, out of the room, out of the house, out of the country. She had left behind everything she'd ever felt for him. All the love and hate. She had left behind her clean job and her safe flat and her sensible life, and now she had Lowell and Eddy and the baby and Liam and Terry and Maureen and Jackie and Bill, and she would see Inez laid to rest and Mrs. Hewston brought to justice, and she would replant the muddy wreck of the asparagus bed and learn how tend to roses. She would get the stock online and look over the accounts and put LG Books to rights. She would live a life. Not filthy, not ludicrous, not chaos. But probably perplexing. Probably permanently perplexing.

She could hear Lowell coming back up the stairs, still talking. He must have made the call with Eddy's mobile. She would keep it to herself, and let this good man be happy. She would accept what the world had just laid at her feet and she would let the memory go. She reached out and picked up the O. Douglas, thinking perhaps it wasn't too sweet after all. It would do quite nicely. For tonight, anyway.

ACKNOWLEDGMENTS

I would like to thank: Donna Andrews, Frankie Bailey, Terri Bischoff, Kevin Brown, Leslie Budewitz, Jessie Chandler, Mathew Clemens, Laura DiSilverio, Cari Dubiel, Barb Fister, Audrey Ford, Beth Hanson, Julie Henrikus, Wendy Keegan, Louise Kelly, Catherine Lepreux, Jessie Lourey, Jim and Jean McPherson, Neil McRoberts, Gin Malliet, Karen Maslowski, Katie Mickshl, Erin Mitchell, Lisa Moylett, Nicole Nugent, Lori Rader Day, Martha Reed, Eileen Rendahl, Sarah Rizzo, Hank Phillippi Ryan, Sarah Shaber, Susan Shea, Spring Warren, Beth Wasson, Molly Weston, Dina Wilner, and Simon Wood, who have all helped me get through this year, fraying at the edges but never quite unravelling completely.

Extra special thanks to Judy Bobalik, Clare O'Donohue, Risa Rispoli, and Terri Bischoff (with a very different hat on). They know why.

FACTS AND FICTIONS

Wigtown is a real place in Scotland and the streets in this book are real streets. There is a cemetery and a harbour and a bowling green. There is even a big house where Jamaica House is imagined to be. And there are *lots* of bookshops and a wonderful literature festival every autumn (www .wigtownbookfestival.com). But none of the specific businesses or other houses in *Quiet Neighbors* are based in reality and none of the characters are related in any way to real individuals, living or dead. Todd Jolly's cottage isn't there, in case anyone goes looking.

The employees of Thorndike Press hope you have enjoyed this Large Print book. All our Thorndike, Wheeler, and Kennebec Large Print titles are designed for easy reading, and all our books are made to last. Other Thorndike Press Large Print books are available at your library, through selected bookstores, or directly from us.

For information about titles, please call:
  (800) 223-1244

or visit our Web site at:
  http://gale.cengage.com/thorndike

To share your comments, please write:
Publisher
Thorndike Press
10 Water St., Suite 310
Waterville, ME 04901